Medusa's Sisters

Medusa's Sisters

Lauren J. A. Bear

ACE
NEW YORK

ACE
Published by Berkley
An imprint of Penguin Random House LLC
penguinrandomhouse.com

Export edition ISBN: 9780593641354

Library of Congress Cataloging-in-Publication Data

Names: Bear, Lauren J. A., author.
Title: Medusa's sisters / Lauren J.A. Bear.
Description: New York: Ace, [2023]
Identifiers: LCCN 2022044783 (print) | LCCN 2022044784 (ebook) |
ISBN 9780593547762 (hardcover) | ISBN 9780593547779 (ebook)
Subjects: LCSH: Medusa (Gorgon)—Fiction. |
Sthenno (Greek mythology)—Fiction. | Euryale (Greek mythology)—Fiction. |
LCGFT: Mythological fiction. | Novels.
Classification: LCC PS3602.E2477 M43 2023 (print) |
LCC PS3602.E2477 (ebook) | DDC 813/.6—dc23/eng/20221031
LC record available at https://lccn.loc.gov/2022044783
LC ebook record available at https://lccn.loc.gov/2022044784

Printed in the United States of America
1st Printing

Book design by Alison Cnockaert

For my mother,

For my father,

For my brother:

the three strands of my braid

It is immediately obvious that the Gorgons are not really three but one + two. The two unslain sisters are mere appendages due to custom; the real Gorgon is Medusa.

—Jane Ellen Harrison,
Prolegomena to the Study of Greek Religion (1908)

CAST OF CHARACTERS

AMONG GODS AND MONSTERS

Gaea—primordial goddess of the earth

Uranus—primordial god of the sky

Pontus—primordial god of the sea

Cronus—supreme ruler of the Titans; god of time

Rhea—wife and sister of Cronus; goddess of fertility and mother of the gods

Prometheus—god of forethought

Epimetheus—god of afterthought

Helios—god of the sun

Selene—goddess of the moon

Metis—goddess of good counsel

Leto—goddess of motherhood

Phorcys—god of the sea's hidden dangers

Ceto—wife and sister of Phorcys; goddess of sea monsters

CAST OF CHARACTERS

The Graeae (Deino, Enyo, and Pemphredo)—daughters of Phorcys and Ceto

The Gorgons (Stheno, Euryale, and Medusa)—daughters of Phorcys and Ceto

Ladon—son of Phorcys and Ceto; a dragon

Echidna—daughter of Phorcys and Ceto; a sea dragon, mother of monsters

Typhon—a monstrous giant; consort of Echidna

Offspring of Echidna and Typhon—the Sphinx, the Chimera, the Hydra, and Cerberus

Doris—a minor sea goddess; mother of the Nereids

Amphitrite—wife of Poseidon; a Nereid

Pandora—a human; wife of Epimetheus

Zeus—supreme ruler of the Olympians; lord of the sky

Poseidon—brother of Zeus; god of the sea

Hades—brother of Zeus; ruler of the Underworld

Hera—wife and sister of Zeus; protector of childbirth and marriage

Hestia—sister of Zeus; goddess of the hearth

Aphrodite—goddess of love and beauty

Athena—daughter of Zeus; goddess of the city

Apollo—son of Zeus and Leto; Artemis's twin; god of light and music

Artemis—daughter of Zeus and Leto; Apollo's twin; goddess of wild things

Hermes—son of Zeus; messenger of the gods

Ares—son of Zeus and Hera; god of war

Hephaestus—son of Hera; god of the fire and forge

Dionysus—son of Zeus; god of wine

CAST OF CHARACTERS

IN THEBES

Cadmus—king of Athens

Harmonia—his wife; daughter of Ares and Aphrodite

Ino, Agave, Autonoë, and Semele—daughters of Cadmus and Harmonia; princesses of Thebes

Polydorus—son of Cadmus and Harmonia; prince of Thebes

Desma—Semele's nurse

Hasina and Annipe—Semele's servants

IN ATHENS

Erastus—a musician

Ligeia—wife of Erastus

Thales—nephew of Erastus and Ligeia; an athlete

Frixoula—a high priestess

Charmion—a madam

Menodora—a hostess

Hagne and Aspasia—Charmion's employees

BETWEEN THE ISLANDS

Acrisius—king of Argos

Danaë—daughter of Acrisius

Perseus—son of Danaë

Polydectes—king of Seriphos

Dictys—brother of Polydectes; a fisherman

Orion—a hunter

Oenopion—king of Chios

Merope—daughter of Oenopion

Medusa's Sisters

PROLOGUE

ENTER STHENO, ALONE

> With or without a name,
> for beings such as me,
> I must begin.
>
> —*Anonymous, "Anonymous"*

I HATE THE NUMBER three.

It is an unholy character—complicated, messy, confrontational. Small and odd and prime.

It was my identity, and then it wasn't. Now I'm haunted by its prevalence.

Mathematicians may argue, three is beautiful! Take the perfection of an equilateral triangle, for instance. Or solving proportions with the rule of three. There exists a theory of triangulation that within the unique power of triangles, truth is always revealed.

Ha!

Scientists slobber like ravenous dogs over three: the states of matter, the dimensions of space. Solid, liquid, gas. Land, sky, water. Sun, moon, and stars.

Three is human life: mind, body, and soul. It is ritual. Morning, noon, and night. Three meals a day. Three trimesters of pregnancy. It is also dramatic. Aristotle's three unities. Aeschylus's trilogy. Beginning, middle, and end. Past, present, future.

Within my own world, threes appear with cruel frequency. Beasts with tri-forked tongues or triple heads. Cronus and Rhea had three sons and three daughters. The oracle at Delphi's tripod. All us "weird" sisters—the three Fates and Furies, three Graces, three Harpies. Or the nine Muses, multiples of three. The triple goddess, Hecate—maid, mother, and crone—whom we would witness transform throughout cultures, beneath hegemonies, across time and place.

Poseidon's trident.

The three maiden goddesses.

The geometry of hearts, minds, and souls, however, obeys no law of balance. There is no perfect trinity, for three connotes competition. Power struggles. Favoritism and loneliness.

We were almost not a trio; although now that she is gone, neither of us feels like a duo. We are not twins, nor will we ever be. Our third was the center, and when we lost her, we also failed each other, collapsing inward upon ourselves.

A broken triplet. Thrice blessed. Thrice cursed.

Our tragedy is a famous one, devoured and regurgitated. Sensationalized, of course. Misrepresented. A trio of malevolents! And the youngest? Well, that depends upon whom you ask. A symbol of wrath and rage, but also sex and desire. Every time her drama repeats erroneously, she dies again. And *our* stories—*our* survival—become even further removed from the annals of history.

We have lived long enough to watch heroes become monsters. We oversaw the emergence of gods and welcomed their disappearance. Kingdoms raised, then set to flames. Endlessly. Over and over again. Different casts and settings, same plot.

Life adapts; it evolves. Yet betrayal—in word and deed, by lover and kin—remains remarkably the same.

Perfidy by jealousy and by love.

For we are women, still, despite what we were made.

To be ageless and anonymous, immortal and ignominious.

Famous and feared, yet nameless.

We know you have never heard of us, but that is no bother. We stopped caring a long, long time ago. Back on those rocks, that beach, surrounded by the waves that crashed unceremoniously at the rite of her immortality. When our sister finally achieved what she was denied at our birth and became a legend.

Our mortal sister is dead.

She was Medusa.

And we are the Gorgons.

AFTER HE TOOK Medusa's head, Perseus threw up.

His bile coated the boulders that were our home; green and yellow chunks of cheese and herb slid viscously into the sea. The resounding splatter both a grotesque knell and a final desecration to our refuge, the altar of our family.

Perhaps the newness of flight upset his stomach—it's not an easy sensation for anyone, let alone an unpracticed boy. But this day has been consigned to the poets, not the witnesses, and those lofty minds would never allow their Chosen One any deficiency. It was her gut-wrenching reflection in his gods-given shield! Blame the hag, men! I can almost hear the smug chortles.

I was there, though, and must differ. The act itself made Perseus sick. It was compunction, the very wrongness of what he did.

Perseus slaughtered a sleeping woman. An unarmed, innocuous stranger to him and his people.

There was no fight—aren't warriors forged in battle?

She didn't even scream.

And she was pregnant.

Yes, Medusa was pregnant and asleep, but Perseus became a hero. For she was only a beast, scaled and feathered, a body for Perseus to define himself upon.

Nobody requested our testimony. The voices of ugly women are easily diminished. Perseus could pretend that Medusa charged, threatened to tear open his chest with her claws and suck the life from his still-beating heart. Nobody challenged his account. He was so human, so young and beautiful, and we were . . . deformed.

Make no mistake, truth and goodness are merely aesthetics. I wish I had known this when I was still pretty.

I have had lifetimes to reflect, and if I ever had a chance of killing him, it was that moment, as he wiped away the runny mess of tears and snot with the back of his hand. But unlike Perseus, I beheld my nemesis in his weakness and, though an inchoate darkness coursed through my veins, I hesitated.

He was no more than a child, younger even than Thales—*Oh, Thales. I'm still so sorry*—and mucus clung to his beardless chin. Strange how I stared at that putrid discharge, how it consumed my focus, when my youngest sister's head dangled from his left hand.

I could not meet her eyes and he—of course—would not meet mine.

A disconnected triangle.

If only . . .

But then Euryale broke through my trance with cries bereft and feral: "Stheno, the babies!"

And so I did not sink my fangs into Perseus's adolescent neck and shred his throat, spilling his life into the blood he took, blending hero and villain for eternity. My remaining sister's words confounded and overthrew me. Fettered me to a reality I no longer recognized but vaguely recalled.

*The baby? No, ba*bies.

And so I faltered, and my enemy remembered to flee.

Perseus grabbed his inherited gifts, and his savage trophy, and escaped into the fog. Disappearing into his name.

Dispel everything the poets—who never met her—penned. Medusa rarely angered. She was ebullient, the paradigm of magnanimity. Liquid sunrise poured into her soul, and she woke each morning full of hope. Even after all her suffering, if she were given the opportunity, I do not think she would have fought back.

I am the vengeful sister. Me, Stheno. The hateful pariah who murdered more men than either of the other two Gorgons combined.

I consider this no accomplishment. I do not gloat, but neither will I atone. I am descended from a brood of sea creatures that humans deem beasts, and isn't that what monsters do? We maim and torture and feast upon the gore. We delight in destruction, drinking our victims' blood from golden chalices and dancing circles to their pleas.

But on that day, the one that mattered most, I paused.

I could have effortlessly killed Perseus—the ancestor of Heracles—and forever changed the mythical record of our age, but instead I chose my sisters.

FIRST EPISODE

STHENO

The way of sisters is more arcane
even
than the ways of gods.

—Erastus of Athens, "The Theater of Sisterhood"

FIRST YOU MUST accept that monsters have families.

My mother and father, two ancient sea deities of notorious danger, gave me eight siblings, but we were not raised together. Couldn't be, for we were separated by more than birth order—by our physical shape, our otherworldliness. Human families, by comparison, are so simple. Maybe one child has brown hair, the other blond. Eye color may range over shades of blue. Oh, how mortal parents dramatize these trite differences! Discussing in laborious detail how one learned to walk *a whole month* before another! Inconceivable!

In my family, some of us had tails.

Deino, Enyo, Pemphredo, Echidna, Ladon, and I share parents, but Medusa and Euryale are my sisters. Just as the Graeae were born together, so were we Gorgons.

We would not be called the Gorgons, however, for many, many years.

My grandparents were primordial beings, the sea and earth themselves, present at the creation of the world. This union between Gaea and her second husband—her own son Pontus—produced my parents. My father, Phorcys, married his sister and female counterpart,

Ceto, and all their progeny came to life during the Golden Age of the Titans, well before Zeus was hidden in a mountain cave on Crete and Cronus swallowed the changeling rock.

Yes, I watched Zeus release the monsters of Tartarus and conclude the ten-year campaign against his father, victorious. His lightning bolts became the harbinger of a new era, the Silver Age, where he was lord.

Though well hidden from the fray, I also witnessed the Titans meeting their punishments. Prometheus and the eagle. Atlas and the world. I should have paid closer attention when these so-called Olympians, denizens of the highest mountain, attacked those who wronged them with dogged maliciousness. Maybe then I would have been more prepared for how they treated the rest of us.

On days when I'm especially cynical, I find it almost laughable that I am older than both Poseidon and Athena, who would wreak such havoc upon my life. No respect for elders in the immortal community, I'm afraid. But then again, so much of age is attitude, and it took me far too long to acquire one.

I sound just like my mother. That happens to immortals, too, when we become old.

And I'm getting ahead of myself. I do that sometimes. Time holds little consequence when you occupy forever.

The story of our birth, then.

My mother, Ceto, resided in a watery cave beneath Mount Olympus, connected to her precious seas through endless tunnels and labyrinthine streams. Though my father adored his wife, he did not attend her labor—a messy, menial process, which he considered a female's work. And for reasons inexplicable—both then and now—matters of the womb are unpalatable to masculinity.

I have viewed battlefields covered in unspeakable gore, but I have seen delivery beds far, far worse.

I am extremely old.

At my mother's side stood her first set of triplets, the Graeae, or gray women. Another trio forced to sacrifice their individual identities for group nomenclature. Born with gray hair and skin, Deino, Enyo, and Pemphredo shared one detachable eye and tooth. I never found them ugly, despite that deficiency. Their gray faces were more interesting than unpleasant, and unlike my sisters and me, the Graeae had a gift: the modest ability for prophesy, to guide those who wander or are lost.

Though if they ever deigned to advise us in those early days, we certainly didn't listen.

When Ceto's contractions commenced, my mother summoned Doris, the wife of her other brother, Nereus, for Doris bore the nearly fifty Nereids and thus had plenty of experience with labor.

Still, complications arose.

I emerged first, en caul—within the protective sac indicative of my immortality. My aunt ruptured the bubble and released me, red-faced and stoic, upon the world. Doris smacked my bottom with her aquamarine hand to summon tears, but I refused to cry. I frowned at her repeated efforts, bringing Ceto great felicity.

"This one will be unforgiving!" she laughed between bites, for our mother ate the caul of all her immortal children. With jelly dripping from the corners of her mouth, Ceto named me Stheno, for she knew, even then, that I would be strong.

Euryale followed moments later, screaming incessantly—even within the bloody veil—demanding attention with her first breath. Another family might have greeted her with the affection she so obviously needed, but our callous community only grimaced.

"Make it stop," muttered Deino, no doubt wishing she also shared a retractable ear.

Though separated by mere heartbeats, Euryale would always be my younger sister. We had to organize ourselves somehow; all living beings crave hierarchy, and we were no exception.

"How do they look?" our mother asked, straining to see her new daughters as her older ones performed the rites of delivery, washing and swaddling.

"Ordinary," answered Pemphredo on a sigh.

"Fins? Fangs?"

"None."

"Talons?" wondered Ceto, riding a hope.

"Not even a sharp nail. Ten fingers, ten toes. Two eyes."

Ceto snorted, then winced as she clutched her lower abdomen. "Doris! I feel another!"

This last baby, however, refused to drop.

"It is breech, I think," worried Doris, removing red hands from my mother's birth canal and pushing green hair out of her eyes with a forearm. "I felt a foot."

"Then go in and grab it!" hissed Mother, gnashing her razor-sharp teeth. Ceto wasn't only the goddess of the largest sea creatures, but also the most lethal ones. "The little demon is destroying me!"

Poor Doris shoved an entire arm's length into my mother's belly, grabbed the baby's leg, and yanked. When Doris would later recount the story, she claimed the din of my mother's shrieks blurred the boundary between life and death.

The babe, however, arrived in this world the same way she would leave it.

Voiceless.

She was small and bluish with a shock of dark hair and no caul. A serpentine umbilical cord coiled lethally about her head and neck.

A being born in conflict with itself, choked by its own lifeline.

"Dead," murmured Doris, with greater surprise than sadness. For my kind, death is more a novelty than an emotional experience. Most of us lack the requisite empathy. Soft hearts aren't meant to last forever; it is why immortals grow selfish and cold.

Yet Doris was softer than most, and she held the lifeless babe gently while untangling the cord.

"What a shame," she lamented. "Three would have been a nice number."

Pemphredo, commanding the communal eye, ran a hard look over the cradled corpse, crown to toe, and her lips tightened. She snatched the tiny baby from Doris's arms and tossed it into the abyss. Doris yelped.

"Daughter!" upbraided our mother, slamming fists against the miry stones of her cavern. "I would have liked to see it before you fed my beasts!"

Pemphredo shrugged, for she was not inclined to apology. There had been an ominous aura to my youngest sister, and Pemphredo felt only respite to be rid of the pernicious little presence. Besides, our kind did not romanticize babies. You had to be strong to survive in such a world, and this one was clearly weak.

"You really are vicious," remarked Ceto with some admiration, exonerating Pemphredo's transgression. "Show me the other two, at least."

Deino and Enyo brought Euryale and me into the moonbeams that descended from the cave's natural skylights, casting our neonatal features in an opaline glow.

"They are common."

A failure.

Later, we would be called "human form." No physical deformities, no aberrations of color. We were my parents' most conventionally beautiful offspring—cherubic, even—and, thus, their least impressive.

"They are *lovely*," corrected Doris, overcompensating. "And their eyes are so unusual!"

"Indeed," Ceto responded sadly, inspecting the four miniscule orbs staring up at her expectantly. Mine were red ocher and Euryale's shone amber. Our mother gave them half a breath of consideration—and tried to find some satisfaction—when the tunnels began to shake, rattling loose stones and dirt from the walls. "Stitch me up, Doris, my husband comes!"

Our brief chance at being special come and gone.

Pemphredo threw the remains of afterbirth to my mother's white-bellied shark, who lingered in a nearby pool, while Doris rinsed and tidied my mother's lower half. Ceto, already beginning to heal, prepared herself for the arrival of my father in his seal-led chariot.

"Bring them to me!" she ordered, flapping her arms impatiently.

Deino and Enyo dutifully—blindly—passed us to our mother, who quickly assembled a maternal tableau: a babe propped in the bend of each scaly arm, her own head tilted downward in a vain attempt at demure. However, to Ceto's disappointment, it wasn't Phorcys emerging from the quaking subterranean depths, but rather, my *other* sister, the she-dragon Echidna.

Half speckled serpent, half maiden, Echidna was—at that time—my parents' most prolific issue. She resided in the fetid, slimy waters of the most arcane depths below the earth. With her monstrous storm-giant consort, Typhon, Echidna birthed some of the most profligate abominations on land or sea: the Hydra, Cerberus, the Chimera, and the Sphinx.

Ceto respected nobody, but Echidna at least commanded my mother's attention.

And at that moment, Echidna made quite the entrance, heaving with anger, the disposed baby pressed tightly against her chest.

"Who did this?" Echidna demanded, seething, her black eyes darting between Doris, Ceto, and the Graeae.

"I did," responded Pemphredo, insouciant as always. I would later nickname her the Wasp, for she seemed both free of fear and full of sting.

"*We* did," corrected the other two Graeae, in unison, for it was innately understood—even then—that our family's triplets elicited collective punishment.

"I understand your vision is limited, gray sisters, but your one eye fails you. This infant lives and breathes."

Our mother gasped—I imagine with some amusement. "Pemphredo, you wretch! Hand her to me, Echidna! Now."

Of course, I hold no natural memory of this day, but each time Doris recounted it later, she would pause at this part—linger on the lone heartfelt moment—for Echidna did not want to release the baby. Connections form quickly in my world. Love can be found at first sight and enmity even earlier. The bond between Echidna and my youngest sister was adamantine, instantaneous. Only reluctantly, and with much haggling, did she surrender the child to her rightful mother.

Many times, I have wondered how the trajectory of our lives might have curved if Echidna refused—even if she kept only the one of us. Are we so attached to our fates? To our catastrophes?

Echidna, after all, would suffer so much more than she deserved.

My mother blew her salty breath into the little face, and the baby's eyelids parted, revealing eyes as green as peridot.

"She is different, somehow," Ceto noted, comparing the salvaged babe to my other sister and me. "This one is changed, in a way I can't describe."

"She is mortal," Echidna claimed. "Her immortality was stillborn."

"Unusual," murmured Ceto.

"But possible," added Deino, yielding the wisdom of the eye. "She was not en caul. She will die."

"Of old age. Or sickness," elaborated Enyo.

"Or murder," finished Pemphredo.

"You see her future?"

"Not clearly," Deino replied. "We cannot tell *how* she will leave this world."

"Or when."

"But she will leave it? You are certain?"

Pemphredo nodded. "Kill the baby now. It will be a mercy." It was an argument born of the most abject pragmatism, and echoed by the other Graeae.

"What can a life mean for one who will die among those who cannot?" wondered Enyo.

"This babe will always be at risk," reasoned Deino. "It will be unfair to the other two sisters, futile, like yoking them to a broken plow."

Ceto deliberated. She operated within her two natures, made

manifest in the twin leviathans flanking her at all times. Sometimes she was a whale, tribal and sage. At other times she was a lone shark. Bite first before you are eaten.

"Your daughter lives," contended Echidna. "Infanticide, especially within a family, is an act of great darkness. An anathema, even among our kind."

Ceto pursed her lips. "And what does Nereus's wife think? Do you side with my gray children or my sea dragon?"

Doris shook her head, wisely abstaining from the family's division. "All your children offer cogent counsel, but you are the mother. It is your choice."

Echidna, intrepid and fervent, locked eyes with Ceto. "As such, you will bear the punishment."

It must have been quite a sight: two monsters, mother and child, engaged in a war of wills.

"If you do not make your claim," finished Echidna, "I will keep her."

And it was this statement that spared my sister from becoming chum. I suspect my mother made the decision mostly out of intrigue: What was it about this divisive baby that inspired Echidna's advocacy, her attachment?

"I will acknowledge this mortal, who is somehow a product of me and my brother-husband." Ceto laid us babies upon a bed of woven seaweed, and we squirmed into our familiar positions. Reunited by touch and feel. "Whether she be an honor or a curse, let none of you harm her." And Ceto flicked her wrist, decree delivered.

Echidna lowered her head, as pleased as the Graeae were jealous and Doris was eager to leave.

"What will you call them?"

"Stheno," Ceto began, like the opening of an invocation, as she touched our brows. "Euryale."

And she paused, lingering on the third infant—the babe who almost wasn't. Ceto bared her teeth. "And the little queen."

Pemphredo scoffed.

Then Ceto whispered the name that would become lore when it was still only a name, nothing more.

"Medusa."

I HAVE HEARD mortals express a similar sentiment, but it felt like we were children for only a few precious, ephemeral moments. One day we were waddling about caves, the next toddling into streams. Unclothed and unkempt, we splashed and submerged, venturing farther from home. We dove headfirst into the sea and, though we lacked any unique, discernible magic, we swam with the prowess of our bloodlines to the farthest reaches of life.

We bored Ceto and Phorcys, who cherished their gruesome pets and their lust for each other with far greater energy than they ever exhibited toward their children. For a time, Ceto sent warm-blooded sea creatures to nurse us: whales and seals, sea lions and dolphins. But after a while, she forgot.

And once she birthed our only brother, Ladon, we were truly left to fend for ourselves, for who could compete with a full-fledged—*male*—dragon?

On rare occasions, Phorcys would take us three for an undersea ride to a grotto off the coast of Ithaca, his haven long before the island found consequence. He did not know how to be a parent, and did not consider us part of his domain, but I accepted his failings just as I could not forgive Ceto's. Unfair, I know, but so are most preferences. Our father, gray-haired like the Graeae and fishtailed like his sister-wife, had spiky crab skin and claw forelegs shooting from his body—neither of which fostered warm hugs. Still, by the light of his torch, Phorcys delivered his best—and only—paternal advice:

"Stay together."

Did he speak directly to me, or have I reimagined it so? Regardless, I more than listened; I drank his words. Ingested them. Branded that two-word command upon my heart, my spirit, my purpose, and my existence.

Stay together.

"We will, Father. I will."

And truly, we did not need parents when we had one another. Our shared commonness became our serendipity, enabling an unfettered independence. I can think fondly of our idyllic childhood, not just because we were a whole trio, but because we were free. Of all our relations, my sisters and I were the least restricted—no offspring to nurture or prohibitive physical size. We weren't fearsome or mighty, intimidating, or execrable. We were beautiful, of course, but unnoticeable, which provided us a false security: we assumed we could forever escape notice and dodge trouble.

We were wrong, of course. Both would find us, but not before we explored the limits of fantasy.

My sisters and I visited Ladon, who guarded the far western garden islands, via the conduits of Oceanus. There, the Hesperides tended to a grove of golden apples, and long before those fruits touched the hands of Atalanta or Eris, we caught our reflections in their amber shine. We giggled and whispered beneath the arbors, in and out of shade, as Helios led his radiant chariot across the sky and our shadows danced.

"Do you think trees communicate with each other?" wondered a child Medusa.

Euryale scoffed.

"See how these trees lean, how they grow toward each other! And then look at those far ahead." Medusa gestured to an apple tree infected with rot, its trunk cankered and black. "The healthy tree beside it bends. I think it mourns. I think trees feel pain."

"This conversation is painful," muttered Euryale, closing her eyes.

I ignored her. "If that is so, Medusa, do I hurt the fruit I eat? Should I apologize to the blade of grass I bend, the flower I pick?"

"No. But perhaps we could be more grateful." Medusa brought a discarded apple core to her eye level. "Thank you. You were magnificent."

I smiled, Euryale snorted, and when the Sunset Maidens commenced their pleasant melodies, we leaned together, like drowsy trees.

"It is peaceful in this part of the world," Medusa murmured, laying a head against my shoulder.

"Tedious," Euryale corrected.

"Serene."

"Droll."

"The only monotony is your bickering," I moaned, lying back between them, physically and figuratively.

As always.

Euryale poked a sharp fingernail between my ribs. "Maybe the trees bicker, too," she rejoined, mocking us.

As always.

Sweet Ladon, who licked honey from our fingers and performed tricks for cakes, sensed tension and padded over, curling his long, emerald-colored tail around our three naked bodies. We had no need for clothes then, half-feral as we were.

I stroked his scales and he purred like a cat.

Before the sun set on the edge of the world and Medusa fell asleep, she cuddled against me and sighed. "If things get bad, we could come back here. Or maybe we should stay."

For it was a chaotic time. When we were still so very small, Echidna's savage and stormy husband rose against Zeus. Even to a child of monsters, he terrified. Typhon was larger than any giant, and though he had a man's torso, he had no legs. Instead, he slithered upon two massive vipers' tails. An enormous pair of wings rose from his muscled back, as well as other animal heads—some that spit poison. He had long, wild hair, a matted beard, and eyes that flashed red with fire. My most prominent memory of my sister's grisly husband is a visceral one: It is a strident sound that ground my teeth and rattled my bones. Typhon moved with the noise of a barbarous horde, a roar so cacophonous I would cower and cover my ears at his approach. His voice alone caused the earth to shake.

But he was Echidna's lover and he treated her with tenderness. She devoted herself to the children of their union. That's monsters for you.

Typhon despised Zeus, whom he deemed a pathetic replacement for Uranus and Cronus. He believed only one such as himself—a father of monsters—deserved sovereignty among the immortals, and thus, Typhon rebelled against the heavens, only to fall by Zeus's lightning bolt. Stunned but not slain, Typhon's mighty hulk was dragged across lands and imprisoned under the mountain called Etna. Once he roused and discovered his entrapment, Typhon continued to rage and revolt, punching holes through the ground and spitting fire to the surface. His behavior prompted Hades to ride from Tartarus in his black chariot, to ensure the border between the living and the Underworld remained secure.

(And if not for this unruly captive, Hades might never have stumbled upon Persephone, gathering daffodils in a nearby meadow. But that's how stories are cultivated. Words and actions are sown, spreading repercussions like wildflowers: monsters begetting lovers begetting conflict begetting heroes. On and on, endlessly.)

After Typhon's castigation, Echidna's embattled heart buckled. And while a more unlikely pair couldn't be imagined, little Medusa spent days and nights in the sea dragon's caliginous lair, mourning by her side, holding Echidna's hand and rubbing her back while she wept, singing in her charming but off-key way. I'm not sure Echidna would have survived this period without Medusa.

It was a life debt repaid.

Though Echidna performed no active role in Typhon's attempted coup, our sister adamantly refused to denounce her husband. To do so would abnegate all her principles, convictions that surpassed reason or self-preservation. Still, Zeus spared her from any punishment. At the time, I considered his clemency a peace offering to the old gods, but generations later the god of the sky's intentions became clear. He needed Echidna because he needed her children. They would all play a part in his plans for the age of man.

Yes, the age of man. Humanity. Zeus's esoteric experiments with creating humans fascinated my sisters and me, and we gleefully observed them go wrong time and again.

We watched atop boulders in the sea when the first humans—all male, in their maker's image—died out within a generation. And while we lolled beside the rivers, feet splashing against the stream, we witnessed Zeus annihilate the second race of men, the ungrateful ones who refused to properly pay homage. We climbed to the tops of the very same ash trees that formed the warlike third race after they inevitably killed each other off.

"This is all so stupid," argued Euryale. "Why does Zeus invest so much time and energy into something that always fails?"

I felt inclined to agree, but Medusa remained steadfast in her support.

"Humans are fascinating!" she insisted. "It's nearly impossible to predict what they will do next."

Euryale rolled her eyes. "I know what happens next, they *die*."

I shot my middle sister a furious look, and she had the decency to blush. The mention of death always altered the mood, for we could never forget that Medusa was mortal. Though her life span was indefinite—a benefit of her ancestry—she lived within consistent limitations and at constant risk. She bled and she bruised. She hungered and needed rest. After hours in the sun, her skin browned and hair lightened.

When she climbed too high, I worried. Same as when she wandered too far or swam too long. Would that mushroom kill her? That whirlpool? That fall?

Medusa's preoccupation with humans, I always believed, was a fascination with their corporeality. She watched them because she needed to see how beings aware of their imminent death chose to live.

In an immortal community, time holds no obvious value, but when time doesn't matter, neither do a lot of things. And Medusa, whose days were limited, desired a structure our aimless wanderings couldn't provide.

Because her life would end, it needed to matter.

As I have already admitted, in our earliest ages, I struggle to remember chronology without glaring anachronisms. However, I do know—without equivocation—that everything changed when Zeus delegated his mortal project to the Titan brothers, clever Prometheus and scatterbrained Epimetheus. Their success with both humans and animals, after all Zeus's failure, forced life into a structure of time, and it altered Medusa. She longed for entities I didn't consider essential: excitement and experience, a richness to her finite existence. A definition.

For as mortality became synonymous with human, what did that make Medusa?

Physically, Medusa matured at the same rate as Euryale and I—that is to say, very slowly. It took many, many years for our bodies to finally shed childhood, and then, just at the verge of womanhood, we paused.

We seemed to be stuck, waiting, but for what or whom I did not know.

SECOND EPISODE

EURYALE

She lifts her dress to wade,
this river girl.
She bares her ankles
and shows her heart.

—Erastus of Athens, "The Illness of Maidens"

WHILE MEDUSA PERSEVERATED on those anemic humans, Euryale pursued a far nobler race.

The Olympians overshadowed humans and outshone the Titans. Their powers were vast and vigorous, their bodies beautiful. They behaved in ways that celebrated decadence and ambition, and the passions and feuds of their personal lives thrilled Euryale. Hungry for snippets of their hierarchical melodramas, she consumed the gossip and obsessed over their increasingly tangled relations.

Beside such sophistication, Euryale's own family seemed crude. On childish adventures with her sisters, while they played in tide pools and built landscapes of sand, Euryale daydreamed about making a home on Mount Olympus. She smiled, imagining Ceto's shock and envy when her benthic-born daughter ascended to the clouds. Euryale's sisters would be invited to visit, but never to stay, for her husband and children would require too much of her attention. After she hosted Stheno and Medusa with divine treats and regaled them with stories of her marital bliss, she would send them on their way—with a fine gift, naturally, for such riches would be nothing to her.

Dry your eyes, sweet sisters, I will find time for you again, soon.

But it would be humankind, ironically enough, who served as the catalyst for Euryale climbing that famed mount.

When Prometheus broke Zeus's trust by gifting humanity with fire, he upset the balance of power. After the Titan's brutal sentencing, Zeus was forced to make peace with the culprit's brother, for he didn't need another embittered god seeking vengeance. Zeus commanded Hephaestus to form a human woman from clay as Epimetheus's consolation prize. Though no lovelier than any immortal, this human woman was *blessed*. One by one, the Olympians honored the dirt-born imposter with a present that outdid the last. Music from Apollo. Majesty from Hera. A sapphire-studded silver gown woven by Athena's own hands. Hermes gave her a name. *Pandora.*

And, of course, Zeus bequeathed a sealed vase.

It made Euryale's blood boil. What an infuriating waste.

In a spirit of unity, Zeus invited the entire pantheon to the wedding he hosted within his palace on Olympus. Euryale and her sisters, as children of the old order, were included, and as they entered the royal complex, Euryale missed no detail of her environs: the heavy fortifications of purest marble and hardest bronze, the golden gates and shimmering pavement. She had never seen so many buildings in one place, stables and chambers and halls—more rooms than she could count. Even the air was immaculate, an ether of luxury, the breezy confidence begotten of worship.

And above it all arched a rainbow. This was perfection.

The sisters watched from the farthest outskirts of the cloistered courtyard as Epimetheus and Pandora beheld each other for the first time. The bride wore an aureate crown, threaded with garlands, and an embroidered veil of spider silk hung suggestively across her face.

"She is more beautiful than I thought possible," murmured Medusa, eyes bright, awakened somehow.

The groom, aglow with Aphrodite's desire, gently pulled aside the shimmering cloth to kiss his new wife.

"He is bewitched by her!" furthered Medusa, raising her voice, and even stoic Stheno agreed, nodding along and—*Did she just sigh?*

This was getting embarrassing.

"She is empty," Euryale rejoined, correcting her simpering sisters. "Her eyes are as lifeless as two river rocks."

"You judge too harshly, Euryale. Can you imagine, coming into the world full-grown?" Medusa pushed herself up on the tips of her toes, angling for a better view over the assortment of demigods and beasts delegated to the rear of the audience. "Perhaps she is dumb, or perhaps she is just young."

"She was born *into* marriage," added Stheno, "which would overwhelm any creature."

"Does she feel and think like a child? Or a woman?"

Euryale's irritation simmered up through her chest, spilling over the lips of her mouth. "She thinks and feels as much as dirt, Medusa. Because that is all Pandora is."

"Ah, but dirt goes deep." Medusa grinned, delighting in the way she could aggravate Euryale. "Does she carry the earth's memories within her? Does she speak its language?"

"Stheno," Euryale whispered, "tell your favorite sister to be quiet."

"You are both my favorite sisters."

Euryale exhaled through her nose, causing her nostrils to flare. Stheno's stubborn ambivalence could be more frustrating than Medusa's endlessly irritating questions.

"Just enjoy the day," Stheno advised.

"How can I enjoy one of our oldest gods, a Titan, debasing himself with the lowest of life-forms?" Euryale shot back. "It's sickening."

Her older sister cringed. "Now you're the one who should lower her voice."

"Is it Pandora's mortality that makes her lesser?" asked Medusa, with no edge, only a patient curiosity.

Yes, Euryale longed to say. Flustered by her private beliefs, she struggled to explain herself. "Epimetheus may love her now, but she will die, and he will live forever. It's like tying your heart to a butterfly."

"A short, glorious flight and a sweet landing." Medusa shrugged. She turned back toward the bride. "A life could be much worse."

AFTER THE CEREMONY, Euryale wandered from the gold-paved feasting hall and past the prodigious banquet, accepting a glass of ambrosial nectar on her way. She stopped beneath a covered walkway at the edge of the palace and admired the crisp, panoramic view provided by the mountaintop: viridescent isles cutting through cerulean sea. Clouds like pink rose petals strewn across a forget-me-not sky.

Euryale spent so much time in the water or belowground with her sisters, what a respite to reach such heights!

The world below belonged to the immortals, but for how much longer?

She sipped at her drink and tried to ignore the merriment behind her, where foolhardy Epimetheus allowed himself to be mollified with this human substitute for his brother.

Were siblings so replaceable, after all?

"You are missing quite the party," came a foreign male voice. "Or is the party missing you?"

His words ran down her body like smooth water, and yet Euryale felt something at the core of her yanked toward him with the strength of a tide. She spun and discovered Poseidon, Lord of the Sea, idling before her, leaning against a column. Hair so dark it shone blue like a mussel's shell, curled lips, chest bare. She nearly dropped her glass.

"Are you not entertained by Zeus's beneficence?"

Ignoring the flickering in the depths of her belly, Euryale kept her voice steady, detached. "Entertained, yes, but never impressed."

Poseidon loosed a low chuckle. "And what of the bride? Her name parts the lips of everyone inside."

"Not my lips."

His gaze dropped to her mouth and he stared openly. "I am aware."

Euryale's mouth was dry. She swallowed. "How did you honor the bride, Lord Poseidon?"

"With a necklace that prevents its wearer from drowning."

"Inspired."

"Not particularly. I forgot then ran out of time." Poseidon grinned. One of his canines was too sharp and slightly crooked. "She herself is a rather apocryphal present, though, is she not?"

Euryale raised an eyebrow. "'Apocryphal?' You doubt Zeus's intentions?"

"My brother is known for many things. Charity is not one of them."

"And so all of this"—Euryale gestured to the lavish festivities, the location itself—"is a ruse?"

"I would call it a wily move to restore balance."

"Between Zeus and the brothers?"

"Between us and them."

Us.

"Prometheus brought humanity fire," continued the Olympian. "He is their redeemer. Now Epimetheus will bring them Pandora."

"And she will be their downfall."

"You see clearly, Golden Eyes." Poseidon closed the distance between them as he also took in the view. "And you know my name, but I do not know yours."

"I am Euryale. Of Ceto and Phorcys."

His expression shifted from confusion to recognition. "Then you are a grandchild of Pontus. I have heard mention of three beautiful maidens living amid a horde of beasts."

Beautiful.

"And your sisters?" he asked, scanning the crowds behind them. "They are here?"

She nodded.

"Show me."

He offered his arm and escorted her back into the clamorous party. Euryale felt the proximity of their bodies like a dizzying blow to the head, and she hoped—she *prayed*—that everybody noticed their entrance.

"There." She pointed, forced to raise her voice over the pandemonium. "Tall and somber. My older sister, Stheno." Poseidon nodded when he located Stheno, standing alone but unbothered at the edge of the crowd, content to observe.

"And the other?"

His face came so close to hers that his beard grazed her cheek, and Euryale struggled to maintain a steady breath. She worried he could feel her erratic pulse.

"Medusa, the baby, is attempting to dance."

For indeed, Medusa, flustered by heat and humor, attempted to follow a dryad in a complicated dance. She was sweating, laughing, and impossibly bad, spinning the wrong way, crashing into guests, and stepping on toes. Lavender petals flew from the sprigs in her hair.

Euryale winced.

"She has no rhythm," commented Poseidon dryly.

"She's an even worse singer."

Yet the hungry way Poseidon stared at her winsome sister made Euryale frown. Medusa, whose brown hair glinted with gold from long hours in the sun and whose cheeks flushed an annoying shade of dusky rose when pleased, clapped along to the music, just slightly off beat and euphoric.

"She's mortal," clarified Euryale quickly. "And odd."

"Clearly."

And Poseidon smiled at her, just once, just enough that any lingering worries about her captivating sister vanished from her mind.

Poseidon's hand curved around Euryale's waist to the small of her back, and he nudged her toward him.

"You've shown me your sisters, now why don't I show you . . ."

But he halted, for Amphitrite approached their periphery. The eldest of Doris's Nereids—and Poseidon's wife—resembled the sea-foam at dawn. She wore a stunning, diaphanous gown decorated in pearls and treasures of the sea, and atop her head rested a crab-claw crown and hairnet. Amphitrite did not walk so much as she drifted, as delicate as a water strider on a pond's surface.

Euryale owned only one colorless, formless shift. No jewels, no sandals. Her hair ran in tangled paths down her back, for she didn't know how to style it. Standing beside the resplendent ocean nymph, Euryale felt uncouth and exposed; she burned with a new shame.

"My queen." Poseidon, the adoring husband, bowed.

Euryale inclined her head. "Good evening, Cousin."

"It's nice to see you looking so well," Amphitrite responded. Her words were airy and light but failed to lift her face. Nereids were enchanting, fleet of foot and eager to dance, but this nymph did not rejoice. Amphitrite's eyes lingered upon her husband's hand at Euryale's hip, and she sighed.

"The girl became lost wandering Zeus's palace, my wife. I have returned her safely."

"Her sisters must be anxious at her absence."

"As my brothers whisper and plot during mine. There are no reprieves from the demands of family, even at a party."

Amphitrite allowed her husband a tight approximation of a smile.

"Give our best to your mother and father, Euryale," she insisted, a polite signal but a signal all the same.

Euryale understood.

"We will meet again," Poseidon murmured in Euryale's ear, secretly stroking the small of her back. "By the sea."

Long after he ushered his wife back toward their illustrious kin, Euryale felt his voice tickle inside her, felt the absence of his touch.

She knew her cousin's story well. Poseidon sought modest Amphitrite's hand, but she fled his advances, hiding below the waves until a dolphin betrayed her hideaway. Poseidon retrieved her, overcame her, and married her.

The order of which differed according to the teller.

The tale made little sense to Euryale then, and now that she had met him? Only a half-wit would resist a union with such an Olympian! Only a prude could prefer chastity to the Lord of the Sea's bed.

What had he wanted to show her? Euryale shuddered. She would have gone with him willingly—she would not have given chase—and that would have been an irreversible mistake. Amphitrite's life illuminated one vital message: the value of virginity. As much as Euryale ached for the pleasures of a male touch, she cultivated a nature more calculating than impetuous. No, she would not run from him, for she was no coward. But Euryale would demonstrate forbearance; she would hold her own maidenhood close until it could be used to her best advantage.

When she met Poseidon again, for she knew she would, by the sea, Euryale would be better prepared.

She returned to her sisters, feeling heavier and lighter.

"Where were you?" wondered Stheno.

"What do you mean? I never left."

"Shall I get us some food?"

And Euryale declined, preferring to savor the deliciousness of her deceit.

POSEIDON PREDICTED CORRECTLY.

When Pandora broke both her promise and Zeus's vase, she released ruin upon the mortal world in abundance: disease and death, greed and vanity, slander and envy, toil, old age, and war. Each misery ransacked humanity, forcing Zeus to send massive rains and floods to wash away the mess. Euryale chuckled to herself at Zeus's plan made manifest.

The rightful balance restored.

She and her sisters oversaw the destruction, perched at a rocky pinnacle like three large seabirds. Far below, humankind floundered in wrathful waters: the symbol of life recast as an instrument of death.

"Poor Epimetheus," remarked Stheno quietly, hugging her knees to her chest as powerful winds smote the landscape. "Hasn't he suffered enough?"

Euryale shrugged. "Don't accept gifts from Zeus."

"Which one, Pandora or the vase?"

"He should have tossed both into the sea."

Thunder pealed so loudly it shook rocks loose from the mountainside. The waves rose and raged. Medusa shivered, and the sisters huddled closer together beneath their seagrass blanket.

"Would you have opened it?" Stheno asked.

"Immediately," answered Euryale.

Medusa nodded. "Me, too."

Stheno's face hardened. She kept her eyes forward, locked on the disaster. "I wouldn't. Never."

An alarming, confusing rush of appreciation and frustration for her steadfast sister swept through Euryale's chest. She wanted to hug her; she wanted to slap her. "You don't always have to be so righteous."

Medusa lay her head against Stheno's shoulder. "We grant you permission to misbehave, Stheno. At least once."

From the other side, Euryale nudged Stheno with her elbow. "Start a fight. Tell a lie. Spread a plague. Eat a baby."

Medusa giggled.

"Leave me alone."

"Because of Pandora, we have an opening to be as wicked as we want."

"Stop blaming that girl," Stheno rebuked.

Euryale drew back. "I didn't know you were so attached."

"I'm not, but this world wasn't ruined by some clay girl and a silly vase." Stheno clutched her hands together in her lap. "The wars between egos have always existed. Fathers kill their sons. Sons overthrow their fathers. And these battles will rage on for as long as too few hold too much power."

Medusa and Euryale exchanged a look over Stheno's head.

"We hear you," Medusa told their sister.

"And you're not wrong," admitted Euryale.

A smile tugged at Stheno's lips. "I'm more than that. I am right."

The sisters sat quietly for a while, lost to their own thoughts, but Medusa could tolerate silence for only so long before commencing her sanguine chatter. She was like a bird in that way, chirping through the torrents. "Do you think there will be more humans?"

Euryale groaned. "I'm so bored of this conversation. I'll rip every hair from my head if we talk about humans one more time."

"Unlikely," commented Stheno. "You are far too vain."

"Although," clarified Medusa, a puckish ring to her voice. "I've been told *I* have the best hair in this trio."

Stheno laughed.

Euryale pursed her lips. "I would push you into this flood, but Echidna would save you."

"And you'd miss me."

Euryale scoffed but allowed Medusa to reach across their eldest sister to hold her hand.

"You'd miss me," Medusa repeated.

Euryale didn't answer, just let her focus drift slowly, naturally back to the horizon. To its shades of tempestuous blue: the watery mass grave moaning beneath a squally sky.

"You'll miss me."

DESPITE ZEUS'S BEST efforts, humanity survived.

Pandora's daughter, Pyrrha, and Prometheus's son, Deucalion, floated on a piecemeal ark to Mount Parnassus and began anew, throwing the rocks of Gaea over their shoulders to form another race of man and woman.

Such resilient creatures, Euryale thought with begrudging admiration. Like a decapitated reptile that immediately regrows its head.

With the generations that followed came an entirely new phenomenon: the city-state. Civilizations sprouted like wild amaranth, and they placed human names on these primal lands. Corinth and Argos. Attica. The large island became Crete, and it was there that Zeus, as a white bull, abducted the princess Europa.

Arguably, this became the moment Euryale acceded to humanity's permanence. Now that Zeus had tasted the spoils—had capitalized on a new prurient venture—there would be no more natural disasters and mass killings. The gods were as hungry for maidens as they were for fresh stories.

Europa's heroic brother, Cadmus, founded Thebes, a city-state of unparalleled dominance and influence in the land of Boeotia. The sisters collected whispers of the Cadmea, of the Spartoi, and repeated them to one another under the private veil of night. It was Medusa who first confessed: "I want to go."

For Medusa was brave enough to voice what Euryale also desired. She could not swallow another acerbic lifetime clinging to the outskirts, as removed from the gilled and scaled as they were from the elite. In truth, the sisters made sense only when they were alone together, and Euryale would rather join the ranks of the Underworld than spend her eternity as a spinster.

"But *why*?" Ceto frowned, stroking the octopus nestled at her shoulder, tentacles draped across her being in a strange subterranean style. Once again, she exhibited more affection for some spineless, toxic creature than for her own daughters, and Euryale's lips clamped down on a sudden gush of vitriol. Their infancy was a bitter recollection. On good days they were raised by whales, but Euryale was no animal. She despised Ceto for outsourcing her maternity, yet Euryale also knew that without a mammalian wet nurse, she and her sisters would have surely starved to death.

It was complicated and confusing, emotions that made Euryale irritable.

"Everybody visits, Mother," Stheno offered simply.

"Well, it should be an easy assimilation. You three are so unremarkable."

The Graeae lurked and listened, their very grayness blending them into the cave, and they smugly echoed Ceto's insults:

"So humanlike already!"

"Could easily pass for mortals."

"Especially Medusa."

Ceto popped a prawn into her mouth like a berry, then spit its tail into a putrescent pile of fish bones beside her. Euryale set her jaw. Ceto affected airs, but she represented the lowest region of an august domain. Sea beasts were revolting, all scar tissue and barnacles, gelatinous tentacles and misshapen accretions, snaggleteeth in constant flux from the viciousness of eating.

Other water beings inspired praise. The salty Oceanids included the lovely, fishtailed Eurynome, who mothered the Graces. The Nereids—not just Amphitrite, but Thetis and Galatea—wore coral wreaths and white robes trimmed in gold. They danced barefoot with their father on a silvery grotto at the bottom of the sea, singing with melodious voices of bounty and breadth. And then there were the freshwater Naiads, who collected tributes for nursing the young, for guiding a human child's passage to adulthood. They were the wives of kings, beloved of gods!

Ceto relished in reaping fear. She reveled in pain and horror, reviled beauty.

Euryale would rather be worshipped—she had been born to the wrong water family.

"They call Cadmus the first hero," continued Stheno, in a futile attempt to sway their mother. Euryale wished she would stop.

"For slaying the dragon of Ares! One just like your brother!" Ceto leaned forward, hissing. "Your *hero* built his city from its teeth."

"And he atoned for eight years," countered Medusa. "Cadmus

wed Ares's daughter, Harmonia. If Ares can forgive Cadmus, why can't we?"

"Ares's love child with Aphrodite?" Ceto barked a seal-like laugh. "A cursed bride! The human fool did Ares a favor by taking her off his hands."

"The Olympians are without loyalty," stated Deino, who held the eye.

"Cheaters and connivers," Pemphredo agreed. "Fickle and fraudulent."

"They cannot be trusted."

"Do not forget how Zeus deceived Metis," rasped Enyo, and Ceto nodded, clucking her tongue.

Metis, a daughter of Oceanus and mother of wisdom and deep thought, was Zeus's first wife. Though a Titaness, she betrayed her kind and gifted Zeus a magical emetic that he used on his father, Cronus. When Cronus vomited up his other five children, Zeus was able to recruit his siblings and stage a coup. Without Metis's divine assistance, the Olympian order would not exist.

Zeus owed everything to his bride, and though he admired her cunning and dedication, it was not enough to assuage his anxiety that any of their children would be too powerful.

And because Metis's womb remained a constant threat, Zeus became what he despised—his father. Just as Cronus had circumvented the rules of primogeniture, so did Zeus—even duplicating his methods. He swallowed Metis whole. But Metis, who was indeed pregnant, was fierce. She fought for her child from within Zeus's omnipotent form, terrorizing him with headaches that sent the mighty king of Olympus limping to Hephaestus for aid.

Create whatever weapon necessary to stop this pain!

Hephaestus forged a double-bladed ax strong enough to cleave open the skull of the greatest Olympian and slammed its edge into his lord's head. Zeus bellowed as his head parted, but what emerged, however, was not the forsaken wife, but their adult daughter in full panoply.

Athena, goddess of war and strategy, who would become her father's staunchest ally.

"The new gods and goddesses behave monstrously but will not be called such. Humans do not see through the guise." Ceto sighed, and for once it wasn't an expression of arrogance or exasperation but an emission full of regret. "I'll never understand why you three spend so much time on land, spying. None of your siblings do."

For a brief moment, Euryale recognized Ceto as a mother, one who struggled to connect, to communicate her worry. If there had ever been a time for Ceto to relay counsel, it was right then. Euryale's breath caught in her throat.

"We don't want to be spies," began Medusa, one hand to her heart as she stepped closer to their mother. "We want to participate."

Ceto's laughter burst forth violently, a resounding smack to the face.

"Participate?"

Euryale exhaled, cursing herself for expecting anything other than derision.

Pemphredo's toothless mouth gurgled in an eerie semblance of a giggle, and the other Graeae hissed and stomped, clutching their sides in snide mirth. Stheno flinched and Medusa's eyes watered, but Euryale shouldered their disdain. She saw right through its green-tinted origin. Like Ceto, the gray sisters could never occupy the human space, would never consider a sojourn to Thebes. They were forever confined to the remote and murky. For a time, being grotesque made them special, but that world was changing.

Euryale and her sisters were a link between the new generation and the old.

"Go, then. *Participate.*"

Euryale straightened her spine, lifting her chin. "We weren't asking permission."

The octopus crawled down Ceto's arm, like something sinuous and ancient, and rested its bulbous head in her lap. Ceto leveled a poisonous glare at Euryale. "Since you don't ask, I won't say what I think. But I know you three are due for a reckoning."

Dread, cold and oily, pooled in the depths of Euryale's stomach. She felt sick, but Stheno gripped her forearm before she could falter. "We are leaving," pronounced her older sister. Stheno took Medusa's hand as well, and the sisters clung to the safety of one another, forming a shield against their family's barbs.

"Oh, but one more thing."

Ceto's voice shot through the dark like an arrow, and Euryale closed her eyes, awaiting the kill.

"Watch yourself, Medusa. It would be so pathetic to die by a human's hands."

THIRD EPISODE

STHENO

Cadmus came before his court.
Cloaked, crowned, colored
in saffron, carrying the
cradle of civilization.

—Erastus of Athens, "The Conqueror"

WE ARRIVED AT Thebes as dawn's light broke through mist, lone travelers despite the worn road. Situated between a lake and a mountain, the city rested in a low, hilly plain still wrapped in a blanket of early fog. Even beclouded, with its people half-conscious, the city and its fertile ground emanated energy. A palpable buzzing, like we had chanced upon a hive of ingenuity and potential—and, naturally, the risk of being stung.

I pulled my shawl more tightly about my shoulders and then reached for my sisters' hands. We did not admit intimidation aloud, but I'm certain I did not battle trepidation alone. Thrill and terror tugged at my heart with equal strength.

I had witnessed war among cosmic entities, called beasts of yore my friends, but humanity would be an altogether different sort of danger.

"We don't have to stay long," began Euryale, resorting to forced flippancy.

Medusa bit her lower lip, and hesitancy gilded her olive eyes. Our mother's final warning still spiraled about my mind—did it torment Medusa, as well? Did my little sister sense death in this strange place? The taste of bile reached the back of my mouth, but I forced it down: Ceto would not ruin this for us.

"Follow me," I told my younger sisters, and I strode forward with the show of faith they both needed.

We descended a gentle slope, passing shepherds and goatherds who obdurately clung to sleep beside their rousing flocks, then reached a stand-alone building on the fringe of the city proper, a checkpoint for incoming goods. We had nothing to declare besides a gift for the king and our own apprehensions.

"Welcome to Thebes," greeted the guard, making moon eyes at Euryale, who stared back with open hostility.

Thebes awoke as we proceeded inside its walls, as if the locals heeded some internal, ubiquitous alarm: *Foreigners! In our city!* Followed quickly by *Invaders or customers?!* We held no coin, a token of our naivete. Economics meant nothing to us then, for immortals bartered in power only, a currency composed of suspicion, strategy, and lust.

We wandered past sleepy-eyed artisans lighting fires in the forges where they crafted copper tools and dishes. Bronzesmiths and goldsmiths, as well. We drifted past an endless array of wool-processing workshops, of chattering women ready to wash, pick, and spin the crude animal fibers provided by the shepherds. Children in various sizes and ages raced past, completely oblivious to our intrusion and far more interested in games of chase.

And there were human men *everywhere*, more than we had ever seen in one place, at one time, and at such close range. Cutlers and bowyers, carpenters and masons, money changers, wine sellers, soothsayers and beggars, farmers and enslaved people. Like the guard at the gate, more than one man paused to gawk as we caught their notice.

What did these men see? Sisters, no doubt, by the traits we shared: light brown skin, dark brown hair, and slender builds. I knew we were all quite lovely, though my own face was the least interesting, as Euryale so often told me. Her beauty could only be described as proud. Severe eyebrows. Keen cheekbones. A haughty chin. Her hair was always a mess, which should have humanized her, but it only provided her an additional air of defiance.

Medusa, our baby, never lost her youthful look: cheeks just a bit too round, lips like an unopened flower, and large, upturned eyes. With the sweet-stepping body of a perpetual waif, she was so soft, so heartbreaking.

Beside them, I was awkward—a truth that didn't much bother me. My eyes were a bit deeper set, my nose slightly too long. And maybe my body tended more toward lanky than lithe. I gave the impression of a squid—an abundance of limbs.

I suppose we were an unusual sight on that typical morning. We walked in wildness then, like deer. Uncultured, fleet of foot, and quick to startle. A trio of fawns entering the hunting grounds.

But I speak now from reflection. My clearest memory from our arrival is actually the smells, aromas never encountered in the briny realms of Oceanus. Freshly baked bread bade us a yeasty *good morning,* wafting up, waving, from outdoor ovens. Merchants lined their stalls with ripe lemons and olives, grapes and figs. Bitter scents with bites of sweetness. Spice and syrup. Women curated domestic gardens of cumin and mint, fennel and celery. Euryale and I did not hunger in the same way as Medusa but still relished the taste of exotic, mouthwatering foods.

Almost reluctantly we reached our destination, the House of Cadmus—a palace that formed the heart of the city's acropolis. In the open vestibule within the portico, we gave our names to the guards and thus, for the first time, to the human world.

Stheno. Euryale. Medusa.

As daughters of two of the oldest sea deities, we were received with reverence and more than a bit of curiosity. A royal herald led my sisters and me through the eastern door and down the entrance hall to an antechamber. Elaborate frescoes decorated each of the walls, detailing the grand events of the king's life: his voyage across the sea, his discovery of the blessed spring and ascent into heroism, his empyrean marriage.

While we awaited our formal introduction, I studied this art. Particularly the image of young Cadmus slaying the dragon, which had guarded this land in its genesis. Here were Ceto's words illustrated: Cadmus burying the serpent, its bones sprouting the Spartoi—the sown men—who would build the Cadmea and become the city's inaugural court.

"He looks like Ladon."

I turned toward Euryale. She, too, had her eyes pinned to the heroic tableau—to the dragon, bashed by a boulder, then backed against an oak tree and stabbed with a spear. Its body pummeled, bruised and broken, blood spouting from wound after wound. *Heroism.* Would these humans consider our gentle brother a threat? Would they celebrate his murder with a similarly graphic commemoration? I felt queasy and clasped my hands together to stop their shaking, particularly as we were summoned into a square-shaped throne room.

Had we stumbled into a trap?

But we were presented before the court and their attendants with much bowing and scraping, and I had to wonder: Do they fear *us*? Or at least our family's reputation? Cadmus, after all, was aged. No longer the strapping youth of legend. Why risk his life and legacy on a second bout with a dragon? And he wasn't known for his prowess on the sea. He might not survive the wrath of Echidna and her children.

Such thoughts provided me comfort. And confidence.

King Cadmus stood between his throne and a massive circular hearth, along with Queen Harmonia and their five children: the princesses Ino, Agave, Autonoë, and Semele, and their only son, the prince Polydorus.

So this was human royalty. An assemblage of average height, some more fair than others. Cadmus was portlier than I imagined, his belly indicative of leisure and ready meals. Is this what becomes of a hero? Who was he before, on that fateful day he left Phoenicia to save his sister, a nobody, and found himself in adventure? Was that boy still in there, buried beneath body fat and expensive cloth?

"Welcome, daughters of Phorcys and Ceto, nieces of Nereus,"

boomed the king of Thebes, interrupting my thoughts on his corpulence. I blushed. "Your presence dignifies our great city, and, tonight, we will feast."

"It is our honor, as well," I returned gravely, hiding a smile. If they only knew how little we mattered in the immortal pantheon!

Medusa conferred the pot of live eels we carried. "A gift, from our home to yours, in gratitude for your hospitality."

He seemed pleased by our offering.

"Such a delicacy," added Harmonia. "I will see that these are prepared with the utmost care."

Euryale lowered her head before the regal Harmonia. The Theban matriarch was a by-product of two Olympians yet had been married to a human man as collateral. Their relationship—as the reverse of Pandora and Epimetheus—proved that women could be traded and gifted whether their blood be ichor or red.

An unsettling realization.

"My youngest daughter will acquaint you with our palace, your home for as long as you should stay."

A princess peeled off the line and stepped forward. Semele, with her swanlike neck and heavy lashes, was the recipient of her fair mother's grace, and clothed in materials I had never touched let alone owned. Fine linen and soft wool, all embroidered with delicate lines of silver and gold. I felt Euryale stiffen beside me.

"Follow me." Semele opened a decorated arm, shepherding us forward like a herd of livestock. We fell into the pace of her languid steps as our group exited the throne room and entered the labyrinthine halls. Safely outside her parents' field of vision, the princess abruptly dropped her polished decorum. Her hands settled upon her slim hips, and her playful eyes darted from one of my sisters to the next. "You are not at all what I expected."

Euryale crossed her arms over her chest. "Why? We're even prettier?"

Semele tossed her head back in laughter. "You are! I thought you would at least have flippers. Or green hair. Besides those strange eyes, you look practically human."

Euryale bristled.

"Oh, now I've offended." Semele lowered her voice conspiratorially. "It's not so bad passing for human. We have our diversions. You'll see. I promise." And the princess winked.

Medusa smiled back.

"Come, my father insists I show off our gratuitous riches. We wouldn't want to disappoint the old goose."

Semele ushered us through her family's magnificent home, talking all the while. We passed rooms filled with elite handicrafts, around pillars of invention, beneath successive architectural feats. In the armory we saw untarnished weapons and spotless riding tack, as well as archives on clay tablets. Medusa paused and traced a finger over the strange figures.

"Do you know what these symbols mean?" she wondered.

Semele shrugged a thin shoulder. "Can I read? Why would I bother?" But then she grinned. "That's not entirely true. I tried but wasn't smart enough." She faked a sigh. "At least I'm pretty."

She was obnoxious. She was charming. Were all humans so complex? Or was this princess unusual?

We stopped in a room of jars, where we encountered oils and spices from lands near and far. Rue and sage, coriander and saffron. We stopped to smell as many as we were permitted to unseal.

"There are also workshops," Semele offered, "the places where we boil perfumes and mix ointments."

I nodded. "Lead the way."

But Semele did not move, only fiddled with the hem of her shawl. Had my answer bored her? I could not figure out what I was supposed to say.

"My nose is a bit sensitive to fragrances," began Medusa slowly. "Perhaps you have another destination in mind?"

Semele brightened. "I'm not explicitly allowed to take you there, but neither was I forbidden. Shall we accidentally stumble into the treasury?"

Euryale arched an eyebrow. "I do have a horrible sense of direction."

"I knew you three would be fun."

We held in our laughter as Semele snuck us into the heart of the palace, ducking behind columns, alternating between delicate footsteps and moments of speed. We nearly crashed into her back when Semele came to an abrupt halt outside a monitored doorway. She motioned that we should hold our tongues, then she raised her neck to its full length and approached the guards.

"The king commands that our distinguished visitors be shown the royal trove."

Semele spoke as if from behind a mask, as convincing as any actor in the mortal theaters.

"Yes, Princess."

"As you say."

To us she pronounced, "Let your immortal kin never doubt the great affluence of Thebes."

The guards moved aside with eyes to the ground as Semele sashayed forward, my sisters and me trailing in her wake. When she closed the door behind us and waggled her eyebrows, I marveled at her ease in switching from mischief to manners.

"Welcome to my second-favorite room."

"And your first?" questioned Medusa.

"The wine magazine, of course."

The interior of Cadmus's treasury dazzled like the inside of an abalone shell or a geode. Bombastic works of lapis lazuli, gold, agate, and quartz covered every flat surface, the overflow heaped in piles. My sisters fingered the cache, murmuring over their workmanship and splendor.

"I'm so glad we got lost," breathed Euryale.

I admired the riches, too, but admittedly, I've never been drawn to gems and metals. I don't understand why a colored stone is any more appealing than a hyacinth in perfect bloom. I'm simple like that yet know better than to admit such a thought aloud.

Semele motioned us toward a plain box, camouflaged by its banality.

"Here is a treasure worthy of a god."

She opened it and beamed at our round of gasps.

"Hephaestus made this for my mother to wear on her wedding day," whispered the princess reverently. "It brings her eternal youth and beauty."

In the bed of the box lay a necklace forged of beaten gold, so smooth I barely noted the hammer strikes. It shone like yellow fire, lustrous and incandescent. Loaded with jewels of perfect clarity and color.

"There is a robe, too, but my mother keeps it in her rooms."

"May I touch it?"

Semele nodded and Medusa placed one admiring finger upon the piece, outlining the shape of two serpents who formed its clasp with their gaping mouths.

"I have never seen its equal," Medusa professed.

"Even on Olympus?" quizzed the princess, eyes eager.

"Not even on Pandora."

Semele waved a dismissive hand at Pandora's name. "What of the goddesses? Hestia? Artemis?" She hesitated and bit down on her bottom lip. "Hera?"

I shrugged. "I did not notice."

Euryale frowned. "Why would Hephaestus gift such a wonder to the daughter born of his wife and her lover?"

For Harmonia, as our mother had thrilled to remind us, was begotten of the illicit affair between Aphrodite and Ares, not the goddess of love and her kindly but lame husband.

"That's between Hephaestus and Aphrodite, it has nothing to do with my mother." Semele closed the box and tucked it away. "It is a blessed gift. And it will be mine next, my parents promised."

FOURTH EPISODE

EURYALE

Wine to loosen my tongue and robe.
Wine to swallow the doubt with delight.
Purple wine for purple nights.
Drink, tonight, to night!

—*Erastus of Athens, "The Symposium"*

FOR WILDLINGS, EURYALE and her sisters settled into palace life almost effortlessly. They bathed and dined, wove and danced as if born into human royalty. The king and queen treated the trio with cautious congeniality, denying them nothing but maintaining distance. Semele explained to Euryale that her parents would not risk committing an impertinence, not to relatives of Echidna.

Semele, of course, delighted in impertinence.

The sisters spent nearly every night in the brazen camaraderie of the princess's suite. Sometimes Semele's siblings joined—Prince Polydorus most of all—but the eclectic parties were usually composed of discreet serving girls, any visitors to the palace of a certain temperament, a daring guard willing to risk censure, and a paid entertainer.

Semele lived to host. In the very center of her rooms, she kept a large painted bowl filled to the brim with wine, day or night. Here, Euryale learned to drink—how much it took to feel pleasantly lightheaded, how much to stumble and forget. She studied how wine affected the mood of the party, and was pleased when she began to identify the effects of alcohol in others—when somebody was about to get too uninhibited, another belligerent.

The guests refilled their cups, regaling each other with ribald toasts and laughter. Enslaved peoples—those taken as plunder by Cadmus's pirates—strummed on tortoiseshell lyres while others sang. The princess pursued debauchery, of course, but also a happiness of mind, soul, and body. When her guests weren't cavorting to wild music, they improvised poetry. Semele favored a storytelling game where each person took a turn adding no more than a single plot point to a tale, and it would circle about the room, around comedies and over tragedies, long into the night.

The humans, Euryale noted, delighted in debate and held the gifts of rhetoric in high esteem. Often Semele's diverse parties coalesced into philosophical musings on a single question: Why do some animals eat plants and others one another? Why do men have nipples but no milk? Is wine a blessing or a curse? What is madness?

Euryale, purposefully fractious, reveled in proposing troublesome topics—discussions that fanned the flames of contention until food was thrown, guests stormed out, and Semele was compelled to force amnesty. When Euryale slyly proposed, "Should mortals and immortals procreate?" the stricken group warred for days until the princess called a cease-fire.

Royal attendants served octopus and salted sardines brought in from the coast, pulses and almonds, blue figs and grapes. On special occasions, they dined upon expensive dishes of tuna with fish sauce. Platters were constantly replenished across the cypress table, every drop of spilled wine immediately cleaned. The princess enjoyed a luxury allowed to the rich in that her sloppiness was quickly expunged. Fixed, forgotten, and forgiven.

Semele was often drunk. She started most nights in her favorite, cyan-colored chair and ended them sprawled across a leopard-skin rug. She alone was permitted to drink from her kantharos—a deep cup with loop-shaped handles rising from the bottom and extending above the rim.

"Fetch my kantharos, Desma!" became the princess's battle cry, signaling the campaign of carousing to commence. And Desma,

Semele's ancient nursemaid, would grumble but oblige. Despite her advanced age, Desma chaperoned all the princess's symposia. She was a part of the scenery, sitting ramrod-straight in the background, eyes closed, but—as Euryale learned—never fully asleep.

"Semele holds the finest parties," insisted a wealthy merchant from Megara, "because she is the arbiter of taste."

"With one exception." And Euryale motioned toward the crone, wheezing slightly in repose. "That old goat."

Desma's rawboned fingers darted out, pinching hard on the soft layer of Euryale's upper arm. Euryale yelped.

"You may be a sea urchin," croaked Desma, "but I am no goat."

Semele howled, as did Euryale's traitor sisters.

"Never underestimate my Desma," advised the princess fondly as Euryale cursed and rubbed her sore arm. "She misses nothing."

Desma narrowed rheumy eyes at Stheno, Medusa, and Euryale in turn. "That one is boring, this one is darling, and *you*." She pointed a gnarled forefinger at Euryale's chest. "You are simply nasty."

The decrepit hag leaned back, coarse white chin hairs twitching as she released a smug snort. Euryale, not one to swallow a slight, ground her teeth, but Stheno clasped a placating hand atop her shoulder.

"She's one hundred years old," Stheno whispered in her sister's ear, breath and tone equally warm. "She'll be dead soon, anyway."

Sometimes her older sister wasn't completely dull.

Desma wasn't the only Theban who preferred Medusa. Semele took to her immediately, and as the favorite princess's favorite companion, Medusa was discussed all over court.

Precious Medusa of the golden hair!

So warm, so modest, so earnest.

She brings a smile to all!

It wasn't long before Medusa was allowed to hold the favored kantharos.

"Why dolphins?" Medusa asked Semele, studying the engravings on the side of the cup: a pod rising from the surf, dorsal fins cutting the sky.

"They hold all the best human attributes, only perfected. Quick-witted, playful, clever. Cruel." Semele's eyes shone above ruddy cheeks. "Is there any creature more joyful than a dolphin?"

"Why, you, of course!"

Semele brought Medusa's hand to her mouth, kissing it. "Oh, Medusa, you understand my vanity so well!"

Euryale groaned at the pair of them, the little sisters who held rank.

"I should learn to make wine," stated Medusa, finishing her cup.

"Then we shall find you a vintner!"

Euryale was exceedingly bored by this routine. Medusa, full of caprice, would wake one morning desperate to learn pottery. The following day, acrobatics. Then knucklebones and dice. Whatever Medusa wanted was provided by Semele's largesse. When Medusa observed an adviser to the king record taxes with a strange new system of pictograms, her hunger for knowledge became insatiable. Semele installed one of the palace's scribes as tutor, and Medusa spent a portion of each day mastering the alphabet Cadmus introduced to Thebes. She would return from her lessons full of symbols and sounds.

"There's nothing else like it," Medusa insisted, settling into a low couch with a glass of wine—a move, Euryale realized, that eerily emulated their hostess. "Eighty-seven syllabic signs! Each with its own phonetic value. And one hundred more ideograms to represent objects and commodities."

Euryale huffed. "One hundred eighty-seven pieces of useless information."

"It will change our culture!"

"*Our* culture, Medusa?" needled Euryale, but her younger sister disregarded the implication.

"Stop bickering like you were raised by sea monsters," scolded Stheno, in a failed attempt at levity.

Medusa locked eyes with Euryale. "Don't you want to be remembered?"

"I don't need to be remembered; I'll always *be*."

Semele, lying on her furs and staring at the ceiling, furrowed her brow. "But does immortality guarantee remembrance?"

"Naturally," maintained Euryale.

Stheno shook her head. "Longevity is not fame."

Semele sat up, spilling her wine, and Desma beckoned for an enslaved girl. "Sometimes dying well is more memorable than a life lived."

"What does it mean, to 'die well'?"

"To perish from an act of great or noble passion."

Medusa's mouth twisted. "I would rather be remembered for what I did, what I said, whom I loved, then how I met my end."

Semele, sensing a shift in the mood, moved to Medusa's side. "Oh, my beautiful one, look at us! Speaking of Hades when we should be celebrating your latest accomplishment. We are young! You keep learning and I'll continue causing trouble!" She raised her cup and winked. "Not a one of us shall cross the river Styx tonight!"

"I will gladly toast to that," agreed Stheno, much relieved.

But when Semele lowered her kantharos, her mouth fell into a moue. "If only you three were my sisters."

Euryale snorted. Drunks and their moods!

Stheno, however, demurred politely. "The elder princesses are sensible and much respected."

"Respected," argued Medusa, in Semele's defense, "but not adored. Nothing at all like Semele."

"They are far too serious," Semele cried out, indignant yet slurring. "They would never join me as you do; they'd sooner drink milk with northerners."

"Some would credit their temperance," muttered Euryale.

Semele took a pointed sip of her wine. "I have everything, and still, I covet what is yours."

"We have nothing, Princess," Euryale responded flatly.

"You have loyalty. And inseparable companionship."

"We are *quite* separable," she returned, ignoring the flash of pain across Stheno's face.

"My sisters compete. For favor, for suitors, for reputation. For our parents' love. We are connected only by secrets and lies." Semele waved her kantharos at Euryale and Stheno, liquid sloshing once more onto the tiled floor. A harried girl hurried forward with a rag. "You three accept each other for all that you are and are not. You share your lives. *That* is sisterhood."

Euryale avoided the eyes of her sisters, refusing to acknowledge their reactions. Did they glow under Semele's praise, or were they racked with a similar discomfort? Though Euryale had yet to detach from her sisters, it didn't mean she couldn't—and still thrive. She did not want to share her life forever; one-third of an existence was no longer sufficient.

"Ino, Agave, and Autonoë—even Polydorus!—don't *see* me. They cannot look past their latest intrigue."

"I see you, dear princess," soothed Medusa. "We do."

Semele blinked rapidly but failed to catch her tears. "So often I feel that I do not belong. Not with my family. Not in Thebes."

And then Semele, a girl born with every privilege and the wealth to buy whatever she may lack, openly cried. The kohl lining her eyes descended her cheeks in murky gray trails.

"You have a good family, a good home, Semele, and you are wrong to believe immortals are so loyal." Euryale felt all the attention fall on her and sat up straighter. She continued, "Remember that Nyx, the goddess of night, gave birth to many demons: misery and trickery, doom and deceit. We who live forever must live with them, too." Euryale pursed her lips. "Do not trust beings that would eat each other."

In the back of the room, Desma listened. Her eyes opened, and she considered Euryale, seriously, sternly. Euryale awaited the inevitable scowl, but Desma rewarded her with one small—goatlike—nod.

Euryale stood and, in a rare display of affection, placed her palm against Semele's damp cheek.

"You are young, Princess. And enchanting. Don't be a fool."

MEDUSA WASN'T THE only sister taking advantage of the education offered by Cadmus's court. Euryale, determined to shed her unsophisticated image, sought out the palace servants to teach her the art of beauty. These two women, originally from Kemet, handled all the princess's toilette, from the crown of her hair to her perfectly trimmed toenails. With the princess's permission, they conveyed Euryale to a table littered with a vast array of bottles and combs, pins, tweezers, wooden spoons, and palettes.

The older servant, Hasina, demonstrated how to keep her skin clean and soft with natural emollients. "Every night, you must draw a bath of honey and donkey's milk." Then she showed Euryale how to decorate her face, the way to line her eyes and brows with charcoal, apply beetroot to her cheeks and berry juice to her lips. "Mix it with beeswax and olive oil so it will last through dining."

"And kissing," added Annipe, the younger woman—and Hasina's granddaughter—with a cheeky grin. "Prince Polydorus asks constantly for you."

Euryale startled. "What have you heard?"

"He begs Semele to play matchmaker, but she refuses."

Euryale frowned. Perhaps Semele thought she did Euryale a favor, but it wasn't her decision to make.

"Help me with my hair," she said instead.

Annipe fingered a wild lock. "Olive oil is a panacea. It will ease the tangles and make it shine."

Euryale owned no jeweled combs or scarves to adorn her head, so the servant women schooled her fingers in complex braids and how to band them into place.

"There are methods to lighten your hair," offered Hasina. "It will glow like your sister's."

Hasina nodded. "It's a simple recipe. Just chamomile, lemon, and—"

"No," retorted Euryale, tightening a fist. "Never."

Annipe flinched.

"I prefer my dark hair," Euryale added in appeasement.

Hasina exchanged a look with her granddaughter and shrugged.

When Euryale later beheld herself in Semele's mirror of polished bronze, she was loath to turn away, for finally, she looked the way she felt.

Not like a savage sea daughter, but a royal—worthy of a king.

She would start with a prince.

Euryale began by deliberately placing herself in Polydorus's way, accidentally bumping into him as he left the bathhouse.

"Euryale!" he exclaimed. "It pleases me to see you."

"I was headed to the women's pools," she explained. "I'm desperate for a long soak." And she paused, just long enough to suggest the mental image. "It's a shame, you know, where I'm from the males and females swim together."

She let her eyes settle on his bare torso, on the dip where chest met neck, and she gave him her most beguiling smile. He swallowed, hard.

"I am a prince. I could arrange for privacy."

Euryale sighed. "Ah, but you have just bathed! Another day perhaps. And I hope you will join us for your sister's gathering tonight."

"Semele does not invite me."

"As you said, you are a prince. Be one."

She swung her hips as she walked away.

That night, Polydorus would not leave her side, bringing her food, finding excuses to touch her. Semele and Stheno eyed their interactions warily, which only encouraged Euryale. Polydorus was attractive, lean and olive-skinned, with black hair and a lower lip that made him always look somewhat pouty, and Euryale did not hate his advances.

Not at all.

"Escort me back to my room, Polydorus," Euryale pleaded, faking a yawn. "I yearn for my bed."

The prince leapt at her command, and outside her room, she let him push her against the wall, accepting his tongue in her mouth and his needy hands upon her body with more objective fascination than excitement. It was her first kiss, after all.

"You are the most intoxicating woman," he moaned in her ear, tickling her, thrilling her.

"But I'm not a woman."

Polydorus pulled away. "What are you?"

"A fantasy."

He groaned and returned his mouth to her neck, but when Euryale felt her body respond too fervently, she worried for her self-control. Gently, she extricated herself from her place between him and the wall, ducking beneath Polydorus's arm.

"Good night, Prince."

Polydorus leaned his forehead against the cold stone. "I will not sleep tonight without you."

"Do not tease me," she chided. "I need you rested. I am sure I will need escorting all over the palace tomorrow."

His lips were swollen, and his eyes glassy. Her heart quickened to see her effect on him.

"Is that a promise?" he asked.

"Would I lie to you?"

FIFTH EPISODE

STHENO

He could repel the wild
and defend his city.
So, more is the pity
he couldn't guard his child.

—Erastus of Athens, "The Conqueror"

IN THEBES, FOR the first time in my life, I found myself idle. Medusa's protean mind kept busy with her various interests—usually assisting the palace scribe, but also pottery painting and wine making, weaving and oil pressing. Her list of obsessions seemed to grow daily.

There are sea animals who completely blend into their surroundings. Fish that appear as rocks or drifting leaves, as sand or seagrass. I have seen an octopus perfectly mimic the appearance of a snake or fish. These are the creatures that came to my mind as I observed Medusa in the human city. But my youngest sister never intended to disappear; she sought assimilation, to become a part of the ecosystem.

To appear normal.

Euryale also adapted. She transformed her skin and face, her hair—even the smell of her breath. She followed the fashions of court and sneered at the old dress I still wore. She beseeched me to do something about my bare feet.

"I have an oil with jasmine you can massage into your heels. And then I can get you a pair of leather sandals."

"Are you ashamed of me?" I wondered, stung.

Euryale did not answer.

And though she delighted in detailing humanity's deficiencies and loved to list their limitations, Euryale never once proposed leaving Thebes. She continued to deny it with great fervor, but I saw the way she flirted with Polydorus, draping her curves and holding her body at ridiculous angles. After lifetimes of being overshadowed by gods and monsters, she was finally exotic, finally special. The prince followed her around like a lovesick finch.

Still, the three of us sisters spent each night together in the same room and same bed, as always. It had become inveterate—a physical need since infancy—and no matter if we lay on the finest sheets or a cavern floor, we slept tangled together like a litter of lion cubs, lulled to slumber only by the security of one another's warmth, the familiarity of one another's breath.

During the days, when I lost them, I would assuage my solitude by walking Cadmus's gardens. Was this loneliness? I wondered. I did not like it. On one afternoon, I retired beneath a lemon tree, well shaded from the piercing sun. I closed my eyes and inhaled the aromas of primrose blossoms and freshly spruced cypress wood, letting their fragrance coalesce at the back of my throat. I listened to birdsong and servants' gossip, smiling at its similar cadence. Still refusing sandals, I wiggled my toes in the soil.

I am content, I told myself repeatedly, *with small, simple things.*

But when a pair of hands came down over my eyes, I gasped. A husky voice filled the darkness: "Guess who I am!"

Though she tried to keep her voice playfully low and disguised, her arms smelled of fennel, her breath of linseed and lime. I would have known that combination anywhere, at any time.

"Princess."

Semele released me and sighed. "How did you know?"

"Your soap."

"I gifted some to Medusa."

"I know. She uses it every day."

Semele wore an ivy wreath atop her dark hair and an expensive dress of cerise cloth, held at her shoulder with an ostentatious pin. Gold bangles jingled up and down her arms. She was entirely too made up for daytime, but such protocols mattered little to her.

"Walk with me, Stheno."

She took my hands and pulled me up, lacing her arm into mine. We traversed the royal ground without speaking. Semele's confidence brought her serenity in all circumstances, but my insecurity became unbearable in silence, compelling me to say something.

"What is that?" I asked, pointing to a stand-alone brick-and-mortar building at the perimeter of the courtyard.

Semele's spirited eyes danced. "The wine magazine."

"Ah."

"During the day, servants rush in and out, in and out. But at night, my parsimonious father locks it down as if it were paved in silver."

"That must inconvenience your parties, Princess."

She smiled then, privately, as if sharing a joke with herself. "The locks work to my benefit."

I frowned, puzzled, but she squeezed my hand and pulled me along.

"Come see my babies."

I heard their babel from afar. In a tangential arcade I'd never visited stood cage after cage of short, compact birds. Brown-feathered bodies, some with light eye stripes and others with white chins, opened their tiny black beaks in a chaotic jumble of noise. Chirps in triplet—*one, two, three! one, two, three!*—with heads bopping to the downbeats of their song. Semele drew seeds from a clay pot and tossed handfuls into the bottom of the cage.

"Feast, my winged loves!"

I watched them peck as Semele deposited an extra handful for the small ones and shooed the more dominant creatures away.

"Quail?" I guessed.

She nodded. "I wanted a pet goose. Or a crane. But my father insisted that quail were more fashionable. I'm afraid I've formed a sentimental attachment to the silly beasts." Semele wiped her filthy hands on her dress, careless of its cost. "So many Olympians have chosen a venerated bird. Apollo's crow. Athena's owl. Hera's peacock. Zeus's eagle. They must sense an interconnection." Semele ran a finger across a sleeping quail's tiny head. "Do you find yourself in their feathers?"

Semele's eyes bored into me. She had an uncanny manner of staring directly into a person's face when she talked to them. Usually, her attention was focused elsewhere. Having it on me was disconcerting. Still, I did not speak. I couldn't answer such a personal question so quickly. "Do you?" I asked instead, hedging.

"They are short-lived, beautiful. Unavoidable." She grinned. "So yes."

"I appreciate their commitment to song," I finally said. "And admire their ability to fly."

"A good answer." And then: "Your sisters are happy here."

Did it bother me how Semele laid claim to them? *My* Medusa. *My* Euryale. Perhaps. But these were emotions I didn't have words for then.

"You attend my parties every night and still I wonder, who is Stheno?"

"I protect them."

Semele shook her head, disappointed. "That's not who you are, that's what you do."

She wasn't wrong, for what had I been doing earlier under that lemon tree? Biding time. Thinking about my sisters. Waiting for them.

"You must always be honest with your sisters. It is the only way to survive. Even if they balk or laugh in your face, force them to talk to you."

I offered her some noncommittal agreement, but in truth, I resisted her advice. Why should I listen to a mortal woman of less than two decades—a girl who spent most nights in her cups, stumbling and giggling about her father's palace? What could she possibly understand about life, about relationships, that I did not? And she had just met my sisters!

Humans and their hubris.

I should have read this conversation for its obvious subtext. The ostensibly candid princess harbored a secret. Perhaps if I had prodded and acted then—heeded Semele's own counsel, forced her to talk to me—it wouldn't have been too late to save her.

NOT LONG AFTER, I woke in the middle of the night to find Medusa missing from our bed. Euryale slept at my other side, her hair in a sweaty black tangle across her face. I laid my hand in Medusa's space; it was cool. The customary alarm nipped at my insides, that parasitic fear for my sisters' safety, and I sat up, gnawed apart with worry.

Where could she be? During one of Medusa's inspirations, she would follow the wisp of an idea, wherever it may lead. Did she stroll the Cadmea? Was she out on the hills? Down in the agora? How far would my sister roam without us, without *me*?

A groggy voice rose in the dark: "She will return."

A small smile touched my lips, and I turned onto my side, tucking my body around Euryale's. She nestled into my touch.

"You don't worry?"

"Never."

"But what if she—"

"She's fine."

"Maybe I should—"

"Don't embarrass her."

I sighed. Euryale was right. I couldn't chase Medusa through the palace like a crazy mother hen. Besides, with guards posted at every entrance, there was no safer place in Thebes. I forced myself to take deep, meditative breaths until I drifted into a light and dreamless sleep.

Medusa returned with daybreak, her nightgown flashing amber as it caught the rays of morning sun. Through bleary eyes I watched her climb over the bottom of the bed into the small space between Euryale and me.

"Semele is in trouble," she told us.

Euryale pushed the hair from her face with both hands and raised an expectant eyebrow. "How bad is it?"

"She's pregnant."

That was bad.

Despite our age, we were new to womanhood. If we had crossed paths with Semele in a later lifetime, our responses would have been different: *Does she want it? Will she keep it?* But we were still so ignorant. We knew men could force babies upon women and then deny paternity, and we'd seen fathers go to ruthless lengths ridding themselves of unwanted sons. But women taking control of their own wombs was a human ingenuity, and we had not yet heard of herbs and methods, timings and tonics that could alter fate. We simply couldn't envision a scenario where Semele's pregnancy didn't come to term.

And furthermore, Semele was unmarried. In the eyes of her father and his people, she was a virgin.

"Who is her lover?" I asked, my mind spinning with the faces of every man I'd seen at the symposium.

"She must marry him immediately," insisted Euryale. "She's Cadmus's favorite daughter. He won't deny her."

Medusa hushed us with a finger against her lips, then checked under the bed and closed all the windows. Euryale started to complain, but when Medusa whispered, "It's an Olympian!" Euryale clapped a hand over her own mouth.

I groaned. "Which one?"

"She refused to say."

"Married?"

Medusa nodded, miserable.

"Zeus? Hades?" Euryale sat up. "Poseidon?"

Medusa shrugged. "I do not know."

"Does it matter?" No immortal would leave his wife to marry a human—even if she was a princess, even if she was pregnant, even if he loved her. "This won't end well for her, Medusa. You must stay out of it. You could be punished."

"She needs me."

I sighed. "Then tell her to marry a mortal substitute. Quickly. One that will benefit enough from the union that he'll pass the babe off as his."

"It must be Apollo," pressed Euryale. "He's the patron of this city. It's the most logical option."

"Euryale! Stop obsessing, it hardly matters." To Medusa I said, "We could sneak the baby out of Thebes. Leave it on a hill."

"She won't consider it," responded Medusa. "She says her god returns her love. She believes they can be together."

"Oh, Semele," I moaned.

"We should leave today," stressed Euryale. "Avoid the disaster."

"I will not go! She has nobody else."

"You fool, she has *everything*."

Medusa clutched my arm. "Stheno, please. Semele's pregnancy will show soon. We cannot abandon her."

My gaze shifted between my two sisters, one pleading and overwrought and the other exasperated and adamant. Euryale noted my indecision and flopped back down, dragging the blankets over her shoulders in a huff.

"Spare me, Stheno," she grumbled. "I know you'll side with her."

"I need to think."

"Please," Medusa begged.

I closed my eyes and bowed my head. My fingers laced together behind my neck, and I pressed up into my grip, straining my muscles. *Stay or go? Fight or flight?*

Medusa or Euryale?

I lifted my chin and delivered my verdict.

"Semele has been good to us. We remain with her until the end."

"Thank you." Medusa hugged me. "Thank you, Stheno."

But Euryale shifted farther away from us, muttering under her breath. I reached for her, but she kicked me backward.

"I'm sorry, Euryale," I said quietly. When she didn't respond, I tried to ignore how her dismissal cut to the quick.

Our choices define us, and I chose this tragedy, our first of many.

SIXTH EPISODE

EURYALE

This campaign against women,
by women,
becomes no one.

—Erastus of Athens, "The Illness of Maidens"

WHEN SEMELE'S STOMACH began to protrude like bloated cattle, Medusa persuaded the princess to confide in Desma. The weight of the secret had certainly become too heavy for Euryale, and if anyone could navigate Semele through this process with discretion and loyalty, it was her fierce old nursemaid. To the sisters' collective relief, Desma took immediate command. She ordered new clothes from tailors outside the court. She delivered Semele's excuses to the king and queen, fabricating a constant stream of illnesses—head colds, stomachaches, contagious rashes. She dismissed Semele's serving girls and prohibited any outsiders from attending Semele's nightly parties—including Polydorus and the elder princesses. Desma keenly knew Semele's sisters posed the gravest threat.

"You are the king's beloved," Desma stressed. "They will happily use this to ruin you."

Still, even to the woman Semele trusted most, she refused to name her lover.

"He loves me and our child," she proclaimed, never wavering. "Our son will be welcomed among the gods."

"He will be a bastard," badgered Desma. "Pick a human prince. Save the child and yourself."

"You will come with me to our home on Mount Olympus, Desma. I will need your help with the baby." Semele hugged her belly, offering her nurse a dreamy smile. "You need not worry, dear one. I am so happy."

In private, Desma wept. "I sheltered her too much," she told Euryale, for despite their tenuous start, Desma had come to appreciate Euryale's sagacity—especially compared to Medusa's and Semele's penchant for the quixotic. "She is incapable of compromise. She can't imagine a scenario where she doesn't get her way." Desma tore at her hair. "This is madness."

Euryale clasped the old woman's frantic hands in a firm grip.

"It is. And you cannot fight it. I am from the ocean. I know that you cannot change the direction of the current, no matter your strength, no matter the desperation."

So Desma dried her eyes and conceded to her princess's delusions.

Within her rooms, Semele celebrated her impending labor. Wineglasses remained full, old stories were retold, and new ones created. Sometimes Semele invited Euryale to feel the baby's kicks.

"There." She beamed, pressing Euryale's palm against the taut bulge of her stomach. When Euryale caught those tiny erratic taps, she gasped. Imagining that little life made her heart ache with such longing. Her own body felt empty and flat in comparison.

"You lie with him? Even like . . . ?" Euryale gestured to Semele's belly.

"I do." Semele's lips curved upward in a smug smirk. "I bring wine to our bed and he pours it into my mouth. It makes me go wild. He says I am the best lover he has known."

If a woman could be the best at lovemaking, then she could also be the worst. Euryale frowned. With animals the act seemed straightforward, instinctual. Ewes had no technique, and rams did not rank them.

What makes you so good? she longed to ask. *What do you do? Who taught you?*

What else am I missing?

But the moment to ask passed. Semele succumbed to the discomfort of her swollen body, and Medusa led her to a couch where she could rub Semele's swollen ankles and knead her lower back.

"If only you were a man, Medusa," Semele moaned, eyes closed. "Wouldn't we have been happy together?"

Medusa brushed the hair back from Semele's shoulders. She pressed her thumbs up and down the top of her spine.

"I could never be scandalous enough for you."

Semele released a soft laugh and settled into Medusa's ministrations, and Euryale watched a single tear drop from her sister's eyes. Medusa rubbed it into Semele's ivory skin, blending one woman's grief with another's comfort. Euryale drew in a sharp breath.

What else am I missing?

EURYALE REQUIRED A safe space to learn about love.

She committed herself to sneaking away with Polydorus, to arboreal alcoves and lonely nooks where they could share their lips and hands. She used him to explore the masculine form and discovered so many pleasurable places along the way—the nape of the neck and inner wrist, the earlobes and scalp. Yet their clothing remained. Polydorus assumed Euryale needed a promise from him first, and in his desperation to lie with her, he offered the world.

"I would marry you," he pledged between breaths.

"I cannot live so far from the water. It would destroy me."

"You would be queen of Thebes."

Though still perched in his lap, Euryale drew back enough that he could see her full face.

"What is a human city to an immortal? You believe Thebes will last, but I have seen many versions of men just like you rise and fall."

She placed a palm against his cheek, not unkindly. "Euryale will survive. Polydorus will not."

He took her hand and kissed it.

"Then bless my short life with your body, just once, before I die."

She would never and felt a slight pang of guilt. Yes, she enjoyed practicing this game of kiss and touch with Polydorus, but there would be no "winning." She didn't know how, and it terrified her. Maybe with Polydorus she could become as good at love as Semele claimed to be, but if Polydorus took her virginity, Poseidon would never want her.

She would be spoiled.

A maiden she must remain, even as she softened to this human prince's worship.

"I cannot," she said again.

Awareness dawned across his face. "There is somebody else."

"Why would you say that?"

"Because there is such want at the core of you, Euryale. I have seen it always. Felt its tremors. Yet you don't want me."

Euryale stood, realizing her error. She had allowed this boy to come too close, and he had guessed at her secret.

"I want to go," she said acidly. He reached for her waist, but she slapped him away and rushed back to her room, disregarding his calls and the ache of her own heart.

Knowing that their affair had peaked, Euryale retracted her claws and retreated from her prey. She ignored his invitations and avoided his presence—even resorting to hiding once or twice, much to her shame. Poor Polydorus moped about the palace and vented his frustrations upon enslaved girls.

"Has the prince offended you?" queried Medusa.

"No, only bored me."

"You are cruel, Euryale."

Euryale flushed, remorse turning to anger by the judgment of her sanctimonious sister.

"I am smart," she fumed, "and surrounded by fools."

Stheno stepped in. "Not now, you two," she beseeched them, rubbing her temples. "Semele's baby is nearly here. Save your energy for that debacle."

Euryale eyed her younger sister in a wary truce. They would need their energy—and unity—for the trial ahead, and that meant prioritizing survival. Polydorus would recover from Euryale's rescinded flirtation. But Semele?

She was in the hands of the gods.

WHEN SEMELE DISPATCHED Desma to the treasury for the Necklace of Harmonia, the faithful nursemaid pursed her lips but obliged. It was especially difficult to deny Semele in her condition.

Desma returned from her clandestine assignment with the treasure hidden beneath her shawl. When she passed it to her mistress, Pandora's name buzzed through Euryale's mind, and though she swatted the memory away like a gnat, the uneasy feeling lingered.

Semele opened the box with a sigh. "It only gets more magnificent. That is what makes it so precious. Too many things in life become less impressive with time."

She placed the golden chain around her neck, and the open-mouthed serpents rested perfectly at the center of her clavicle.

Disease and death, thought Euryale. *Greed and vanity, slander and envy, toil, old age, war.*

But Medusa said, "Beautiful."

From across the room, Desma's world-weary eyes caught Euryale's.

"I will wear this at my wedding, just as my mother did."

"You will honor both her and the necklace."

Pleased, Semele removed the piece and handed it to Medusa. "You must try it on, Medusa. I insist."

Medusa rose too quickly and teetered on her feet. Euryale frowned.

Her little sister had been drinking too much wine of late, and on that night, she was quite drunk.

Cadmus and his court had been openhanded hosts, but even with their borrowed wardrobes, the sisters had never worn jewels, had never possessed anything fancier than a tortoiseshell comb whittled by their own hands. Medusa held her curls aloft while Semele laid the most famous necklace in existence over her head, adjusting its majesty upon her chest. As she watched, Euryale tasted copper on her tongue.

The evening descended further into strangeness.

"Ah," exclaimed Semele, nodding in satisfaction. "Just as I thought. The serpents become you."

Medusa modeled the treasure, giddy with wine and glee. Though the golden snakes circling Medusa's throat augmented the green of her eyes, she radiated with a noisome energy. Her lissome sister was overwhelmed by the piece, by a force somehow reptilian and despondent. It did not hang right on Medusa, and some pesty, primal instinct warned Euryale not to touch it.

Then again, it was not offered to her.

"Take it off, Medusa," commanded Stheno, her voice taut.

Medusa's face crumpled. "Why?"

"I don't like it, take it off!" Stheno, standing now, made a grab for the necklace.

"Stop it, Stheno!" Medusa covered the necklace with one hand and moved backward toward the princess.

"Don't be ugly," scolded Semele, lacing her fingers through Medusa's.

"She is my sister." Stheno reminded Semele. "And for a moment, she wasn't."

Medusa, looking a bit stricken, removed the necklace and returned it to Semele. "Satisfied?"

Euryale awaited Stheno's reaction with some fascination. It wasn't often that her sisters clashed, and a wicked part of her enjoyed it.

But Stheno, looking mortified by her cursory tirade, simply turned and fled.

Semele immediately put the necklace back on.

"I'm sleeping in this tonight," she proclaimed defiantly. "And only this."

At the rear of the room, Desma rose to her feet. "The princess needs her rest." She drove the two sisters toward the door. "No more trouble tonight."

Before they left, Medusa apologized for Stheno's behavior.

Semele shrugged. "She feels the need to protect you. Even from me." She grinned. "Worry not. Tomorrow we shall kiss and be friends again."

In the wide hallway, Medusa, a bit heady with drink, tripped and stumbled sideways, crashing to the floor.

"Who put that wall there?"

Euryale helped her up and slid a steadying arm around her waist. "A stonemason, I'd wager."

"A tricky one."

"Very."

Euryale bit back a smile. She led Medusa toward their room, grip tightening as her sister teetered beside her.

"It was just a necklace," she murmured into Euryale's shoulder.

"And a garish one."

Medusa giggled. The crown of violets she wore had slipped over one eye.

For it *was* just a necklace. Nothing sinister, nothing transformative. Stheno could be overprotective and easily excited; Euryale would not.

The sisters collapsed into bed fully dressed, beside Stheno, who pretended to sleep.

"It was just a necklace," Medusa repeated into Stheno's face, a husky whisper against Stheno's fake, steady breath.

Then Medusa rolled onto her side and almost immediately began to snore.

◆ ◆ ◆

MANY HOURS LATER, Euryale startled, awoken by the sound of laughter.

Beside her, both sisters slept soundly, unmoved and unbothered, but Euryale's skin tingled with unmistakable alarm. She smoothed a hand down her arm; the hairs stood on end. Could that voice have been the cackling echoes of a dream? *No,* screamed the instinctual voice at her core. She crept from the bed and padded to the door, opening it so slowly, so quietly. No hilarious specter haunted the hall. No giggling ghosts.

Feeling foolish, Euryale made a move to retire, when she heard it again.

Unmistakably manic. Nefarious and female.

She could ignore the night's strangeness no more.

Euryale chased the sound, hurrying across the tiled floor as the peals crescendoed. Her anxiety grew with each glissando.

Far ahead, a form emerged from the darkness outside Semele's door, and Euryale jerked to a stop. She retreated into the shadows, placing one hand against her thundering heart and the other over her mouth.

Who came from the princess's room at such an hour?

Only Desma. Euryale snorted, bemused by her jitters. But then a violent laughter racked the nurse's body, throwing her off balance. Desma caught herself before she fell, extending an arm to the wall.

A surprisingly sturdy arm.

Desma sensed Euryale's presence. She cocked her head, and an inhuman smile lifted the sagging flesh of her cheeks.

"Can I tell you a secret, girl?"

Euryale did not nod, nor did she shake her head, but her stomach clenched into a small, tight ball.

The top of Desma's head began to glow, spreading details with its descending light—first a metal band, then the tips of a diadem. Robes embroidered in lotuses shimmered and then solidified, replacing the simple servant's gown, and the nursemaid's frail figure morphed into a crowned goddess, tall and hale, manifest and stunning.

The fully corporeal goddess winked at Euryale and then vanished, dissolving into an iridescent ether.

She of the heights, white-armed, protector of men, and queen of the gods.

Hera.

Semele's lover wasn't Poseidon.

Trembling from fright and nauseated with relief, Euryale hurried down the corridor and into Semele's room, calling the princess's name. It was empty. Alive or dead—the girl was nowhere to be found.

Euryale needed her sisters. She turned on her heels and rushed back toward her room, spewing invectives. She cursed the slowness of her feet and the passage of time. She cursed mortal girls with their madcap dreams and immortals who struck in the dead of night, when wine and slumber weakened their prey.

Returned to her room at last, Euryale yanked the blankets unceremoniously from their communal bed, exposing her sisters to the cold and the night and the danger.

"Wake up!" she yelled. "Wake up! It's Zeus. Semele's lover is Zeus!"

SEVENTH EPISODE

STHENO

Theban bird,
do not sing for the King.
Theban bird,
do not take seed from his Queen.

—Erastus of Athens, "The Tragedy of Trickery"

EURYALE CALLED FOR me, but I was lost in the seas of deepest sleep, sailing through a heavy fog, confused by the words reaching me in brief glimmers of light. Her voice blazed like the fire atop stone columns at harbor, guiding ships homeward, signaling me back. But I couldn't find meaning in the flickers. They were too separate, and I was unable to hold them together.

Wake . . . danger . . .

As my consciousness returned, I recalled the previous night. My apprehensions and embarrassing confrontation. I would not heed Euryale's message; none of this was my problem.

I will remain in this boat and avoid it all.

But while my mind moored in another world, my body continued to live and breathe in this one. I inhaled a heady mix of sweet wine and fennel that broke through my malaise.

Medusa.

I opened my eyes. Medusa stood before me in her plain shift. No jewels shackled her neck; no legacy weighed her down.

She was my baby again. Safe. Unscathed.

"Get up!" thundered Euryale as she leapt across the bed and grasped my shoulders. "We may already be too late!"

I had never seen her so distressed.

"What has happened?"

"Skies, Stheno, are you deaf?" exclaimed Euryale, in a state of utter frustration. "Semele carries Zeus's baby, and Hera has been here tonight, impersonating Desma."

Oh, Princess. You couldn't have chosen worse.

Medusa flew out the door.

"Medusa, wait!" I cried. But there would be no talking sense with her, not now. Euryale and I each grabbed a small bronze lamp and dashed after Medusa. The smoky light cast our images against the palace walls. Burning shadows racing through chaos toward ruin.

Medusa headed for Semele's rooms.

"She's not there!" Euryale insisted as we caught up, but Medusa needed to see the empty bed for herself.

It was perfectly made, blankets untouched, but on the floor, the box from the treasury lay open. Its necklace missing.

Medusa barreled into a small annex. There, Desma slept heavily upon the low couch, a thin line of drool spilling from the corner of her mouth. My heart ached for her, the constant guardian caught unawares, for the first time—for the last time. I roused her gently but urgently.

"What do you want?" Desma rubbed at tired eyes with her fists. A half-finished tray of food perched on a modest table.

"Where is Semele?"

Desma scowled. "Where is Semele? I put her to bed!" But she saw our grim faces and faltered. "I ate my supper and . . ." Her forehead creased and she shook herself. "Why I . . . I can't remember."

"Who brought your meal, Desma?"

"A new girl, I did not ask her name."

My sisters and I shared a dark look.

"I think your food was poisoned with a sleeping draft."

Desma scoffed at me. "Who would dare?"

I swallowed. "Hera."

Medusa knelt at Desma's side. "Euryale saw Hera tonight. In a disguise."

"She was you."

Desma clapped both hands over her mouth, but it did little to cover the harsh mewling that rose from her throat.

"My poor Semele! What did that witch say to my girl?" Desma choked on her devastation. "What did *I* say to make her go?"

Those wails scratched at my resolve, and I collapsed inward, considering surrender. It was all too much, too fast. I wet my lips with my tongue and prepared myself to admit, *We are too late.*

"We will find her," soothed Medusa, clasping the old woman's shaking hands, "but we need your help. Tell us, where does she go when she meets her lover?"

"She never said," sobbed Desma.

"Hush," Euryale scolded. "I need to think."

Euryale stood straighter, ascendant, and I welcomed her leadership. My muddled mind saw only sorrow, not strategy.

"I will check every bedchamber. Medusa, inspect the servants' quarters and workshops. Stheno, head to the gardens and pools." Euryale laid a surprisingly tender hand on Desma's shoulder. "And you stay here, to wait for Semele should she return."

"Find her," begged Desma. "Please."

We parted in three directions. I traversed the property, moving slowly along paths blighted by darkness. I tripped often. Fog filtered the moonlight, distorting its guidance, obscuring my vision and sense of reality. Was this truly me, dashing through nocturnal mists to rescue a human princess from an immortal's vengeance?

I paused beside Semele's quail. The covey slept huddled together, heads nuzzled into their own breasts, blissfully impervious to their owner's fate. How I longed to crawl inside the security of those cages, lay my head down among the warm bodies, and succumb to my weariness!

I never confessed as much to either sister, but when I reached that avian arcade, I stopped searching and sat in the dirty mix of loose feathers, spilled seed, and pebbles. I pulled my knees to my chest and held myself tightly, listening to the cicadas' shrill buzz, watching the palace's wild residents continue on. Frogs and mosquitoes and bats and spiny mice, all oblivious—to me, to this complex, to our comedies and tragedies, all our silly positing.

I told myself it was a temporary respite, that I simply needed a moment to think, and then I could get up and continue with renewed conviction. But I barely believed it. A part of me knew it was already over, that Semele would never get the life she wanted. It was always going to end badly, and I was in no rush to behold the ghastly resolution. If I had kept looking, would the night have ended differently? I do not think so. Hera had laid a trap, and women hopelessly in love never see truth.

Semele was no match for a goddess, and neither was I.

So I waited.

I did not have to wait long.

A thunderclap broke across the grounds. I covered my ears, crying out as my body physically echoed the boom, as my head split in two. My heart stopped beating, I'm sure of it, and if I hadn't been sitting already, the cataclysm would have thrown me from my feet.

For such a disturbance—for such destruction—it was all so brief. One scream piercing the heavens, one lightning bolt slashing the earth.

Then total, gut-wrenching silence.

When an animal or a human is screaming, at least you know it's alive.

Or maybe I had lost my hearing.

My trembling body rolled with waves of shock, so I pressed my face against the ground, embracing its solidness. I felt steady beats against my cheek—human feet running—then distant yells, confusion, and terror. I wasn't the lone survivor, nor was I deaf.

Battered and benumbed, I struggled to my feet, brushed the loose filth from my nightgown, and limped toward the wreckage.

◆ ◆ ◆

SEMELE WAS DEAD.

The news repeated in hushed conversations as people gathered outside Cadmus's scorched and severed wine magazine.

"The princess is dead."

"Princess Semele has been killed."

"Struck by lightning."

"Why was she in there?"

"There wasn't even a storm!"

The roof had split; the ground was torn. Columns fell at awkward angles like fractured bones. People stepped over crumbled white stones and cracked clay bricks. I hung toward the back, nauseated by the crowd and its collective mix of despair and macabre excitement—that sadistic thrill when calamity befalls another, and you get to safely bear witness.

The humans have a word, *phthonos*. I did not know its meaning then, but I understand it now. It describes a type of delight in the misfortune of those one envies.

It is an ugly word.

I heard Medusa's scream from inside the ruins. The onlookers beside me froze, petrified by her raw, corrosive keening, but I jolted forward, leaping over rubble and ducking beneath the splintered, slanted doorway.

Medusa's back was to me, and I entered just as her knees buckled. I caught my sister and held her close in the center of that sulfuric hellscape.

The room stank of burnt hair and meat, like an outdoor altar after a sacrifice. I retched, then pressed my mouth against my shoulder. *Medusa is alive and whole,* I told myself. *You can stomach anything else.*

But then I saw the body.

The vibrant princess was a log too long in the fire, charred beyond recognition, past all humanity. A few dark curls held firm to a diminished skull, shrunken by omnipotent heat, and the features of her expressive face had melted, leaving sunken divots where convivial eyes once sparkled. Fingerless arms stretched outward like the branches of an emaciated tree. Tendrils of gray smoke twisted and twirled as they rose from her smoking corpse.

The majority of the wine magazine was similarly seared—only the Necklace of Harmonia, still clasped about Semele's neck, escaped the inferno's rage. Disturbingly bright amid the black ash, taunting me.

"Stheno?" Euryale called from outside.

"In here."

Euryale crept toward us on hesitant steps. When she saw the carcass, she stumbled back and bit down on her wrist to suppress her gagging.

Or screaming.

Or both.

I struggled to hold Medusa, whose slender form convulsed with ragged sobs.

"Help me with her."

Euryale and I managed to lift Medusa and lead her through the remains of the building.

"Poor Semele," Euryale murmured to me. "And that poor baby."

"That poor *what*?"

King Cadmus stood before us, wearing his sleeping robe but holding a sword.

"Where is my daughter?"

His eyes were a blue maelstrom of agony, torturous confusion, rage, and helplessness. I wondered, How can a soul hold so much emotion and still look so empty? It was a tension I couldn't yet process.

But I would. Oh, how I would.

"She was pregnant," pressed Autonoë, grouped with the other royal siblings. "I knew it."

"She had gained so much weight," whispered Agave.

"Vile, jealous bitches," swore Polydorus.

"You are a good brother," Ino said tartly, "but Semele was a drunk. This is what happens."

"Silence!"

I could see the king's heart pounding through his thin robe. Harmonia, eyes wet, clutched his hand. "Send for Desma."

There was so much Cadmus needed to learn to process his favorite child's death. I could've shared what I knew, the part I played in her subterfuge, but my sisters and I did not belong here beside this grieving family. We snuck away—cowardly, maybe—and left the royal family to their complicated domestic dance of shock and mourning, guilt and accusation. Euryale and I dragged Medusa back through the hallways, hushing her as best we could.

But in the privacy of our room, we released Medusa to her misery. She sank to the floor while Euryale barred the door. I inhaled, deeply, slowly. My head still pounded from Zeus's eruption.

"She's dead," sobbed Medusa. "My first real friend."

"Be quiet," hissed Euryale, annoyed. "The entire court can hear you."

"She trusted me, and I failed her."

"Semele rolled around with the king of the gods. She doomed herself."

"Semele loved him, and he *killed* her! He murdered their baby!"

"Hera did this," I stressed. "Somehow."

"She will not suffer a rival," added Euryale. "Even a mortal one."

Medusa hurtled toward a table, where the knife from our last meal lay gleaming, waiting to be made animate.

"Medusa, no!"

I saw her plunge the blade into her heart, watched her slide it across her wrists and throat.

My mind played cruel tricks on me.

In truth, Medusa held the blade at her hair, right below her chin, for human women cut their hair in mourning, and Medusa was more human than not since we had come to Thebes.

I yanked her hand down and she wrestled half-heartedly against me. "Don't cut your hair."

"I will! I must!"

"You simpering fool," snapped Euryale, her stores of patience and compassion dried up. "It is your greatest beauty."

"I don't care what I look like, not now, not ever!"

Euryale snorted. "You're a liar, Medusa. Just like Semele."

Medusa's nostrils flared. "And you are heartless."

"Enough!" I thrust my body between my two sisters, riding a wild anger that reared and leapt. The knife clattered to the tiles, blade ringing, and Medusa fell into my arms. I held her tightly, rubbing her back, and we gradually sank to the floor.

"She's gone," Medusa bawled into the front of my dress.

"She is."

"It can happen that quickly."

Smoothing back her hair, I knew I should be grieving the princess—and regretting our final confrontation—but I thought only of Medusa. *She will die too,* an inky voice crooned. *It may be slow and laborious. It may be within the blink of an eye. And either way, you will break into a thousand pieces, and you will wish for a knife as well.*

Medusa's forehead rested against my shoulder. "I can't remember. Did I say good night to her?"

"I don't know. I wasn't there." I sent a pleading glance at Euryale, who watched with open disgust from the other side of the room, arms folded over her chest. She glowered at me but gave Medusa her answer.

"Yes."

"I am glad." Medusa sniffled. "Do you think he loved her?"

"I do."

I answered honestly, but would Zeus mourn Semele like Cadmus? Like her nurse or my sister?

Never.

To him, she was another pretty girl, the latest in a disturbing pattern: Zeus—disciplined enough to organize the successful overthrow of the Titans, but unable to harness his own carnal impulses—would obsess over a mortal girl, coerce himself upon her, and then abandon her to his wife's punishments.

We should have seen the experience for the warning it was—the cowardice of lovers and the creative range of vengeance when the wronged hold infinite power.

But we didn't, and that is our shame.

THE FULL STORY of that night traveled quickly along the immortal and mortal circuits—Hera made sure of it. Why would she want her husband's indiscretion made public? Because it presented a dual opportunity to brag and to warn: lie with my husband and I will use the person you love most in retribution.

For Hera, masquerading as Desma, tricked the Theban princess into demanding her own death.

But how do you know, my dear one, that he is who he says? That he isn't that trickster Hermes in disguise?

Why would he lie to me?

To win over a prize such as yourself? A hero's favorite daughter, wealthy and lovely, adored by all of Thebes? A man would say anything.

If you saw him, Desma, you would know. He is tall and muscled with a face that has seen every darkness! But when he looks upon me, he lightens like the breaking dawn.

My lovesick girl, before you bear his child, make him swear on the river Styx that he will deny you nothing.

He has already promised.

But has he proven his love? Demand he lie with you in his purest form, the way he would lie with his eternal wife.

In a thundercloud?

Ah, then you admit—it is Zeus. I thought so. Yes, Princess, ask to see his lightning bolt. That will prove he is no imposter.

While the real Desma lay drugged in a back room, Semele met Zeus in the wine magazine, their covert place, and begged him to reveal his true glory. For Hera, in her great maliciousness, knew what Semele did not: a woman born of a human father could never survive such a sight. And because he had indeed sworn on the Styx, Zeus unveiled himself.

His thunder and lightning consumed the hapless girl almost instantly.

I do not know what became of the Necklace of Harmonia, which slave or servant was tasked with prying it from the molten corpse, but I wish they had thrown it into the ocean.

EIGHTH EPISODE

EURYALE

She will feed on you from the feet up
so you can watch her eat.
The cruelest beasts know
to save the mind for a treat.

—Erastus of Athens, "Ode to Monsters"

THEY BURIED SEMELE in the family tomb, on a hill outside the seven-gated city.

After Semele's immolation, Thebes lost its luster. The city dimmed without the sparkling laughter of its beloved princess—and so did Medusa. Euryale and her sisters attended the funeral and then immediately planned to depart, leaving Cadmus and Harmonia to grieve and navigate the storms raging across their court.

The Theban king bade them farewell, red face swollen in agony. "Your companionship brought my daughter joy in her final days."

"Her joy was ours, King," insisted Medusa.

Cadmus bequeathed a heavy bag of coin and a name: "Should you enter Athens, seek out the artist Erastus. He is a friend of mine from Crete, and he will treat you with decency."

Euryale and Stheno bowed, but Medusa—always terrible with formalities—stepped forward. She laid a hand against the old man's cheek and murmured something in her sweet voice that caused his chest to shake. The king pulled her to him in a tight embrace.

A man can be a ruler, prosperous and powerful, a legend among his kind, but that will not keep a daughter safe. If a mortal had ravaged Semele, Cadmus would've sought justice at the end of his sword. But with Zeus there would be no condolences, no apologies, and certainly no recompense.

It was the Olympian way.

As the sisters left the throne room, Euryale felt the skin at the back of her neck prickle. Somebody was watching. She whirled and spied Polydorus leaning against a far wall, eyes pinned to her.

"Give me one moment," she told Stheno and Medusa. "I will meet you outside."

Euryale did not love the prince, but her heart still lightened at his lanky frame, those brooding brows and lips. No, she could never love him, but she had enjoyed him.

"I should despise you," he offered by way of greeting, "yet I only loathe to see you go."

She gave him a soft smile. "Fantasies do not last."

"If you change your mind, come back and be my queen."

"You could be married by then."

"I'll have her killed."

Euryale couldn't help herself; she threw her head back and laughed. Polydorus grinned. He took her hand and kissed it.

"I know you wait for someone else," he added, and his tone became serious. "I still do not know whom, but I fear for you. Do not become my sister."

Euryale flinched. She tried to retract her arm, but he clung to her.

"Please, Euryale."

"I do not heed the fears of children," she seethed, shaking him off. "And you are only a boy."

He rolled his eyes. "A boy who's trying to help you."

"I did not ask for any!"

Polydorus lowered his voice, but Euryale still heard him as she stormed back to her sisters.

"I do not want to see you humbled."

But he would never see her again, anyway.

◆ ◆ ◆

THE SISTERS EXITED the city through the main gate, heading toward the mountains. After much discussion and more than a few arguments, they decided to seek out Echidna's daughter, the Sphinx, who inhabited the Cithaeron range. Stheno insisted their destination remain a secret, for the Sphinx's proximity to Thebes had caused trouble for Cadmus.

Messengers had brought the king graphic rumors of a creature—half woman and half lion—ravaging young men in the countryside, devouring organs and licking bones clean.

Apparently, the Sphinx had quite an appetite.

Stheno led as they traversed the steep, dry slopes of Mount Phikion, wild hares bounding through the brushwood while blackbirds and partridges rustled in holm oaks. Palace life was too stationary, and the walk invigorated Euryale. She could walk all day and barely feel the strain, swim all night without suffering a cramp. Movement became her.

Medusa, diminished by grief, remained quiet but kept pace, sweat beads collecting across her copper skin. They had never met the Sphinx, and new experiences revived Medusa's spirits. Euryale assumed it was curiosity alone that kept her moving forward.

Stheno stopped to pluck a small red berry from an arbutus.

"Sweet?" asked Euryale. "Or sour?"

Stheno passed the fruit to each of them, and Euryale took it between her teeth, breaking the juice onto her tongue.

A bit of both.

Medusa accepted another.

In the days that followed, the sisters immersed themselves in the mountain landscape—foraging food, building temporary shelters, negotiating scree and ravines. Euryale removed her sandals to wade streams, her toes clutching rocks, perching like a bird. During those evenings, dark as pitch, Euryale attempted sleep, but a burning restlessness consumed her like tinder. And in those fiery moments, she left her sisters nestled together to walk alone. Only in perfect solitude could she tend to the simple questions that blazed within:

What do I want?

What do I need?

There must be more for her than an angsty human prince and his clumsy caress. Semele was an idiot and so was Polydorus, but she had learned much from both. Great love awaited her, surely, and she would be ready. Euryale schemed and dreamed until dawn's first light.

THEY FOUND THE Sphinx's cave by following the trail of bodies—small game, yes, but also goats and their shepherds. Scavenger foxes grinned over the skeletons, viscera dangling from their teeth. A vixen dropped a decomposing human foot before her kits.

Medusa vomited.

Stheno rubbed Medusa's back, but Euryale threw her hands in the air. "The Sphinx is a predator. She must eat."

Medusa wiped the spittle from her chin against her forearm. "There are plenty of deer."

The naked bones stopped at the base of a tall limestone cliff, where a cave's entrance broke the granular rock face. Euryale saw deep claw marks slashing through the shades of yellow and gray, between the sedimentary deposits of tiny shells. Clear-cut warnings to any would-be trespassers.

"Hello?" tested Stheno. Euryale held her breath.

The Sphinx materialized in the void—without a sound—for she walked on the tips of her pads, muffling her movements. She was, undeniably, a creature of their kin. Though smaller than Euryale anticipated, the Sphinx was, nonetheless, the perfectly mismatched jumble of Echidna's and Typhon's bloodlines.

Her upper half resembled a woman, with bare breasts, long brown hair, and pale cheeks. The look on her face was open—unguarded—in the honest way of animals. From the waist down, she turned leonine—muscled hindquarters, four golden paws. Upon her back sprang the most glorious wings, and behind her twitched a markedly serpentine tail.

"Aunties," she purred in a silvery voice.

"You know us?" marveled Stheno.

"Anywhere. My mother told me of your eyes."

They presented her with Theban goods: lamb meat, red wine, a woven blanket, and a beautiful clay amphora—a gift from Desma at their parting. The Sphinx inspected each offering carefully, nodding her acceptance.

"Come inside."

The cave felt surprisingly cool and airy—a welcome break from the sweltering day. The Sphinx set the meat to roast upon her hearth while Stheno poured wine, and they settled upon the soft earthen floor. Though strangers, Euryale experienced no discomfort. Between their shared family and the humble environs, it was like easing into a warm bath.

"I have not seen Echidna in such a long time," Medusa began.

"She yearns for you, as well," replied the Sphinx.

"For all her babies."

"For you more than most. A natural child can never compete with one chosen."

A harsh sentiment, but the Sphinx bore no anger. Why complicate the incontrovertible?

"Tell me of your life with the humans."

Stheno narrated their Theban sojourn: the feasts and parties, human rituals and hierarchy, the countless man-made marvels. She did not mention Semele. Euryale watched the Sphinx's reactions, somewhat mesmerized. Though sharp and articulate as any woman, the Sphinx was characteristically feline—scratching at her back with honed claws, tail flicking back and forth when she fell deep into thought.

"You enjoyed them, then? The humans?" the Sphinx surmised, and the flames reflected in her cobalt eyes danced. She seemed a creature more suited to the Underworld.

"We did."

"I enjoy eating them."

Medusa tensed.

"My sister has a tender heart," Euryale explained to the Sphinx. "And you give Theban children nightmares."

"With the dragon of Ares gone, I am the mightiest beast in Boeotia."

Medusa chuckled, soft and cynical, staring into her cup.

"You doubt my influence?" pressed the Sphinx, amused but dangerous.

"Only your legacy."

The Sphinx's mouth set in a hard line, and Euryale's fingers twitched at her side. Oh, how she longed to slap her stupid sister sometimes! What would Stheno do if Euryale tossed her wine in Medusa's self-righteous face? Would either of them fight back?

"There are plenty of monsters," Medusa continued.

"Yes, but not many can claim my father, my lineage."

"And Typhon lives in infamy because of his staunch beliefs. He fought for the old order and lost his life." Medusa set down her cup. Her hands moved when she became impassioned. "You are formidable and frightening, but those qualities alone will never inspire a legend."

Euryale sensed the Sphinx's rising discord, and her mind sprang toward more conciliatory topics. Boar hunting? Beekeeping? *The weather?* But tedious conversation was Stheno's jurisdiction, not hers. If their elder sister wouldn't intervene, why should she?

Maybe the Sphinx would bite Medusa. That might be fun.

"And how, Lady Mortal," the Sphinx asked, lingering on the loaded epithet, "do I ensure my notoriety?"

"Don't kill arbitrarily," Medusa maintained. "Give yourself a purpose."

"I must eat."

Medusa gestured toward the land outside the cave. "This mountain is teeming with game! It's a hunter's paradise."

"This is my territory," snarled the Sphinx. "The humans should respect my boundaries and stay in their city."

Stheno turned over a log on the fire. Sparks flew just as Medusa shot up from her seat. "Why not *protect* the city instead? Scare away the invaders, not the citizens."

"I do not belong to Thebes," scoffed the Sphinx. "I owe them nothing."

"Of course you don't," Medusa reassured. "But imagine the tributes they would bestow—the glory placed on your name!—if you plagued any would-be intruders."

The Sphinx considered but demurred. "It is not enough. My brother Cerberus already guards the Underworld. I cannot compete with the hound of Hades."

"In Thebes we learned that the humans love a challenge," put in Stheno. "All the best stories involve a test."

"Like a footrace?" The Sphinx sneered. "That is no contest."

A wide grin spread across Medusa's face. "A battle of wits! Set to each person who dares enter Thebes. Solve this problem—this *riddle*!—and you gain entry. Otherwise . . ." Medusa paused, then performed an exaggerated gulp.

"I get to eat them?"

"Yes."

Stheno raised her cup in triumphant toast. "To the making of an epic—"

"I want to know what Euryale thinks."

Euryale's head jerked up. Did somebody seek her opinion?

Stheno lowered her arm.

The Sphinx waited, mouth resting in a smug curve, and her sisters hung in the balance. Medusa wanted to stop the murders and Stheno wanted to make Medusa happy, yet Euryale could deny them both. With just one sentence. What a hedonistic thrill!

Still, Euryale considered her own feelings before her words. This was all a question of ethos. As an immortal, Euryale prided herself on remaining unethical, but an unwelcome image of Polydorus being devoured by the Sphinx stopped her cold. She still did not love the idiot, but neither did she love the idea of his organs pecked apart by crows.

"Make it an excruciating riddle."

Medusa clapped her hands.

The Sphinx's tail flicked back and forth in amusement. "All right," she conceded, "but you three must provide the riddle."

The group deliberated.

"What can run but cannot walk?" suggested Stheno.

"What has no wings but will one day fly?"

"What goes up but never comes down?"

"What is always in front of you but can't be seen?"

The Sphinx scrunched her nose and shook her head. "A river, a caterpillar, age, the future. These are too obvious. I'd sooner kill myself than become a farce."

Medusa hushed her sisters with frantic hands. "I have it." And she inhaled a long breath, solemn and grave. "A thing there is whose voice is one. Whose feet are four and two and three—"

"Stop!" the Sphinx stammered, excited. "I don't want anyone else to hear!"

Medusa beamed. She skipped to the Sphinx's side and whispered the rest of the riddle in her ear. And the Sphinx giggled in a way that was perfectly feline and female: the cat who swallowed a bird and delighted in her conquest.

Stheno caught Euryale's attention. "Thank you," she mouthed.

Euryale rolled her eyes.

NINTH EPISODE

STHENO

Decision-maker,
myth-weaver,
fate-bringer.

—*Erastus of Athens, "The Theater of Sisterhood"*

WAKING IN A cave was a confusing mix of foreign and familiar: my sisters' smell, cavern walls and spilled wine, but also *fur.* I remembered the corpse-lined hike, the Sphinx's smile illuminated in flames as Medusa convinced her of the riddle. With a deep sigh, I removed myself from Euryale's hair and legs, and walked outside to find Medusa and our other sister's child seated together on the rocks. Quiet, watching the wilderness rouse.

Medusa made space for me, and when I sat beside my sister, she laced our fingers together. It was the first sign of affection she had shown me since Semele's death; my heart sang.

The Sphinx spoke first. "We were discussing where you three might travel next."

"Home," I answered. After Thebes and its failure, I assumed we would return to the safety of the sea, to the channels and waves that raised us.

"If you go back to Ceto and her blasted eels," rang a steely voice behind me, "then you go without me."

I turned. Euryale stood in the mouth of the cave, hands at her hips, daring me to leave her behind.

"And you, Medusa?" I asked.

My sweet, determined sister squeezed my hand. "How could there be anything worse than what we have already experienced?"

"You need more for your own legend," agreed the Sphinx, somewhat slyly. "It's only fair."

I sighed, overruled. "Then where?"

The Sphinx rose and arched her back, lifting her hips and flattening her forelegs. She yawned, unaware of her own impressive grace.

"To the northwest is Delphi. Or you could travel straight west and cross the gulf into Corinth. But on the peninsula to the southeast," she said, settling back onto her hindquarters and folding in her grand wings, "lies Athens."

Athens.

The way she pronounced its name sent a shiver up the small of my back, an augury of consequence.

"That was Cadmus's recommendation, as well," relayed Medusa.

Euryale joined us on the rocks. "What do you know of the city?"

"It's a very good story," the Sphinx teased. "There's even a challenge."

"Tell us, please."

The Sphinx's tail curled as the storyteller's gaze settled upon her eyes. It's a look I've come to recognize, when a speaker inhabits the faraway and the present, retreating to memory, invoking language, and assembling both for an audience.

"Athens's first king and founder was Cecrops," imparted the Sphinx, "and he reigned for fifty years. He brought culture to his humans—the rites of love and death—but also politics and religion.

"In those days, the gods were actively laying claim to all the human cities. Patronage guaranteed worship and sacrifice. Rhodes, Argos, Sparta. But the jewel of all was Athens, and two of the greatest immortals fought for guardianship."

"Athena, obviously, and . . . ?"

"Poseidon."

Euryale stiffened beside me. She tried to cover her reaction, but it was too late. I felt it.

"Zeus refused to settle the dispute between his darling daughter and formidable brother, for no decision would benefit him. Instead, he delegated the choice to King Cecrops. The poor man, tasked with navigating two monstrous egos while protecting his populace—and possibly his own life—proceeded to issue a challenge: *Our city's tribute will be rewarded to the Olympian offering us the best gift!*

"Athena and Poseidon convened at the top of the cliff-sided hill, witnessed by Cecrops and the other gods. Poseidon presented first. He raised his mighty trident and cracked open the stony ground, raising a spring of ocean water."

"Miraculous," applauded Euryale.

"Indeed, and Cecrops was impressed. But never underestimate the gray-eyed goddess," cautioned the Sphinx. "Athena thrust her spear into that same crack. The waters ebbed, and in their place sprouted an olive tree, the first of the region."

"The people cannot drink seawater," mused Medusa, "but an olive tree provides edible fruit and valuable oil."

"The judges concurred, and Athena won the city."

Euryale raised an eyebrow. "Surely Poseidon didn't take such an embarrassment well."

"Not at all. He flooded the western plains of Attica in a fit of rage."

My middle sister laughed.

"Despite its early conflict, Athens is a curious city," finished the Sphinx. "One open to ideas and innovation."

Could this be a suitable location for Medusa to heal? Nothing revived my sister like a fresh discovery.

"Will it be Athens, then?" Medusa asked me.

On my other side, Euryale picked dirt from her fingernails, purposefully aloof, but she couldn't fool me. Athens was her choice, as well, but she would never condescend to admitting it out loud.

The decision would be mine.

I could demur, suggest an entirely different land: Illyria or Thrace, Ionia. But I could not disappoint my sisters, and their hearts were set on this small southern city in Attica.

"When shall we depart?"

Euryale bit back a grin. Medusa lay her head on my shoulder.

The decision was all mine.

I would never forgive myself, afterward.

THE CHILD

FRAGILE MEN SHOULD never receive prophecies.

Long before Medusa and her sisters decamped for Athens, King Acrisius of Argos cast his daughter and infant grandson out to sea in a wooden chest.

What?

Yes, you heard that right.

Why?

Following a precedent set by Cronus himself, Acrisius feared a Delphic prophecy in which Danaë, his daughter and only child, birthed a son who would kill him.

How do oracles—with the knowledge of foresight—deliver such messages in good conscience? Apathy? Lassitude? Or is it sadism, a love of chaos and bloodshed? In a world where the competitive tension between fathers and their male heirs is already palpable, this prophecy was inescapably fatal.

Once the blameless Danaë reached her first blood, Acrisius had her contained in a doorless, windowless bronze chamber where no man could defile her. She was far too lovely and, therefore, far too dangerous. Danaë was a young woman damned twice over, once for her beauty and again as an innocent trapped between one man's ruin and another's triumph.

In the years that passed, Acrisius portrayed himself as the over-protective guardian, affecting a preoccupation with Danaë's carnal treasure. "She is my daughter! I must keep her safe!" When his wife, Queen Eurydice, protested, Acrisius relented slightly. He allowed a narrow skylight built into the roof so their daughter could breathe fresh air.

Poor mortal mothers, who cannot swallow their children whole or whisk them away to forgotten isles!

Danaë hated that box. She screamed, she pleaded. Banged her fists until they bled. How did she maintain her sanity with only the clouds as friends, with only the sun and moon to bide her time? Well, in moments of exhausted acceptance, she sang—a pure soprano in perfect tune. Her voice rose higher and higher until it reached the wanton ears of Zeus himself.

Acrisius should have anticipated how tempting a comely virgin in a gleaming box appears to a god. A gift waiting to be unwrapped.

Zeus transformed himself into a golden rain and descended into Danaë's chamber through its skylight, painting the blank walls of her lonely world with shimmer.

Did she welcome the rain, did she open her mouth and taste the drops on her tongue? Did Danaë dance in the puddles? And when she saw the wonder for what it was, a violation, did she rage? Kick and spit and splash?

I'm sure no poet thought to ask her.

The insatiable god of gods filled the girl's womb with his seed and then he left. The skies went dry; the walls went flat.

Young Danaë braved those nine months of pregnancy alone. The nausea and fatigue, the backaches, the cravings that could never be satisfied. Always alone. And when she birthed that baby, she was her own midwife, her own husband. Danaë tried to keep her son quiet, but an infant screams to keep itself alive. *Nurse me! Burp me! Love me!* A cruel irony.

Imagine Acrisius's chagrin when he heard that newborn's wail. He would have gladly offered the baby to the wolves, but he feared the Furies' wrath. The king couldn't shed his family's blood without risk of divine retribution, but to let the babe live would ensure his own demise. Racked with stress, he devised a diabolical plan that would ensure his daughter's and grandson's deaths by indirect means.

Acrisius's men broke open the chamber and removed the filthy children. The king had them both secured in a new tomb, a wooden chest, and released them to the sea.

"She is my daughter! Mine to do with as I choose!" he yelled at his wife, on both defense and offense. "I am no kinslayer! I set them free!"

Semantics.

The chest rocked with waves and swirled with storms. Danaë, dying herself, held her baby close, wrapped in their red cloak, and sang him to sleep—the long sleep she knew awaited them both.

Hush, tiny baby, it will be over soon.

Not too soon, for Poseidon calmed the waters and saved his lord and brother's bastard—or so the story goes. Perhaps the chest drifted to the shores of Seriphos of its own free will. Why must every moment of good fortune be claimed?

An honest fisherman by the name Dictys chanced upon the chest, thinking it nothing more than lost cargo from a merchant ship. But when he opened it—oh! A feral young woman and a half-starved newborn!

Danaë had no reason to trust any man after the life she had lived, but she took a gamble.

"I am Princess Danaë, daughter of Acrisius of Argos. This is my son by the lord Zeus. Please do not reveal me. Please do not turn me away."

Acrisius and Zeus, who had taken so much from her, could not take away this choice. Danaë chose to survive. She chose to be brave, and perhaps she also chose revenge, for she named her son Perseus, the Destroyer.

Do ewes call their lambs such?

Dictys brought Danaë to his home, a fisherman's hut on the shores of Seriphos, and Perseus, another child who was never meant to be, would grow into manhood desperate to honor his mother and reclaim their worth.

And above all, deserve his name.

TENTH EPISODE

EURYALE

Meet me on the Panathenaic Way,
where the drums and flute will play.
Will you dance with me, only me?
Or are there other girls you see?

—*Erastus of Athens, "The City"*

THEIR LAST NIGHT on the road to Athens, Euryale slept. And though it didn't happen often, she dreamed.

It began in the sea.

Euryale swam, naked as a newborn. The water, cool and salty, filled her ears and nose, her mouth and eyes. It didn't matter. Euryale couldn't drown. She *was* ocean, a part of its currents long before it had a name or a ruler. A milky white horse emerged through the sandy floor beneath her. Detritus flew from its body as it loped off, the sounds of its pounding hooves swallowed by the sea. Euryale followed in its wake, her fingers barely touching the tips of its bleached tail. She trailed the stallion until the waters warmed and ocean met island. They rose from the surf in tandem, an unlikely pair wading through the shallows. The horse shook out its mane, sprinkling droplets like rain, but Euryale let her own hair weigh down her back and chest. She wore her sopping tresses against her nudity like a hooded cloak.

The horse neighed once, then led her inland, over rocks and pools, to solid ground where a small fire burned.

"Will he come?" she asked the horse.

The majestic creature carefully folded its legs beneath itself and settled down beside the flames. Its eyes closed and its breath steadied. Soon, though, the horse's stomach bloated and began to quiver—faster, stronger, until the poor beast rippled and rocked and tore open. Dozens of snakes slithered free from the bloody fission.

Euryale jumped backward. She opened her mouth to scream but made no sound.

Some snakes scurried right into the fire and immediately crisped, turning the flames blue and the smoke black. Others joined together, melding into larger, conjoined horrors. Through the thick, hissing air, Euryale watched in deranged amazement as three snakes morphed into young children, two girls and one boy, all with black eyes and forked tongues. One of the remaining serpents began to steadily consume the others, becoming more and more giant as it ingested its slithering siblings.

Soon, all that remained of the gorgeous steed was one monstrous serpent flanked by three attendant children.

The first child approached the snake's mouth, cocked her head to the side, and wordlessly offered it a honey cake. The snake, its master, refused.

A second child—the boy—came forth. He placed an open palm against his chubby cheek and stroked his own face in a palliative gesture. But it was only a temporary calm, for the boy jabbed pudgy fingers into his eye socket and plucked out an eye. Grimacing, he dropped the bloody ball before the snake, who lifted its head from its coils but did not eat.

The final child waddled forward. So blond, so young—Euryale felt an inexorable need to hold her, to protect her from this depraved scene. The girl's arms hung limply at her sides, and the fingers of one hand curled loosely upon an obsidian blade. The little one studied the honey cake and eyeball in turn, then raised the blade. With an expedient movement somehow innocent and violent, graceful and ruthless, the child sliced off her own head. When it tumbled to the ground, the snake lunged forward, fanged mouth protracted, and swallowed it in one gulp.

Finally, satisfied.

Finally, Euryale screamed.

The creature turned toward Euryale.

Can snakes smile? This one surely did.

Panicked, Euryale turned and fled, leaping from rock to rock until she reached water deep enough for a dive. Returning to the water should have been a solace, a familiar embrace, but this water felt hot, not warm, and tasted sweet when it should have been salty. Euryale choked as it seeped through her parted lips. She opened her eyes and flailed against the golden fluid once she understood what it was, into what she had submerged.

Perhaps she *could* drown, for this was ichor.

Immortal blood.

THE SUMMER SUN brought relentless heat as the sisters approached Athens, and Euryale wished its searing rays could infiltrate her mind, burn away the images from last night's repugnant dreamscape. She saw them still: the horse, the snake, the children. Another dreamer might scour the sequence for meaning—the Graeae, for instance—but Euryale refused to believe the vision held any presage. She did not share the nightmare with her sisters, sought neither their counsel nor calm.

Dreams were only dreams, and Euryale was not hysterical.

The city's countryside lay before them, lovely yet deserted. Everywhere, hardy goats abounded—billies, nannies, and kids with short legs and thick black hair—eating grass and butting heads. Where were the farmers? The gatherers? Who tended these flocks and pastures?

Did Euryale's sisters share her misgivings? They said nothing, offered less.

"Are all the humans dead?" Euryale finally demanded, exasperated by the silence. "It would be just our luck to arrive at Athens in the midst of a catastrophic plague."

Medusa pointed to divots in the dry dirt beneath her feet, then raised her hand, gesturing at the hill beyond. "They are all in the city."

She was right. Intersecting patterns of heels, human feet, and horse hooves all followed the same direction.

"Why?"

Medusa gave Euryale half a smile. "I assume we'll find out shortly."

And as the sisters got closer, they could hear the evidence: the humans were very much alive and extremely loud.

"Hold our coin tightly," Euryale told Stheno.

Medusa sighed. "You judge too harshly."

"Thank you."

Stheno frowned. "That wasn't a compliment." But she tied their shared purse to her belt.

They came into Athens through its northern gate and were immediately whisked into the chaos. Dense crowds of raucous humans congregated in narrow streets that spread haphazardly in every conceivable direction, eating and drinking, angling and jostling for better views.

Stheno yelled something to her sisters over the discordant rabble, but Euryale didn't catch it.

A cheer raised and spread through the masses, ubiquitous and deafening. Euryale startled, then lifted herself up onto her toes, straining her neck to see over the heads and shoulders of the Athenians. A dozen hippeis in full panoply entered the streets, and people leapt clear of the warhorses' hooves. Hoplites armed with spear and sword followed on foot, removing the stragglers.

"It's a parade!" Medusa exclaimed.

"Has there been a battle? A new king?"

The soldiers, basking in the attention of the crowd, marched by the sisters. Next came older men in the robes of the elite waving olive branches, followed by women carrying baskets of freshly baked breads and cakes—the emanating aroma a welcome respite from the malodorous mix of horse dung and human sweat.

Medusa tapped two fingers against an elderly woman's shoulder. "We are visitors to Athens. What is this marvel?"

The woman gawked, missing teeth on full display.

"You do not know? It's the Great Panathenaea!"

Medusa shook her head, perplexed. "Forgive me, the Panathenaea?"

"The second day of summer, Athena's day," explained the grizzled man holding the woman's arm.

The formal procession concluded with a cadre of adolescent girls wearing necklaces of dried figs. Some held bowls of barley, others first fruits. Two in particularly beautiful white gowns held up a woven dress between two poles.

The woman pointed. "The arrephoroi bring that peplos to Athena's statue at the temple, to clothe the goddess until next year."

"Arrephoroi?" wondered wide-eyed Medusa.

"Maiden daughters from our noble families," clarified the old man. "They are chosen to live with the priestesses for a year."

Euryale's eyes darted among the column of neophytes—most of them rather plain and ordinary looking—but recoiled when one stared back at her, smiling. She could not have been more than ten years of age, hair the color of sunflowers.

Her hands clutched a black stone knife.

"One hundred cattle are sacrificed at the outdoor altar," the old man was saying, voice thick with deference.

The woman nodded. "The smoke drifts all the way to Mount Olympus. The whole city feasts."

Disgust curdled Euryale's insides, and rising bile spoiled her composure. She turned away from her sisters and the crowd, clenching her jaw and eyes shut.

Her sisters prattled on to the couple about tributes and virgins, but Euryale stopped listening. She pushed against the crowd, seeking respite from the throbbing humanity—the galvanizing mix of celebration, piety, and bloodlust—for she was spinning, in and out of reality, above and below sanity. Images and questions whirled through her mind.

Girls with knives.

Children without heads.

Blood on hands, on throats, on white dresses.

Snakes everywhere. Endless coils.

Why did the horse bring her to that island? What did he want her to see?

Nauseated and overwhelmed, Euryale placed a hand against the nearest wall, focusing on the cool mud bricks, solid and real.

Harmless.

Her sisters found her at the back of the crowd.

"Euryale! There is a torch race tonight, then singing and dancing until dawn!" Medusa clapped her hands. "What an auspicious day! We must follow."

Euryale's head pulsed, and panic circled her chest. One desperate word clawed its way to her lips. "No!"

Medusa frowned. "Why?"

"It's too loud," Euryale stuttered, grasping at a reason as she gasped for breath. Her sisters were staring like she'd grown horns, so she added, "And these people reek. I'd sooner dance with swine."

Medusa looked expectantly at Stheno. "Isn't this what we came for?"

Their eldest sister, in a quandary, bit at her lower lip.

Euryale inhaled. She closed her eyes.

Choose me, Stheno. For once in your cursed life, choose me.

Stheno cleared her throat. "This is . . . perhaps . . . a lot."

Medusa's face fell.

"Have patience, Medusa," Stheno consoled. "We will see all of Athens."

As Medusa waved to the last of the pageantry, Stheno came to Euryale's side. "What troubles you?" she worried.

"I don't know," Euryale confessed. "But I'm fine."

"You don't look fine."

"I look gorgeous."

Stheno scoffed but offered her hand. "Come, gorgeous, lying sister. Let us find Cadmus's friend."

ERASTUS, THE SISTERS were told, lived among the city's other craftsmen—the potters and dyers, shoemakers and carpenters. They followed the given directions and passed through a menagerie of stray animals: trotting dogs and slinking cats, indignant winged creatures clucking and pecking. Feathers and feces littered the walkways. In Thebes, they never left the manicured Cadmea and its perfectly polished image of luxury. Here, in urban Athens, beggars caked in dirt waited for alms or deliverance. Impoverished children led donkeys laden with baskets. Humanity made itself present—in all its states, under every force: the crippled and ostracized, the derelict and disenfranchised, the favored, the free.

Medusa reached for the coin bag at Stheno's waist, but Euryale intercepted her hand.

"Harden your heart."

"Grow one."

"Grow *up*."

"Stop it," Stheno seethed.

Euryale pointed an accusatory finger at Medusa. "She would give all our money to strangers."

"It is the king's money."

"We may have need of it, Medusa," said Stheno decidedly. "We will not be rash. Whatever is left, you can give away."

Euryale smirked and Stheno shot her a withering look.

In Erastus's neighborhood, all the buildings were whitewashed brick and terra-cotta tiles. The artist's home, they had been told, had one discernible—and expensive—difference: a light silverwood door decorated with a dried laurel wreath and a painted raven, the symbols of Apollo. The sisters all scoured the workshops and homes for the telltale door, but it was Medusa who found it. She laid a finger upon the bird and traced the shape of its folded wings.

Cadmus never defined Erastus's style of art, but Euryale's mind conjured a workshop full of the finest marble, surrounded by torsos and busts, aquiline noses. She imagined paints in every hue and tone of Iris's arch, those belonging to nature and others found only along the heartstrings of creation—the colors one sees in dreams but can never recall when conscious.

Stheno rapped her knuckles against the door. Nobody answered, so Euryale, already bored of waiting, pushed it open.

"Hello?" she demanded, crossing the threshold and leaving her sisters with no other choice but to follow.

"Hello?" echoed Medusa. "Master Erastus?"

"Apologies for the intrusion!" Stheno added.

The main room was crowded with projects: tortoise shells and animal horns piled in corners, horsehairs laid across tabletops, pieces of resin and tools and hand drills. Variegated strips of boxwood and holm oak leaned against a far wall, and stringy sheep gut hung from the ceilings. Euryale paused, waiting for a voice, a bump or thump or cough, some indication that a human lived and breathed inside these walls. Instead, she heard the opening strains of song.

Erastus, the artist, was actually a musician.

"An artisan of sound," whispered Stheno, coming to the same realization.

The sisters followed the trail of notes on the tips of their toes, hesitant to disturb the melody, but came to a sudden stop at the entryway to a bare, windowless room.

There, the musician sat, eyes closed, holding an upright instrument like a lover. Despite the sisters' obvious intrusion, the musician did not cease strumming, did not stumble upon a single resonant note.

But that wasn't why Euryale's mouth fell open.

Erastus, the musician, was a woman?

ELEVENTH EPISODE

STHENO

My music sings the cosmic order.
My music plays the human soul.

—Erastus of Athens, "On Art"

OH, EUTERPE, BLESSED be your works and wonders! Did you stand beside me, did you shine, as I surrendered to your sound?

Never had I encountered such pitch or timbre, such melody, such a virtuosic progression of chords! Of course, this vocabulary is new. On that day, in that workshop with my sisters, I lacked the language to describe what I heard or how it moved me.

I had heard music before, during Pandora's wedding, at Cadmus's banquet, in Semele's symposium, but had I listened? Those songs were all up-tempo and intentional: *During this piece you dance! For this one, you eat!* But they were also derivative. What did it mean to play music for no audience? With no instructions? With no lyrics telling you how to feel?

This music whimpered and trembled. It was discordant in ways both insensible and perfect. This music sounded like living.

A woman could do this?

She was small and angular, all bones and edges, with thin gray hair pulled back from a sallow face. She sat with her legs crossed beneath her, and I sensed that even at her full height she would barely reach my shoulder. This was a woman who stayed indoors, who held little regard for her appearance.

Euryale extemporized into her hand, and even Medusa's eyes began to wander. Yet Erastus—for who else could this be?—would not pause midsong, and my admiration grew.

I could have listened to her play forever.

When the piece concluded, she lowered her lyre-like instrument, placing it horizontally across her lap, and raised her eyelids.

"What was that?" I asked, not caring how I pounced.

The musician shrugged. "I don't know yet." She took several lengthy sips from a bronze drinking cup by her side, completely unbothered by our stares.

"You come for lessons?" she finally inquired. "Or to commission a piece? I have time for neither."

"We come from Thebes."

Her mouth quirked at the corner. "Cadmus sent you."

"The king told us to seek out Erastus of Athens, who is generous to travelers in need."

"The king takes advantage of my husband's loyalty."

"Your husband?" puzzled Medusa. "Then you are not Erastus?"

She scoffed. "Do I look like an 'Erastus'?"

"How can you not be the famed artist Cadmus praised?" I stuttered. "I have never heard another play like you!"

The woman ignored my outburst. She squinted, inspecting us closely. "What are you? Not human. Clearly."

Medusa gave her our names, those of our parents. The woman contemplated, then came to some sort of internal decision, because she rose to her feet, rubbed at her lower back, and walked straight toward us. We parted awkwardly as she passed through the doorway and headed for a window, which opened onto an inner courtyard.

"Erastus!" she beckoned. "Come inside! Your royal friend has tasked you with another labor."

Euryale snorted.

A man entered, middle-aged and short like his wife, but bald and sunburnt. He held a gardening tool in one hand, a clump of mint in the other. His creased face broke into a ready smile.

"A labor? Ligeia, look at those faces, those eyes! They are labor's foil. What would be the word? A merriment?" He wrinkled his nose, thinking, then snapped his fingers. "A revelry!"

Medusa's cheeks pinkened, and the woman—Ligeia, I suppose—folded her arms across her chest. "Cadmus sent them. They are looking for a place to stay."

I offered up our bag of coin. "We wouldn't dare inconvenience either of you. We can pay."

He noted the royal insignia on my pouch and shook his head adamantly. "Cadmus's money holds no value here, and there is a room upstairs that we don't use." Erastus settled onto a stool. He was small, without a pinch of fat on his whole body, but his affable warmth filled the space—as did the aromatic leaves from his pruning. "How goes my old friend? Have those daughters destroyed him yet?"

An awkward pause stretched between us.

"Then you haven't heard?" asked Euryale rhetorically.

Ligeia's mouth hardened. "Out with it, girl."

"Princess Semele is dead."

"She was the best of the litter." Erastus's eyes took on the cast of his wife's haunting music. "You must tell us the full story later, but I have heard enough tragic tales to know they all begin differently and end the same." He sighed. "Nevertheless, I am sorry for the king."

"I am sorrier for the princess," chided Ligeia, and Erastus inclined his head to her.

"Our nephew, Thales, runs our errands," continued Erastus, shifting in his seat and in conversation. "He can navigate the agora for you. He knows the best farmers, the more honest merchants. He was born in this city, and you can trust him with your coin. Otherwise, foreigners—especially the female ones—tend to be swindled. I will send him a message."

"He is competing today," Ligeia said, correcting her husband.

Erastus put a hand to his forehead. "Bah! But of course." He grinned at us. "I am a lucky man for many reasons. One of which is my wife's mind. It's big enough for two!"

Ligeia disregarded his praise. "Thales is an athlete," she explained. "He is entered in the Panathenaea's stadion and pentathlon."

"Your boy attends the festivities, yet you remain at home." Euryale raised an eyebrow. "Why?"

I groaned internally.

Ligeia seemed unbothered by Euryale's question. She plucked a string on a nearby instrument, then another, focusing on their alternating sounds. "I am governed by my work, not by Athena."

"It seemed fun," argued Euryale, the hypocrite. Medusa shot me an incredulous look.

"Most distractions are. Spending money, drinking wine in the streets, admiring pretty girls on parade. Slaughtering innocent beasts."

"My wife does not eat animal flesh," interrupted Erastus in a loud whisper.

"The people we met seemed genuine in their worship," Medusa began, letting her voice trail off, softening the pushback. *She is just as tenacious as Euryale,* I thought, *but she knows how to be gentle.*

Ligeia, however, held firm against both my sisters. "The Panathenaea is a reminder of rule, not religion. Athena won't allow us to forget who holds power here."

It was a strange sentiment. I was not sure how it made me feel or how to respond, so I forced a diversion; I yawned.

"The spare room is . . . upstairs?"

Erastus blinked. "Ah, yes. Do you need me to show you?"

"I am sure we can manage. Thank you again, both of you."

The room above the workshop was ascetic compared to the opulence of the Theban palace, but it was private. Erastus and Ligeia would not bother us, and there would be no snooping servants or prying courtiers. I have never needed much or expected anything, and already in Athens, we had coin for food, cups for our wine, clean-enough blankets, and a window overlooking the street. I stood at its sill and admired the star jasmine growing up the wall. I inhaled its intoxicating sweetness, and, in that moment, I truly believed this city would be a restorative experience for me and my sisters.

Maybe Athens could be home.

But Euryale saw only the fine layer of dust, the austere furniture, and the oddness of our hosts. She crossed her arms. "She's incorrigible. And he's ugly."

Medusa curled herself atop the bed. "You're incorrigible. And ugly with ingratitude."

"This space," I insisted, "is ideal."

Euryale only scoffed.

But while I reveled in the comfort of our new simplicity, my sisters were already plotting. Thebes hadn't sated either of their tastes for human life. In fact, the very opposite was true. When the next day dawned, they rose, full of plans they cooked up without me.

"Would you like company?" I wondered aloud, too ashamed to beg, *Take me with you.*

Medusa licked a stubborn remnant of breakfast fig from her finger. "I want to see what remains of the Panathenaea. I doubt it would interest you."

Why wouldn't it interest me, Medusa? But I said nothing.

Euryale finished tying her sandals. "I should be back by dusk."

"Where will you be until then?"

"Seeing people."

"You don't know any people in Athens."

"Not yet."

I forced a smile, watching them go, and pretended busyness by adjusting our few possessions about the room. Why couldn't we explore the city together? How else would I keep them safe?

I have always known Fear. She was the fourth sister, and my most intimate acquaintance. And I also knew that I couldn't sit alone with her all day long. Anxiety thrust me to my feet, and I descended the stairs, pausing in my surreptitious step when I heard Erastus humming and fumbling about the kitchen.

"Do you drink ptisanē?" he called up.

I hesitated, somewhat flustered to be caught creeping—with nowhere to go and nothing to do—but I kept my momentum moving forward. "No," I answered, entering the kitchen. "What is it?"

He gestured in the direction of a small hearth. "Come. I will show you."

I followed his directions, lighting the fire and bringing barley water to a boil. I strained the puffed grains and added honey from a small jar.

"While you wait for the honey to dissolve, add a sprig of mint and oregano."

I found his herbs, and while I waited for the drink to set, Erastus restrung an instrument, the one Ligeia played the day before.

"And what is that?" I asked, so desperate to know I would expose my ignorance.

"This?" He seemed shocked. "Why, it's a kithara!" He strummed the fastened strings and smiled at the sound.

"Your wife, when she plays, she is . . ." I fought myself for the right word. "A marvel?" I shook my head, frustrated. "No, more. Her playing is nothing like magic. It's far too real."

Erastus smiled at me tenderly. "I understand exactly what you mean."

"Is the tea ready?" called a voice, and Ligeia came into the kitchen. "Oh! You." She was surprised to see me. "You're not out chasing life and love with the others?"

I shook my head.

"I have taught her to make ptisanē," announced Erastus, "and she learns quickly." He removed the herbs and poured us three cups. I took a sip. Hot and clear, with a light sweetness and slight spice.

"Do you like the drink?"

I nodded.

"It fills the belly," Ligeia declared. "It keeps me full enough that I can work without pause."

"I insist she eats dinner," put in Erastus, and I saw the way her hand brushed lightly against his arm, a signaling of the affection between this unusual pair. I was completely flabbergasted by their relationship, their arrangement. He gardened, he cooked. She played the kithara. Yet Cadmus called Erastus the artist.

"I have to ask," I blurted out. "Which of you is the musician? Cadmus said . . ."

"Cadmus, like all men, sees what he wants to see." Ligeia wrapped both hands around her cup—tightly, for I saw the whites of her knuckles.

Erastus leaned toward me, embodying the open candor of his personality. "I am a great performer, but a passable musician. My wife is a *creator*." And he imbued that word—*creator*—with all his being. "She composes the music, and I play it in contests and festivals and rites, in courts and theaters the land over."

"But," I sputtered, unable to repress a sudden surge of sadness, "it's her music. And you are famous for it."

Erastus nodded. "Yes."

"I am a woman, Stheno." And because it was the first time Ligeia used my name, I sat up straighter. "No man wants to see me outperform another man. It would disrupt the order imposed on our world. They can prohibit me from playing in public, but not what I do in my home."

"And I make sure she is heard," finished Erastus, "even if it is just a poor reproduction."

"Have we settled all your uncertainty?" Ligeia's voice was hard but brittle.

Hardly. Was this how Medusa always felt, to be so curious? But there would be time—I hoped—to learn music, and how this fascinating couple navigated the unjust parameters of their art. For now, there was another question that nagged, pulling at the carefully made corners of my mind.

"Yesterday you said the gods hold no power over you, yet your door so clearly commemorates Apollo."

"I play his instrument," answered Ligeia, speaking for them both, "yet you won't ever find me in Delphi. Apollo's light has shone brightly on our lives, but I create boundaries. I do not crave closeness to the gods."

I considered her words and recognized their wisdom. "Nor do I."

"And your sisters? What do they desire?"

But I could not answer, for I did not know.

TWELFTH EPISODE

EURYALE

Let this secret remain
between the waves and me.
And, you, of course,
always you.

—Erastus of Athens, "Her Dark Love"

THALES HAD THE look of a kind boy, just at the cusp of manhood. Honest eyes and bronzed skin, shoulder-length auburn hair that he kept tied back, broad shoulders and big hands—like a puppy that hasn't yet grown into himself.

Different from Polydorus, who was dark and lean and brooding, spoiled and entitled.

Indeed, young Thales was handsome enough, and Euryale entertained the thought of a flirt. If he knew Athens as well as his uncle Erastus claimed, the boy's adoration could have its advantages. Plus, it would irk Stheno to no end.

But it had ended so bitterly with Polydorus, she recalled their farewell like an unwelcome storm.

She barely listened as Stheno and the boy discussed shopkeepers and payments. Why bother herself with banalities when her sister so happily handled them? Instead, she wickedly wondered what Thales looked like without his clothes.

But then Thales saw Medusa.

She came floating down the stairs, as soft and light as a cumulus cloud on a spring day, and when Thales looked up, his eyebrows nearly lifted off his forehead. It was as if he beheld Hebe herself.

"Oh! Hello." Medusa tucked a lock of that obnoxiously gold-streaked hair behind her ear, almost shyly. Thales stood so quickly he knocked over a stool.

"This is Thales," explained Stheno, biting back a smile. "I think he may know everything about Athens. And everyone, too."

"And as we know nothing," added Medusa, "you have arrived at the most opportune time."

"Only tell me what you need," he announced, a bit too eagerly.

"I'm sure my sister has already burdened you with too many of our desires. I wouldn't want to bother." Medusa took an open seat at the table, crossing her ankles as she tucked her legs beneath her. Stheno may believe in Medusa's naivete, but to Euryale, this deferential child act was no more genuine than any rehearsed drama. And she had watched this scene play out before.

"I promise you are no bother," insisted Thales. "My aunt and uncle asked me to help."

"Well, I went to Athena's temple yesterday, on the acropolis, but was so overwhelmed. Do you know the place well? Could you take me?"

Thales beamed. "I can do even better. I know the high priestess, Frixoula. She is close with my mother. I will introduce you."

Medusa clapped her hands together in delight, and the boy grinned from ear to ear.

Euryale sighed, intentionally loud enough to disrupt the mood.

"I'm off to sully myself." Her gaze lingered on Thales. "But best wishes with the chaste."

And then she strode out the front door without another word.

THERE'S AN INHERENT joy to walking without a distinct destination in mind. On previous days, Euryale circled the city, but today she needed to pass beyond its walls. To remain inland was to reside in a trap, and Euryale missed the rhythms of the sea. Athens, unlike Thebes, enjoyed an easy access to the water.

She would sully herself; she would pace and wander and think. But she would do so with a view.

Euryale exited the agora by the southern gate and followed the western coastline. She had no way of knowing how far south the land went—perhaps if she could fly like a seabird, she could soar above it all and find her place on the map. Find her place anywhere, really.

Euryale passed through forests and farmlands, over hills resplendent with amethyst wildflowers. She ate from a wild fig tree, opened a pomegranate and savored its seeds.

"How far does it go?" she asked some men weeding crops on a large estate.

"What, the coastline?"

She nodded.

"Until Sounion."

"Sounion?"

"The end of the peninsula. The end of our world."

"Our part of it," corrected his friend.

"Is it much farther? I have already walked most of the day."

The first man put down his mattock and wiped the sweat from his face. "It is worth it."

Encouraged, Euryale continued, and when she reached the cape, she rejoiced in her decision. Sounion, its azure waters and verdant green hills, felt like kismet. A destined destination. She stood alone, not yoked to her sisters, owning the vista for herself.

Perfect seclusion. Blessed isolation.

After long hours under the summer sun, Euryale stepped into the pellucid waters without pause—walking straight and true until the water covered her head.

Welcome home, child, sang the sea.

Below the surface, she blew bubbles and ran fingers through the tendrils of her hair. She was a jellyfish, floating and free. She removed her sandals, let her toes curl into the marine detritus—shells and tiny rocks, sand and seaweed—rooting herself like a crab. She spun forward, head under feet, over and over. A playful seal.

The salt water infused her blood and she connected—she synthesized. In the sea, Euryale was unaffected by temperature or pressure. She was weightless, powerful, and graceful. She kicked through strong currents like they were flimsy reeds. The waves hugged her close like a cherished daughter.

Did her sisters yearn for the water like she did? They never mentioned it.

Sated, Euryale retrieved her sandals from the sea bottom, then ascended just as afternoon waned into dusk. A rocky promontory formed above her, and she spied a manageable path to its peak. With her wet dress clinging to her body, Euryale scaled the rough, slippery rocks of the cliff side, sure-footed despite a frisky breeze. She wondered what mortals experienced when they climbed. Fear, probably. Not ecstasy, not the rush she felt in her own eternal strength—her perfect, infallible form. It was a far climb, but when she reached its zenith, she exhaled.

It was the closest to happy she ever got.

Euryale pulled off her damp clothing, irritated by its clutch and confinement, and lay naked upon the sunbaked boulders. The sky broke into shades of mauve—from the soft pink of a shell to the rich purple of a grape. Far out, a lone trireme passed between islands.

Did she wonder where it went, or how many of its sailors would return?

Did she care?

"What are you looking for, daughter of monsters?"

His voice, sudden yet silken, startled Euryale. Once again, he had come up behind her, catching her unawares. She sat up.

"I have always watched the sea."

Euryale reached for her discarded dress and held it up against her chest. She heard Poseidon's sandals step across the dirt and rock—

such a normal, ordinary sound for a god!—and then he settled beside her on the rock.

"I would have asked, *Who* are you looking for? But I could not stand the disappointment if your answer wasn't me."

She did not look at him. "A girl thinks of many things when she is alone, in a place such as this." Euryale gestured to the horizon.

"And when she is naked?" Poseidon brushed a knuckle against the back of her arm, and Euryale could not stop the shivers. He chuckled at her gooseflesh and openly laughed when she thrust his hand away.

"I worry you prefer humans to the immortals, now that you have been to Thebes and Athens."

How did he know? Euryale's cheeks warmed, but she shrugged noncommittally.

"You came with your sister, the mortal one?"

"With both my sisters."

"Ah, yes. You are three. The serious one, the little rose, and you."

Euryale did not want to talk about her sisters, and she could be cruel, as well.

"We arrived during the Panathenaea."

She faced him finally. Saw the tension in his shoulders at her mention of the festival, a slight clicking in his jaw. His anger reminded her of his power. Euryale should be careful.

"You know, then, of my trial with Zeus's daughter?" Ire sharpened his words.

"I heard of her tricks, yes." A demulcent offering, for Euryale did not seek him as an adversary—not in the slightest—and she wanted his grin, not his grimace, on her.

"I would have bested her in simple combat... Athena has become far too proud."

"Pride is rewarded among the gods. Punished in the rest of us."

"Yet it is beautiful in you, Golden Eyes." He cupped his hand beneath her chin, lifted her face. The sea god wore a headband over his black hair that made him seem young; his muscles relaxed as he studied her, though Euryale suddenly struggled to breathe.

"You find me beautiful yet call me proud. Your words confuse me, Lord."

"I think I am perfectly clear."

"I think you are purposefully ambiguous." She tasted salt on her lips, licked it away. "Why are you here?"

He grinned then, decadent and dangerous. "I came with a gift." He leaned into her, mouth hovering just above her ear. "Cadmus's daughter lives."

Euryale nearly dropped the careful drapery of her dress. "I attended her funeral! I saw her remains enter the burial tomb." She shuddered, remembering. "There was barely enough of her left."

Poseidon shrugged a shoulder. "I would not lie to you, Golden Eyes, and I will give you the story for a kiss."

Euryale hesitated, then laid a quick, chaste peck upon his cheek.

"That's not what I meant." He frowned.

"Then you should have been more specific."

Poseidon sighed. "I am outmatched." And he shifted beside her, finding a more comfortable position as he settled into his tale. "After Zeus revealed himself to the princess and killed her, my brother pulled the babe from her womb and placed him in his own thigh."

"*Him*," Euryale whispered, a mix of jealousy and awe. "Semele had a boy."

Poseidon nodded. "And Zeus hid him in his own body to keep it secret from Hera. He brought their son to Mount Nysa. The rain nymphs raised the child in their caves. Now, full grown, he is the twice-born Olympian, Dionysus."

"He is a man already?"

"He is Zeus's son. Human time cannot define him."

Euryale's mind reeled. Semele's baby, alive, *an Olympian*.

She grabbed Poseidon's arm. "But you said Semele lives."

"I did. But only because of her son. Dionysus longed for his mortal mother so desperately that he risked Hades, traveled to the Underworld, and freed her. Semele walks and breathes again, on Olympus by the name Thyone."

"She is a goddess?"

"To Hera's eternal frustration." Poseidon reached over and wrapped a lock of Euryale's hair around his finger. "Her affair with a married god ended well for her, no?" And he gave her curl a light tug.

Euryale would not answer, would not acknowledge his smugness. Instead, she studied how the clouds manipulated the sun's last rays, darkening them as they bent around indistinct shapes in the distance.

"Perhaps I will see more of you, the next time, by the sea," mused Poseidon, and his steely gaze lingered on her bare legs. Euryale flushed, her stomach clenching in a way both terrifying and pleasant.

"I am living with the musician, Erastus."

"A fortunate man indeed."

Then the sea god, the great earthshaker, stood and walked off the side of the cliff, vanishing into the evening's evanescence.

Euryale released her dress and rubbed her free hands against her face until they ceased to shake. She dragged her fingers down the sides of her cheeks and neck, and settled her palms, one on top of the other, against her chest—over her heart and its throbbing pulse.

WHEN EURYALE RETURNED to the workshop, Medusa and Stheno were still awake, talking over a late supper. Medusa spoke passionately of Athena's temple, the details spilling forth in a chaotic jumble with no regard for transition or timeline. And Stheno, who Euryale suspected was, in actuality, dreadfully bored, sat through the long-winded litany with appreciative murmurs, nodding and raising her eyebrows at all the right moments.

How clever! Ingenious! Inspired!

Euryale took the empty seat. Nobody asked where she had been.

And so Medusa prattled on about shrines and purifications, oaths and officiants, and Stheno pretended to care, and Euryale suppressed her rage. A besetting rage, an ardent rage. Rage at Medusa's self-absorption and Stheno's forced equanimity. Rage at her own duplicitous participation.

"The temple is a place for women to be independent. The priestesses earn their own money. Some of them even hold property." Medusa paused to drink water from a clay jug on the table. "Thales introduced me to Frixoula. She's from a noble family and was chosen as an arrephoros at a young age."

Arrephoroi, Medusa explained, were the young maidens carrying the peplos during the Panathenaea.

"Now Frixoula is high priestess. It is a public office, a prized position for any woman."

Euryale snorted. A *prize*? A life of forced virginity, without love, without children?

"She asked me to return," Medusa announced, full of glee. "Frixoula wants me to instruct her in the writing system I learned from the Theban scribes."

Stheno smiled, but it barely lifted her face. Medusa wouldn't notice; she never did. "Wonderful," their older sister said automatically. "You should share your talents."

Unable to tolerate another word, Euryale let her rage loose.

"Yesterday," began Euryale, fully aware of what she was about to instigate, "you were a hanger-on of a court, the dearest companion of a louche princess. Today you're an acolyte priestess? Only you, Medusa."

Stheno winced.

"I am *curious*," Medusa insisted, but Euryale only laughed.

"You are a fair-weather supplicant."

"I have many interests," rejoined Medusa, and her voice was tight, her words clipped. Euryale's rage purred, enjoying itself. "What do you have, Euryale?"

"A story."

And Medusa perked up, intrigued despite herself. Stheno eyed Euryale warily. Suspiciously.

Euryale did not immediately explain herself. She moved from the table and settled upon the low bed, administered a handful of oil to her ravaged feet. It had been a very strenuous walk, after all. She took ample time, drawing out the moment.

Let Medusa be bored for once.

"Tell us, Euryale."

Her sisters remained at the table. Medusa raised the jug, took another sip of water.

"Semele and her baby survived."

The jug struck the floor, shattering. Cool well water spread around and under the burnt-orange shards, yet nobody made a move.

"How?" Medusa whispered.

Just as Poseidon had done, Euryale first told her sisters of Dionysus's rescue and rebirth, finishing with the new god's redemption of his fallen mother. And as she narrated, Euryale appreciated its beauty; namely, the lengths a son would travel to rescue a mother he never met. It might be the truest love story she had ever heard, and touched by its poignancy, she almost regretted the way she had behaved toward Medusa.

Medusa went to the window. She stood in its frame for a long moment, and when she turned back around, her cheeks were wet.

"Why do you cry, Medusa?" Stheno exclaimed. "This is serendipitous news!"

Medusa seemed to struggle for words. "Semele must know how I've mourned her, and yet she did not come for me." Her voice wobbled and her thin frame shook. "She sent no word."

Euryale's regret vanished as quickly as it had appeared. She threw up her hands. "You are impossible! The object of your sorrow *lives*! The child she died for *lives*! Yet you mope because their reunion didn't include *you*?"

Medusa's jaw dropped, but she did not speak. Stheno fell to her knees and began stacking the pieces of the broken jug.

"Stop it, Stheno!" snapped Euryale. "This is *her* mess!"

Silently, Medusa made her way to Stheno and took the shards from her hand. She placed them on the tabletop. "I will go purchase another jug and fill it," she said, only to Stheno, then she went down the stairs and through the workshop. Euryale heard the front door open and close.

Stheno lingered on the floor, unbothered by the water soaking her dress. When she finally raised her head, Euryale met her stare, defensive and exasperated.

"I thought she would want to know."

"You know how she is. What she wants," Stheno replied wearily. "And you know what words will hurt her most."

And there it was, out loud—almost. The thing about Medusa they never acknowledged.

Rage and regret gone, only Euryale remained. Returned to herself, far from happy.

"I like to share my talents, as well."

THIRTEENTH EPISODE

STHENO

If you want my music, you will pay
in skin and blood
and bended bone.

—*Erastus of Athens, "On Art"*

"I HAVE NO TALENTS."

Ligeia raised an eyebrow. They were thick and dark still, despite the gray of her hair, and stood out on her face. She continued strumming her kithara and neglected to comment.

Admittedly, it was an odd conversation starter, even for one as unpolished as me, but I persisted.

"I do not paint or weave. I cannot ride a horse or throw a discus."

"Does that matter?"

"How can you say that? You are the most talented person I know." Emboldened, I continued: "I want you to teach me to play music."

"No."

"I will pay you."

"I do not want money. I want you to leave me alone."

I was not aggressive, but I was trenchant. "Do not mock me. Please." I had brought coins from Cadmus's purse. I laid them before her in that tiny windowless room. "Every mortal desires money."

Ligeia heaved a great sigh and set down her instrument. "Of course, money is indispensable to a mortal life."

"You are a woman. You cannot have fame, but you can earn money." I placed a hand on my chest unnecessarily. "I can reward your talent."

She shook her head. "You misunderstand. Money provides the food and drink I need to create, yes. It gives me a warm, dry place to build and store my instruments. But Stheno, money does not inspire my work."

"Then why do you play?"

She chuckled a bit under her breath. "You are so old and yet so young."

Shame burned my cheeks. "You mock me yet again. I asked you not to."

"I forget how earnest you are. Forgive me, I do not laugh to be snide." She gave me an appraising look, then said something I will never forget: "I would play music even if I had no food or drink, no warm, dry home. I will play music while I die, holding each note like a tether to life for as long as I can. I will let go of this world on a song."

I fell quiet. It hurt me suddenly—my jealousy of her.

"And yet you will not teach me to play."

"No. Not if your reason is to be good at something. Music deserves better than that."

"It's not my reason."

"Then what is it?"

"This is the first thing I've wanted to do for myself. Perhaps ever."

She snorted once, short and sardonic. "Nobody is that selfless."

"I don't have the words." I wrung my hands, cursing my inadequacies. "I never do. I can't explain it. But I am genuine, I swear."

"Maybe you are bored. Maybe you want to impress someone you love or prove someone else wrong. Maybe this is all some competitive horseshit with your sisters." She rolled her eyes. "I am far too old and impatient for any of it."

I stomped my foot like a petulant child, then apologized, embarrassed.

Ligeia pointed toward the door. "Go, Stheno. Think. And come back when you have a better reason."

I slammed the door as I left the shop, heading out onto the Athenian streets with nowhere to go, nobody to call upon. One sister tended to her self-righteous anger, the other nursed a self-centered melodrama. They were free to do so. I would not reprimand either. And yet I never dared play the injured sister. That wasn't my character; those weren't my lines. We were no different than any theatrical performance. An actor does not change roles halfway through the play because they are exhausted by the part they are given.

You cannot recast sisters. Not after so much time.

And besides, I wouldn't have the right words.

I did want to learn music. I knew it in my soul with perfect clarity. My frustration with Ligeia had nothing to do with her, and everything to do with me.

Ah.

Awareness engenders serenity. My mind fell still, ready, and with my frustration subsiding, I began to think.

By the time I returned to the workshop, I had my answer.

"Teach me to play so that I may finally speak."

Ligeia nodded, then motioned to a low stool. "Let us begin."

I APPROACHED MY kithara lessons with the solemnity and precision of a spiritual ritual. I brewed the ptisanē with Erastus, then together we served Ligeia, who would suffer no morning platitudes. I received no niceties, no transitions, she simply jumped into the lesson when she was ready.

"Sit," she commanded that first day. "You are as timid as a deer."

"Not when it matters," I returned evenly, accepting the seat. I settled into the worn cushion, folding my legs before me as she did. Ligeia closed her eyes and began to play. I marveled at the way her hands complemented each other, how they danced in perfect coordination.

"What do you call this song?"

"Hardly a song. Scales."

I must have worn my confusion, for she offered a terse explanation. "Scales are sounds organized by pitch. They can ascend"—she demonstrated—"or descend."

"But what you played when we arrived. That was a song, yes?"

She nodded.

"But there were no words."

"I don't sing. I have the ear and the hands but lack the voice. I write those parts for others to perform."

"Like Erastus?"

"Yes, he is a lovely singer. I use lyrics when I have a point to make, a message to be remembered, but if I am honest, I prefer music without all that mess."

Though loath to admit it, I liked lyrics. "Then how does your listener know what the song is about—or what to feel—without words?"

"Ah, that's the inherent magic of music. This theme of five notes"—she plucked the corresponding strings—"says something. What it says to me may be different than what it says to you. Because we are different women who have lived different lives. And neither of us would be wrong."

The cup of ptisanē cooled in my hand, though my mind was heating up. "You have an intention as you compose, don't you? That must be the right answer."

"You can try to assume a creator's intention, but you will never truly know what their work means to me." It was not a challenge, but a statement of fact. "Meaning belongs to the individual. You can only assess your own reactions."

My thoughts jumbled together, and I wished for eloquence. Semele's symposiums thrived on philosophical conundrums like these, but I never dared to contribute. I listened, worried that I would only appear trite or foolish.

But today I could not be satisfied without saying something.

"Not everything in music, in art, can be so boundless," I stammered, trying to articulate my confusion. "There must be limits."

Ligeia smiled at me. She was not a handsome woman, but when

she smiled, she could be radiant. "Indeed, there are. For while personal interpretations and preferences may be endless, one issue is never up for debate." She became serious then and leaned toward me. "Some art is done well; other art is not."

"And yours is?"

"The best."

I looked up. Erastus had answered my question from the doorway, arms folded over his chest and eyes twinkling. I had been so engaged in our conversation that I'd failed to notice his eavesdropping. "People can like bad art that brings comfort and entertainment; people can dislike good art that chafes."

"But art itself must be judged by criteria," I said, finishing for him.

"She is an excellent pupil," Erastus told Ligeia, and I glowed. I even relaxed, sipped my drink.

"Bah," admonished Ligeia, "she hasn't even begun."

And then she put me to task.

Each morning, Ligeia began by explaining a theory of music, demonstrating its technique, and then assigning me a set of skills to practice. Afterward, she returned to her compositions, and I played for hours alone on my borrowed instrument.

The work was repetitive, but it was purposeful.

I loved it.

At first my fingers bled, but they soon grew protective calluses. Erastus whooped and congratulated me when I showed him my new fingertips. Sometimes my lower back ached in the night from grueling hours holding the kithara's wooden frame in my arms, but I did not mind. The instrument filled me, and I ceased to feel lonely.

Who is Stheno? Semele had asked me once, in a garden filled with quail.

Then, I was just an older sister, but maybe now, I was this.

FOURTEENTH EPISODE

EURYALE

She was never meant for loom or wheel.
A different thread. Spin again.
Unwoven woman.

—Erastus of Athens, "The Theater of Sisterhood"

WHERE ARE YOU *when you aren't with us?*

It was the unspoken question that Euryale would not answer.

Her sisters were simple, obvious. Medusa and Thales wandered the acropolis. Stheno and Ligeia kept indoors, plucking away at monotonous chords.

But Euryale would not settle for mediocrity in Athens. Not after Thebes, and certainly not after Sounion.

Besides, it wasn't any of her sisters' concern where Euryale headed. She did not need their wide eyes or pursed lips, their mawkish judgment or control masked as concern. Medusa could traipse about temples, playing priestess, and Stheno was more than welcome to ruin her posture, playing artist. Euryale didn't care.

There was one important lesson to be learned from Thebes, and she was pursuing further education. Semele had found her god not on her knees, but on her back.

"He says I am the best lover he has known."

What do I want?

What do I need?

Euryale knew both now, but not the way. She did not dare ask Erastus or Thales, so she was forced to impose upon a stranger. The first man she approached only shook his head, and the second warned her away. The third, however, provided the information she required with an oily sneer.

"You want Charmion's Little House."

He told her where to find it but took her hand and pulled her toward him. Euryale stuck her nails down—hard—into his fleshy palm, and the man yelped. He brought a hand marked with little half-moons of blood to his mouth.

"You know what will happen to you there," he growled, licking his wounds. "With those men."

"Or maybe *I* will happen to *them*."

And when Euryale gnashed her teeth in his face, the man flinched backward and stumbled. She laughed, leaving him cursing in her feral wake.

What freedom exists when men find you dangerous!

Euryale followed the city's long walls to the Bay of Phaleron, Athens's harbor on the gulf. She wrinkled her nose, unaccustomed to the odors of a wharf—rotten fish and human bile, sea brine mixing with the copper of tools and blood, all of it salted. Outdoor fireplaces roared with industry. She passed over cart tracks, passed by haggling shoppers and recalcitrant vendors hawking baskets of octopus, crustaceans in all manner of shells.

How Ceto would have roiled! Just the thought made Euryale smile.

And Charmion's, of course, was marked by a tiny scallop shell etched into its cornerstone.

Even at this early hour, the front door was propped open. In this place, business operated under both moon and sun. Others might have paused at the threshold, taken a deep breath to consider the line they were about to cross. But Euryale had never likened herself to others. She strode through like a brazen conqueror, a warrior queen in full command.

In another life, the building might have been the private residence of a wealthy man. Its inner atrium prioritized human comfort—cushioned seats, vivid rugs, and low tables, a pleasant fragrance. But there was an unmistakably transient energy to the atmosphere, a sense that—despite its homely charms—this was not a place to settle in and stay.

At its center, a woman wearing a fine chiton stood before a statue of a satyr. She greeted Euryale and offered her a cup of honeyed water, which Euryale declined.

"I must see Master Charmion, please."

"*Mistress* Charmion?" corrected the woman, who, upon closer look, was no more than a girl. Her face paint intimated maturity, but Euryale saw behind the mask. "We have no master here. Does she know you?"

"Only my family," Euryale responded. "But that should be enough."

The girl's eyes widened just a bit, allowing the tiniest bit of curiosity to slip through the carefully assembled visage. She bowed and disappeared behind a shrouded doorway on the atrium's perimeter.

Euryale inspected the other visitors. Settled upon benches, two very different men waited their turn. One, a grizzled sailor with a burnt face, drank from an ornate goblet of wine. Fresh carnelian stains dotted his tunic, and he offered Euryale a lopsided smile. The other, far more advanced in age, sat in straight-backed meditation, eyes closed, as if readying himself for a medical procedure. Thick gold bracelets adorned both his wrists.

A lavender mist heavied the air, begging Euryale's mind to submit to the senses. But she could've more readily leapt from her skin than settled into the aromatic miasma.

She wasn't nervous, she reminded herself.

The girl returned and beckoned Euryale forward.

"You are fortunate," she remarked. "Last night was profitable, and the mistress is in good spirits. Come with me."

Thoughts of Stheno came, unbidden, as Euryale followed the girl through the curtained door and past a line of finely arranged bedrooms. *Not now, Stheno. Don't you dare.* Somewhere, a harp rang, followed by a peal of high, coquettish laughter.

And she heard moaning, of course. Percussive breathing. Thumping that was fast and far from gentle.

Though Euryale's stomach tightened, she only raised her chin higher. She banished the images of her incorruptible sister, brushing them away like a pestering fruit fly.

Be gone, Stheno.

And I am not nervous.

The girl halted before a closed door and spoke in a detached—and obviously rehearsed—voice: "Mistress Charmion has little leisure time to spare." But then the girl lowered her voice to add, "Be brief. Be clear. And don't stare at her hands."

Euryale nodded, appreciative of the informal advice, then entered.

Mistress Charmion sat at a wooden desk, coins piled before her. A ready dagger lay on the tabletop between her and the door. Without an upward glance, the mistress clucked, and the girl slipped away.

Alone and without invitation, Euryale helped herself to a seat.

The woman finished her counting with no evident hurry, forcing Euryale to wait. Euryale nearly smiled. This was one of Ceto's oldest tricks—she'd been playing these power games for generations. While Mistress Charmion concluded her chore, Euryale arranged her body into a position of consummate nonchalance, exhibiting no signs of impatience, and she met the older woman eye to eye, steady as ever.

"So, what are you? A mountain nymph who's lost her way? Some demigod bastard?"

"A daughter of the ocean," returned Euryale, evenly, "but no Nereid. My brother guards the golden apples, and my sister is the matriarch of beasts."

"Yet you are unremarkable."

Another of Ceto's ploys. The barb had become so predictable for Euryale, it lacked any sting.

"Perhaps at first glance."

"You are comely though," admitted Charmion, devouring Euryale's face and form with a woman's critical eye. "Considering such a monstrous lineage."

Euryale accepted the compliment.

The mistress took a coin in her hand, turning it over absentmindedly. It clicked rhythmically against the gemstone rings she wore, and drew attention to her grotesquely deformed fingers. Gnarled and knobbed like the branches of a tree long misshapen by wind. They undoubtedly caused her great pain, but she managed to move them quickly, the coin rolling over and over with adapted dexterity. Was she daring Euryale to look, to gawk at her difference?

"I know everyone. Every merchant and sailor, at least half the royalty. And the worst monsters I've known have always been the most beautiful."

Mistress Charmion, too, was beautiful—blue eyes, a slightly overlarge mouth. But her looks fell flat, worn and tired, like a once favored and now threadbare dress. And so, as women do, she overdecorated herself with tiny disguises. A wig of light hair, jewels to detract from her swollen knuckles, a sash tied extra tightly around her waist to suggest curves—though if the bones in her wrists were any indication, this woman was reduced to little more than skin and skeleton.

She couldn't be that old; she must be sick.

"Why are you here, immortal? I am an Aphrodite abiding in Athena's world. I have little choice but to offer these services. What do you aim to do here, besides cause strife between me and your primordial father?"

Euryale took a deep breath, steeling herself. "I want to learn the art of love."

The woman cackled, displaying a dimple in her left cheek. Euryale wished the laughter didn't burn.

"*Love?* Oh, Hera's immortal teat! Who have you fallen for, sweet one? A prince? Or someone more poetic, a handsome fisherman?"

"Both, of a sort."

"And you desire the secrets of the pornai? To seduce him?"

Euryale shook her head. "The hetairai."

"Isn't that presumptuous!" Mistress Charmion put down the coin.

In Thebes, Euryale had listened closely to how both genders discussed the pleasure girls. The pornai were cheap women for poor men: quick and disposable. But the hetairai entertained the elite. The ones she had seen in Cadmus's court were physically stunning, but also influential. Redoubtable.

"Those women are companions. Accomplished. Well versed. I sense little charisma in you—despite your noble bearing."

"I am far from common."

"Fair. A common girl would never make such an unusual request." And Mistress Charmion scrutinized Euryale again, this time with the authority of a merchant, before she added, "You are a maiden; I would wager last night's earnings."

Euryale answered with a frigid silence.

"No matter." Charmion shrugged. "Virginity is a commodity. A token to trade and a treasure to allure. You are smarter than most to keep it for your advantage."

"I will pay a fair price to your house," Euryale said. "I only want to watch."

"You're not the first to ask: there are men who try to be faithful to their wives, others with unseemly diseases. But you are the first woman and certainly for such reasons." Mistress Charmion considered. "I have a suitable room and an amenable girl, but if I take your money, will I also receive your unsightly kin pounding at my door demanding my head?"

"Nobody will know. Nobody would care."

Again, she saw Stheno's coral-colored eyes at the forefront of her mind. Pained. *How could you say such a thing, Euryale?*

It was such a grievous lie.

"Come back tonight with plenty of coin."

Euryale nodded once, brisk and conclusive, as binding as any handshake.

"Everything you wish to discover about men you will find behind these doors. Just don't ask for a refund when you're disappointed."

Charmion's militant business acumen seemed to fade, leaving behind a lingering sadness and perhaps even a sense of loss. Euryale noticed, of course, but refused to ruminate over the madam's inner turmoil—the financial forces and emotional armies at battle. That was another woman's war. The negotiations between Euryale and Charmion were settled, and Euryale would not be deferred nor threatened with disillusionment. In fact, she strode back through the wharf with a light, elated step, feeling more at peace than she had in a long while.

And anyway, what could an old whore know about true love?

FIFTEENTH EPISODE

STHENO

Pretty penitent taken by the Temple.
Psalms and silence,
rose blood rising on the altar.

—Erastus of Athens, "A Prayer"

WE WERE NOT in the city long before Medusa met Athena. I had wondered when one of us would happen upon the city's protector, and with Medusa at the temple nearly every day, it was only natural that my youngest sister met the gray-eyed goddess first.

She detailed their encounter over a dinner shared with our human hosts. Ligeia sat at the head of the table, and Thales—who regularly walked Medusa home from the acropolis—took Euryale's vacant seat. Erastus passed around platters of food.

"Today was a holy day," began Medusa, "the start of a new season. Because the first dew settled upon the olive tree, Frixoula sent me and the arrephoroi to deliver the holy offerings."

My sister explained that this was the girls' final assignment in their yearlong service. After depositing a collection of sealed baskets in a hidden sanctuary and retrieving those from the year before, they were free to go—to return home, to marry. Their service to the temple concluded.

"Where is the sanctuary?" questioned Thales between mouthfuls of egg. I had never seen any creature—mortal or immortal—with such an appetite.

"I shouldn't reveal too much," vacillated Medusa, but then she broke into an impish smile and lowered her voice. "There is an underground passage! It starts in the acropolis, descends beneath the precincts of the city, and opens in a garden's cave."

"And I thought I knew everything about Athens!" Thales pushed a reddish lock from his forehead and grinned at my sister in a gesture so young, so unaware of its tender charm, that my heart warmed for him.

But Ligeia clucked her tongue in disappointment. "Don't be a man who presumes to know everything, even in jest."

Erastus winked at their nephew. "Ligeia may not know all, but she always knows better."

"Better than *most*," she retorted primly.

"What was in the baskets?" I asked Medusa.

"Honey cakes? The girls certainly grind enough meal." Medusa dipped a piece of bread into her watered-down wine. "I am only guessing; I didn't dare look."

"Ah," I exclaimed, "then you aren't a Pandora, after all!"

Medusa met my half-hearted joke with full bewilderment. "I don't understand."

"After the flood, remember? You and Euryale said you would've opened the vase, just like Pandora?"

Medusa shook her head slowly, a slight wrinkle to her perfect forehead. "I don't remember that."

I tried again. "You teased me mercilessly when I said I would not?"

"I don't think I would have said that. I wouldn't open it."

It shouldn't have stung. She probably held memories I had forgotten, as well. And so I smiled. "Ah well, it was a long time ago."

"Finish the story, Medusa," bade Erastus. "You and the girls met Athena at the secret altar?"

"Only me. I lost my way in the tunnel. There are so many barely noticeable rooms, like little tombs, and it's quite dark."

"Sounds ghastly," Ligeia muttered.

"The others were certainly quick to retreat, but I found it all quite thrilling."

"Tell us of Athena."

"She is tall!" Medusa confided. "And lovely, which I had not expected. I imagined her more serious. More . . ." Medusa did an imitation of a rigid soldier that made Thales snort. "But she was wildly articulate and bright. I've never spoken to anyone with such an extraordinary mind."

"I'm insulted," deadpanned Erastus.

"What did you talk about?"

"Oh, everything. The purpose of voyage, the pursuit of knowledge. How to prioritize emotional honesty." Medusa seemed incandescent. "I look forward to meeting her again."

"Then your service to Frixoula is not over?" I surmised.

"I'm not an arrephoros or a hiereia. I'm . . ." She considered, her head cocked slightly to one side. "I'm something else."

Ligeia leaned back in her seat. "Everything about this is unusual."

"Why?"

"The goddess does not visit Athens often. In fact, I heard she was awaiting a more grandiose temple." Ligeia cleared her throat pointedly. "Something in marble."

Medusa frowned. "That does not sound like her."

"You know her so well already?" I jested.

"She cherishes this city!" defended Medusa. "She braved Poseidon for its patronage. Construction on such a scale would require decades of human toil. And the cost? Incalculable."

I watched my sister's eyes flicker, her mind awhirl with the numbers and letters she adored.

"Olympians demand as much all the time," put in Erastus gently.

"Maybe Hera. Maybe *Zeus*." There was no mistaking the heat in Medusa's voice. "But not Athena. She is wise."

I understood the dubious look cross Ligeia's face. My sister had found a new idol; she would not hear reason. And I wondered what Euryale would've said tonight. She admired the Olympians but struggled with Medusa's flights of fancy. It was an easier conversation in her absence, and that awareness made me sick.

I did not finish my meal.

Ligeia, Erastus, and Thales seemed such a unified family. Why wasn't mine? What had I done wrong and how could I fix it?

Afterward, Medusa went upstairs, and Thales departed for the gymnasium. I cleared the table as I always did and washed down the plates and jugs outside.

"She's not a baby."

Startled, I nearly dropped the plate I handled. "Who?"

Ligeia stood just outside my periphery, at the entrance to the courtyard.

"You coddle her in all respects. Her wishes and words. Her feelings."

I did not meet Ligeia's eye.

"Is it because she's the prettiest?"

I shrugged, continued drying the dish with a rag.

"Why, Stheno?" Ligeia demanded, stepping forward. "Why do you believe she matters more than you?"

"Because she does."

Ligeia scoffed, and frustrated by her mockery, her judgment, her lack of understanding, I blurted out, "She will die one day."

And then I sat, suddenly depleted, because confessions are exhausting, and this one held such weight. Ligeia came over and joined me in the dirt, and I started to talk. As I recounted our birth story—how Ceto rejected Medusa, tossed her away like an oyster shell, and how Echidna just barely saved her—I experienced a minor sort of liberation. Admitting our truth aloud didn't expedite Medusa's mortality in any way, and it allowed me a moment of sacred release.

Ligeia stayed by my side for a long time after I finished, staring calmly up at the sky. Did the stars listen to us? I wondered. And would I want them to? For if, indeed, that dusting of celestial souls heard my fears this night, were they twinkling with laughter or tears?

Could I bear either?

"You think you can save her again?"

"I have to try," I answered, with words so quiet they were barely audible—even to myself. "By giving her a full life."

"But, Stheno," interjected Ligeia, with a considerate patience I'd never witnessed in her before, "who gets to determine a life's fullness?"

"I don't understand."

"What is a full life to you?"

I fidgeted a bit, wringing the rag between my hands. "I suppose it is the things Athena and Medusa discussed. Voyage and knowledge. Happiness?"

"I do not travel, I work. I compose and I dream, but I do not smile all day long. My life is small and straightforward. And I will die, leaving behind no children. By such a judgment, will I matter?"

"Yes! You create! Your music is your legend."

I thought I complimented her, but Ligeia seemed frustrated by my answer. "You forget that Erastus holds my legacy, not me. I will not be remembered correctly, and I've accepted that." She cleared her throat. "Stheno, allow me to put this another way: If Medusa lives a 'full life,' by your standards—or hers—will either of you be less afraid of death?"

No.

No matter how we spend our years together, I will always dread losing her.

But I was ashamed by my weakness so I said nothing, running a dirty rag over a clean, dry dish in an act appropriately symbolic of my choices.

"There is a song somewhere in all this, Stheno."

"Would you write it for us?"

Emboldened, I turned toward Ligeia. Her eyes had fogged over, as they tended to do when she lost herself to the music of her mind.

She shook her head once, held up her hand, and murmured, "No. I can barely hear the notes." And then she hummed a piece of a minor scale, fingers dancing through the air. "And the phrasing must be yours."

"I'm nowhere near good enough."

"Then don't. You're right, of course. You are only a novice. An imitation of an actual musician."

Ligeia's words hit their intended mark, and she delivered them with one of her more disdainful looks. "You want a talent, but you're afraid of it. You desire a voice but won't speak up."

"I'm sorry I frustrate you."

"And then you apologize with no sense of irony."

She seemed done with me, but I felt worse for disappointing her. Ligeia was my mentor, but I also considered her my friend. I doubt she reciprocated the sentiment, especially now.

"I won't bother you tomorrow," I said in farewell; I didn't know what else to say.

"If you don't 'bother' me tomorrow," she retorted, moving inside, "then you will only prove that I do know better." She paused to look back at me one last time. "For once, Stheno, I'd like to be proven wrong."

I watched Ligeia leave, rubbing at her lower back, and just as I knew she was still my friend, I knew I would be at lessons in the morning. Alone in the dark, I allowed myself to smile.

SIXTEENTH EPISODE

EURYALE

She thought love a perfect pain.
Come then. Break me, bend me.
Hurt me flawless.

—Erastus of Athens, "Her Dark Love"

CRYSTALLINE STARS CUT through cobalt sky when Euryale returned to the harbor. Lantern light and laughter floated among docked boats, Athena's wooden image carved into many a prow. Euryale passed the other shadow people—the nocturnal ones whose errands and identity relied and thrived upon the murky twilight. Covered by a plum-colored shawl she'd stolen from Semele's wardrobe, Euryale felt as luxurious and powerful as a Theban princess, but also mysterious and sovereign.

For no matter the dressing, Euryale would always embody the deep ocean: plutonic, unaccountable.

At the entrance to Mistress Charmion's, a topless girl played a flute. Inside, men of all sorts filled the establishment with their boasts and body odor. The pleasure house did not discriminate when it came to age or attractiveness; the only requirements were lust and the ability to finance it. Some guests lingered in the crowd, enjoying the prelude to the night's final act, and others pawed at the ground like gated horses. Should one have snorted, Euryale wouldn't have been at all surprised.

Unlike earlier, plenty of women wandered through the atrium—

some pouring wine, others holding trays of figs. Some perched themselves on the guests' laps like erotic birds; others rubbed shoulders and feet. Euryale took note of every shoulder shrug, each smile. The way a woman arched an eyebrow while she talked or threw back her head with laughter, exposing a sinuous neck. How one coiled a man's curl about her finger as she stroked his bearded cheek and another—*oh!*

Euryale startled, for the pleasure girl nibbling a customer's ear had an unseemly bulge in the crotch of her thin gown. Upon second glance, she noticed a clean shave to the otherwise girlish face. It was a young man, but one built more like Medusa than Thales.

The hostess approached. She followed Euryale's wide eyes and her mouth twitched.

"Mistress Charmion obliges many tastes."

By night, the girl seemed even younger—even more incongruous with this place—yet Euryale felt relief at the sight of her. How silly to find comfort in a pubescent girl! Euryale shook herself.

"I did not think you would come back."

I had to, Euryale thought, but instead she said, "What is your name?"

"Menodora."

"I am Euryale. I will come back often."

The girl nodded, nonplussed. "Follow me."

Menodora led Euryale into Charmion's private room. The table now held a small platter of olives, cheese, and nuts—all untouched. The piles of money were nowhere to be seen. The mistress had not finished dressing, and Euryale spied naked flashes of the woman's feeble form. It made Euryale feel guilty, somehow. Similarly exposed. She looked away as Charmion's twisted hands tugged at her sash.

"Menodora," the madam sputtered, "tie it tighter."

The girl administered to her mistress efficiently, pulling and pinning fabric, smoothing troublesome wrinkles with an intimate familiarity.

Why was Euryale seeing this? Was it a test, a game?

"So, the daughter of sea beasts returns!" Charmion held open her arms in facetious welcome. "Courage must run in your family; your father would be *so* proud."

Euryale's lips tightened. "I don't scare easily."

"Ah, but it's early yet." The painted colors on Charmion's face were freshly applied and darker than their first encounter, making the gold in her ears shine all the brighter. Despite the expensive shawl, Euryale wished, not for the first time, that she owned at least one piece of real jewelry.

Soon, she promised herself.

And she presented a pouch containing a goodly portion of Cadmus's coin.

"As promised."

Charmion tucked the purse into her robes, and Euryale caught the briefest glint of a blade. Were all the women here armed? Should Euryale have brought her own weapon? And what else did the mistress hide beneath that constant derision? Feeling herself at a disadvantage, Euryale cursed her lack of judgment.

Mistress Charmion whispered instructions in Menodora's ears, then snapped a bone-thin finger in Euryale's direction, interrupting Euryale's frantic regret.

"Shall I show you to your room, immortal? Before you change your mind?"

"You may continue to doubt me, but I will only continue to surprise you."

"You may not scare easily, but I am never surprised."

Euryale and Charmion, face-to-face, were the sum of intransigent forces—an impasse of wills. What Euryale lacked in experience, she made up for in temerity.

Or so she hoped.

"Let us not waste the night being stubborn," spoke the mistress, with a disaffected air. "Come, let me show you why men come to Athens."

Euryale followed Charmion past rooms with doors veiled and open, some crowded and others private, but all in use. It was a sensual overload—snippets of song and conversation, a few shouts, plenty of giggles, the heady smells of human sweat.

But there came one sound for which Euryale had not prepared, and it stopped her cold.

"Was that a baby?"

Mistress Charmion sneered. "You do know what happens when two animals rut? Or must I include that in your lessons, as well?"

"I just didn't expect . . . here . . ." Euryale stumbled on the words, faltered on the feeling of nausea.

"All my girls drink copper salt in water at least once a season. And they eat the seeds and flowers of wild carrot. I buy them silphium sap from the Cyrenaean traders." Charmion's eyes hardened like twin sapphires. "I do what I can."

Did Euryale detect a note of defensiveness? What wound had she touched upon?

"This prevents a woman from conceiving a child?"

"Or destroys what already exists."

Euryale's mind raced. How had she never heard this before? Why had nobody taught her? If Ceto had actually cared, would she have taken Euryale aside and imparted these lessons? Or was her mother ignorant, as well?

Euryale could perfume her hair and line her eyes, but she was still that barefoot, tangled, ocean-cave barbarian. An ignoramus. The familiar shame flushed her cheeks.

"Sometimes a seed sneaks through, of course," continued the mistress, raising a dismissive hand in the direction of the cries. Euryale heard a woman's frantic voice urging her babe to stay quiet. *Please, little one. Please.*

"Those children are raised here?"

"The girls."

Mistress Charmion continued walking. Euryale rushed forward to keep up.

"I may keep one or two of the pretty boys, but the others I sell.

The ugly infants are left at the outskirts of the city, for the mama wolves and childless shepherds of song."

Euryale could barely conceal the odium in her voice. "And their mothers allow you to enslave their children or leave them for dead?"

"The *mothers* must survive in a world where men and gods—and men who think they are gods—limit their choices." Charmion's nostrils flared. "To have choices is to have power. Most women have neither."

Euryale remembered Semele's expectant belly and her own envy, how she longed to place her own palms against the baby's tiny kicks. But Euryale could no longer divorce that image from the princess's desiccated carcass—Semele's pregnancy marked her and killed her.

"I do not keep slaves in my house; the girls are free to go at any time. But women can be slaves to their bodies, too. Riches, even freedom, matter very little if you cannot control your own womb."

Mistress Charmion escorted Euryale to an empty room, primed for service and saturated in the aromas of aphrodisia: sandalwood and jasmine, orange and vanilla. Beside a low bed rested a basin of clean water. Lewd frescoes decorated the walls, paintings of nude men and women on their knees, women bent forward and back. Euryale wanted to study the images, to memorize their details, but didn't want to be caught curious. She kept her gaze resolutely fixed on the mistress.

"Now this is a room with a secret."

On the far wall hung a woven tapestry depicting the Fates. Charmion pushed it aside, revealing a hole the width and height of an average-sized man.

"You may hide in here and watch Aspasia work. Do not interrupt her, and do not reveal yourself until she's done for the night."

"She is . . . aware of my presence?"

"Yes, but her guests cannot be. And they pay well, so not a cough from you."

Euryale stepped into the narrow recess, and Charmion returned the tapestry to its proper place. Euryale could easily view the room through the weavings made loose at eye level, and she wondered at the countless others who had stood here before. What were their purposes? She shuddered.

But Euryale was no perverted voyeur satisfying an urge or spying on a rival. She was a student. Her intentions were scientific in nature, not born from some petty, nurtured human emotion.

She was incomparable, as always.

"I told Aspasia to put on a show for you." The mistress halted at the doorway to deliver one final aspersion: "Perhaps later we can discuss what you've learned about *love*."

Euryale reminded herself how little some emaciated city madam's opinion mattered. For if she ever got her chance with him, nights like these would make all the difference. Euryale would know what to do. She would be his best.

The mortal women—Charmion, Aspasia, even Menodora—could laugh all they wanted at her humiliation.

They would be dead soon, anyway.

SEVENTEENTH EPISODE

STHENO

Like a bouquet of sweet flowers,
this moment cannot last.
It wilts; its first aroma
lost to memory.

—Erastus of Athens, "The Illness of Maidens"

MY ATHENIAN LIFE began to shape into something routine, and I found peace in its familiarity. In Thebes I relegated myself to loneliness, but in this vibrant city by the sea with Ligeia's lessons and Erastus's good cheer, I would even say I was happy—for a while, at least.

Yes, Medusa spent most days at Athena's temple and Euryale continued to disappear each night, but they always returned home—to me—unscathed and all parts accounted for. Nothing had changed, not really, and I repeated this mantra to myself like a refrain. *There is no danger in their independence, nor in their secrecy.* With my kithara in hand, I could almost believe myself.

The mornings, however, remained a sanctuary. In those brief moments, before Medusa disembarked and after Euryale returned, our separate worlds eclipsed. My sunny sister, her lunar opposite, and me, grounded and stationary, monitoring their constant orbits.

Did I take that time together for granted? Our banter? The messes they made—the loose hair and dirty clothes and half-finished food? Even my sisters' friction?

Of course I did.

Afterward, Euryale would wash and sleep; Thales would arrive for Medusa. And I would seek out Ligeia and what she offered—pure human magic within these four walls.

A day came when Ligeia began the music without me. I found her holding an aulos, a reed pipe, to her mouth while Erastus held the beat on a hand drum. By now I knew better than to disturb her mid-song, so I settled upon the floor, holding her hot drink in my lap. She repeated a series of notes, forehead wrinkled and eyelids fluttering, lost in the throes of creation.

Her frustration was palpable.

"No lesson today," she managed to grunt between piping, and Erastus shot me an apologetic look. I rose to leave, somewhat downcast, but then Ligeia summoned me back.

"Wait, Stheno. Close your eyes. What colors do you hear?"

I frowned, baffled by her request.

"When you close your eyes," Ligeia explained, "you sharpen your ears. Now close your eyes and listen." She played the phrase again.

"Red," I answered.

Ligeia's hand beckoned impatiently. "More, more."

With my eyes still closed, I released the room, her presence, his, even language itself. I sang the melody in my mind, letting the notes splash like paint against the black walls of my imagination.

It is not so easy to think in streams of sound and color, but I was learning.

"Red like sunbaked mud," I clarified as the whirling images solidified around the memory of my sisters fighting in our room upstairs. "Red like clay shards, shattered and sharp, in disparate sizes."

Ligeia pulled the reed from her mouth, abruptly stopping the music.

"Red brown?" she confirmed on a frown.

I nodded, reluctant to provide the wrong answer, but certain she would never forgive me if I lied.

Ligeia exhaled a long breath and crossed her arms. "It should be red like a ripe pomegranate, like a summer tomato's juice. Like swollen lips." She threw the wind instrument down with some force. "It is all wrong."

"What are you composing?" I asked.

"A commission for an extremely rich—and extremely impatient—patron," answered Erastus. "He demands a piece for his young mistress by the new moon."

"And he wants an ode to fruit?"

Ligeia barked a dry little laugh. "Your comedic timing is unparalleled. A love song, Stheno. In four parts—aulos, lute, kithara, and drum."

My eyes widened. "The new moon is only days away."

"Thank you for the reminder."

"What I meant to say is, can I help?"

"Perhaps later. You can strum chords while I experiment with melodies but..." She trailed off, lost again to her imagination. Ligeia tapped a series of beats with her feet and hands, nodding and murmuring to herself.

"But?"

"But it would be more *instrumental*"—she lingered on the pun—"if you could compose the verse."

My jaw nearly dropped. "Love lyrics?"

"Yes. Some exhortations of passion, praise for subliminal beauty, the transcendence of the carnal act." And those expressive hands were in the air once more, waving flippantly. "You've lived long enough, Stheno; you know the pattern."

"But I'm no poet."

"You are today."

She picked up a lute and plucked a simple theme.

"Color?"

"Red purple. Like a tongue stained by new wine."

One corner of Ligeia's mouth quirked upward, and she nodded at her husband. "Better." She played the passage a few more times, adjusting a minor chord and adding a decrescendo. "Stheno, write a verse to that."

I grimaced—I truly couldn't help it—and Ligeia took note, although in misunderstanding. "Do you need to count the beats again?"

I shook my head. "No, it's not that. Ligeia, please, I—"

"It's not so serious, Stheno! For one day, pretend you are a lovesick crane, a heart-weary suitor. Now leave so I can concentrate." She kicked a leg at me, which I easily skirted.

"Ligeia!" admonished Erastus, but she ignored him.

"Out! Out!"

I sighed, submitting. To write verse I would need to concentrate, and I couldn't do so upstairs while Euryale slumbered. So, with nowhere to go, I began to walk.

I sought love in all the corners of Athens, but the moments I collected were hardly the reasons wealthy, infatuated men contracted art: I saw a man stroking the neck of his dog, a middle-aged woman tickling a giggling child. I walked by artisans who delighted in their craft, friends enjoying a meal. I watched elderly citizens commune outdoors, enjoying the weather. But, at this early hour, I did not encounter couples dancing beneath shady trees or feeding each other grapes.

For what was love, if not another's head upon your shoulder, hands intertwined?

When had I witnessed romantic love in my life? Echidna protected her family and honored her husband. Ceto cherished her pets. Semele relished the idea of Zeus, and perhaps he returned that affection for a time. I had seen grooms enchanted by their virginal brides and husbands committed to marital complacency, but neither felt worthy of song.

I strode steadily through the crowds, setting my pace to the beat of Ligeia's new work, hoping my musings would lead to lyrics. Instead, my feet brought me to the top of the acropolis, past the venerated olive tree to the center of its plateau. It seemed inevitable to arrive at the base of Athena's mighty temple. How could I write poetry without the assistance of my starry-eyed sister, whose ability to love came as naturally as her beauty?

It was a rectangular building, with six columns at the front and rear and twelve along each side. Incense drifted along the hilltop breeze, the sweet-smelling smoke of saffron and turnsole. My eyes followed the scent to the periphery, where priestesses fed the ceremonial fires ruminating in braziers. Above me, and sculpted into the pediment, the triangular piece below the roof, were unsettling images of Athena and her father Zeus slaying giants. I frowned.

I passed through the limestone colonnade and into the pronaos, the outer vestibule, admiring the marble pieces supporting the ceiling, the pristine tiled floor beneath my dusty sandals. I wondered at the many laborious hours acolytes spent on hands and knees, scrubbing the mosaic. Did Medusa, who never cleaned at home, engage in such chores here? Should it bother me if she did?

The building seemed constructed to guide me inward—channeling me into the cella, its heart—where the wooden statue of Athena held court, commanding the obedient visitor's attention. I inspected her likeness, allowing myself to get closer than I would ever dare with an animate Olympian. This Athena stood tall and solemn. She held a blank shield, Zeus's aegis, and wore a helmet, subject snakes at her feet, combining around her ankles. There was no softness to her face.

This was not a joyous god.

And I respected the goddess, I truly did, but I could not understand my sister's obsession. For this was the antithesis of Semele. Did Medusa abate her grief with the idol least like the previous? Was this an intentional part of her mourning process?

A woman approached who could only be the high priestess Frixoula. For a virgin, she was certainly matronly: just nearly plump and wholly red-nosed, with a chin that disappeared into her neck. This was no ascetic standing before me. She wore clothes edging on ostentatious and an elaborately fashioned hairdo. I supposed both were as indicative of her status as the ceremonial key hanging from a belt about her thick waist.

"You are Medusa's sister."

It was the first time I was called such in this temple. It would not be the last.

"One of them," I replied evenly.

"You look just like her. The brown skin, the strange eyes, only . . ."

Say it, I dared her. *Not as pretty.*

"Only older."

"We were born of the same day," I said. "I must not carry my years as gaily."

"Few do."

I dipped my head, acceding her point. "Is she here?"

"No." She gave me an inscrutable smile, devoid of warmth, and I knew then that I could not trust this Frixoula, no matter Medusa's approximation.

I frowned. "She is . . . ?"

"Long gone," supplied the high priestess. "She is so cherished here, a favorite. Such spirit! Such a face!"

And then Frixoula bowed, hands pressed against her chest. It was difficult to interpret this maddening woman. Was she sending me on my way? Was she offering a benediction by proxy? *Let this compliment to your sister bring you honor!*

I accepted neither.

"Medusa will . . . return?"

Another small smile. No teeth. Smug with the knowledge she possessed and I sought.

"As the goddess wills."

Hardly an answer. And Medusa did not belong to this temple, to this goddess, or to this infuriating woman! If I hadn't been properly frustrated before, by Ligeia and her assignment, I certainly was now.

"You will tell *my sister* that I came." It was not a question.

"And which one are you?"

"I am Stheno."

The priestess echoed my name, jabbing each syllable as if I were a bug to be further squashed into her perfect floor.

"I need her help," I added, and I despised the way I qualified myself almost as much as I loathed the patronizing way Frixoula raised an amused eyebrow, like she didn't quite believe me.

"I will tell Medusa that her sister, Stheno, asked for help."

We played against each other in a vexing contest I didn't quite understand, and there were no more moves. The priestess and I stood a few paces apart, locked in a tense silence, pulling back and forth on a rope of forced politeness: Frixoula seemed as eager to release me as I was to leave.

Behind the high priestess rose an altar. I couldn't help but envision its cycle of sacrifice, the endless parade of sheep and goats, a special ox or bull. Oblation made odious. Bright red blood splashing against white marble, cleansed and repeated.

But there were stains. There must be stains.

I thought then that the cloying, scented air might make me gag, so I let the mental rope drop.

"Good day, Priestess."

"Goodbye."

My awkward encounter with Frixoula stymied both my creativity and my mood. I left the acropolis in a torpor—diminished, consumed by failures. I couldn't write music and I couldn't keep account of my sisters. I thought I understood where Medusa went each day, what kept her so busy, but Frixoula had illuminated an age-old truth: I knew nothing.

And then I considered Euryale and my stomach turned over. How had I allowed her nightly roaming to continue for so long? Was she safe? Did she make trouble?

My sisters were slipping away from me like the petals on a bouquet of dying flowers. No matter how delicate my touch, the slightest movement led them to crumble.

I almost laughed. Here, finally, were the beginnings of a poem! Would Ligeia's patron accept a song about ruptured sisterhood?

My pitiful state indulged a part of me that yearned to drop even lower. To punish myself, I sought oblivion. Obliteration. I purchased a jug of wine from the nearest vendor and drank as I walked the marketplace, wiping my mouth with the back of my hand. Wine would either numb my anxious mind or provide the conduit to inspiration. I finished my jug and purchased another. If I had known of stronger substances—or where to find them—I would've washed those down, too.

I was Stheno the Insatiable!

This wine tasted sweeter than I liked—cheaper—but I was in no mood to care. I never drank with abandon. At Semele's court, I'd make half a glass last the night, knowing I needed to remain alert, to keep an eye on my sisters. I never lost control, fairly certain that drunkenness wouldn't agree with me.

But today my sisters were long past my protection.

I could be Stheno the Reckless!

Unaccountable. Carefree. Drunk and sloppy.

I waved to groups of men. Peed in an alley. Hummed to myself and danced a bit. Raising my spirits by raising my arm, mouth to rim, over and over. I reveled in my disarray. Thrilled by the chance that *somebody might see me like this*!

I was untethered, a boat adrift. Set loose. I wanted to bob forever in such unmoored delight.

"Dionysus!" I heckled, spinning in a circle. "Come to me! I knew your mama!"

Shockingly, the god did not answer.

And those turns made me dizzy. I paused for a moment at the Eridanos—the stream that ran through the Athenian agora from the outer foothills—to observe the tortoises. The odd little creatures were common in that area, and I liked them. I appreciated their long life spans and protective coverings, the way they moved at their own pace.

This particular breed had oblong, almost rectangular shells, and spurs on their thighs. I was watching one with a perfectly symmetrical design nibble at a dandelion when a smaller tortoise approached, encircling it. Though *my* tortoise—the larger one—lumbered away, the little antagonist was too persistent—and much quicker. Mouth open and squeaking, it began ramming the big tortoise, biting at its limbs.

And I realized, with dismay, that the mating dance had begun.

So this is love.

Disgusted, I scooped some rocks and pebbles from the riverbed and hurled them at the unworthy agitator. "Leave her alone!" I yelled. But the female tortoise either failed to appreciate my efforts at rescue or had lived long enough to understand the futility. Despite my barrage of stone, she succumbed, allowing the pugnacious male to mount her.

No. Not that. Anything but that.

Her eyes closed, and I knew she was waiting for it to be over.

It wasn't fair. She was bigger. Better. She had tried to flee and given up.

I wept. A father pulled his child close to him as they strolled past. I overheard the word *crazy* and thought I might be. I needed to go home.

My jug sloshed with the dregs of wine as I approached the workshop. I could hear Erastus inside beating a goatskin drum and Ligeia humming. I tripped on a loose stone at the road's edge and tumbled forward, hitting my head into the doorframe and collapsing inside.

The music stopped, and Erastus cast an alarmed glance my way.

"You are a mess," Ligeia commented flatly.

I belched. The watery sediments of wine spilled across my dress and the floor, making me laugh. I lifted the jug to my mouth, but only a drop remained, so I threw it across the room in frustration. It crashed, upending a lyre.

Ligeia frowned. "Go to bed, Stheno."

I took no notice of her. "Tell your patron it's not love if you pay someone else to say it." And I laughed, so sure of my cleverness.

"You sound like a fool."

"Good."

"Go to bed."

Her dismissal enraged me. "You are a liar, Ligeia. Just like my sisters. You tell me to find my own voice, yet you'll write songs for any philanderer. You like rich, adulterous men more than me."

She bristled. "They certainly pay better."

"I offered to pay! But I had to *prove myself.* Why, Ligeia? Because I am nobody?" I threw up my arms and felt the back of my head hit the wall. "No magic. No music. Nobody."

Erastus stood, but Ligeia swatted his arm.

"I will help her," he insisted, firm but soft.

"No." Ligeia held my stare. "You think you're nobody? Well, maybe I just hold 'rich, adulterous men' to a far lower standard than I hold a talent like you."

Mortification and wine burned my cheeks. She respected me, and I disappointed her. My vision blurred and I sniffled.

"Oh."

"I shouldn't have asked you to write the lyrics." Ligeia paused, a silent sadness. "Just go to sleep."

Erastus approached me now. He was old, of an age with Cadmus. Why hadn't I noticed it before? I lurched to unsteady feet, and he assisted me as I climbed the steps to our loft, catching me from falling at least twice.

The room, of course, was vacant. Sisterless. I grabbed another bottle of wine and sat at the table. Erastus shook his head, but I took another drink. This wine seemed sour, and already the front of my head ached, but I wanted to drink until I purged.

He sighed but seemed to understand.

Erastus laid a hand on the top of my head. "She cares for you, Stheno," he murmured. I snorted. And then the good man did a good thing: he left me to my pity.

Hours later, as I heaved into an already full slop bucket, Medusa returned at last.

"Oh, Stheno!" she cried, joining me on the floor and pulling strands of rank-smelling hair from my cheeks and chin. "You poor thing! Let me get you water."

Medusa cleaned my face and the foul mess I'd left on the floor; she even changed my clothes. Despite my resistance, Medusa forced cold water down my throat, cup after cup, and when I finally kept it down, she cajoled me into eating a piece of bread. Afterward, she led me to bed and tucked a blanket around my shoulders as if I were a baby.

It felt so nice I cried some more.

"Do you want to talk?" she wondered, eyes heavy with concern.

"What is that?" I pointed an accusatory finger at Medusa's new snakeskin headband, the recognized covering of the hiereiai, the female priesthood.

She tossed it off, blushing. "It's just a token, Stheno. Nothing more." And she gripped my clammy hands in hers.

"You weren't at the temple, Medusa. I looked for you."

Did she flinch? I think she might have.

"I was. Earlier."

"Why does Athena need you so badly?"

Her lips parted, then closed. She struggled, I could tell, and I knew her to be a liar. "I am learning the consecrated mysteries," she replied at last.

I scowled and pulled my hands free.

"Stheno," she implored, "tell me what happened today."

I wanted to resist her. To pout and huff, retract into my shell. Instead, I let her dominate because she was my Medusa—not theirs!—and I loved her so much.

"Ligeia asked me to write a song," I began, voice quavering as my body continued to shake from toxins.

"And?"

"She wanted a love song, Medusa." I barely recognized the spite lacing my voice. "What do I know of love?"

She softened; she glowed. "No sister could love me more—could love Euryale, certainly!—as you do."

Medusa attempted to reclaim my hand, but I thrust her away. "Not like that."

"Oh, Stheno," she murmured.

I inhaled.

"I've never even been kissed."

The words were less than a whisper, beneath a breath, and I wasn't sure she heard. It was a truth I'd never admitted aloud, though my sisters must have known. I avoided the topic, hoping they'd forget or think I didn't care.

But, of course, they didn't.

And, of course, I did.

Medusa reached for my hands again, and this time I let her take them.

"I would like to kiss you."

So many generations spent side by side and she could still surprise me. I searched her face for a trace of mockery but found none.

Should I giggle, wave her away? Instead, I nodded.

Medusa scooted closer. She took my cheek in the palm of her hand, and I closed my eyes, dropping my face into her touch. The pad of her thumb faintly grazed my cheek, and then my sister kissed me. Her soft lips made mine feel coarse—stars, even her kisses were pretty! She tasted a bit musky and sweet, like a flower, and I worried about the burning bile still ruminating in my throat, but then her mouth parted slightly, and I thought, *Oh, she's done this before.*

Medusa pulled away, laid a chaste kiss on my nose.

What should I say to her, the sister who gave me my first kiss so I would know what it felt like?

Did I do it right?

Thank you.

I love you, pure and simple.

We said nothing.

Medusa settled onto our bed, and I took my place beside her, just as we had almost every night of our lives. She fell effortlessly into a deep sleep, exhausted by her day—whatever that was—while I lay awake, head and stomach still rolling and throbbing. I couldn't relax. When Euryale entered with the lavender dawn, she came straight to us and cuddled into my other side, nuzzling her face against my arm, just once. Just enough.

She smelled of sandalwood and musk.

My two sisters, the loves of my life.

And I worried for them. Men and women never pay the same price for passion—not in the human world, not in ours. Medusa was accustomed to kissing and being kissed. But how much more? I knew men watched her. Had she disrobed, been taken to bed? Thales could not keep his eyes from her. She must have noticed, responded in kind. It was the natural way of things. Frixoula was connected to his family; did she cover for their liaisons?

And what of Euryale? She would never be satisfied by a boy like Thales. Whom did she seek?

Had they both abandoned me to my virginity? Why couldn't we talk about these things? Romance and kisses? Men?

I wished we did. If only we had.

I never wrote those lyrics either.

I did not know it then, but my days in Athens were nearly over.

EIGHTEENTH EPISODE

EURYALE

And in the offerings,
olives and oil,
all of the offal,
was her only life.
Only a life.

—Erastus of Athens, "Her Dark Love"

MISTRESS CHARMION, DESPITE the sordid nature of her transactions, ran an honest business, leaving Euryale no cause for complaint. Each night, she deposited her coin with Menodora, who kept the front of the house. Then, clothed in shadowy fabrics, Euryale drifted through the atrium, fixing to the walls of the nightly party, casting herself behind others until her room was available.

When the time came, Menodora, accustomed to Euryale's undemanding presence, simply nodded in her direction and then Euryale quietly left, floating along the twisting, turning hallways to her home in the wall.

She hadn't heard a baby's cry since the first night, but nonetheless, Euryale covered her ears each time she passed that certain door, that certain room, where Charmion's girls were allowed to be their own women.

Euryale loathed the hole in the wall in the same way she revered it. She took greatest issue with the tapestry, for she knew every knot and string of its weaving—a depiction of the three Moirai, spinning and measuring the thread of life. Stars, how Euryale detested the sounds and smells trapped within its fibers!

And yet, behind that damned cloth, Euryale learned more about every ilk of man than she ever had on the sunny Athenian streets. She knew the regulars and the first timers, the desperate and the heartbroken—who cried afterward. There were rough men seeking power, and others who arrived drunk and needy. Men who were grateful, men who disgusted themselves and pushed the girls away like filth when they were done. Some men had strange desires their wives wouldn't—or biologically couldn't—fulfill.

And so many men could be more than one man in a single night.

The women showed her how to handle the entire gamut—when to play meek and when to take control, which men needed to be held and which craved a strong slap across the face. Euryale learned to anticipate, to measure what a man said he wanted with what he needed.

She conquered her initial disgust with the sex act and came to watch the nocturnal pairings with a detachment akin to a doctor observing a patient in surgery, for any sight, any experience can become rote. Euryale forfeited her ability to be shocked—a significant but necessary accomplishment.

So, without having touched or been touched herself, Euryale mastered the erotic arts. From her hiding place, Euryale mimicked where to place her mouth and hands, her legs. What to do with her hair and hips to appear most attractive, which motions gave a man his utmost pleasure. Euryale doubted Aphrodite herself held more carnal tricks.

Mistress Charmion's little house was both temple and theater, religion and drama. Euryale paid tribute and admission, became the penitent and the audience; she memorized all the prayers and lines.

A night came when Menodora joined Euryale on the walk to her room. Euryale liked the girl—well, as much as she ever liked anybody. But she admired how the girl could be both hard and soft at the same time.

"Aspasia is not here tonight," Menodora confided. "She is . . . sick."

Sick.

Euryale envisioned vials of copper salt. Wild carrot and silphium, vomit, blood clots, placenta. Images she blinked away.

"Hagne will use the room instead. I might warn you; she is . . . different."

Euryale pursed her lips. "Say what you mean, Menodora. Sick? Different? I don't pay for mystery."

Menodora's face scrunched into an unreadable expression. "Hagne is . . . Hagne *was* a—"

But then a man's impatient voice broke through their camaraderie, and the young hostess stiffened.

"Hurry!" she whispered, urgently pushing Euryale through the door. Euryale dashed into the crevice and steadied the swinging wall hanging with the lightest touch of her fingertips. Outside, Menodora stalled the customer with a perfected—and perfectly obsequious—bow and greeting: "Welcome, Master Lykos. Our house rejoices at your return."

An anemic-looking older man brushed past Menodora impatiently. "You have the girl I want?"

"We have summoned her from prayer."

He grinned, wolflike, and sank into a seat, knees cracking like twigs in a fire.

Through the peephole, Euryale could just make out a sylphlike shape appearing in the doorway.

"Hagne," cooed Menodora gratefully. "Master Lykos awaits the ritual."

The woman—Hagne, Euryale supposed—entered the room in a chaste white gown. She wore a necklace of ceremonial figs and a headband across her brow. The same one Medusa wore. Euryale's stomach flipped over itself.

"Come, hiereia. Let me inspect your maidenhood."

Tonight, this man would fulfill a lurid fantasy; Menodora made a hasty retreat.

Hagne knelt before the man, who lowered his leer from the crown of her strawberry hair to her bent knees.

"Worship me," he ordered, in a voice that rumbled low and hoarse with lust.

Hagne obeyed—just as she would obey every man that followed, who all demanded she perform the same sordid role of spoiled virgin. And through every reenactment, the girl did not utter a single word. Aspasia would moan or sigh, make playful jests. Not Hagne. An insidious melancholy infected the atmosphere, seeping between the threads of the tapestry and sinking into Euryale's chest.

The men failed to notice its infiltration.

The tapestry, Euryale realized with a start, had also changed: the Fates were replaced by a spider. This was a tableau of Arachne, emboldened by her talent, punished for her victory. Was this a request of the men? Some signal from Charmion?

For the first time, Euryale wished she could leave early. She should have fled with Menodora. And because she could not escape, Euryale closed her eyes, squeezing them so tightly that her forehead ached. And the unspeakable night passed far too slowly to be real, for surely this was some trick, some dream, some torturous manifestation of the Underworld. Was Euryale truly trapped in a wall, in a brothel, in the seedy wharves of Athens, praying for Selene to finally relinquish the sky to her brother, Helios?

She was, oh, she truly was. Euryale pushed her forehead into the palms of her hands.

And then.

Morning, at last.

The final tryst came to its predictable end, and Euryale heard the last man exit. When Euryale finally blinked open her bleary eyes, Hagne was washing herself from an earthen bowl beside the low bed. The girl removed the ceremonial headpiece, placing it carefully upon a worn pillow, and then turned toward the tapestry, staring straight into the hole, directly into Euryale's line of sight. Euryale startled and hit the back of her head against the mud-brick and stone.

Sometimes Aspasia would wink in the tapestry's direction—like she and Euryale were both in on a grand secret. But Hagne did not nod at Euryale, nor did she smile, and now Euryale must face her. With her heart racing erratically, Euryale pushed aside the hanging and entered the room. Neither spoke, and though Euryale had seen the other woman undressed repeatedly, in the most intimate and compromised of acts, it was Euryale who felt naked.

Hagne's blue-green eyes trailed Euryale's path to the door, watching her struggle between holding her head high and succumbing to flight. Those indelible eyes saw Euryale stumble, fumbling upon her own steps, and Hagne did not have the decency to look away.

A loud yet voiceless accusation.

She hates me, Euryale thought. *Should I defend myself? I closed my eyes! I couldn't watch!*

But she had embarrassed herself enough tonight.

In the atrium, now empty of guests, Menodora collected the night's littered relics: half-filled chalices, a lost sandal, spare coin, even an abandoned dress. Euryale interrupted the girl's work, yanking her aside.

"What were you about to tell me?" she demanded. "Of Hagne?"

Menodora nervously scanned the room before lowering her voice. "The men call her hiereia because she was one. And an arrephoros before that. Supposedly she was a great favorite of Athena."

Euryale lessened her grip on Menodora's forearm. "Then why is she here?"

"She fell from favor at the temple, and the high priestess brought her to Mistress Charmion. Frixoula said there was no other place for her."

"Why? What did she do?"

Menodora shrugged. "Nobody knows. Not even the mistress."

Euryale's eyes narrowed. "I hardly believe that."

"I swear on the river Styx."

"Then I will ask Hagne myself."

"It won't matter," murmured Menodora sadly. One finger traced the wine-stained brim of a cup. "She will not talk to you."

Euryale's rising frustration was met only by her exhaustion. She tossed her hands into the air. "And why is that?"

"Because she can't." Menodora released a deep breath from her nose. "Before Hagne arrived here, somebody cut out her tongue."

AS A RULE, Euryale did not concern herself with others. Insouciance was a sign of her strength. Weak souls—like Stheno—worried. Soft ones—like Medusa—empathized. Euryale likened her own soul to that of a crocodile. Sly and solitary, a hunter fending for herself.

But after she met Hagne, her mind broke rank with her credo. Euryale could not rid herself of the prostitute's image: recumbent, degraded. How did the men not see her fractured spirit, the scars of her trauma, and recoil? How could they take her tongueless mouth upon themselves and find pleasure?

Euryale had heard mention of such punishment before, but mainly in acts of war. Tongue mutilation was a form of torture, of course, but also a way to control the spread of information. Hagne was no warrior. She had been a priestess—and no more than a girl—so why had she been muted? For punitive reasons or because she knew too much?

Euryale had to speak with Medusa.

She found her younger sister in Erastus's courtyard playing petteia with Thales. Euryale never bothered to learn the rules, but the two of them spent hours over this rectangular board, moving black and white pebbles into squares and hollering like they had actually achieved something.

Euryale positioned herself before them, hands at her hips. "What happens to girls who misbehave at the temple?"

Medusa raised an eyebrow. "Nobody says hello quite like my sister."

Thales grinned.

"Hello, Medusa. Good evening, Thales."

"Hello, Euryale."

"What happens to girls who misbehave at the temple?"

Medusa shrugged and returned her attention to the game at hand. "Chores, I assume."

"But Frixoula could administer physical punishments, correct? As high priestess."

"I suppose so. But it would have to be a grievous wrong for her to react in such a way."

"And what would be considered a grievous wrong?"

"Frixoula's loyalty lies foremost with Athena, so anything that could harm the goddess. Heresy, perhaps." Thales moved a black token beside a white and scooped it into his hand. Medusa cried out, then pouted at Euryale, blaming her for the loss.

Euryale hardly cared.

"And castigation would be what?" Euryale continued. "A slap? A whip?" She paused, ran a tongue over her dry lips. "A knife?"

"Euryale!" Medusa stomped her foot as Thales gleefully pocketed another white pebble. "I need to focus! What is the meaning of all this? Do you fear for me? Frixoula would never cause me harm." And her cheeks bloomed in the color of spring flowers. "I am protected."

Thales, turning equally pink, looked away.

Euryale nearly gagged. She left them to their foolish games.

The only way to get answers was to be direct, which meant Euryale must consult with Frixoula or Hagne, and she was decidedly more comfortable in Aphrodite's house. Though Hagne could not speak, Euryale was clever. She would parse the truth from nods and headshakes. She thought again of Hagne's baleful eyes boring into the tapestry and shivered, but Euryale needed to know if her sister's involvement with the temple put her in danger, and, for that, Euryale could stomach Hagne's condescension.

The port at Phaleron sat strangely under the midday sun. There was shipbuilding and excitement, the slightly chipper aroma of freshly cut wood, and the pervasive daydreams of foreign coasts and future wealth. It was an assiduous energy, one of hope and adventure and hard, honest work.

A façade, thought Euryale bitterly. It was a whole other world in the night.

Euryale knew Charmion's door would be open. Inside, Menodora and the slender man who typically dressed as a woman sat together, casual and comfortable, talking over a shared plate of food.

"Euryale!" greeted Menodora, in welcome surprise. "I did not expect you until dusk."

"I must speak with Hagne. Immediately." Euryale raised a hand. "I have not forgotten that she is mute. But I have questions she can still answer."

The hostess drew her bottom lip between her teeth. "The mistress will not take kindly to a girl being bothered, especially for unpaid purposes."

"Menodora, I would not ask if it weren't important. It concerns my younger sister. And her safety."

Menodora wavered. She exchanged a glance with the man, who gave her a slight nod. "Just be quick," Menodora relented, "and try not to upset her. Please, Euryale. Hagne is sensitive."

Menodora snuck Euryale past Charmion's office and the room where the baby cried, then beyond the room with the tapestry.

"Hagne does not board with the other girls," Menodora explained in a whisper. "She prefers to sleep on the floor in a storeroom."

They stopped before a thin wooden door, and Menodora rapped twice.

"Hagne?" she called softly. "It's me. Menodora."

Euryale prepared herself, reviewing the questions she needed to ask. They must be pithy, meriting yes-or-no answers. She would be courteous and brief, and, if necessary, she would tell Hagne about Medusa—appealing to Hagne's sense of sisterhood.

Assuming the girl still had one.

"Hagne?" Menodora repeated.

As they waited, Euryale tried not to alarm, but her body tensed regardless. She sniffed. "What is that odor?"

"I don't notice anything."

But Euryale had smelled such a fragrance before.

"Menodora"—and oh, how she fought to keep her voice steady!—"open the door."

She did, and she screamed, but Euryale was ready. Menodora fell into Euryale's open arms, and they clutched each other tightly. Just as Euryale and Stheno held Medusa on the night Semele burned.

"Shhh," Euryale hushed. "Do not look."

For Hagne hung from a wooden lintel in the roof, still slightly asway, choked to death by her own girdle.

A MANSERVANT CUT down the body, and Charmion's other girls conducted the prothesis, the first part of the death ritual, for Hagne. They began by closing her mouth and engorged eyes, then washing her body and anointing it with olive oil. They dressed her in clean clothes and wrapped her body in a winding sheet, leaving only her head—and that vibrant red hair—exposed. Like crimson poppies in a white vase, fresh blood splattered upon the ceremonial stone.

Then, with Hagne's head propped on a pillow and feet facing the door, the women sang a ceremonial dirge.

Within three days, they would bury her in a mass grave outside the city walls, to preserve Athens from her corpse's pollution. There would be no cremation for a low woman such as her. No urn in a family tomb, surrounded by loved ones and preparations for a rich afterlife.

Euryale sat alone in Charmion's office, holding a proffered glass of wine and not drinking. A trio of voices approached.

". . . but we are within the gods' possession, it is a crime against them to take our own lives."

"Not if the god sends a compulsion upon you," argued another.

"I don't belong to anybody but myself."

"Ha!"

"And gods demand worship, not death."

"They demand sacrifice."

"Then they ask too much."

"Silence."

Euryale recognized a fourth voice, a stentorian one. Charmion.

"There will be no more talk of Hagne. Or gods and death. Return to your rooms and prepare for tonight or face *my* consequences."

"Yes, Mistress."

Charmion stormed into her chamber and closed the door. Euryale couldn't identify all the emotions rolling over the woman's features. It was a confusing conflagration: umbrage and disappointment, nihilism and sadness.

"And what does our immortal guest believe?" Charmion wondered, motioning toward the hall and the conversation just ended. "If humanity belongs to the divine, is it immoral to hang yourself? What if a god tells you to?"

"God or goddess?" dared Euryale.

Charmion's lips tightened. "That is dangerous speech. We have enough trouble here."

Euryale set down her glass of wine, only for Charmion to pick it up and take a massive swig. Euryale had never seen her drink before. The mistress collapsed into her seat and shut her eyes.

"I apologize that you had to see that. I should have . . ." Charmion sighed. She rubbed absentmindedly at the knuckles on her swollen hands. "You have one night left."

Euryale gave a slight nod. And then she had no more money—a very mortal problem. She could ask Stheno for more, but she had seen enough. One more night and then never again.

The art of love, she had called it. Euryale grimaced.

"I do not think it a crime to kill yourself," Euryale found herself replying, unable to get up, to remove herself from the horror of the day. "Yet I still wonder what Hagne had to say. If she could have told her story, would she be alive? Or would it have damned her sooner?"

Charmion settled back. "Perhaps a better question is, Why does it matter to you? There is an easy answer, one that will let you remain complacent, sleep well at night, continue. And there is another answer, but this may demand you become more than you are." The madam crossed one leg over another. "You and I have already spoken of choices. Of power. Hagne had very little. When you or I choose to remain silent, whom do we empower?"

Euryale would stop asking questions.

A crocodile will always choose herself.

THE CHALLENGE

PROUD MEN SHOULD never receive competition.

For King Polydectes, his younger brother Dictys was not meant to matter. He was unambitious and entirely manageable. When Polydectes inherited the throne of Seriphos, Dictys happily accepted a cottage by the sea. Out of sight, out of the way. And the brothers cohabitated on the isle in the manner of opposites—one always hungry and the other easily sated, one who devoured and one who provided.

But this story, like any story, is dependent upon a succession of ifs.

If Dictys had not been relegated to a life of fishing, he would have never encountered a strange coffin bobbing among the waves. He wouldn't have opened it to find a dehydrated young mother and her starving infant.

Did Danaë look beautiful? Not at all—how could she?

If Dictys had not been raised to believe he was lesser, to be humble and charitable, he might not have saved her.

But the good man rushed the pair back to his modest home along the cove, offering the ragged woman and her sickly babe not just hospitality but life. Dictys rubbed olive oil against Danaë's chapped lips, fed her simple food, and offered his own clothing. (Of course, he closed his eyes when she removed her soiled dress.) He washed the salty mix of tears and ocean from her babe while the mother sipped fresh water, and—huddled so small in his robes!—she gave Dictys all she had in return: three names.

Hers. Her father's. Her baby's.

After living so many years alone, Danaë needed time to find language again. After being so long confined, she needed to strengthen her atrophied muscles. So Dictys spoke softly and slowly. He held her arms while she relearned how to walk, waiting patiently as Danaë returned to her body and beauty and herself. He purchased a she-goat to feed young Perseus until Danaë's own milk came in. He commandeered blankets for swaddling, and while Danaë rested, he recited poems to the fussy baby about the ocean. About sea monsters and heroes, pretty girls and fools.

And these two lonesome hearts became a part of something communal.

And the baby cooed and smiled.

He grew.

Danaë and Dictys funneled all the unrequited love of their own childhoods into little Perseus. Danaë, who had only suffered abuse by men, kept gentle Dictys at an arm's length. And Dictys, who cherished this woman from the sea, told himself that to be near her was enough.

Years passed in that pine cottage on the sandy beach with the boy and man catching tuna and carp, swordfish and octopus. The mother, who had spent too many years in a box, never tired of the fresh air. She spent her days outside, no matter the weather, fulfilling the role she assumed a woman to provide. And perhaps it was to her benefit that she had no real model for the proper wife or mother, for she never lost her childish appreciation of life.

She liked to name the clouds. She made up songs about fingers and toes. Danaë played with her boy, and Dictys joined them, celebrating in her imagination—the only friend she'd ever had.

Because Dictys and his brother barely maintained even a fraught relationship, Danaë and Perseus were fully ignorant of their dear Dictys's royal lineage. Similarly, Polydectes knew nothing of his brother's long-lasting guests until one day, a courtier gossiped of an Argive princess living by the sea with her child and a bachelor fisherman. The villagers said the trio kept to themselves but radiated happiness. These rumors festered in Polydectes's suspicious heart: Could it be? Could his lowly brother have a woman? A son? And even worse, a *story*?

Dictys was not meant to matter!

The king summoned his chariot and descended upon the cottage where he had exiled his kin so many years before. On the beach, a golden young boy mended a hull with Polydectes's brother, laughing. When Dictys spied the approaching entourage, he placed a protective hand against the boy's chest—a small act, but one of such familiarity, such love.

Polydectes fumed.

And then Danaë—windswept and sunburnt, as lovely as high summer—emerged onto the scene, calling her son to her side. With an ax in one hand and a harpoon in the other, Dictys positioned himself between the king and his home.

All the rumors were true. And Polydectes's worst fear, as well.

The king demanded Danaë leave with him that day, to take his arm and his name, but she refused, demure but firm: "It is the honor of a lifetime, Your Majesty, but my life is here with my son."

"You are the daughter of a king, not a peasant. Your son would be a prince of Seriphos."

"My son will be a fisherman."

How could such a spirited woman prefer a simple man like his brother? Rejected and enraged, Polydectes raced his horses back to the palace in a fervor, whipping them until foam spilled from their mouths and white sweat dripped down their chests. He stormed across the marble floors of his elaborate rooms, struck servants in the face. He wanted this woman like a madness, and her denial inflamed all his most immoral impulses—of which there were plenty.

What had Danaë said?

My life is here with my son.

The son was the problem.

Polydectes could kill Perseus easily; in fact, he yearned for immediate action. One snap of his ringed fingers and a soldier in full panoply would sever the boy's head, return it to him in a sack. But, of course, the murder must not be so obvious. Dictys would rile the island people and usurp him.

Thankfully, the king boasted an excellent memory, and he recalled how the boys' eyes dimmed when his mother proclaimed him a fisherman. Young Perseus desired more from manhood than a rural subsistence among martens, fawns, and porcupines. He was naive and poor, and that—Polydectes chuckled—was a catastrophic combination. He would send Perseus on a fool's journey. Let the child prove his manliness! When he inevitably failed, his mother would assume her rightly place in Polydectes's marital bed.

All the king needed was the perfect fatal errand.

NINETEENTH EPISODE

EURYALE

And such men as these,
only wield
the power you hand them.

—Erastus of Athens, "The Tragedy of Trickery"

EURYALE DID NOT return to Mistress Charmion's until after Hagne's ekphora, her funeral procession from Athens.

Aspasia reclaimed her place in the room with the gods-forsaken tapestry. And on that interminable last night, Euryale barely paid attention to what she saw, so eager was she to be done, to bid good riddance to her hole in the wall and move onward with her life.

When it was over, Euryale laid a small jar besides Aspasia as she cleaned.

"For you."

The woman's large mouth curved into a generous smile. "A gift?"

"It is pomegranate oil. For your skin," explained Euryale. "It will keep you young."

Aspasia laughed. "Not in this house. And not like you." She pulled the stopper from the jar and brought its rim to her nose, breathing its sweet tartness. "But I like it."

Euryale found Mistress Charmion next. The madam seemed blanched by the morning light. She had removed her jewels and hair ornaments and sat, dressed down to a simple shift, staring at the wall, at nothing in particular. Lost to thought or lassitude. Her lip stain was smudged from talk, and her eyelids sank heavily beneath cracked paint. A cup of untouched water waited beside her. For the first time, on Euryale's last day, the woman did not bother to hide her infirmity.

The mistress was wasting away.

"I will not come back," Euryale announced, by way of greeting.

"Well, there's nothing more we can show you, unless you want to learn about animals."

Euryale wrinkled her nose.

Charmion released a croak of a laugh, dry in its delight, brittle with irreverence. "Still squeamish, immortal?"

"You might be, as well, if you knew the same beasts as I."

The madam clucked her tongue. "You were Aspasia's favorite customer. Far and away the easiest to satisfy."

"Then I hope my money flows to its rightful destination." Euryale hedged a look toward Charmion's table, where the mistress tallied her nightly totals. "You have enough rings."

"And I earned them all," quipped Charmion.

"But the girls—"

"The girls need me far more than I need them."

"Hagne certainly needed you," Euryale snapped back, shocking even herself.

"I didn't maim that girl. And I paid all her expenses." The mistress leered at Euryale. "You wasted your money here. What you learned will not matter. The first time is too painful for artistry. And if it's truly a god or king you await, the first time is all he wants."

"I didn't know you sold counsel, too."

"I sell whatever people will buy." Charmion stood and shook a finger in Euryale's face. "Stay away from powerful men, ocean girl."

Not another mortal giving her unsolicited advice. Euryale could not bear it. "Let me remind you, Mistress, of my bloodline, of my age."

"Immortal years!" chuckled Charmion. "Frivolous. Meaningless. Barely worth a human day."

"Do not condescend."

"I do not talk down to you when I speak the truth." And though Euryale was the taller woman by far, she would always remember Charmion as meeting her eye. "I will walk you out."

Most mornings only Menodora occupied the atrium, sweeping up fallen food, mopping spoiled wine, and brushing down compromised linens.

But on this day, Menodora was missing.

Charmion immediately noticed. "Where's—?" And then she interrupted herself with a sharp intake of breath.

In a far corner, a slovenly customer pinned the hostess against a wall, one hand under her dress and the other on himself. Menodora protested, struggling against his chest, but his weight held her in place. Tears rolled down the girl's cheeks.

Charmion sprinted like a panther across the tiled floor, unsheathing the dagger she kept beneath her robes and thrusting its point into the man's lower back. He howled and raised both arms as a bloodred rose blossomed across his tunic.

"I will have your kidney if you take this girl," snarled Charmion.

"This is a whorehouse," he barked, globs of spittle striking Menodora's terrified face. "She's a whore!"

"It is *my* whorehouse. I decide what is for sale and what it costs." Charmion pressed the dagger harder into his thick flesh. "And you cannot afford her." The man screamed and Menodora flinched.

Charmion was leonine; she was merciless.

"I'll tell everyone about this!" sputtered the man. "You crazy bitch, I will ruin you."

"Then I will reveal to all of Athens how your wife despises you and sleeps with her slave. I will let every elite, every general and trader, know what you like shoved in your arse and when." The mistress lowered her voice to a hiss. "I would reconsider your threats, Simonides."

Euryale grinned. She wished she could see the look on his horrible face.

Simonides grumbled but released Menodora with a shove. The

girl's knees buckled, and she slid down the wall. Simonides, perspiring from the alcohol and shame, spit on the tiles before Charmion.

"Do not come back here. Ever."

At the doorway, he kicked over a clay pot. It didn't even break.

Pathetic.

Charmion crouched upon the floor, surveying Menodora—the bruises already ripening her arms and chest, every rip in her dress. "Did he . . . ?"

The girl shook her head, but her lower lip quivered. "I apologize, Mistress. It was my fault. He demanded more wine, but he was already so drunk. I told him I would fetch some water, and he grabbed me . . ."

Charmion placed a hand on each of Menodora's cheeks and brought the two of them face-to-face.

"We do not apologize for the sins of men, Dora. Not today. Not ever."

Charmion rose wearily—no longer the wildcat that sprang across the atrium. She lent Menodora a hand, propelling her to her feet.

"Now you've seen what men want, daughter of the sea. They want to feel big by forcing you down. If this man you cherish would make you feel small and you would *still* give yourself to him, then you are a fool. And I feel no pity for fools. Only disdain."

Euryale swallowed.

Charmion lifted her gown and returned the dagger—still covered in Simonides's blood—to its sheath. "Last lesson. On the house."

"Goodbye, Euryale," whispered Menodora, and she attempted a smile.

It was in that forced movement that Euryale noticed a telltale dimple in Menodora's left cheek.

Those children are raised here?

The girls.

Euryale left the older woman and the young, to be alone together.

But before she crossed the threshold, she righted that clay pot.

◆ ◆ ◆

EURYALE WASTED LITTLE time before returning to Sounion. She gave herself a few days to rest—she'd developed some unsightly circles under her eyes from continuous nocturnal escapades—and to bathe. She washed her hair, then administered emollients and scented each part of her body. When her sisters were gone, she practiced caressing herself, smoothing her palms along every curve and inside each crevice, searching for imperfections, feeling herself as he would.

And she was satisfied. Euryale had never been more in command, been more excited by her own body. There was no other moment but *now*.

Everyone expected Euryale to stay in bed all morning, so she relished the shock on her sisters' faces when she rose with them.

"You're up early," commented Stheno.

"I have plans."

They finished a quiet breakfast, and Thales arrived to escort Medusa up the acropolis. *It's on my way,* he always said, though nobody believed him. Euryale watched Medusa lean her head fondly into his shoulder. What would the boy do if Medusa committed herself to the temple? What would Stheno do if Medusa committed herself to marriage, to a new family?

When Stheno left to brew Ligeia's gods-awful tea, Euryale departed the workshop, heading south out of Athens. It was a straightforward trek, but a lengthy one, and to make the cliffs by sundown she set a determined pace. This would be *the* night, after all. Had Ceto fretted before she consummated her marriage? Celebrated? Euryale had never considered her mother as a youth, as female, as anything other than the virulent womb that expelled her. But she must have felt *something* before bedding her husband. Did Ceto's mother, Gaea, prepare her?

Doubtful.

Neither her mother nor her grandmother chose their mates. They were overtaken by their own kin.

But Euryale would take charge of herself.

She was confident in her preparation—maybe overly so—and it produced a strange emotional detachment. Would tonight be an act of passion or just the physical culmination of her careful studies—an occasion to finally prove what she knew?

No, Euryale was still flesh and blood, for less than halfway into her daylong hike, she began to feel flushed. True, Helios bore oppressively upon her back, heating her dark hair like coals in a brazier, but that was only a partial explanation. There's also a type of fever that overtakes a person before rapture. A shivering ague of anxiety.

Tonight. It was happening *tonight.*

Finally.

Her cousin's husband.

Unimportant.

She walked and she remembered. Forget all Charmion boasted about mortal days; immortal time mattered, too—especially the years spent pining. Euryale had awaited this improbable moment for longer than she cared to acknowledge, and she was ready.

Euryale would be no maiden tending cows, unaware. She would not shriek or run.

She would rise up to meet him.

Euryale did not stop for food or drink—she had no coin, regardless of need—and kept to the path as straight and true as an arrow. When she spied the headland of Sounion, surrounded as it was on three sides by the sea, she struggled against herself. For Euryale was hard-pressed to see water and not dive in, but the day was already beginning to turn.

There will be time for a swim later, she chided herself as she scaled the cliff side and tossed aside her filthy dress. Naked and free, delighting in the earthy heat of her body, Euryale shook her hair free from its binding and lay across a flat rock. She arranged herself on one side to accentuate the natural curves of her body—one arm propped up her head, and the other snaked around her jutting hip bone.

She had timed her arrival perfectly, and while the sun began its descent, Euryale indulged her imagination. She pictured him watching her, approaching from behind and laying a salty kiss on her neck. She would allow herself just the tiniest hint of a moan and then curve into him, under him. Euryale became light-headed. Wet. Desperate to be touched.

Would he be gentle? Rough?

Would he tell her he loved her?

Yet in all her fantasies, Euryale hadn't considered how long she might have to wait. She always dreamed that Poseidon took her for the first time just as the sun met the horizon—twin joinings in perfect unison. As darkness settled, Euryale shifted her expectations. Wasn't the moonlight preferable, anyway? What could be more romantic than stars?

Lying upon that rock grew more and more uncomfortable, and goose bumps spread across Euryale's skin as an evening zephyr blew across the ocean. Euryale retrieved her crumpled shawl and draped it over her bare shoulders.

This look was more suggestive, she told herself. The allure of what's hidden.

Twice, Euryale nearly fell asleep. *Be present,* she scolded herself, *he comes.* She shifted her weight, realigned the cloth. Even ran a hand between her legs, waking herself up.

But when night reached its pitch-black center and even the cicadas ceased their song, Euryale abandoned her posing. She sat up and pulled her knees into her chest, hugging them close.

He was *so* busy, the lord of the *entire* sea! How presumptuous to think his appearances would honor her precise timeline! She laughed under her breath. How could a magicless immortal ever understand such responsibilities? He ruled one-third of the known world, and she had given him no signal to meet. It was her fault, really.

Of course, other possibilities remained. Maybe he spent this night with his wife, the bland Amphitrite. Or maybe he enjoyed yet another—a nymph or princess, some perfect new face that induced men to battle. For there was always a new girl somewhere, even more beautiful than the last, to be wanted.

When a chorus of birds heralded the dawn, Euryale conceded. She reassembled her dress and her pride. No lowly goatherd would catch her weeping. Not Euryale, the golden-eyed daughter of sea beasts.

Euryale steeled herself. She began the long walk north.

SHE MADE TERRIBLE time returning to Athens.

Thinking of the workshop loft, the starkest reminder of her spinster existence, filled Euryale with dread. For how much longer could she maintain this communal reality? Sharing everything with her sisters, with no possessions or entanglements to call her own?

Sterile and safe. Celibate.

No better off than the grotesque Graeae.

And Euryale was pretty! Everyone said so. Yet all around her ugly girls led fascinating lives. It made Euryale sick.

Polydorus had acknowledged the want at the core of her. Perhaps she should have stayed in Thebes. It wasn't the story she coveted, but at least she would have a part. In Athens, she had nothing.

So, no, she was not in any mood to return to another couple's house and lose another day to a room that wasn't hers, watching Medusa prance and listening to Stheno practice the most infernal exercises.

Stheno, always content with the bare minimum. No vision or purpose. Certainly no desires. Sometimes Euryale dreamed of screaming in Stheno's face, spewing the nastiest insults. Anything to get a reaction. What would it take to make Stheno steam? For her older sister was a volcano, and one day, Stheno would erupt.

Euryale entered the city at the end of the day, unsure of where to go. There were too many people in the agora, too many complications at the port. She had no money, no friends, no real interests besides *him*. But then, just outside the housing district, she found a walled garden. Euryale wasn't one for random explorations—she was no Medusa—but at that particular moment she was in a contrary mood with few better options.

Euryale stepped under the archway and into a lush green world. Ivy vines climbed and twirled about the light-colored stone walls, baked by the late-afternoon heat. Just beyond the threshold stood a terra-cotta bowl filled with hallowed water. Euryale paused, cupped the warm water with her hands, and splashed it across her face. She let it drip down her cheeks and chin, licked one herbaceous drop from her lip. Rosemary? Thyme? Flavors she recollected from Cadmus's prodigal feasts but could not name.

She had discovered a piece of the wild in the midst of civilization. Euryale strolled beneath bay laurels and myrtle trees, past lilies and lavender. The garden was overgrown, unkempt in a way that enhanced its mystifying allure. She sat beneath a pear tree in its prime, plucked a succulent piece from its bough, and took a juicy bite. She felt eyes upon her and looked up to a limestone statue of Eros, forever in puckish flight.

Of course, *of course*, she ended up in a sanctuary to Aphrodite.

Should she pray? She'd rather not.

Euryale finished the pear and made to toss its core into a nearby bush, when a familiar noise caught her attention. She froze, arm in midair, and strained her ears, listening more closely. There was no mistake. A woman's laughter, slightly muffled, tumbled with the wind—light and high, like the music of a bird's wings.

She would have known it anywhere, anytime.

But where was it coming from?

Euryale shot to her feet. She pushed past dense foliage and lifted palm fronds as she navigated herself toward the sound's origin. There, at the back of the garden and blending into the garden's perimeter, was the entrance to a natural cave.

Intrigued, Euryale crept inside, ducking just slightly at its low entry. She followed a narrow tunnel to a small rock shelter. There, three sealed baskets rested upon the floor.

Euryale peeled one open and peered inside. She raised an eyebrow. "Interesting."

More laughter echoed against the cool walls, and the hairs pricked up along Euryale's arms. She traversed another passageway deeper into the earth. Without any light or ball of yarn, Euryale descended—hoping this network of caves didn't end at the gate to the Underworld. She walked slowly, blindly, recalling a game she used to play with her sisters when they were young. Two of them closed their eyes and tried to catch the third, who would caw like a bird, offering up little hints to their location. Euryale always won, not because she was a good listener, but because she peeked.

Giggles and murmurs—still undiscernible—continued up ahead, and Euryale spotted the wavy light of a glowing candle. Her hands shook as she approached the illuminated cavern, and she held her breath in her chest as she peered inside, allowing no more than half of an eye to slide across the opening.

Euryale shot backward and whirled around, slamming herself into the dank cave wall. Her fist flew into her mouth, and she bit down hard to keep from crying out.

It wasn't the pain, but what she saw.

Medusa lit up. Naked and arched. Writhing.

And decidedly not alone.

TWENTIETH EPISODE

STHENO

An aunt can be a mother, too.
You will learn this.
Let you learn this.

—Erastus of Athens, "Thales"

I DID NOT NOTICE when Euryale began to change, so I cannot say if it was a gradual metamorphosis or an instantaneous transformation. I was too consumed by music, by my camaraderie with Ligeia and Erastus. I took eyes off my sister for just a moment, and that's all it took.

I wasn't present. I wasn't there to talk, to offer sage counsel. If I had been, we might have kept what happened between ourselves.

But I was brewing ptisanē and tying strings of sheep gut. I was measuring happiness in chord progressions. And thus, it was Ligeia who first alerted me to Euryale's altered demeanor.

"Your sister has been quiet," she told me.

"Medusa?" I replied, puzzled, for she had been more cheerful than ever. Only the day before I caught her humming in bed, off-key as ever, a blithe smile on her face.

"No, Stheno. Euryale." Why did Ligeia say the name like an accusation? And why did I take it that way? "She is subdued."

Subdued?

I set down my kithara. Full of quips and snipes, Euryale was haughty, and never quiet. But then, when had she last argued with one of us? I couldn't recall.

Perhaps Ligeia was right.

I monitored Euryale over the next few days, and my middle sister, all sharp edges and prickles, had dulled. She seemed taciturn, almost shocked to be standing and moving and seeing, like her body and mind had become so disjointed, one was barely aware of the other.

It wasn't sadness, per se, but a gloomy inwardness. What troubled her? How could I help? These weren't questions I was brave enough to ask, and now, I can't believe I was so afraid. Would it have been so awful if she laughed at me? Insulted me?

Considering all the sins we committed against each other later?

I wish I had sat her down and asked for the truth, but I didn't. Instead, I pounced upon her with my own selfish anxiety.

"Did I do something to upset you?"

Euryale groaned. "It's not you, Stheno. It's never you."

We sat in the modest courtyard, bearing the thick autumn humidity as best we could. I offered my sister a palm frond fan, which she accepted without making eye contact. Her gaze was empty, locked on nothing, but I knew her mind pulsed.

Thales appeared, grinning, and Euryale stiffened.

"Is Medusa here?"

"No," sniped Euryale, cold and clipped.

"Not yet," I amended.

He nodded. "I'll go meet her at the acropolis, then. Bring her home."

I smiled at his earnestness. I liked Thales for my sister. "I'm sure she would appreciate your company."

Beside me, Euryale clenched her fists. "Leave her."

"Euryale! Don't be rude."

My sister rose, and the fan fell from her lap to the ground. I stared at the abandoned palm for too long, forcing a distraction, avoiding the confrontation. When I glanced up, Euryale had a finger pointed into Thales's chest. "Stay away from Medusa. And that temple."

Thales drew back, dumbfounded. His mouth opened and then

closed like a netted fish, and the poor boy turned to me for deliverance. I grabbed Euryale by the elbow and pulled her close.

"Enough of this," I whispered harshly, but my sister shoved me backward and I stumbled.

"You blind old bat," Euryale seethed. "You can't even see what's right in front of you. You understand *nothing*." Her eyes glistened as she delivered a final warning to Thales: "Stay away from my sister."

Then Euryale stormed past, leaving us both bobbing along in a wake of awkward confusion. Thales tried to mask his pain; I cleared my throat.

"I apologize, Thales. Euryale is . . . unpredictable. You've been a godsend."

"She does not like me."

"She doesn't like most."

"I am an athlete, not a warrior. A man"—he blushed—"barely, and no immortal. I understand her disapproval."

"Do not justify her cruelty, and do not let this mar your friendship with Medusa."

He looked at me, into me, and I recognized how hopelessly lovesick he had become. "I do not wish to be Medusa's friend."

I placed a hand over my heart, overcome.

"I will fix this," I insisted, panged by the guilt of a false promise. I bore little confidence Euryale would allow me to speak with her, let alone change her mind. Thales departed with those broad, strong shoulders slumped, handsome face cast downward. I ached for him.

Ligeia emerged from her practice room. I could tell by the rigid way she folded her arms that she overheard our scuffle. I sighed and prepared myself for more criticism.

"I will never understand the world you come from," Ligeia said, before I could even begin to explain. "With its beasts and magic, its endless possibilities of life and ability. I'm sure immortals get bored easily and you must look for diversions where you can. But let tonight serve as a reminder: I have welcomed you three into my home when you were strangers. Should you violate my hospitality and wound my nephew, regardless of intention, I will spend each day until my dying one ensuring that you never know peace again."

Her voice was calm, made even more eerie by its careful control. "I will show no mercy, call on every favor—and Erastus and I count kings among our friends, Stheno, you know this. I will compose song after song of your transgression until I may rest comfortably in my grave knowing each generation on every land and isle bears witness to your crime."

I swallowed. "That's quite a speech."

"That boy is an innocent. He is under my protection."

In the way she glared upon me, this woman I considered a friend, I saw her for all that she was. Not just Erastus's hermetical wife who lived and breathed for art, who taught me chords in exchange for some tea and company, but the brains behind a massive institution. Her power, I realized, was bound to the human record. A mortal's only lasting monument is their story, and Ligeia was the builder. Her musical creations—her odes and epics and paeans—would survive even after the mortal body crumbled into the clay of its formation. In this brutal civilization, her masterpieces would remain—which is why she could demand a premium, why men of means would do whatever necessary to preserve the influence and grace of her song.

If Euryale hurt Thales, if Medusa hurt Thales, Ligeia would guarantee our three names were forever bound to ignominy and disgrace.

I could apologize to Ligeia, but I barely understood what transpired between my sisters and this city.

"I'll fix this," I said instead.

She left me and returned to her beloved instruments. There was no need for her to say she didn't believe me; I already knew.

And I could whisper it again and again, *I will fix this I will fix this,* working repetition like a spell, casting for a miracle, but words alone would never reverse time, would never rebuild or undo.

Believe in myself? I was struggling to believe in anything.

TWENTY-FIRST EPISODE

EURYALE

Forgive me, forsake me,
for it is done.

—Erastus of Athens, "Her Dark Love"

LOOKING OUT AT the water provided Euryale an unspeakable calm. Even if the seas raged and the foamy waves rose like white birds from the blue, she felt only serenity. For despite her lineage, her emotions weren't influenced by the actions of the sea, nor did they serve as any mirror into her soul. Euryale held no powers to pull tides at a whim or concoct eddies of retaliation. She couldn't summon giant squid or breaching whales, sights to shiver even the most seasoned sailor.

No, for Euryale, it was almost the opposite. She allowed the ocean to drown her emotions. When she looked at its eternal blue expanse, in all the shades and iterations—cerulean to cobalt, aquamarine to midnight—she felt nothing. Thought nothing. She was scoured empty. Maybe even scourged a little.

After the past few days of downfall and tumult, coveting and grieving, it was a gorgeous void.

This was where she came from, not Athens or Thebes. The waters called to her but also reminded her how little she mattered. And wasn't that what *home* meant?

Following her harsh words with Thales, Euryale escaped the

city's confines at the gate between the Hill of the Nymphs and the Hill of the Muses, heading toward Piraeus, Athens's other sea outlet. She could've gone to Phaleron, but the port was crowded at night, and she would recognize too many people—men she had now beheld at their most compromised.

Those images, after everything in Aphrodite's garden, made her stomach turn.

The Athenians called this small strip of Piraeus Votsalakia for its light, round pebbles. Euryale couldn't care less about the beach's consistency, but she appreciated its rocky cliffs and the way they sheltered her on either side. She felt protected, not unlike how it felt to sleep between her two sisters.

The way that *used* to feel.

What Medusa had been doing in that cave . . . Once the shock had settled, Euryale was left holding a ravenous, rotting secret. One that devoured from the inside like a fruitworm.

How could Euryale confess to Medusa that she spied on her? How could she tell Stheno that everything they assumed about their sister was wrong, so egregiously wrong? The information she carried was an onerous burden, and one far too dangerous to share with any mortal. Not that she had any human friends.

And because she was truly alone, in every sense, Euryale screamed. Her cry raked up her throat like the claws on a caged animal longing for release. She let loose a second time, eyes closed, head thrown back. Nobody cared. The ocean persisted, with no regard for her grief. Waves in and waves out, carrying on. Euryale laid her face in her hands.

But then a powerful wind lifted the hair from her shoulders.

"What consumes you tonight, Golden Eyes?"

Euryale snorted. Of course he would appear now, on this night of all nights. She kept her face down until she regained her composure.

"Just imagining a life without siblings."

Poseidon laughed and settled beside her in the sand. Damn it all, how she savored the bass of his voice, the way it thrummed inside her, against her! He wore no finery, carried no trident. He wasn't here to impress or intimidate. He came to listen.

Somebody did care.

"I am also the second of my brothers." He held up three fingers, folding them as he spoke. "First, dour and gloomy Hades. Next, me. Then, Zeus, whose survival has become the ilk of legends."

The umbilical cord, the Graeae, Echidna's rescue. Euryale knew a thing or two about miracle births.

"Everyone has heard how our father did not want children, how he swallowed us whole, one after another. And my mother did nothing, not for Hades, not for me. But then along came Zeus. *He* was the one she chose to save and he, in return, got to become our savior." Oh, he was so bitter! Even more so than Euryale. "I was middle born then, and hold that ground still, trapped between one brother in the sky above and another below the earth." Poseidon shot her a sideways smile. "Let me say that I, too, understand the need to sit alone on a beach and imagine myself an only child."

His awareness, his sympathy, was more than Euryale could have asked for, even better than making love beneath a sunset—although, Euryale couldn't keep herself from fantasizing about twirling a finger through his blue-black hair and pulling his mouth to hers.

No! she internally scolded herself. *Control your emotions.* The Lord of the Sea was still talking. Euryale forced herself to focus.

". . . are allegedly equals, yet the golden boy calls himself king."

She pursed her lips. "My sister's name means *queen*."

"Medusa. I am told she is a great favorite with my niece."

Euryale stiffened. "I do not enjoy speaking of Medusa."

"As I dislike talking of Athena, my brother's favorite child, the very same who stole this city from me." Poseidon scowled. "I would have provided these people a bounty of fish, the most convenient currents, a safe harbor." He gestured toward the ocean before them, and truly, Euryale could imagine no gift more munificent.

"And they preferred a tree."

She tilted her head softly toward him. "There is no accounting for taste."

Their eyes met; their kindred spirits touched. Poseidon surely felt it, too, for a genial wave rolled forward, depositing a mollusk at Euryale's feet like an offering.

"Open it."

The shells split apart magically in her hands, and within the soft tissue lay a nacreous, iridescent pearl, one of the largest Euryale had ever seen. She gasped.

Poseidon took both halves from her. He tossed the empty half over his shoulder and then placed the other at his parted lips. Tipping his head back slightly, Poseidon poured the contents into his mouth. Euryale watched the movements of his jaw, pictured his tongue penetrating through and around the salty flesh. He swallowed, and when he winked, every part of her body tingled.

The gem shone clean and bright between his front teeth. He guided Euryale's hand toward his mouth and dropped the pearl into her palm, letting his lips brush against the inside of her wrist.

"For you," he murmured.

Control her emotions? She could barely steady her breath.

Under the light of the swollen moon, Euryale inspected the sphere, twisting it back and forth on the tips of her thumb and forefinger. He must know, as she sat there in her quotidian dress, that she had never owned a treasure of its caliber before.

"Flawless," she whispered.

"Indeed."

But his eyes belonged to her, not the pearl. She felt them tracing her profile—the point of her nose, the dip of her lips—etching her face into the night, making her feel permanent.

"Why you are here, Euryale? Why does a woman who looks and moves like you, whose tongue makes mortal men quiver and gods laugh, sit alone on such a night? Tell me the truth."

And then he waited. Patiently. It is a small act—to give someone time—but it was a kindness Euryale craved. Everyone assumed the worst of her character: *Euryale likes to fight, Euryale gets irritated, Euryale is too hard, too cold, too honest, too vain.* What she needed was some gentleness every now and then, just like anybody else, and Poseidon noticed her, he made space for her, gave her a gift.

"I saw something I wasn't supposed to," she finally said.

Poseidon raised an eyebrow but kept quiet. And because he applied no pressure, the story began to leak out on its own. Haltingly, at first, but with increasing fluency as she settled into her role as narrator.

She told him of Ligeia and Erastus. Thales. Hagne—though not how or why she met her. Athena's temple and Medusa. The Garden of Aphrodite.

Afterward, Poseidon broke into a round of rich, sardonic laughter. Euryale felt bewildered by his response, disquieted, and more than a bit frantic to reclaim her words. What had she done by telling him? Whom had she hurt? *Please, tide, wash away the memory of all I said!*

Then Poseidon remembered her presence and collected himself. He laid a kiss against each of Euryale's cheeks, yet when he cupped her chin in his palm, she thought not of affection but of his size. How large his hands were! Her own body seemed tiny—inconsequential—in comparison. Could he crush her face with that one hand? Crack her cheekbones and grind her nose to dust? She forced down a shiver.

"You were brave to share your story with me, Golden Eyes. It is a terrible one, but I'm here now. You need not worry anymore."

She reeled. "Terrible? I don't—"

"Such a disturbing transgression. Indecent. If word spread, she could be ruined."

Euryale frowned, confused, like she had lost comprehension of their conversation. She struggled with how to reassert herself, to regain control of not just her emotions but her story, her family's secret.

"My sister is like a child," justified Euryale. "She is only curious."

"This will be a learning lesson, won't it? But I am happy to instruct."

He smiled, and in his teeth Euryale saw all the sea beasts that were or would be: white sharks and moray eels, Cetus and Scylla, the Hydra.

She saw her mother.

And, like a blanket torn from her shoulders in the chill of winter, her body went cold.

"I don't want—"

Poseidon raised a palm, and her lips shut. Was this magic he used against her? Or did she obey of her own volition? Which would be worse?

"I promise you, Golden Eyes, a heinous wrong will be made right."

Poseidon kissed her again on the top of her head and jumped to his feet. As he entered the surf, a triton materialized in his right hand. A chariot led by four massive fishtailed horses came riding a wave, and he climbed aboard. The Lord of the Sea departed, and he did not look back.

Euryale's hands were empty. Though she dug through the sand in a panic, breaking her fingernails on rocks and jagged shells, she did not find it.

The pearl either was lost or had never been.

TWENTY-SECOND EPISODE

STHENO

The dreaming lilies awaken tonight.

—*Erastus of Athens, "The Illness of Maidens"*

THE DAY OF our doom dawned like any other.

I boiled tea with Erastus and then practiced with Ligeia. She and I muffled our misapprehensions over Thales with the music we shared, gradually blending our bothers, melting them into melody. If only all the world's woes could be settled so soothingly!

I had fixed nothing between her nephew and my sisters, but for the love of song, Ligeia would tolerate me.

"Tomorrow," she said, putting down the plectrum that strummed her kithara, "I will play the tremolo lines and the beat rhythms. You will play the theme."

It was the closest to a compliment she ever gave me, and I smiled—so hapless, so unaware, of course, that I would never get to play it. By this point, I was already damned.

Emboldened by a bit of pride, I sought out Euryale. I was a good sister; I was also a bad sister. As attentive to one as I was dismissive of the other. But perhaps it was not too late to forge a balance, to correct the angles of our trinity and redistribute the energy more fairly.

Nothing is as dangerous to the soul as hope!

I asked Euryale to visit the agora with me, in my clunky and ungraceful way, and she rightly saw through my charade. I could almost hear her thoughts, they thundered so loudly: *After hundreds of years placing Medusa first,* now *you want to coddle and dote?*

"I am busy," she mumbled. Meanwhile, she had not risen from our bed.

I had been unmindful of Euryale since our sojourn to Athens, but I had noticed her share of our coin was depleted. Nothing raised Euryale's spirits like luxury. "I will buy you something beautiful," I cajoled.

The blankets slipped down her face. "I won't talk to you about the other night."

I almost smiled. "I would never expect you to."

And she relented.

The agora was a bazaar of clay and cloth, metalworks, spices, and fish. We ambled past foot soldiers, both at work and at play, a feisty public meeting of pale-faced old men, and a slave market where prisoners of war were auctioned like livestock. Later, I would miss the street culture of Athens, the wash of color and the mix of noise, the unorganized jostle of hundreds of legs and crisscrossing intentions. Human shouts and laughter, heckling and greeting, animals and children and deliveries, servants running errands, friends out visiting. It was impossible to be bored in such a place.

Yes, living in this city was crowded and clamorous and sometimes cruel—a far cry from the airy silence of Cadmus's high-ceilinged palace, the restraint of the rich. I knew I could never be contained behind stone walls again—even if they were marble. It was little wonder Semele talked to birds.

Under a stoa, Euryale and I caught some shade and sampled the wares of a cloth trader.

"These beauties just arrived! Dyes from the black lands to the east."

Euryale fingered a turquoise cloth.

"Like the bluest water in the world," she breathed.

"You miss home?" I wondered.

"No."

"But you like the cloth?"

Her silence was telling.

"How much?" I asked the vendor. He responded with an exorbitant price, but I happily paid.

Afterward, Euryale held the fabric folded in her arms like an infant.

"You should have bargained," she reprimanded, her way of thanking me.

"You are pleased. The merchant is pleased. It is a good day."

I bought us pastries laced with walnut, honey, and goat cheese from a food stall, and we ate them on foot. We passed a home, pulsating with a shrill female voice. The ground itself seemed to quiver with her shrieks.

"Every time I walk by here, the woman is berating her husband," I gossiped to my sister, nodding my head in the house's direction.

"She threw his laundry out the window two days ago." Euryale gifted me a small, conspiratorial smile.

I chuckled. "I cannot understand marriage."

"What part?" And she seemed genuinely interested in what I had to say. We came to a standstill as I collected my thoughts.

"It feels like an act of abandonment, a trading of one family for another. I am you and Medusa. Ceto and Phorcys. Even our other sisters and brother. If I married, I would become something else."

"You don't see it as a fresh start? A chance to reimagine yourself?"

I swallowed the last of my pastry. It stuck in my throat, and I longed for water. "I cannot exchange this self for another, Euryale, and I wouldn't want to. I am happiest as a sister. I have never wanted to be a wife or mother."

For a moment, I worried Euryale might cry. Her skin flushed and she blinked her eyes rapidly, looking away from me. I hurried to remedy my blunder, whatever that might have been.

"But that is just me, Euryale! I am the simple one, remember? You and Medusa are so much more."

"Medusa and I will never marry. You must know that."

I startled. *Did* I know that? Suspicions rose in my mind, floating free and scattering like wayfaring dandelion fuzz, but I blew them away. Remember, I was the sister who wouldn't have broken Pandora's vase. It was so easy for me to dissociate when my sisters were concerned.

Euryale awaited my response. When I said nothing, she seemed disappointed, then resigned. Considering the alternatives, I told myself to be content. I told myself not to wonder at the opportunity I might have missed.

When we returned to the workshop, Erastus lay flat on the floor with Thales hovering over him, leading his uncle through a series of exercises—pulling the older man's arms across his chest, bending and straightening his knees. From a chair, Ligeia watched, bemused.

"Your back would be less sore if you moved around a bit more," chided Thales.

"Unfortunately, your aunt has me at the lyre most hours of the day."

"If he's going to play my pieces," quipped Ligeia, "he had best play them perfectly."

Thales gave him an affectionate pat. "Then you must stretch every morning and night. As I have been telling you for years."

Ligeia coughed into her hand pointedly, and the men turned to face us.

Euryale regarded Thales warily, but I would not let the past overshadow our bright day together. I placed my hand at the small of Euryale's back. She leaned into it.

"We brought sweet breads and cheese," I announced, and I laid the food on the table, fully aware of its symbolism: this was a peace offering.

Thales leapt forward, so eager to accept our penance. He tore off a flaky piece of pastry, pushing it between open lips in hasty communion. So did Erastus, but sly old Ligeia demurred, first fixing my sister with an appraising eye.

Euryale lifted her chin; my stomach dropped.

But then Thales broke the bread and brought it to Ligeia. "Here, Auntie," he said as he knelt before her. "Eat with me. Eat with us."

I recognized then how much she loved him, for Ligeia received the bread. "You are fortunate that I am hungry."

I could have wept.

We feasted in silent ceremony. Thales laid one piece to the side. "For Medusa."

"She is not home yet?" I asked.

"Only for a moment," answered Erastus, easing into a chair beside his wife. "A message came for her earlier in the day, and when she heard it, she left again."

"It must have been urgent. Is everything all right?"

Erastus twisted his neck to both sides, and his bones made audible pops and cracks. Thales made a *tsk*ing sound.

"I know, I know," Erastus grumbled good-naturedly, "exercise every day."

I repeated myself. "But everything is all right with Medusa?"

"I assume so. The messenger said, 'Frixoula needs Medusa in the hidden sanctuary. At once!'" Erastus raised a closed fist in the air, emulating the visitor. Ligeia rolled her eyes, but Thales cocked his head.

"Frixoula? You are sure?"

"I may be stiff and old," Erastus griped, "but I am quite capable of recalling a name."

Thales frowned. "It's just that my sister went into labor. Frixoula left with my mother for their estate outside the city. The baby is head up." He shrugged with a young male's easy ignorance. "Mother implied they would be gone for days."

Nothing about this story settled together, and it left me uneasy, discomfited. If Medusa was at the temple all day, she would have known of Frixoula's absence. Who, then, did she believe she was meeting tonight?

"I don't know about any baby, but he said Frixoula."

"'He'?"

Ligeia threw up her hands. "*He* interrupted me in the middle of a piece, and though I yelled, 'Go away!' multiple times, the bastard kept knocking. I sent Erastus to the door to order him away. I only saw the brute from afar. Tall, with a cloak over his head."

"Did he give his name?"

Erastus shook his head. "No, but he had a beard and bright blue eyes."

My sister gasped and I spun around. She raised a trembling hand to her mouth.

"What is it?" I demanded, but Euryale ignored me.

"How long since Medusa left?" she queried, and her voice was breathy, disembodied.

"An hour, at least."

Euryale chewed at the inside of her cheek, a bad habit from our youth. I hadn't seen her do it in years.

"Euryale," I pleaded. "Tell me what is happening. What do you know?"

Four sets of expectant eyes watched my sister pace across the workshop, back and forth, to and fro. Her lips silent but moving. Since when did she talk to herself?

"Euryale," pressed Thales, "is Medusa in danger?" I cringed; the question seemed so melodramatic when spoken aloud, but it was the same one that gnawed at me.

Finally, Euryale halted. She spoke to me alone. "We must go to the Garden of Aphrodite."

"The one outside the housing district?" wondered Erastus.

"Yes."

I tensed. "Why?"

"Because that is where Athena's priestesses leave the sacred offerings. That's where the secret underground temple is located."

"How do you know?"

"I found it by accident."

"When?"

She waved her hands, flustered and frantic. "It doesn't matter! We must leave *now*."

"I will accompany you," offered Thales, already grabbing his cloak.

"No. You must stay here."

"If there is trouble, I can help."

Euryale intercepted the boy before he reached the door. "Please." She placed a hand over his, the one clasping his cloak. "If it is . . . what I think . . . then we will not need you."

Thales sagged, crestfallen and frustrated by his own innate obedience.

"Do you need a weapon?" Ligeia had risen from her seat. "I have my father's sword."

A *weapon*? *Us?* I had never so much as held a sharp stick before.

Euryale's mouth set into a hard line. "It wouldn't matter."

Forget unease, my stomach sank. I moved to the doorway.

A light rain began to patter against the clay-tiled roof, dotting the dirty streets. Little drips, tiny spots, multiplying beyond individuality, amassing into puddles and then streams. Propelled by the wind and the city slope, pushed by forces beyond their control.

How quickly an autumn rain becomes a downpour.

Euryale joined me at the threshold. "There's something I should have told you."

"We will speak on the way."

TWENTY-THIRD EPISODE

EURYALE

Gather at the altar
and place your heart
where I can taste it.

—Erastus of Athens, "A Sacred Tripod"

EURYALE AND STHENO sped across Athens through sluicing rain—no athlete could have been faster—and as they raced, Euryale talked. For the second time she told another about the day in the garden, about what she stumbled upon in the cave.

Stheno stopped—had to—not because she tired but because she struggled with what she heard. "I have been so blind," she finally whispered, wrecked.

"There is a girl I met," continued Euryale slowly. "A former priestess, another favorite. She . . . they removed her tongue."

"Do you think she . . . ?"

"Yes."

Stheno gaped. "You have told nobody else of this, right?"

Euryale wanted to disappear, she wanted to lie, she wanted so much more than this harrowing sprint through the rain. But instead, she told the truth.

"I told Poseidon."

"Poseidon?!" The pupils in Stheno's coral eyes darkened, pulsing with an anger as red hot as any forge. If Euryale hadn't been so anxious, she might have been mesmerized. This was the Stheno she'd long awaited. Ignited, impressive.

"You have been seeing *Poseidon*?!" Stheno wrung her hands. "Oh, Euryale. What have you done?"

They entered through the garden's archway, its charm diminished by their urgency, by the primal scent of petrichor, and its nefarious role in their little sister's deception. Ivy snarled and stems stung. Flesh-eating birds perched above bloodletting brambles. The statue of Eros held court, grotesque and fiendish. Euryale shivered.

As she led her sister through the dark, branches scratched at their arms, and rocks seemed to shoot from the soil just to break their stride. Something with wings fluttered against Euryale's face and she recoiled, flapping at it with her hands.

She drew in a breath, collecting herself. "It's not much farther."

They arrived at the cave, and Euryale brought Stheno to the room of offerings. One of the ceremonial baskets had been kicked over, another shattered as if flung.

"It was not like this before," stated Euryale, looking around.

"This ground is freshly broken," observed Stheno, crouching down and running a finger through the displaced dirt, "as if there were a scuffle." She stood. "How far did you take the tunnels before?"

"Only to the cavern where . . . I found Medusa." Her heart thumped against her breastbone.

"She says they run under the city and all the way up to the temple."

"Do you think she ran there? In the dark?"

"I do not know where else she could be."

They hadn't brought a torch, and Euryale cursed her oversight. In Thebes, the first time the sisters fought against the lethal night, battling to save a woman from her mistakes, they at least remembered candles. Euryale should have known better, for with each additional step into the rocky network, they lost moonlight. Right before they descended into profound blackness, a delicate glimpse of color caught Euryale's eye. A violet on the ground, the exact kind Medusa wore in her hair. Oh, how efficiently an object can rally memory! Medusa picking flowers. Medusa weaving crowns. Medusa, lying in a field, that gorgeous gold-brown hair spread amid the blooms.

She showed it to Stheno, the petals drooped.

"What if we are too late?"

"She is alive," insisted Stheno. "I would feel it, otherwise."

The sisters stumbled onward, below Athens and into the depths of the earth, so low they brushed against Hades's kingdom. Euryale kept one hand to the rockwall always, to hold herself upright, and the other atop the shoulder of Stheno, who led the way.

They tried to run but kept falling—onto their knees and into each other. They were as sightless as worms, deaf to any noise besides the other's labored breathing. Euryale could measure their journey only in the types of steps she took. First, down down down, holding her weight back to protect her ankles. Then, up up up, until her thighs burned and her chest ached. Down and up, up and down. She yearned for claws and wings to tear through the ground and fly into fresh air, where she would breathe and see and never ever grovel in the dirt or gloom again.

Now she understood why people feared the dark.

And because they had to navigate the passageways by touch alone, it took them far too long to reach the acropolis and the concealed entrance into Athena's temple.

They emerged in the adyton, a small room just for the priestesses. It, too, was empty.

"Where do you think she—"

And Stheno, with mud smeared across her stricken face, did not finish her sentence. There was no need.

Euryale, for as long as she lived, would never forget Medusa's screams.

TWENTY-FOURTH EPISODE

STHENO

The girls unbound their hair.
It fell and fell and fell.

—*Erastus of Athens, "A Sacred Tripod"*

WHEN MY MIND journeys along the course of my life, I cannot stop here, at this moment, to rest and drink. It is a poisoned well I avoid at all costs. Even when I thirst for memories of her—just a sip of who she was in those final moments as herself—I abstain. For it is too toxic. Noxious. To consume it over and over would surely kill me, immortal or not.

But I will tell you what I saw, because it happened. And it is her story and my story, too.

Listen closely, for I will share it only once.

I cannot recall whether the night ran warm or cold, whether the stars twinkled or hid. Was it raining still? Did Euryale and I pass any people as we dashed through the city, and did they call out to us, wondering at our clear distress? Did my sides knot up in pain? Was I wearing sandals?

And was the cave truly that dark, or had I temporarily lost my eyesight? Were we in the tunnel for hours or days?

I remember hallucinogenic fear so complete it paralyzed my senses, silenced the voice inside that spoke fact and reason. I remember a primitive focus: nothing existed beyond finding my sister. Shaking her. Asking her why, why, *why* she learned nothing from Semele. "We are sea creatures," I would remind her. "Lesser descendants of an old order, and we do not tangle with Olympians!"

But Medusa was screaming and screaming.

No no no no nonononono.

We opened the door into the temple's cella and entered Tartarus.

At the other end of the chamber, beneath Athena's statue, the Lord of the Sea knelt atop Medusa. One of his hands easily restrained both her delicate wrists, pinning them above her head. The other held her jaw in place, just below her neck, so that she could not look away from his fixed stare, his open mouth.

The top of her dress was ripped open, exposing her small breasts, bruised and bitten. Its hemline bunched at her waist so that her slim, trembling legs were bared—and forced open—as Poseidon, fully nude, thrust himself into her, again and again.

Like a beast, like a god, like a male who could be both with impunity.

Like she was nobody beneath his omnipotence.

Beside me, Euryale collapsed to the floor.

And my soul—or whatever one calls the force that animates my face and kicks my feet, that lengthens my hair and nails, that powers my being, my idea of me—cleaved.

Neither Euryale nor I protested when Poseidon flipped our little sister onto her stomach and seized her by the hair, yanking back her head so they could face the statue of Athena as he finished.

With a grunt, Poseidon released his grip. Medusa's chin cracked against the floor, and the rest of his seed shot across her back. He closed his eyes for a moment, panting, and I saw that he still clutched strands of her long hair in his hand. He regarded it with a mix of disgust and disinterest, then flicked the pieces away.

They stuck to the glistening mess on her back.

She is dead, I thought. No mortal could survive that. But then I heard her moan, and hot tears leaked through my eyes. Still, I did not run to her side. I did not leap upon Poseidon's bare back, I did not punch or pull, bite and claw him away.

Because I was too craven—too afraid of what he'd do to her, yes, but also to me.

Allow me this: terror is witnessing your sister brutalized; horror is knowing you are incapable of stopping it.

I wish I had summoned the strength of the monsters who bore me or at least enough courage to send him away. *You are done here, Lord,* I would have said, cold and commanding. *I will tend to her.* It is possible he might have left, and I could've wrapped Medusa in my own dress and walked her home to our loft, to clean her and feed her, heal her and hold her. Played my kithara by her side for as long as she needed me and the music. And when she was ready, we would leave Athens. I would take her wherever she wished to go. Maybe we could have started anew, rebuilt love and trust and joy.

But I said nothing, did nothing. It is my infinite shame.

I remained cowering in the shadows, and Poseidon did not leave. For the god was finished with my sister, but not with his revenge.

Around me and above me, the temple seemed to animate, and every candle flickered to life. Amid the constellations of light, I wondered many inane things. *Is it over? Was it even real? Have we entered the world beyond the stars?* I could not process reality. I could not fathom how my sisters had been broken—one for him and the other because of him.

The eyes on Athena's statue kindled with a silver fire that sparked and sent a shining sentience throughout her form. The wood rippled as it became immortal flesh, and the real goddess arrived, emerging through her inert form.

Graceful but unsmiling. She wore full armor and carried both her lance and the aegis.

Though I still reeled in partial stupor, something lifted in my chest. Athena was regal retribution. Athena, with her martial wisdom, would do what I could not. She would redeem Medusa, who honored her and loved this city.

"The goddess returns!" jeered Poseidon.

Athena pointed the tip of her spear at the sea god. "Get out," she commanded, and her voice shared the thunder of her father. The foundations of her temple shook.

Poseidon, still naked, seemed to luxuriate in the discomfort it caused his niece. He leisurely retied his robes, lips twitching. "It appears, Athena, that your people *do* want me."

"I will not repeat myself."

Poseidon straightened. At his full height, he towered over her, but Athena did not balk. "It is clever what you've been doing here, Niece, with the cave and the tunnels and the girls. But this one? You shouldn't keep such a delight underground." He poked Medusa's hip with his foot. "A flower like her deserves fresh air. And water."

At his touch, my sister curled further into herself. Moonlight limned Athena's helmet, making it gleam.

"Your words mean nothing to me, Uncle."

Poseidon ran a hand down his beard. "Ah, but I think they do, Athena *Parthenos*." He paused, savoring the tension. "If you still go by such."

Athena's jaw clenched. "You may try to use my name as bait, but I am not one of your fish."

"And you are no maiden either." He chuckled. "My brother's most cherished child. His standard of perfection: the modest female. He would be appalled to learn of the mysterious rituals you conduct here. I'm not sure he would recover."

At the mention of Zeus, something like worry flickered across Athena's face. Poseidon saw it, too, for his lips curled.

"Let our accounts remain between us, Poseidon," she declared. "I took Athens, and you have taken her. We are settled."

His eyes flashed. "And I am satisfied."

Athena raised a finger. "Go."

Words can be lethal, and with only one, Athena made clear her intentions. What would happen if Poseidon ignored her command?

Would the clash of power between these two destroy the temple, the city? All of us?

Poseidon hedged, torn between making peace and waging war. He settled upon one final blow: "I wish you had been here before, when she moaned for me."

Athena bellowed and hefted her spear. Poseidon grinned. He whirled off the altar, cape rippling behind him, and strode across the cella. His eyes landed upon us, still hiding in the dark, and my heart beat once, twice, three times. Recognition crossed his face. He winked.

And then he was gone.

Athena exhaled, and half the candles extinguished. The lance fell from her hand, clanging against the marble and rolling away.

Medusa managed to rise into a sitting position, whimpering as she pulled the pieces of her dress together. Athena knelt beside her in the dim light, itemizing injuries, summing up the superficial extent of Poseidon's damage—the sallow eyes, the contusions binding her wrists and circling her thighs, the rings around her neck. Two kinds of blood dripped and stained, one dry and brown, the other wet and red.

Sadness clouded Athena's handsome features.

"Oh, Medusa, my little beauty." She placed one palm against my sister's cheek, and Medusa nuzzled into her touch.

"I did not . . ." Medusa began, struggling to make words. "He lied."

Athena retracted her hand. "It won't matter."

"I thought you sent me a message. I went to meet you, but he was there instead, waiting for me. I saw it was a trick and I fought him. I ran."

But the goddess barely listened. "He ruined you."

"He used me," Medusa insisted, forcing the words through her cracked and swollen mouth, "to hurt you."

"But how did he know, Medusa? Why would Poseidon believe I cared for you more than any other priestess?"

Euryale drew in a sharp breath.

Medusa raised her shoulders, then dropped them, lost and shattered. "I don't know."

"You must have told him."

"I told no one! I would never betray you. Or us."

"You gossiped about me. To *him*." Despite her stiffness, Athena's lips quivered. "After I shared my heart with you."

Tears streamed down my sister's battered face. "Never. You are everything to me, Athena."

I yanked Euryale to her feet. "You must tell her," I whispered fiercely. She struggled against my grip, but I was relentless. "Speak, Euryale. Now."

"And say what?" she hissed.

"That you told Poseidon, not Medusa!"

"Who is there?"

Athena's voice shot out against the tiled walls and floors, ricocheting with fury. The lance had returned to her hand.

Euryale stilled, but I tugged her with me into the center of the cella, into the circle of light.

"Medusa's sisters."

Medusa cried out and stretched her arms in our direction. I longed to hold her, but once again, an Olympian barred my way.

"What have you heard?" the goddess demanded, and there was danger in her tone, in her stance, in the very air around her. There are no rules for handling dangerous people. I did not have the time to run through every scenario, so I acted on instinct. I chose honesty.

"I heard—I saw—all of it."

Euryale groaned.

Athena's eyes narrowed. "Then you know your sister has desecrated my temple."

"I know that Poseidon forced—"

"Her maidenhead defiles this holy space. She contaminates our purity with her filthy lust."

I gaped at Athena's sudden transformation. Only moments ago, she caressed my sister's face and called her beautiful. Now she stood as cold and rigid as her statue had been.

"But—"

"This temple is a sanctuary for virgins."

I frowned. "You are not . . ."

"A virgin?" Athena slammed the blunt end of her spear into the floor. "I have never lain with a man."

The candles surrounding me guttered, a warning made manifest. *Be careful, lesser creature. Guard your tongue or she will take it.*

Yet I did not doubt Euryale's tale: Medusa and Athena in the holy chamber, feasting upon each other. Deep kisses and sweaty collapse, arms and legs tangled, knotted with love. In love.

"Say something, Euryale," I begged. "Tell her about Poseidon. About Hagne."

Euryale lowered her head. She would not speak.

So I did.

"You lay with my sister."

Five words. That's all it took to damn us forever.

Athena's face paled, but she recovered quickly. She scoffed. "You have a vile mind. Disgusting."

"And you lay with other girls before her."

The goddess forced a laugh. "You would dare say such to *me*? A daughter of Zeus and protector of Athens. You are nothing, derivative, the lesser offspring of lesser offspring. Nobody knows your name. Nobody ever will."

Because Athena understood only pride, she assumed insults would deter me. But I had no pride. I took a few more steps forward.

Medusa laid a hand against Athena's thigh. "My love. Please."

Athena kicked my sister away like a cur. "Do not touch me."

"Athena," entreated Medusa. "We can still be together. They are only my sisters."

"Stop talking!"

A snake materialized from the ether, resting atop Athena's

shoulders and then languidly descending. It coiled down her body, tongue flickering, seeking the blood scent. When it landed on the floor and slithered toward Medusa, head raised and hissing, fangs exposed and ready to strike, Medusa quaked with fear. She scooted backward across the tiles with her hands, leaving behind a liquid trail.

Beside me, Euryale murmured something incoherent about a dream.

"Enough!" I yelled. I grabbed a copper candleholder and dashed to my youngest sister, placing myself between her and the snake. The flame went out, but I held the long metal base before me like a sword, swinging at the serpent.

Athena whispered a string of cryptic words I couldn't comprehend, and the snake disappeared. I tossed the candleholder aside and fell to my knees, clutching Medusa to my chest. Her heart pounded into mine, and it gave me a mad sort of courage.

"You say that I am nobody," I maintained. "Fine. But my sister is somebody to you."

"She was. Now your sister is just another whore."

Medusa flinched and my fingers flexed—as if gripping for a source of magic I knew I didn't have, some force I could summon and unleash upon my sister's lover, this perfectly formed malevolence before us.

"You do not deserve Medusa," I said instead. "Her heart is pure, and her love is brave."

Athena pointed her lance at my sister's chest. "She betrayed me."

She is going to kill her, I realized, and all Ligeia's lessons spiraled through me. *Claim your voice, Stheno. Claim your power.*

"Hurt her, and I will tell everyone the truth. I will spend each day of my immortality ensuring that you never know glory again. I will show no mercy, call on every favor—and I count kings and musicians among my friends. I will repeat this story over and over until each generation on every land and isle bears witness to your crime. The name Athena Parthenos will be forever scorned."

Euryale began to sob. She understood then what I did not. And Medusa, eyes wide, protested: "Athena, my sister is harmless."

Athena's eyes bored into mine. "You will tell no man of this."

"Take it back, Stheno," beseeched Euryale.

"Never." For I still could not fathom any fate worse than Medusa's death. I thought I was defending her.

I saw the magic assembling within Athena—emotional, otherworldly, vicious—and I knew there would be no placating her even if I wanted to.

Time slowed and I wondered, *Whose fault is this? Medusa, for loving a goddess? Euryale, for whispering their secret? Mine, for threatening the truth?*

Silver magic exploded in three directions.

And then I wasn't me anymore.

In my unmaking, I was only pain.

Searing. Incomparable. An agony that split me and my life in two—whoever I was before, the Stheno who wondered and loved, who slept and smiled, and this nascent being, this creature constructed only of hurt.

I didn't breathe.

I couldn't.

How am I still awake?

How can I withstand this?

How do I end it—me—us?

How could any of us, in a hundred lifetimes of a thousand mistakes, ever deserve such punishment?

Primal energies eviscerated me. My insides tore. I was shredded, shedding, flayed. Unknown parts thrust through my skin, things of bone and cartilage, spiked and serrated. My spine twisted and then fractured, thrusting my balance forward under some strange new weight. I contorted violently—held up only by unnatural forces—but then I fell to my knees, biting through my own tongue with sharp fangs. I spit and watched in horror as my hands hyperextended and bloody claws pierced through my fingertips, leaving discarded clumps of flesh on the tiles.

I managed a gasp of air.

Where were my sisters?

A winged creature cried, prostrated beside me. It turned its head, laying one cheek against the floor.

Euryale.

Euryale had *wings.*

I moaned, I keened. And I longed to awaken. For surely the torture had lulled me from consciousness, and I lurked in a nightmare place. My sisters and I were ordinary. Lovely.

But then I caught sight of Medusa, clawed and winged, crawling toward Athena. Where did she find the strength? I could not move.

"Please," my sister implored, and her voice was still light and sweet. "Please."

The goddess regarded her with silver eyes of burning ice, of frozen fire.

"I still love you."

Athena closed her eyes. She leaned down and kissed Medusa—hard—upon the mouth. When she pulled away, streaks of my sister's blood smeared her cheek and chin. But then the goddess lifted her hand, like a conductor of some inimical symphony, and she delivered the coda.

"Let no mortal man lay his eyes upon these serpent-heads lest he be turned to stone."

She was not finished with us, after all.

Magic struck me again, and my head cracked open. My mind separated, elongated, and slithered from my skull. I heard nothing but sibilations, a visceral, vibrating hissing so loud I could not make out my own shrieks. I clutched at the sides of my head, covering my ears with my palms, but my fingers gripped . . .

Where was my hair?

There, on the ground, sleek and black, in clumps and strands.

All of it. Gone, gone, gone.

Yet my head moved. It *lived.*

Because Medusa bowed before me, I saw hers first. A nest of wiry green snakes. Dozens of them, thin and activated, curling and unfurling where silky waves once fell. And I understood that this curse was Athena's protection—from me—from the threat of my testimony. Our sins demanded a punishment far more creative than the taking of tongues. There was still wisdom in her sadism.

"Little beauty," Athena lamented, "you were my favorite of all. And now I can hardly bear to look upon you."

The remaining candles sputtered, then died, and Athena, coward that she was, fled from her lover. There would be no farewell, no last, lingering touch. The end of their romance was a tragic tableau: three destroyed sisters, prone upon a holy floor, and one heartsore goddess weeping in the night.

I needed to do something, to speak or move, but I couldn't seem to connect my words with my tongue or my mind with my arms. Maybe in this transformation I was mute and dumb. Paralyzed.

Maybe that would be a blessing.

But not two heartbeats passed before Thales arrived, running and rain-drenched. Ready. A starry-eyed hero, a steadfast friend. How long had he waited at the workshop, pacing and struggling with his conscience, before finally rushing to our aid? Had he perceived the commotion from afar—the angry Olympians and their magic—and panicked? Pushed his mortal body to its limits to reach us before disaster?

Dear, dearest boy.

"Medusa?" he called into the dark, halting at the cella's edge. His voice sounded wary yet unafraid, for he was too innocent to fathom the depths of this evil.

I recovered my voice just in time to warn him. "Do not enter!"

He remained at the wall of columns on the threshold as my sisters and I crept on all fours into a shadowy corner.

"I heard screams."

"We are alive."

Thales stepped inside the temple tentatively, searching for us, left and right.

"We must leave this place," I told him, "but not until you go."

"Let me bring you home."

Home. I nearly laughed. "There is no home for us any longer. You cannot see us again."

"What has happened, Stheno?"

"I cannot speak of it." My mouth could barely form sentences. I felt like I talked through water.

"I don't understand!"

Me neither, I longed to say, but reality loomed in the impending sunrise. We needed to escape Athens before the city awoke to our chaos.

"We have no more time. Go away, Thales. I do not want to harm you."

"Harm me?" Thales edged closer, peering into our shady corner. "What have you done? Where is Medusa?"

"She is here," I said.

"Is she safe? Why can't I speak to her?"

"Thales," Medusa uttered. It was all she could manage, but it was enough. He seemed to release a bit of tension from his body.

Euryale pointed outside to the rising dawn. We could linger no longer.

"Close your eyes, Thales, and do not open them until day breaks."

"Why won't you let me help you?"

"We cannot be helped. Not anymore. Now you must close your eyes or leave."

"Promise me," Medusa implored. "Do not look."

And because she asked, Thales assented. "I will go."

He left the temple, and I heard his footsteps crunch against the acropolis's dirt.

I breathed deeply and shoved my sisters into a line behind me.

"Follow," I ordered them both.

We emerged from the dark—and that accursed temple—to the dawn's hazy bronze breaking across the acropolis.

And to Thales's expectant face.

His mouth parted, but there was no time to scream before he calcified. The gray began in his eyeballs and then spread outward, rock rolling across his face and sliding down his neck. Stone swirling into each crevice of carefully honed muscle, from arms to abdomen, thigh to toe. So quick, so irreversible. Hardening his sweet heart forever.

Thales eternal, an athlete in his prime, young always, victorious forever. I took defeat from him just as I took his life.

Dear, dead boy. My first kill.

TWENTY-FIFTH EPISODE

EURYALE

A day will break upon you,
after the night made you a killer.
The sun spits in your face.

—*Erastus of Athens, "Thales"*

WE CANNOT FLEE like this," Stheno told Euryale. *Like this*—meaning faces and bodies capable of murder. Thales was dead. Stheno killed him at first sight.

My body, my face, what am *I? How can I possibly look like her? Or her?*

Stheno bolted awkwardly into the temple, weighed down by her wings, and ripped the ceremonial peplos from Athena's statue, rending it into two large pieces. Medusa made to protest, and Euryale fought the urge to slap her.

You would still honor her image, you insipid fool?

Stheno wrapped the linens over and around her sisters' heads and hair—no, not hair, not ever again—and tied the covering tightly at their necks.

"I cannot see," protested Euryale, squinting through the fabric, fighting thoughts of Charmion's tapestry.

"I will see for us." Stheno's own head remained unbound.

"You will hurt more people," wept Medusa, and Euryale knew she cried for Thales, the dupe who pined for her while she craved a woman's touch. His statue would remain on the acropolis as a tragic testament: both an altar to unrequited love and evidence of a flourishing wickedness.

"And my soul alone will suffer the consequences," returned Stheno stiffly. "We must make haste."

"Where will we go?"

"The sea."

It was barely an answer, but Euryale had no alternative ideas. She was too hazy, too drunk on curses and bitter devastation to think properly or care.

Stheno took Euryale's hand in her own, and their claws clacked and scratched against each other. Medusa clung to Stheno's other side. They fled the Athenian acropolis, never to return. Through her hastily constructed mask, Euryale could discern only vague inanimate shapes, building and trees, walls. The birds had commenced their chirping—their bright hope so incongruous with Euryale's misery—but the day was still too young for people.

Stheno held them to a light jog. Euryale could not see Medusa, but she heard her moans and whimpers. Medusa was still a woman between her legs, and she had been ravaged.

"I know it hurts," Stheno murmured, "but we have to reach the water soon."

Euryale did not question Stheno's lead. She barely thought of the wings on her back or the fangs her tongue discovered. She did not even consider whatever rested upon her head, replacing her messy locks. No, Euryale's mind could not look past one burning image, seared into her memory, branding her very being.

Poseidon, for whom she had saved and groomed herself, dreamed and desired, wanted and needed so desperately, generation after generation. Poseidon, *her* Poseidon, releasing himself into her little sister.

Medusa, who stole everything. Attention and praise. Echidna's love. Stheno's. Semele and Thales and now *two* Olympians.

Nobody loved Euryale and now nobody ever would.

Would she ever see anything—feel anything—besides this scorching betrayal again?

It made her scream.

"Be quiet!" scolded Stheno, snapping Euryale's arm like a rein.

But Euryale was no unruly mule, no domesticated beast. No easily placated middle sister.

"I hate you," she seethed, directing it to both, to neither, to all. "I hate you," she said, again and again, feeling better each time.

Medusa sobbed.

"Speak another word," Stheno hissed—or was it her snakes?—"and I will gladly leave you behind."

They passed through the city center, and Stheno headed for Piraeus. It was the prudent choice. Phaleron was too populated, at any time of day, and morning had cracked open the sky, yellow sun spilling like a yolk over the earth.

Euryale, breathing heavily beneath the veil, monitored their progress by the ground she felt beneath her feet. It changed from stone to packed dirt to loose sand, and then she knew they had reached the beach. Euryale smelled the brine, heard the waves overlapping with welcome and warning: *Hurry, hurry!*

But she also caught a faint airy tune. A sailor's whistle, the music of his morning work. Stheno stopped short, and Euryale was flung forward. She crashed into Medusa, and they sought to right themselves, sightless as newborns, groping at each other and struggling for purchase.

The unfortunate mariner managed only a truncated scream before he was turned. One guttural wail before Stheno scared the very life from him.

Euryale sniffed, and then wrinkled her nose.

Urine.

A man saw us and soiled himself.

"No," Medusa intonated, "no, no, no."

"Do not remove your wraps." Stheno's voice tightened. "More approach."

And Euryale, in a recreant act, closed her eyes unnecessarily beneath the shroud and allowed her sister to dispatch one man after another. Stheno became a murderer to get Medusa to safety. Stheno became a murderer so that Euryale didn't have to.

"Come," Stheno finally announced, grim and guilty and resolute. "It is done."

The sisters scrambled across the expanse of beach, and the water beckoned louder and louder against Euryale's muffled ears. When surf licked her toes, Euryale wrestled against Stheno's grip.

"Release me!"

"Wait, Euryale."

But asking Euryale to refrain from water was akin to barring a lamb from pasture.

"Why?"

"Someone comes."

Euryale nearly laughed. More? But she stilled herself enough to catch a break in the regular rhythm of the sea, and she sensed a slight change in the wind, a rustle, a whiff of the past.

Figures emerged from the salty depths. In their silhouettes she perceived something familiar.

"Stheno, Euryale, Medusa."

Euryale startled. Such a voice was hard to forget. She vividly remembered its sardonic gravel, its coarse laughter when they announced their expedition to Thebes.

Pemphredo, undoubtedly holding the eye, flanked by her two sisters. The Graeae were in Athens.

Three on three in a grisly reunion. Brought back together in a macabre mirror, reflecting and refracting the others' abhorrent image.

"I thought you might come," Stheno confessed.

"We saw."

But what had they seen and when? How long had they known? Had they been waiting here for days? Years? Could they have prevented this calamity?

"We need a safe place," imparted Stheno. "Far from here."

"We know."

Euryale detected no smugness in Pemphredo's tone. Why wasn't her sister gloating in their misfortune, delighting that Euryale and her sisters had failed so spectacularly? Could it be that she *pitied* them? Euryale's throat filled with bellicose bile. She needed to scream again but feared that this time, once she began, she might never stop.

"Come," enjoined Pemphredo. "We will travel beneath the sea."

Stheno urged her sisters forward.

"You may remove your shrouds," the gray woman added, somewhat gently. "You cannot hurt us, at least."

THE SIX DAUGHTERS of Ceto and Phorcys traversed—by whatever strange power the Graeae commanded—through the deep-swirling, back-flowing waters of Oceanus. Down rivers of space and across streams of time. Around eddies, over rapids, under lakes of fresh water and salt. Euryale, too numb for contemplation, simply moved her body onward, staring only at the gray women's backs so she could not view her other sisters—and, thus, herself.

Nobody spoke.

The Graeae conveyed them to the far western streams of Oceanus, the same mystical realms where their younger versions once cavorted with Ladon. They passed the Hesperides, the red isle of Erytheia, and just before reaching the utmost place of Night, the sepulchral company arrived at the rocky, near-impenetrable shores of a lone island.

Exactly like the one from her nightmare, Euryale registered, with little surprise.

Pale moonlight backlit several arching and rugged cliffs. Hints of juniper and cypress floated up and out from the isle's core.

"This is called Sarpedon," Deino disclosed.

"And we will be safe here?"

Enyo shrugged. "Very few come this far."

Hysteria threatened to overwhelm Euryale. To be immortal and trapped in this body, on this forgotten lump of land—stranded, imprisoned—with only Stheno and Medusa, forever, might be worse than death. She bit down hard on her tongue to stifle the rising laughter, then winced, spitting blood into the bits of shell below. She had underestimated the severity of her new teeth.

Underestimated so many things, really.

"Will you stay?" Stheno wondered, with a hint of desperate hope. Euryale understood. The longer their gray family remained, the longer the sisters delayed the inevitable: facing what had happened—and each other.

"No."

"Where will you be?"

"The island of Cisthene."

"How will I know the way?"

"It will be found," answered Deino, who controlled the eye.

Stheno frowned, one eyebrow arching higher than the other, as it always had. And it was strange, Euryale thought, that her sister's face could emote in such a normal way when she was otherwise so changed.

"You leave with our gratitude."

Pemphredo grimaced as their trio returned to the surf. "Do not thank us yet."

Euryale scowled. She preferred their snide condescension to this cryptic righteousness, and as the Graeae disappeared beneath the waves, Euryale selected a rock the size of her palm and hurled it in their direction.

She hated them.

Because now the three of them stood together, and there would be no more running, no more hiding. Medusa's tear-streaked face. Stheno's chapped lips. Two pairs of haunted eyes.

And endless serpents.

Dozens of green snakes, slender as a lady's finger, twisted atop Medusa's head. Spiraling gradients of green—from near yellow to emerald to dark moss. Stheno carried only three, all in a red the shade of coral. Euryale felt a perverse need to inspect her own but didn't yet dare. For once she beheld her reflection, there would be no return. Her image of herself would irrevocably change, and she would soon forget the beauty she used to be. The longer Euryale waited, the longer she preserved that girl's image.

Stheno cleared her throat. "We should find a place to sleep. Then we must talk."

"What is there to say?" Euryale snapped. "Athena was quite clear. Medusa is a whore who damned us all."

Euryale aimed for Medusa's heart, hoped to slice off a bit of whatever remained. And while Medusa gave no reaction, no indication that she had even heard, her sister's knot of snakes rose to strike.

"Watch your words, Euryale."

But Stheno's admonition was more of an entreaty; Stheno was too exhausted to argue. She took mute Medusa's hand and guided her carefully over the rocks and up the island. Euryale, frustrated by her lack of options, followed. Her sisters stopped at the first flat, open ground, but Euryale kept a begrudging distance. She watched Stheno collect moss and other soft vegetation and then fashion it into a sort of slipshod nest. Their older sister held Medusa by the elbow and gently lowered her down.

"I will find you something to drink," she crooned.

Silent Medusa lay on her side in her ruined dress, wings folded behind her. She stared in Euryale's general direction, and her green eyes were oddly glassy. Was she even awake?

"Keep watch of her," Stheno instructed Euryale.

"From what?" Euryale shot back. "Ants?"

Her sister leveled a black look at her.

"Do not judge me, Stheno," she warned. "Not now."

Stheno gestured incredulously toward her head, then Euryale's. "Judgment? We are far past that."

Then she headed farther inland, toward the best chance of finding a freshwater source.

Alone with Medusa for the first time, Euryale understood her implicit duty: offer mendacious comfort, happy little platitudes. But she would not prioritize Medusa's suffering over her own. And considering her sister's present state, nothing Euryale said held any value. She might have cooed, *I love you despite it all*, or berated her with invectives. *Watch your words*? She doubted Medusa listened or cared.

So, self-justified in her nonaction, Euryale sat apart from her shattered sister and nursed her hate instead.

STASIMON

ENTER CHORUS

HOW TO DESCRIBE a life with snakes on—*of*—your head.

Sentient hair.
Conjoined pets.
Opinionated tumors.
Extensions of self, yet distinct.
Permanent pregnancy?
Not at all. A mother's child is only half her own.
And these snakes were a sole production.
Fatherless offspring, conceived by curse.
Slithering from one mind, through one skull.
Serpentine heartstrings.
One for each love.

Accomplices in murder. Accessories. Aiders and abettors.
Witnesses to the unforgivable.
Shedding, transforming:
turning bodies into weapons,
daily lives into acts of war.

Never again to market or port,
to games or temple or festivals or
banquets. No bread from the baker or
dances or kisses.
No more duets.
No idle chatter.
No others,
not ever
again.

Why didn't she take their tongues?
She wanted to hear them scream.

Descended from beasts and to beasts they shall return!
Misunderstood, maligned.
Whipping, thrashing, winding, twisting, contracting.
Solitary. Lethal.
Venerated. Venomous.
Hated, hating, hateful.

THE FOOL

VICIOUS MEN SHOULD never receive gossip.

For while Polydectes was consumed with jealous thoughts of his brother's beautiful houseguest and how to depose her son, he first heard word of three monstrous creatures, newly cursed by the gods, wreaking havoc upon mortal men.

"Tell me again," he ordered the merchant, just in from Athens, who joined his table. This time, Polydectes would listen without distracting visions of Danaë in his bed.

"The monsters are female, winged, with claws of brass and fangs sharp as any lion. But most terrifying of all, their hair is made of snakes! Just one look will turn a man to stone."

The king leaned forward. "Then they are unkillable?"

"Two are immortal," answered the merchant, sipping from his wine. He belched.

"And the third?"

"She is mortal," the merchant granted, "but you'd have to battle with your eyes closed." He shivered. "It's a death wish. Suicide! I'd rather drink hemlock."

Polydectes could barely contain his smile.

"What do they call these beasts?" asked another courtier.

"The songs out of Athens name them Gorgons, the dreadful. The mortal one is Medusa."

"And the other two?"

The merchant shrugged. "Nobody knows."

Another traveler to court chimed in: "I have also heard of Medusa. She was caught boasting of her beauty. Proclaimed herself lovelier than Pallas Athena! The goddess came to Athens and cast a spell on her."

"The bitch learned her lesson, then," another man chuckled. "Not so lovely now!"

Polydectes delighted. These Gorgons were the answer to his prayer!

Though no hunter himself, Polydectes would set a trap for young Perseus. Mother bears, as everyone knows, can always be captured through their cubs.

The king initiated plans for a massive celebration and ordered a precise message be delivered to Dictys's cottage. "Speak only with the boy. Tell him the king would have him as an honored guest at tomorrow's feast but to say nothing to his mother or the fisherman—for they would never approve of the merriments I have planned!"

And what young man, trapped in the doldrums of a solitary fishing cottage, could deny such a tempting invitation? Perseus was as good as snared.

The following afternoon, as Dictys and Danaë prepared dinner, Perseus snuck away—his very first foray into deception—and hiked to the palace on the hill. He arrived dusty and disheveled, smelling of fish guts and adolescence. Polydectes's courtiers sneered at Perseus's homespun clothes and common manners, the calluses on his hands and dirt caked into his feet.

"Where is your gift?" a favorite of the king asked on cue.

"A gift? I did not know . . ."

"But it is customary to bring a tribute! Especially on such an occasion—King Polydectes is to be married!"

Perseus stammered. He bit his lip.

"Come, boy! Ease your worries with a drink!"

And the hapless child, without a friend in sight, mitigated his discomfort with drink after drink. Soon, he was smiling and laughing, too. This was not the watered-down wine Dictys served at home, and though he had been too nervous to eat his midday meal, he didn't feel drunk. He felt *good.* A part of the audience that offered up toast after toast to their leader.

"You must drink the whole cup," one devious older woman instructed, eyeing his perfect skin and young lips with greedy delight. Perseus obliged.

The king made quite a show of opening his presents, tossing each aside with spurious displeasure. He sighed.

"What ails you, King?" they asked.

"Alas, no man-made gift could ever measure the worth of my future wife. None of these will impress a queen of her preeminence!"

And the crowd played along, for nothing assuages elite ennui like a cruel game.

"What about a lyre that keeps its tune?"

"Bah, no need with a singing voice like hers."

"A necklace strung of perfect pearls?"

"Her beauty is greater."

"A sword sharp enough to split a hair?"

Polydectes considered. "I do need to keep my wife safe. But what is one sword against an army of men?"

"Your Highness, I have the answer!" And an associate of the Athenian merchant stood. "There is no greater weapon on earth than the head of a Gorgon!"

Naturally, Perseus did not know the word Gorgon, but he roared his approval with the rest, nonetheless.

Polydectes clapped his hands together. "With such a trophy, I could keep my family—and all you good people, our entire island!—safe from any harm. No vile foreigner would dare invade Seriphos if its king wielded a Gorgon's head!"

"But who would dare slay a Gorgon?" called out one guest.

"You mean Medusa," corrected another.

"Not I, for I am too old."

"Nor I, for I have too many young children at home."

"And I am neither strong nor brave."

The king's men lamented their shortcomings, and Perseus saw so clearly how he would make his name. He blushed at his earlier gaffe—visiting court without a present—but he could compensate with the ultimate tribute. Perseus would impress their king, honor his mother, *and* protect the entire island!

"I am young and have no issue," Perseus announced, stumbling to his feet. "I am afraid of neither sea nor beast." He swayed and just barely caught himself on the table's edge. "I am Perseus, and I salute this impossible quest. King Polydectes, you have welcomed me to your table, and for that, I will bring back the Gorgon Medusa's head!"

The royal audience cheered. *Such courage! Such fortitude! Our hero, son of Seriphos!* Perseus grinned, face flushed, as the wealthy and powerful slapped him on the back.

The king placed a hand against his chest. "Noble Perseus, I am overcome. My personal ship sets sail tonight. Go now, and do not tarry. We all await your inevitable victory."

Perseus let the men lift him to their shoulders. He waved his fists in the air as they roared and stomped and carried him outside, placing him in a chariot that was already tacked and waiting.

Hours later, Perseus stood on a trireme deck, head pounding and anxious. He did not recall exactly how he got there. The details of the day were spotted and shaded, and he certainly could not remember why he had to leave so soon.

"I must tell my mother," he insisted, but the sailors barred his way.

"The king will take care of her," their leader crooned.

And Perseus, miserable and alone, closed his eyes and covered his ears.

But he could still hear their laughter.

TWENTY-SIXTH EPISODE

STHENO

Shaken soul and bound body
anguish in the shadows,
fallen far from Olympus.

—Erastus of Athens, "Exile"

THE FIRST NIGHT on the island proved the easiest. I collapsed behind Medusa, benumbed in mind and body. Too weary to worry for tomorrow, to fret for our subsistence—even to fear. I doubted a worse turpitude existed beyond what we had already endured. I slept without the freedom of dreams, the weighted slumber of the dead.

But if that night proved the most innocuous, the following morn had to be our worst. We had yet to behold our transformations beneath the sun's honest and injurious light.

When I woke that day, my arms were under my own head and not around my sister. Medusa was gone. Euryale—and the thick golden snake curled atop her head—still slept at the distance she designated. Close enough to remain in sight, far enough that we couldn't attempt comfortable conversation.

I didn't mind the quiet. And I chose not to wake her.

I found Medusa on the beach, returned to the scene of our arrival. She stood at the water's edge, completely nude. Her soiled dress tossed aside.

"Burn it," she said. Her back was to me, and water dripped from the tips of her wings.

"I will. Of course I will."

I drew up beside her cautiously. She did not turn my way, so I followed her gaze to the flat line of distant sea. As smooth as a seal's fur or worn leather. A false peace.

"I tried to bathe," she began, in a voice I did not recognize. "But he tore me open so many times. The salt stings more than I can bear."

I wish I could kill him, Medusa.

I'm so sorry.

You didn't deserve this.

I promise—I promise—*I do not look at you any differently.*

Instead, I offered pragmatism: "I found fresh water last night."

She nodded.

I led her up the island, toward the stream, stealing glances. In many ways, Medusa remained unchanged: same waifish, tawny body and full face. But those incongruous snakes! How could they be a part of my sister, a girl with no cunning, no bite?

I did not consider what I looked like. Knowing that my image alone could kill was answer enough.

On our way, we passed the makeshift camp—assuming a few piles of dead leaves and space for a fire constitutes as such—where Euryale sat cross-legged. Catching sight of us, she fell into a horrible bout of shrieking hilarity. Angry, darting laughter lashing in every direction, regardless of whom it pierced.

"Stop," I scolded.

"You are hideous!"

Euryale raked her claws up and down her thighs, leaving angry trails upon her own flesh. Medusa's eyes watered, and exasperation filled me. I stomped forward and grabbed Euryale's wrists, pulling them from her legs.

Her golden snake pulsed; it bared its fangs at me.

And I felt the trio atop my own head rear back, preparing to strike.

I knew there were three. I don't know how.

"You want to fight me, Stheno?" goaded Euryale.

I did not trust myself enough to answer her. "Down!" I commanded my snakes, but the wily creatures did not heed.

Euryale's face cracked into a mad smile. "Admit it, Stheno. You've longed to throttle me for years. Now is your chance." She lifted her chin, exposing her throat.

I wanted Euryale to stop talking, and I'll admit, I imagined grabbing her by the nape of her neck and shoving her mouth down into the dirt.

I felt my snakes rise, stretching the skin below my scalp. Taut. Tense.

Down! I repeated, this time speaking through my mind. *Down. This is not who we are.*

It might feel nice to silence her, but lay my hands on her? Never.

Euryale is coiled fury, but I will not be.

Two snakes submitted, but not the obstinate third, the creature insulted by Euryale's tempestuous tongue. I reached a nervous hand upward. *Would it bite me? Could it bite me, if it* was *me?* I tapped a forefinger atop its flat head—once, twice. When it did not attack, I ran a flat palm along its scales.

Down, I soothed. *Save your venom for our enemies.* Slow and smooth, the snake retreated into the others.

I sighed.

Euryale observed it all with stormy eyes. "You will never tame me."

I met her gaze. "And you will never bite me."

Euryale turned away first.

NEITHER SISTER OFFERED to help as I scrounged for our survival on Sarpedon. These were long, hard days with little joy. I forgot how to smile, and my voice cracked from disuse. Medusa kept quiet and immobile, lying on the ground tucked into herself, most often affecting sleep. Her constitution was shaped by melancholy—

vacant eyes and lifeless mouth, the yellow tinge to her skin. Her ribs began to show, and I agonized over her health. Begged her to at least drink water.

Euryale paced like a big cat, up and over the craggy rocks and hills, in and out of the ocean. Made restless by hate.

Wrath and woe, rage and regret. And then there was me, channeling trauma into industry. Sometimes I pretended we were back on the Sphinx's mountain, when living off the land was a novelty. I would hum Ligeia's melodies to myself while I worked, imagining my sisters the way they used to be.

I set traps for fish and filleted them. Caught crabs and cooked them over the stone firepit I built. I foraged horta—peppery arugula and aromatic chervil, dandelions and prickly lettuce, chicory and sea lavender. Some wild strawberries. I searched for olive trees, for I missed their oil. Collected firewood. Carried clean water from the stream. I wove baskets from grass and the splints of fallen trees, weaving one, two, three, one, two, three in a fixed pattern. I learned that sleeping mats braided in waxy roots better repelled water. We needed a shelter for foul weather, so I bound branches together in a rustic latticework. I hoped to build a sturdy roof that I could raise for a real house. I did not need a knife when my brass claws were sharper than any hero's sword.

We made do. We had grown too accustomed to human comforts, but we had never been human.

One day, while I fumbled at constructing a rope, I heard a far-off scream. *Euryale.* I dropped the bundle of dried stalks and the hairs rose on my back.

"What has happened?" croaked Medusa, rising from her nest.

"Stay here."

I retrieved the rock I hid from my sisters, buried behind a poplar in a shallow hole. It was triangular shaped and fit perfectly in my palm. At night, or when I was alone in the woods, I worked at sharpening its edges until it made for a serviceable weapon. Medusa's eyes widened.

I chased Euryale's voice to the beach. She pointed to a humble fishing boat, washed ashore.

"Look," Euryale exclaimed, "a gift! A wonderful gift."

I motioned her behind me as I approached, rock in ready hand. What menace awaited us in its bottom? But when I peered inside, I gasped, for I beheld a veritable stockpile of goods. Blankets and reams of cloth, strips of leather, an adze and tools, plates and cups, jars, a set of clay lamps. Euryale pushed past me and eagerly rifled through each treasure.

"Don't touch anything," I warned, knowing she would ignore me but feeling it a duty, regardless. I scanned the coast, checking for floating bodies. Was there a marooned sailor somewhere on the island? I circled, I inspected. No footsteps exited the boat, and I discovered no sign that any soul had lived or worked inside its hull. Each item was pristine, untouched, as if convened by magic.

"Who would do this?" I murmured. "Nobody knows we are here."

"Who cares! We are beggars."

I cared. I felt uncomfortable accepting this trove without knowing the source—or that source's intention.

"Maybe the Graeae?" she suggested with a shrug. "Ceto?"

I snorted, and for a moment, Euryale forgot she was supposed to hate me. She grinned. "Perhaps not Ceto."

I wondered if our benefactor could be Ligeia, but that was pure fantasy. My friend would have included a kithara—she would have considered it more essential than any fabric or blade. Also, she was no longer my friend. Not after I broke my promise and killed her pride and joy. She wouldn't care that it was an accident.

If I thought too much of Ligeia, I would not be able to care for my sisters. The grief and guilt would disable me. I bade her image goodbye—for now, at least.

"We cannot keep these things," I said ruefully. "Not without knowing their provenance."

"Of course we can!" insisted Euryale. "They were sent here, for us."

"How do you know?"

"I don't. But it doesn't bother me."

I gazed longingly at the adze, at the chisel and hammer. The hemp fiber rope, expertly crafted.

"Leave it there for three days. If nobody comes to lay claim, it is ours."

Euryale and I whirled around. Medusa stood on the beach, wan but upright.

"Three days," she said again.

Euryale allowed Medusa a brisk nod.

"All right," I agreed.

Three days passed and we brought our gifts home.

THE NIGHTMARES BEGAN soon after.

Every night I slept beside Medusa with one hand resting atop her slight frame. I did this to comfort her, to remind her of my presence. But also so that I would rouse should she try to leave, should she attempt to dig up the weapon I buried in a new place each day and hurt herself.

On the first awful night, her whimpers awoke me and I snapped up, instantly alert.

"Medusa?"

But my sister slumbered quietly. I watched her chest rise and fall, and she seemed to have settled. I relaxed enough to lie back down, but then her moaning became louder, more anguished, and she thrashed with a face contorted in pain.

"Wake up, Medusa," I demanded. I placed my palm against her heart, and she drew away from my hand. I tried again to the same result. Touching her, I realized, made it worse, so I spoke into her ear, keeping my voice measured and language accessible.

"Medusa," I murmured, "Stheno is here. You are safe. Whatever you see is not real."

I repeated these simple sentences in a chant, providing the directions back to me. There were moments when I broke through the veil, moments when her breathing stabilized and her eyelids fluttered, only for her to descend once more into Epiales's deepest realm. I could not reach her, and I fretted over the dream's strength and her weakness against it.

"Come back, Medusa," I called. "Come home."

I wished to shake her awake, but I feared provoking her—or the snakes flailing around her face.

"Fight it," I whispered.

It took far too long for her to wake. When her eyes finally opened, her face shone with sweat and her voice rasped, hoarse and raw.

"Is he here?"

Poseidon.

"No," I promised. I lied to her rarely over our hundreds of years, and only when pressed. But I did then: "Never."

She rocked back and forth, and I matched her rhythm with my reminders: *I am here . . . I am your sister . . . you are safe.*

But was she? Were we?

Medusa rubbed closed fists against her eyes, forcefully, brutally, as if she longed to remove them from her head and see no more. I hummed melodic exercises from my music lessons, hoping I could lull her into some semblance of serenity. By then, the night was nearly over.

These terrors became a nightly ordeal. Each time I managed to bring her back to consciousness, she would relay glimpses of the images haunting her. These were fragments of her story—how her imagination translated the conditions of her trauma. Only in the dark did she find the words. I could not see her eyes, could barely make out the flutter of her lips. But sitting beside her, listening, I felt her tremble.

She dreamed of trickery constantly. Lying with Athena—willing to please and be pleased—only to discover it wasn't Athena, but Poseidon in disguise. It was Poseidon's lips she savored. And once he fully materialized, Poseidon stung her senseless, paralyzing her body. He would enter her mercilessly. While she couldn't move, couldn't speak, he broke her open, again and again.

In one iteration he caught her in a net, dragged her body down into the sea. In another he pierced her side with a harpoon.

"I fought him," she whispered aloud. "I knew I stood no chance on my own, but if I just made it to the temple . . ."

She did not finish the sentence; there was no need. Medusa believed that if she reached the temple, Athena would help her. Together, they could overpower the Lord of the Sea. But we both knew the ending. Athena loved her name more than my sister, and she would not risk her reputation for a mortal love.

Night after night, I sat beside Medusa's hunched form as she fed her torment to the shadows. If Euryale also heard, she gave no indication. Her heavy breathing filled Medusa's pauses.

One night, the dream differed, and Medusa woke wailing, pounding fists against her abdomen and hips.

"He's still inside me!"

I was ready for I no longer slept—how could I?

"Medusa," I began firmly. "Breathe. I am here. I am your sister. You are safe. He is gone."

She rolled into me and sobbed against my lap. Her tears soaked through my dress, and I felt warm wetness on my legs.

"He is here. He is *in* me."

"No, Medusa. He is not. We are safe on our island. I will not let him come here, not ever."

So many false promises. I had lost count.

"Stheno, I feel him." Medusa placed her hand on her stomach, just below her navel. "*Here.*"

And then, she froze.

I froze.

Her eyes sought mine, and our fragile world shattered into infinite pieces.

We would have no peace, no matter how tenuous.

Give me Erysichthon's hunger, Ixion's wheel. Eagles, take my liver. Sisyphus, pass the boulder.

I would happily take any other punishment.

Euryale loomed over us, cackling with a rage that sparked in the night.

"I knew it. I knew. She carries his child."

A snake hissed.

TWENTY-SEVENTH EPISODE

EURYALE

Find delight in your pain, she said,
and rejoice in your longing.
If it still hurts,
you are alive, you are alive.

—Erastus of Athens, "The Theater of Sisterhood"

EURYALE STORMED SARPEDON, feet pounding up and down, on and on, until night merged with morning. Medusa was her misery, and movement her vigil. Maybe if she took enough steps, it would stop hurting.

She bisected their gods-and-everyone-forsaken island, then circled it, noticing nothing.

Not the birdsong or the fresh dew.

The clumps of aromatic herbs or animal markings.

The heaviness of her new wings.

The blood staining her palms and soles.

Blood? She must have fallen. Once? Twice? She couldn't recollect, couldn't force herself to care. She was only a beating heart, straining, banging, wet and hot against her cheeks and eyes. Flushed with humiliation and jealousy.

Feet alone could never mitigate this pain, this gravest injustice of all her life's injuries. Medusa carried Poseidon's offspring. Medusa would be a mother. And there was nowhere for Euryale to go. She would remain here, on this patch of rock, bearing everlasting witness.

Her snake lowered its head to her cheek and drank her tears.

At least I have you, she thought, which only made her angrier.

She heard her sisters quarreling from afar. Euryale paused beneath the poplar tree to eavesdrop, precisely where Stheno buried her stone dagger. Her older sister thought herself so stealthy, but Euryale noticed the turned-over ground each morning. Maybe she would dig up the blade and kill Medusa right now.

Snippets of Medusa and Stheno's conversation reached Euryale on the breeze, like notes from a distant elegy.

"How do I get rid of it?"

"What do you mean?"

"There are ways. Human girls have ways."

Wild carrot. Copper salt. Silphium. None of which would be easy to procure, but they could call for aid. Euryale was no human girl, but she knew the ways.

Stheno, however, so callow despite her age and rank among the sisters, could not comprehend Medusa's plea. "You would kill your own baby?"

"I would end a pregnancy I did not want."

"This sounds dangerous, Medusa. You could be hurt."

"It will hurt me more to keep it!"

As Euryale approached her sisters, they fell silent. Stheno regarded Euryale's entrance with a face drawn and pale. Medusa, conversely, was flushed and ruddy, feverish with demand. So rarely did these two engage in a standoff, so rarely did Euryale break the tie, but they turned to her now in need.

It was a powerful moment for Euryale. Which sister would she choose? Liberate Medusa from Poseidon's child, or chain her to him in agony?

After that night of manic, restless wandering, Euryale cared only to cause pain. And in that moment, she hated Medusa more than she loved Poseidon.

"You cannot kill an Olympian's child," Euryale admonished, selecting her champion.

Stheno relaxed her shoulders the slightest bit. "I have told her as much," she sighed. "Poseidon is Zeus's brother. We cannot risk further ire from the gods."

"It is mine, too," Medusa insisted. "*My* burden. I alone will bear the responsibility."

Euryale's laughter split the air—split her sisters—like lightning.

Flustered, Medusa pivoted. "It will be a monster, born of depravity. Help me stop this now, before it is too late."

"That's what the Graeae said about you," retaliated Euryale, and Medusa's eyes flashed.

"It is a baby, Medusa, and innocent of the crime of its conception."

"It is a thing," spit Medusa, but then she quickly swallowed her fury. She held a beseeching hand toward Stheno. "I was innocent, too. Please, help me."

And Euryale knew Stheno would relent. After centuries of cosseting, who Stheno was—and how she treated Medusa—could not be remade . . .

Or maybe she could . . .

For Stheno, though clearly devastated, did not take Medusa's hand.

"I did not want this!" cried Medusa, gesturing to her stomach—though she would not touch it.

"Do not speak to me of want." Euryale barely recognized her own voice, hardly understood how she could encompass ice and fire in the same breath. "Do not *ever* speak to me of what is fair."

"Then I will kill myself. And this abomination in my belly, too." Medusa announced her intention so simply, the way you would give your predilection for food or desire to bathe, and Euryale worried she might choke on her own indignation.

Euryale swallowed, hard, then said with as much control as she could muster, "You stupid, spoiled *slut*."

Stheno's jaw fell open.

"If you hurt yourself," Euryale continued, "you will prove all my worst suspicions. That you are the most selfish creature on land, sea, or air."

"Euryale, that's not necessary. She—"

Euryale held up a hand. "Stheno, I am speaking."

When magma meets snow, it creates a dangerous mixture that steams and floods. This was Euryale now, primed for mass destruction. She would burn this entire island down just to feel its warmth.

"Our entire existence has centered upon *her.* Why? Because she is weak. We have protected her, and now we are entrapped by her."

Stheno closed her eyes. She had never looked more tired.

"If I throw myself and this baby from the cliffs," Medusa shot back, "you can be free of me."

"If you were going to kill yourself, you should have done so after Thebes." Euryale's mouth twisted into a sneer. "We can never be free of you; you cursed us!"

And then her hands were on Medusa's chest, shoving her backward. Medusa's eyes widened in shock.

"I did not bring the curse on us!"

"Well, I did not have a secret love affair with Athena. And neither did Stheno." Euryale shoved Medusa again; this time her little sister hit the ground. Euryale glowered, she glowed, she thrilled in the glorious cruelty of it all.

And she still had so much more to say.

"We should have known the cities would be too dangerous after you fell in love with Semele."

"No, Euryale. We must move forward." Stheno wrung her hands, panicking, for there would be no turning back from this conversation. "Why argue over the past?"

But Euryale had released a force of havoc she could not recall.

"I am being *honest,* Stheno. I can't pretend anymore. Medusa has always desired women, yet we have avoided the truth like a steep drop or a strange smell."

"I did not think either of you would understand." Even in the dirt, even transformed, Medusa maintained a quiet pride.

"I am your sister," Stheno said, as pained as if physically wounded. "I don't have to understand to love you."

Euryale rolled her eyes. "I hoped in Athens you would find a human girl to return your affection. Someone simple. Innocuous. But our Medusa—our *exceptional* Medusa—couldn't be satisfied with anything less than the patron goddess of the city!"

"Stop," Stheno begged as she helped Medusa to her feet.

Medusa tossed Stheno's arm from her shoulders and scowled. "I did find someone who loved me back," she insisted, and then, in a move that surprised everyone, she shoved Euryale with an unexpected strength.

Euryale stumbled to remain upright. How dare she! Her heart galloped like a horse, with an anger that left her breathless, and she abandoned control of her mouth, tingling with unbridled, scintillating freedom.

"Not anymore. Whether you bear the child or not, you are too damaged for Athena. She probably has another priestess in her bed already."

Medusa's nostrils flared, and she hurled herself at Euryale a second time. The sisters toppled to the ground, rolling in a tangle of claws and scales, wings, elbows, and fangs. Grunting and slapping at each other with open hands. Euryale bit down on Medusa's arm. She screamed, then kneed Euryale in the stomach, harder than Euryale had ever been hit before. Euryale's stomach spasmed and she could not breathe.

Stheno entered the fray, attempting to pull Medusa back by her shoulders. Euryale grabbed a handful of dirt and threw it in her older sister's face. Stheno cursed.

"I never thought you liked me," Medusa disclosed, sitting up and licking a drop of blood from her split lip while Euryale gasped for air, "but you must truly hate me. I know you told Poseidon about us, Euryale."

Panting, on her hands and knees, Euryale managed to lift her head. "I did. I thought he would help. But then you had to seduce him, too."

Medusa reeled. "You think I wanted . . . what he did to me?"

"I think you want attention. Everyone's. Monsters and royalty and gods and family. Look what you did to Thales!"

"Enough!"

The snakes on Stheno's head stood with such taut tension Euryale thought they might leap off. "*You* wanted Poseidon, Euryale. Not Medusa. And he used both of you."

He used both of you.

He used me.

It was a realization that fractured, that fissured her entire being. "I did want him. I've wanted him for so long." Euryale felt tears on her chin, on her neck, felt them nestle between her breasts, yet did not know she had been weeping. "And she took that from me."

"He is a monster, Euryale." Medusa spoke with an eerie coolness. No sympathy, but no anger either.

"And now we are monsters."

Euryale cried. She cried for first love and lost love, for the coins spent on a hole in the wall, for Hagne, hanging from that rope with her swollen mouth. For Medusa's blood and her own empty womb. She cried for herself and her lost beauty, into the arms folded around her knees.

"Come with me."

Euryale cracked open her swollen eyes. Stheno waited before her, offering a hand.

"I hate you, too."

"I don't care."

Euryale accepted Stheno's arm and let herself be escorted to the slipshod hut Stheno was building from planks of the marooned boat. Her sisters slept there every night—without her—for Euryale refused them, over and over, again and again. But today she lay down in blankets that smelled like childhood.

"I will protect us," murmured Stheno. "I will fix us."

"We will never be the same, Stheno. Accept us for what we have become."

And Euryale slept.

◆ ◆ ◆

A DAY CAME when they received a visitor.

Euryale counted gulls on the beach when she first spotted the shape materializing upon the distant shore. She tensed. Could Athena have found them? Did she come for more torture, to complete their transformation into animals? Or was it Amphitrite, demanding answers?

No. At second glance, the trespasser moved with soft pride, with a gait eroded by humility. This was no arrogant Olympian, no spurned wife.

Euryale nearly collided with Stheno as they both headed toward the new arrival, side by side, with wings nearly touching. Stheno's eyes met Euryale's, conversing in an unspoken language forged over forever, and Euryale dipped her chin, just once. Timid Medusa waited far behind, partially obscured by a tree—her stomach poking out—peering.

The visitor, slim-waisted and slender-armed, stood as tall and thin as a pillar. White-blond hair fell to her navel and glowed beneath a shimmering veil. Though modestly attired, her loveliness surpassed that of Semele and Pandora, Harmonia, and Medusa. Yet Euryale felt no envy, only awe. She wished she had the means to cover her snake, not because it could hurt this clearly immortal being, but because it felt rude to present ugliness before such divinity.

The woman held up a basket of woven palm.

"I brought dates. From my island."

"And what island is that?" prodded Stheno suspiciously.

"Delos." The female lifted her veil. "I am—"

"Leto."

And she smiled, acknowledging her identity in a manner both demure and regal.

Stheno bowed. "Welcome to Sarpedon."

As the sisters brought Leto up the island, variations on *Why?* circled Euryale's mind. *Why here? Why us? Why now? Why bother?* Euryale beheld their rugged home from an outsider's view: the primitive hut and rough firepit, their few washings hanging from tree branches. Naked bones from a previous night's rabbit in a small pile, licked clean. Euryale's cheeks burned, but her embarrassment was somewhat assuaged by Leto's easy comfort, the way she settled upon a log as if it were any throne, with no air of judgment—as if it were perfectly suitable for the mother of two great gods to be received amid dirt and rock.

Stheno begged forgiveness, nonetheless. "We have welcomed no other company since our . . . change in circumstance."

"If you know my past, you will understand why I am not bothered in the slightest." Leto settled her hands into her lap. "Which Gorgon are you?"

Gorgon as in gorgos? *Dreadful?*

Stheno frowned. "I do not know this word."

"It is what they call you three."

"They?"

"The men. In all the songs that come out of Athens."

Stheno's lips tightened. "I am Stheno. She is Euryale."

"The sisters." Leto turned her head from side to side, searching the encampment. "But where is Medusa?"

"I am here."

A small sound, a timid voice, for Medusa still hid along the periphery, crouched in the shrubbery.

"Do not fear me," chided Leto gently. "I did not travel so far to inflict more harm. Please, child, come closer."

They had not been children for a very long time, but to be called such by this woman was a strange repose. Medusa stepped forward hesitantly, testing the safety of Leto's maternal aura.

"The snakes are . . ." Leto frowned, searching for the right word, and Euryale braced herself for the blow.

"Breathtaking."

A single tear dropped from Medusa's green eye to her rosy cheek. She did not wipe it away, and it perched there, like dew on a petal.

"Eat with us, Medusa."

They consumed the dates from Delos, and when they finished, Stheno brought forth cups of the watery wine she fermented herself.

Leto eyed Medusa's belly. "Are you sleeping?"

Medusa shook her head.

"Lie on your left side, it will be more comfortable for you and the baby. Do you eat?"

Medusa stared at the tops of her hands, flexing them, bringing the bulge of veins to the surface. Then she shook her head a second time, a movement so slight as to be nearly imperceptible.

"Tree nuts, child. If you cannot stomach animals right now, they will fill your belly."

"This is sage advice," answered Stheno, in Medusa's stead. "I have found pistachios here."

"A wonder, isn't it? What these islands can provide." Leto took a chaste sip of her drink.

But Medusa, apparently, did not want to talk of diet or vegetation. "You have heard what happened to me," she stated.

"I have heard Athena's version." Leto paused before adding delicately, "And Poseidon's."

Medusa's leg began to bounce, her knee bobbing in restless rhythm. Stheno placed a quieting hand upon her thigh.

"But as someone who has been *loved* by an Olympian," continued Leto, "I believe neither." They had arranged themselves in a companionable square, but Leto spoke directly to Medusa. "Would you like to hear what happened to me? From me?"

"Yes." An admission in a shade above a whisper.

Leto adjusted herself on the log and rearranged her skirts. Then, in a measured cadence—the way one recites a story after time has smoothed down the sharp parts—she began:

"My parents, Coeus and Phoebe, were two of the Titans who fought against Zeus in the Battle of the Gods. After Cronus fell, they were exiled to Tartarus for their sins. At our parting, Mother and Father told my sister, Asteria, and me to beware, for we were beautiful, and the new order had an appetite for such. I feared for our survival.

My starry sister married another Titan and birthed a child, but that mattered little to Zeus. Once he saw Asteria, he had to possess her. He chased her across the skies, through night and over day, but Asteria would not submit. And before he could take her, she threw herself into the ocean. I never saw her again."

Euryale noted the wistful way Leto pronounced her sister's name. If she disappeared, would Medusa or Stheno speak of her with such longing? She doubted it. If Medusa vanished, however, Stheno would never recover.

"Terrified, I hid myself in forests and meadows. For years I lived like a nymph, making friends with the fawns, conversing with my reflection in lakes and pools. Still, Zeus found me. And he desired me—perhaps for me, but perhaps more for my sister, who got away, for my parents, who warred against him. 'But, Lord, you are married,' I protested. 'Your wife is without equal! I am nobody.' But he liked that I was nobody; it made him somebody greater."

A small bird with a downward-curved bill flew into the encampment, perching in the poplar tree. Its bright plumage, iridescent blues and greens, caught everyone's eye.

"A bee-eater," said Medusa, interrupting Leto's tale. "They are angry birds. I like to watch them remove the stingers."

Euryale nearly screamed at the impertinence, but Leto seemed to understand.

"It took me many years to find the right words, Medusa, and many more to say them aloud."

Medusa did not respond. She studied the bird.

"I am going to continue," Leto told her. "But I will not force you to listen."

And though Medusa stared upward, into the trees like an imbecile, her snakes collectively turned toward Leto.

"Zeus gave me no title nor assurance. He put life in my belly, and in doing so, he took my own. He is terrified of his wife, I'm sure you know, and soon after my pregnancy began to show, he abandoned me to my disgrace. When his queen learned of my condition, she banned me from all terra firma. She sent subterranean beasts to attack me wherever I settled. Enormously gravid and desperate, I wandered the earth in search of mercy, of any place that might offer sanctuary. I pleaded on my knees. I sobbed and ripped my hair. Even the uninhabitable lands refused. No king, no location, not one daring soul would risk the wrath of Hera.

"The exhaustion I felt was indescribable. And more so, the loneliness. Even now, it is a visceral wound. I poke it with memory, with language, and it releases horror like a pus. The sufferings of a violated woman can feel like a disease without a cure." Leto swallowed. "No male could ever understand.

"When my labor pains began, I sought death. Which benevolent power could I call upon to end me? Send me to the Underworld with my mother and father, please! I even cried out to Hera, 'You have won!' for my spirit could be reduced no further. But either she did not hear me, or she enjoyed my torture. The ban remained.

"And then, in my delirium, I heard a song from the sea, and its lyrics were my name. 'It is only a siren,' I bemoaned. 'A malicious trick.' But the melody persisted, and it sounded like the music of my youth, of midnight laughter and barefoot dancing. Of Asteria! Half-delusional, I tracked the voice to the floating isle of Delos—an island with no foundation on this earth and thus the only place which escaped Hera's dictate.

"Wild and barren, tossed between wave and wind, the homeless island welcomed me gladly. And there, without a friend to my name, I gave birth to my raven-haired daughter, my Artemis.

"It was a difficult delivery—I will not scare you, child, with unnecessary details—but I struggled for nine more days to birth my golden boy, my Apollo."

The twins. Moon and sun, wild beasts and sweet music.

"Did you ever hate them?"

The way Medusa looked at Leto was more stonelike than any of the men Stheno left behind in Athens. Euryale gripped her hands together to keep from striking out. How could Medusa ask such a preposterous question of the Great Mother? A goddess worshipped for the children she bore, and the kind of mother Euryale yearned for: delicate and polished.

But Leto tilted her head, considering. "I have never been asked that." She gave an airy chuckle. "I appreciate that I can still be surprised after so many lifetimes."

"You do not have to answer," interjected Euryale, shooting Medusa a furious look.

Leto held up a placating hand. "I came to help. If it will ease your suffering to know the truth, then, yes, child, I did hate them. In the beginning, I would've clawed them from my womb if I had the strength or chance. But as time passed, and they grew within me, I decided that they could become the family Zeus stole. Why permit him to take any more from me? Hera would not diminish me, but neither would he. They were *mine*, after all. Proof of *my* survival.

"And I am grateful for them now, my two darlings." Leto held Medusa's gaze and added, "Yet I feel no shame for the time when I did not."

Medusa's features softened.

"You said you understand what it is to be '*loved*' by an Olympian." Stheno faltered, frowning. "But you were being facetious; you don't think them capable of love."

"I think love bores the gods unless it is violent. They achieve the ecstasy of love through ravishment and ravage. Zeus chases innocence; Poseidon drowns it."

Athena silences it, thought Euryale. She wondered if Leto suspected the truth of Medusa and the gray-eyed goddess.

"Will Amphitrite seek retribution on Medusa?" Stheno asked. "Or her child?"

"Amphitrite has prudently chosen to remain undersea with her kin. And she was tricked by Poseidon, as well. I do not believe she will harm you."

From a woven bag at her side, Leto removed a satchel of dried herbs and several red berries. "I brought another gift. This is artemisia, the mother herb." It smelled of sage and had purple stems with dual-sided leaves: one green and the other silver. "Burn this and breathe the smoke," instructed Leto. "It will relieve cramps. Or help turn the baby."

Then Leto placed three berries one by one in a neat line before Medusa. "Fruit from the lotus tree. If the labor pains become too great, these will help you rest. One should be plenty."

Medusa rolled one berry into another with the tip of her finger. The line staggered, and Euryale longed to correct it.

"I appreciate your kindness," Medusa managed.

"And I must leave now, before nightfall."

The three sisters escorted Leto back to the shoreline and bade farewell. But as the goddess approached the water, Medusa panicked. She darted after Leto and grabbed her by the arm.

"I am scared," she quavered, snakes twisting and lips trembling.

Leto placed a hand under Medusa's chin, lifting her face. "I will remember you, dear child. All of you."

An odd response, but Euryale would only realize much later and long after Leto disappeared.

EURYALE DREAMED OF talking islands. She wore a veil and ate a stolen berry. Her belly rose like the moon, and she birthed a warrior son of stars.

Her snake flicked its tongue against her eyelids, and Euryale awoke. Medusa sat beside her, in the dark.

"There is so much movement," she whispered to Euryale. "The kicks are too numerous, too strong."

Euryale did not answer, but she listened.

Medusa tightened the blanket about her shoulders. "It cannot be just one. I will need you, Euryale. Will you help me?"

Euryale nodded.

"I will," she said.

She turned over and fell back to sleep.

TWENTY-EIGHTH EPISODE

STHENO

Seabirds cut the sky
so high
with salty wings.

—Erastus of Athens, "Exile"

MEDUSA ACCEDED TO motherhood because of Leto, but also because of me. And since I pressured her to bear this burden, I took on the responsibilities of a father. I would need to protect our island, to provision us against storms and droughts. I couldn't depend upon boat deliveries from our mysterious benefactor or unannounced visitors bearing advice and goodwill. I had no experience with children, but I would give this one the best chance I could.

I had these teeth and nails. These auric wings.

I needed to fly.

But first, I had to teach myself to maneuver my wings. I cleared an empty space for exercise, and I practiced using the muscles of my back and shoulders to open and close my wings. Up and down, in and out, over and over, until I shone with a sweaty film and my torso ached like a common laborer.

"What are you doing?" wondered Medusa, watching my determined repetitions with some bemusement.

"I intend to fly," I announced, and for the first time since our exile, Medusa's eyes brightened to an emerald green. My little sister enjoyed nothing more than a problem to solve or path to explore.

"Truly?"

I wiped my forehead. "Truly."

"Then we must study the birds," she announced, and her use of the plural was not lost on me.

Medusa and I spent day after day acquainting ourselves with the winged inhabitants of Sarpedon: I doubt there was a species we missed. Seabirds with sleek builds, diving at high speeds; hawks with wingspans designed to soar; the gliding albatross and the hovering, manic wings of a hummingbird. We became consumed by birds, scrutinizing them over breakfast and long into the night. Medusa and I analyzed wing shape, feather length, and layout. We carefully dissected the birds we trapped to eat, marveling over their delicate, lightweight bones—nothing like mine.

I wonder now if all the talk of wings seeped into Medusa's womb and shaped what lay sleeping. I admit, I fancy the idea. But at that time, I had more exigent worries.

"How will I launch myself?" I worried aloud. "I am too heavy." For I had moved clumsily in my old body and that was a basic form. I couldn't imagine carrying my odd new shape with the grace of a swan, the elegance of an owl, or the agility of a falcon.

But Medusa remained hopeful. "The Sphinx can fly. The Harpies fly. You will fly."

And because Medusa would not forgo her belief in me, I continued the investigation. We observed how common birds leapt off tree branches, utilizing the sky's pull to initiate flight. But these were the smaller ilk of birds, and I was their complete antithesis.

"Do I just . . . jump?"

Medusa looked up—far up—to a tree branch that might bear my weight. She frowned.

My own mouth went dry, and I swallowed. We were ocean born, and I'd gained wings, not a love for heights. "I'm not sure I could even climb that high, Medusa."

She smiled a bit at me. "We did when we were younger."

"We were wild then."

"And we are wild again."

My heart warmed.

"I wish I could fly with you." She sighed, soft and plaintive. Though only halfway through her pregnancy, Medusa had become too large for most physical activity. She could barely maintain balance while walking. Sometimes when she stood too quickly, she toppled over.

I touched her hand, so confident—so ignorant. "You will. Soon."

Of course, Medusa would not fly soon. Not with me, not ever. She would never again leave our rocky island, never enjoy the wondrous perspective of a view from above.

And Euryale, who pointedly ignored our daytime inquiries and evening discussions, brushed me away when I asked her to join.

"I am not a bird," she spit.

"Then what are you?" I demanded, patience wearing thin.

She had no answer.

Since I preferred all my bones in one piece, I opted against a launch from on high. Instead, I sprinted up and down the beach, flapping my wings, until moisture soaked my light dress and my stomach knotted and I worried the immortal heart and lungs in my chest would expire. I ran with wings open, then closed, with one higher than the other, with wings placed at every conceivable combination of angles. But I never left the ground. I cursed, kicked the sand. Caught Euryale spying from up island, smirking.

"It's in the legs," Medusa cried out, just as I was about to quit.

"I'm moving my legs!"

"Listen to me, Stheno," she explained, patient but excited by her epiphany. "You are relying too heavily on your wings to ascend. Flex your legs and push yourself into the air."

"I'm not strong enough."

"You are." Her grip on my arm was firm, her eyes ablaze.

I wasn't convinced, so Medusa spent the remains of the day dragging me about the island, from bird to bird, while she proved her theory. We lay on our sides in the dirt, observing birds take off from land. Some ran into the wind. But others leapt, just like Medusa said.

And so, the next morning, I leapt.

And I flew.

Not far, that first time, for I was too startled by my unexpected success to focus. I crashed to the other end of the beach but barely felt it for the adrenaline coursing through my veins. Medusa came running—waddling, really—arms thrown in the air. We hugged and screamed.

"Did you see?" I shouted unnecessarily.

"You were magnificent!"

And I wondered if happiness alone might lift me as I allowed jubilation to expand my chest and stretch my cheeks. I lightened on bubbles of elation. I nearly giggled.

But my victory was short-lived. Though I was airborne, I still did not understand the mechanics of actual flight.

"You are a crane," Medusa said one night, rousing me from sleep. "You must fly like one." She pulled me from my pallet and sketched a diagram in the dirt with a stick. "See here? A crane flies with its legs stretched behind and its neck stretched ahead. It puts its center here." She pointed to a spot between the wings. "You should be able to maintain short distances with just steady beats."

She sat back, triumphant. A smudge of dirt across her nose.

So I became a crane. I adjusted my center and gradually increased my distances. I learned what currents could hold me, how to soar on warm thermals with my wings spread, the trick of spirals—circling upward, then retracting my wings to a narrow point, gliding in the direction I wanted to go. I mastered the art of zig and zag, gaining lift and flying until I lost altitude, then zigging and zagging again.

Flying, in the way it demanded practice and discipline, reminded me of music. And there was a rhythm to its technique; I heard its beat as I plucked my wings through the air like kithara strings. My body sang.

Landings continued to brutalize me. I rolled my ankles and sprained my wrists. Smashed my face into a shrub. Medusa watched a gaggle of migrating geese for days until she derived a solution.

"First, you must slow down," she instructed. "And then bring your wings higher. It will make you heavier against the wind."

Naturally, she was correct. And I learned that the lanky birds I imitated also used outstretched feet to slow their arrival. Though I sorely lacked their style, I managed to execute a similar routine—enough so that I could descend without dire harm.

I flew with a religious fervor. Every day, like a ritual prayer, pushing myself to islands farther and farther from home. When I left Sarpedon behind to raid and scavenge from sleeping villagers, I sometimes thought, *If Euryale and Medusa can return to each other, if we can summon sufficient love for this unwanted baby, if I can fly, maybe it will be enough. It could still be a good life.*

Did I ever fantasize about leaving my sisters, about starting again on my own? Once or twice, but it was never a serious consideration. We were three, stronger together than alone. Flight would be Medusa's parting gift to me, a path to future freedom, but I knew then what I had always known: I would not be separated from my sisters until they both left me first.

I TRAVELED OFTEN to an island rich in kumquat fruit, bringing home sacks of it for Medusa, who craved citrus. When I returned, I liked to land in a treeless area of the island, coincidentally the same location where Euryale often bided her time, drying and pressing strips of kelp. She would grind the seaweed into a fine powder and apply it to her skin, turning her face and body as green as Achlys. She claimed it maintained her youthfulness. I don't know where she learned such nonsense, and I'm not sure it did any good. She always looked the same to me. But since I couldn't interest her in anything that aided the homestead—she would neither cook nor clean, garden nor forage, trap nor fish, build nor wash—I supported her frivolous endeavor. I'd rather her keep busy than sulk and start fights.

"Where is Medusa?" I wanted to know, shifting the weighty sack of fruit to my other shoulder.

Euryale rolled her eyes, but I did not mind. Medusa had struggled lately. She complained often of nausea. Her stomach seemed painfully—abnormally—large, but then again, what did I know of gestation?

"Ill," my sister answered, turning over a piece of sunbaked kelp. "As always. She's lying in that hovel you call a house."

I bristled a bit, for I was proud of what I'd built from repurposed plank and branch. It was no home, not yet, but with a roof and three walls, it at the least resembled a room. When it rained, Euryale joined us—which I might have pointed out, but the regenerative flight had me in a forgiving spirit.

"Have you checked on her?"

"No," replied Euryale, exasperated. "This island is smaller than some palaces. I'm sure if she cried out, I would hear just fine."

I stopped at a rain barrel I maintained, and filled a gourd for Medusa. If she ailed, fresh water might offer relief. I passed through the familiar growth, the foliage constituting landmarks—a twisted mastic tree, the fluffy pink tamarisk, the shallow stream I discovered our first night.

In our homestead, Medusa lay atop her pallet, groaning and turning. Thinking she suffered from another nightmare, I quickened my pace, but as I dropped to her side, I found she was wide awake.

Medusa moaned my name and gripped my hand. "You are back."

I laid my other hand across her forehead. Her skin was humid. Clammy.

"You feel warm."

"It's my stomach. Such cramps! It feels like my menses has begun."

"What have you eaten?"

"Nothing."

Medusa rolled onto her other side. As she shifted, I noticed a viscous fluid staining her dress. It was pale yellow and speckled with blood.

"I will find you something simple to eat," I told her, careful to keep my tone neutral.

Instead, I sped back to Euryale, yelling her name as I retraced my steps. True to her claim, she heard my call and met me halfway.

"I think Medusa is in labor."

Euryale frowned. "It is much too early."

I described the thick mucus I found. "And her stomach has dropped, I noticed a few days ago."

It was a terrifying admission, and Euryale swallowed tightly. Neither of us had ever attended a delivery before. I recognized my own fear reflected in her eyes.

"Does she still have Leto's berries?"

"All three."

"Do we summon help?"

I shook my head. "She has both of us. That's more than most women."

Euryale seemed uncertain, but selfishly, I wanted us to accomplish this ritual together. I pictured the three of us on the other side of the birth, and I imagined how this experience would heal the wrongs we had done each other. We would bond as sisters, as aunts and mother. I did not want to share the moment with anyone else.

And, of course, I could not have guessed that Medusa's murderer approached.

Medusa's death would be a summation of little decisions, minute pauses and hesitations, tiny insignificant mistakes that accumulated over time. If I had flown to Delos and retrieved Leto, would Perseus have dared to attack? If I had begged Oceanus for Echidna's arrival, would she have come in time to kill and eat him?

Or what if I had shouldered my pride, my absolute disdain, and demanded Poseidon's protection? Would he have speared Zeus's son with his trident?

Could any of these possibilities have saved Medusa's head?

The choices made by so many led to our tragedy. Too many of those choices were wrong, and they were mine.

This moment, my answer, was one of those.

We would bear the day all alone.

THE HERO

IGNORANT MEN SHOULD never receive challenges.

What was a Gorgon, after all? How do they die? And where do they hide?

These were the questions accompanying Perseus as his ship docked on the mainland. The men onshore unloading cargo told him to seek out the Pythia at Delphi.

But what was a Pythia? Why had Dictys and Danaë taught him only knots and tides, and nothing of any importance?

The Pythia was an oracle, he discovered, at the house of Apollo.

Perseus, who had never left Seriphos before, traveled farther inland to reach the famed peripteral temple. The Pythia resided in its inner sanctum. A girl, really, seated upon a tall, gilded throne. Two other priestesses—just as young—waited on her either side. Perseus frowned. *She* would speak for the gods?

"Wonders the boy who would kill for them."

Perseus startled. Had he spoken aloud? After journeying alone for so long, he could not be sure.

"I act of my own accord," he insisted, and the Pythia sniffed. Offended by her derision and desperate to justify himself, Perseus continued, "I am Perseus. I will behead a Gorgon."

"The Gorgons turn mortal men to stone," responded the Pythia, her voice made spectral and supernatural as it cut through the incense smoke. "Only the one named Medusa can be killed."

Perseus coughed. How did she speak or think in such fumes? "How will I kill Medusa?"

"I cannot say."

"Cannot or will not?"

The Pythia smiled without showing her teeth. Her eyes reminded him of the cats who stalked the market stalls in his village.

"I can only say where you must travel next. See the priestesses in the land where men eat acorns in place of grain. Perhaps they will find you worthy."

A sly dismissal. But he was a mouse, desperate for crumbs, and he must follow their meager path, wherever it may lead.

Perseus went farther west to Dodona, the Land of the Oak Trees, but the elderly oracle, devoted to the Great Mother, Leto, took one look at him, consulted her goddess, and simply shook her head.

Perseus wandered, deplete of coin and favor, bemoaning an adventure ended far too soon and in such spectacular failure. He longed for home: he missed his mother's arms and quiet moments with Dictys. He hoped they forgave him. Perseus now understood Polydectes's great deception, and he knew he could return to Seriphos only in victory.

If he could not fulfill his promise to the king, he would be better off dead.

When Perseus's spirit dropped to its absolute nadir and the dark thoughts consuming him could get no bleaker, a handsome savior appeared—one with a herald's wand and a cunning smile.

Hermes.

"We share a father," the trickster god explained, "and I am destined to assist you."

Divine intervention! At last! Perseus knelt and kissed the god's feet.

Hermes brought Perseus to the nymphs of the Hyperboreans in the far north. They provisioned him with winged sandals, a magical sack, and a cap of invisibility.

"We do not know where the Gorgons lie," a nymph clarified. "But the Graeae do. Go to their island, the gray place. Beneath the shroud of twilight, you will find the strange sisters and, perhaps, the answer you seek."

"Take my sword," Hermes insisted, presenting the hilt to Perseus. "It will take a mortal's head with one true strike."

Still, Perseus fretted. "How will I tell the Gorgons apart?"

"Easily," came a low, lovely voice, a resonant alto. "Medusa is the most beautiful."

Both Perseus and Hermes stepped back, for the mighty Pallas Athena shone before them.

"I thought they were all ugly."

Athena wouldn't deign to comment, but she removed the polished silver shield she wore across her chest.

"Look upon Medusa only through this," instructed Athena, handing over her breastplate. "The reflection will guide your hand and preserve your naked eye from the curse."

Around her wrist, Perseus noted a lock of golden-brown hair—a bizarre bracelet for an Olympian.

"Why would you help me?"

"I have no love for Medusa."

But her eyes burned like silver fire, and Perseus shivered.

"Steal the Graeae's eye," Hermes counseled. "They will deny you nothing to get it back."

It seemed a cowardly move, but Athena nodded. Perseus held his tongue.

Armed with more advice and accessories than he could handle, Perseus flew—by winged sandals—past Oceanus, to a dim island visited by neither sun nor moon. He spotted the Graeae from on high, three lumpy forms distinguishable from the rocks only by their subtle movements, by the slight warmth radiating off their bodies. Wearing his cap of invisibility, Perseus landed on the beach and watched them. The gray women were indeed hideous, but harmless, and his heart sagged heavily with guilt. But picturing his mother married to that tyrant, and Dictys, imprisoned or dead, hampered any misgivings.

He waited patiently until one sister plucked the eye from her forehead. As she passed it to another, Perseus sprinted forward, grabbing it from her spindly fingers.

He tried not to cringe at the little orb's texture: hard but springy. Moist.

"Sisters! A thief has stolen our eye!"

The gray women shrieked. They contorted with such fury and frenzy that Perseus feared their necks would snap. They chased him blindly, with outstretched arms, like dead trees, risen and rootless. He retreated from this nightmare of skeletal women in colorless rags, from their wailing and mourning, from the overly large mouths he would never stop seeing. Rotten gums and deep, black voids.

"Tell me where to find the Gorgons," he managed, "and I will return your vision."

"The Gorgons? We do not know!"

"He means Stheno and Euryale," one whispered. "He means Medusa."

They paused. And though they bore no eyes, they faced each other. They *looked* at each other somehow. Perseus shuddered.

"How can we trust you will keep your word?"

Perseus straightened up, then blushed, for what was the point of posturing when they couldn't see him? "Because I promise you on my honor. As a hero."

"A *hero*," jeered one.

Another snickered.

"Just tell him, Pemphredo."

The gray sister holding a single tooth stepped forward. She cocked her head to the side, sensing him. Sniffed, then spit.

"You will find them on the isle of Sarpedon."

Perseus relinquished the eye.

TWENTY-NINTH EPISODE

EURYALE

Boy hero, baby man.
Does your mother know you're here?

—Erastus of Athens, "Thales"

MEDUSA SPENT MOST of that day confined to her pallet, immobile with nausea, in unabated discomfort. But when the striking pains commenced, she could no longer remain still. Writhing, straining, bucking, and breaking, she shot upward in pain and paced back and forth through their homestead. A rhythm gradually established itself: stumble, stumble, stumble, *stop!*—and Medusa would halt, lurch forward, on convulsions that left her breathless. It was the ending note of a cryptic passage that immediately replayed from the top.

"My spine is breaking," she gasped, red-faced and breathless, while Euryale looked on in dismay.

Stheno pressed her palms against Medusa's hips, hoping pressure may counteract the intense pain.

"Harder," Medusa cried, bent nearly in half, one hand propping herself against a tree trunk. "Harder!"

And so Stheno trailed Medusa, slamming her hands into their sister when she began to moan. Handprint-shaped bruises formed along Medusa's lower back—a swollen butterfly just below her wings.

Medusa did not notice, which told Euryale all she needed to know about the agony of labor.

The day was hot. Oppressively so. Sweat dripped from the tip of Medusa's nose, off her chin.

"We should move her to the beach," Euryale suggested. The breeze would cool her body, the sounds would soothe her soul. It was what Euryale herself would want. "Maybe water will ease the contractions."

Stheno agreed, but it was no simple feat to transport Medusa, for she moved so slowly and required frequent stops. It took the remainder of the night to reach the shore, and by the time they approached the sunlit tide pools, Medusa crawled before them on hands and knees.

The blood between her sister's legs brought Euryale back to Athena's temple. Vivid and violent slashes of red. She nearly gasped.

"Help me lift her," Stheno ordered, summoning Euryale to the present.

"It hurts," wailed Medusa. "It hurts so badly. Everything."

"It is almost over," promised Stheno, as if she knew.

Euryale and Stheno each took a side, lifting Medusa from under her arms, then lowering her into a shallow pool. The salty water just barely blanketed her legs, and it lapped gently against her belly. Medusa wept with relief.

"I will get more bark for her to chew," said Stheno, weariness weighing at her words, and she trudged off.

Medusa closed her eyes and leaned her head back against the rocks, snakes slithering out of the way.

"My body is not strong enough," she moaned. "I do not think I can bear them, whatever they are."

For Medusa never called it a baby. Never referred to it as one.

"Don't speak nonsense," Euryale scolded. "Your baby is coming. Stheno is right, it is almost over."

"It should have been you."

Euryale's heart skipped a beat. "What are you saying?"

"It should have been you. Carrying his baby. Becoming a mother."

And then Medusa became incoherent with suffering. Her hands dropped into the water and gripped at the sand as she rambled once more that her back would break, that she would sever, split in two forever.

Euryale began to fret. Leto labored nine additional days to deliver Apollo, but she was an immortal goddess. How much more suffering could Medusa handle? Euryale cupped water and poured it down Medusa's forehead and neck.

When Stheno reappeared holding strips of tree bark, Euryale pulled her aside.

"I am worried she will not survive this."

"How dare you say such a thing!" Stheno lowered her voice. "What if she hears you?"

"Listen." Euryale rested a hand on Stheno's arm, hoping to calm her. "I am only being practical. Her mortal body may not be able to withstand a natural delivery. We don't know its . . . *form*. And her hips are so narrow."

"What are you implying?" Stheno chewed at her lower lip.

"We cut her open."

Stheno thrust Euryale's hand from her as if scalded by her touch. "No. Never. She will bleed out."

"Then we risk the baby—or babies—getting stuck and they *all* die."

Stheno rubbed her face, pushing her cheeks up into her eyes, then tugging them down toward her chin. It was a remarkably human gesture, Euryale thought. Not something Stheno ever would have done before Thebes.

"She just needs to rest. She has been at this for more than a day. I will give her one of the lotus berries to help her sleep."

"And if rest does not work?"

"I will fly for help."

Though Stheno only delayed the inevitable, Euryale consented. Arguing with Stheno about Medusa was more pointless than the debates she overheard in the Athenian square. Old men talking in circles, around and around one another, then settling back on their own opinion from the beginning. Euryale would conserve her energy for later.

Stheno opened a small pouch at her belt and removed one of Leto's berries, holding it delicately between her thumb and forefinger.

"Eat this," she said, placing it on Medusa's tongue. "You will sleep."

Euryale watched Medusa's throat rise and fall as she swallowed.

"Another," she rasped.

Stheno hedged. "They are strong, Medusa. I don't want—"

"Another."

Stheno relented. Medusa took the second berry into her mouth with some clean water from their gourd.

"When I wake, it will be different," Medusa stated, and then she gasped, clutching at her hips and thighs at yet another tightening.

"Yes, yes," soothed Stheno, settling at Medusa's side and humming as Medusa's groans gradually blended into sighs and her shallow breaths turned steady. The melodies were familiar—Ligeia's work—and Stheno had a pleasant voice. Euryale waited nearby, and though she kept her eyes on the horizon, she listened attentively to her sisters.

"Medusa?" Stheno sang. "Medusa?" But Medusa did not answer, for even the green snakes slumbered, draping themselves down and across her face like seaweed.

Peace, at last.

"How long do we let her sleep?" Euryale wondered.

Stheno stood and stretched her upper body. "Long enough."

"That's no answer."

"I don't know, Euryale. I don't always know." Stheno's coral snakes twisted and rose at her tone, weaving through each other in anxious dance. "Oh, stop!" she cried out, swatting them away.

Her elder sister's eyes were rimmed in pink with purple shadows.

"You should rest, as well."

Stheno scoffed and gestured to Medusa, whose head had fallen forward onto her chest at an awkward angle.

"I will watch her," insisted Euryale. "And I will wake you when she's ready to try again."

Stheno's mouth twisted as she considered Euryale's offer, duty and exhaustion in clear conflict. But, for once, Stheno's physical needs overruled.

"Wake me before nightfall, even if she is still asleep."

Euryale nodded. Stheno climbed upon a rock both flat and large enough for her body. She lay on her side, resting her face against her forearm and pulling her knees up toward her stomach. She seemed small, even with those mighty wings. As Stheno drifted into sleep, Euryale marveled that her sisters' breathing synchronized. Could it be they shared one heart, after all? And did Euryale's own internal cadence match theirs or syncopate?

Euryale perched atop a high boulder that afforded a better view of the distant ocean, hoping that its consistent blue would provide serenity. She longed for stillness, but her obstreperous mind refused to settle. She thought restlessly of gilled beasts and finned monsters, angry gods and innocence chained. A pearl that was lost.

Her fists clenched. *No,* she told herself. *Stop.*

And then she saw again the image she would never unsee: Poseidon pleasuring himself with Medusa.

Not now.

If only she could shake such images from her mind! Slap them out.

She needed to relax.

And then Euryale spied Stheno's pouch, as tempting as any golden apple. A single lotus berry remained. If she ate only half, she would not fall unconscious. Half a berry could calm her wild imagination, allowing her to properly focus on her sisters.

And didn't Euryale deserve a moment of respite? She had checked between Medusa's legs. The birth canal had opened only slightly, and there was no sign of a scalp. Medusa would not go into active labor anytime soon. Euryale had plenty of time.

Euryale crept up alongside Stheno and almost giggled as she reached for the pouch. It felt like a wayward game—a childish dare. As Euryale removed the tiny red orb, Stheno murmured. Euryale leapt back, but Stheno only snorted and rolled over.

One of the snakes awoke, however. It peered at Euryale with beady eyes.

"Shhh," she commanded. It lay back down.

Euryale bit the berry with her front teeth, spitting half back into her palm and setting it aside. The other she chewed slowly, letting the juice soak her gums, pressing its soft skin into the roof of her mouth with her tongue. She tiptoed away from her sisters and found a comfortable spot in the sand. Euryale eased back, relishing the drug's slow absorption into her blood, the way it tickled and tingled as it streamed through her arms, her legs. And when it hit her head, she exhaled. This wasn't the chaotic buzz of wine; it was blurry bliss.

Euryale settled into the high. She watched her hands make shadow dances with the sun, rolled her fingers through the amber air. Was she body or was she wind? She drifted, as light and weightless as she felt in the sea. Nowhere to go, guided by forces beyond her understanding and control.

Freedom!

Oh, she was going to need more of these berries. Stheno should try one, too.

She floated like gold rising. The sky became lavender, and Euryale walked through its fields, smelling herbs and hyacinth. She took a bite of cloud and it tasted like dusk.

And as she wandered—without moving a muscle—she dreamed a boy. He emerged from the twilight, a human child pretending to be a god, soaring above her with a familiar aegis and sword far too heavy for his frame. *Such a preposterous helmet,* she thought. *What silly sandals!* Euryale laughed.

He landed on their beach—the first human to touch Sarpedon, and Euryale cheered. For it was all impossible. No mortal could find their way here unaided.

The oneiric boy tensed, the muscles in his arms quivered. Had he heard her? How? He was a daydream. Euryale rubbed her eyes with her fists, and when she opened them, blinking, he remained. Some slithering instinct told Euryale to move, and she sat up. She frowned.

"Boy!" she called out, but he would not look at her. "Boy! Are you real?"

He hefted his sword and approached Medusa's sleeping form, studying her through the reflection of his thoroughly polished shield. The boy was strong enough to handle the sword's weight, but graceless. He fumbled with the hilt, like one unaccustomed to such a weapon, but there was no question, its blade aimed for Medusa.

Cognition washed away the dregs of lotus. This male was neither mirage nor visitor; he was an intruder—a predator—and Euryale had allowed him into their nest.

"Stheno!" she screamed, and Euryale knew she should move, should run, should fight, but she was a barnacle attached to this rock. "Stheno, wake!"

As her older sister jerked upward, shrieking, the boy panicked. He swung his noble blade across Medusa's throat, waking her from sleep with one slice.

"No!"

Medusa's head flew from her body. Sailing through the air, then plummeting into the sand. It continued to roll with the force of the blow and tumbled to a halt right before Euryale. Medusa's snakes stood on end, stiff with rigor mortis, above two green eyes, forever large with recognition.

Euryale stared into her baby sister's perfect face.

This is not real. I can put it back.

The boy—*who was he, where did he come from, why did he hate us, why, why?*—hunched forward, spewing vomit across rocks and his own feet. Stheno stretched to her full height, wings open and fangs bared. She held her hands up, curled and clawed, and Euryale barely recognized her older sister, this bastard offspring of misery and vengeance.

The boy caught sight of Stheno's image in his shield, a lurid vision made more distorted by metal, and understood he was about to die, that this she-beast would kill him slowly.

And for the injustice of his crime, he would deserve every excruciating second.

The boy scrambled away from Stheno and toward Euryale, tripping on the sandals that did not fit. With his eyes scrunched closed, he picked up Medusa's head, gripping her by the dead snakes, and dropped her into a sack hung across his chest.

But she is ours. She does not belong to you.

Tiny wings on the boy's sandals fluttered to life, thrusting his body into the air, and he struggled to maintain his balance—and his grisly trophy. He clutched the bag tightly against his body.

Stheno rose behind him in pursuit. She would retrieve their sister. And then that boy would die.

Just as they departed, movement from the tide pool caught Euryale's attention and she turned, watching in horror as Medusa's dead body begin to animate. Her headless sister convulsed and thrashed. Was she healing herself? Could she still be alive? A mixture of dread and hope washed over Euryale. But no, some force that was not Medusa fought its way up her corpse.

Something that refused to be left behind.

Despite all Euryale had witnessed in her immortality, nothing could compare to this sight: life, finding its way, wiggling through severed neck, pushing past cords and bone and liquid toward the promise of birth.

She understood what was happening and very nearly keeled over.

"Stheno!" she cried, flinching at the shrillness of her own voice. "The babies!"

THIRTIETH EPISODE

STHENO

Faithless woman.
It was far, far worse—
you were far, far worse—
than any false priest.

—Erastus of Athens, "Ode to Monsters"

I ROSE ON THE strength of my wings and my fury. No run, no jump. I made to follow the boy, to track him through mist and past night, to hold him in my hands and tear him apart, tossing his pieces to Ceto's sharks.

I would reclaim my sister's head.

But the other sister's cries tethered me to land, to the living.

I looked away from the fleeing villain's back. Below me, Euryale pointed a trembling finger toward the tide pool.

There, over Medusa's body, stood a horse unlike any that has lived before or after. Coat and mane of pure white, like fresh snow or a jasmine's petal. It reached seventeen, perhaps eighteen hands in height. A creature that would cause any Persian warhorse to cower.

My heart caught in my throat, and my vision blurred, for decorating its back were the most exquisite wings, beyond anything I could have imagined. Each one taller than me, lined in rows of perfect flight feathers. He shook himself, and one of those ivory feathers caught the breeze. I caught it on my palm as I floated back to land, allowing the boy to gain more and more distance.

"Where did it come from?"

"He sprang from her neck." Euryale barely whispered. Her golden eyes were wide, pupils dark.

The beast neighed, stomped its front hoof. Splashed pink sea foam against my dress.

"Your father is Poseidon," I told him. "You must know. So that you can survive."

The horse leaned down, sniffing at Medusa's corpse. He opened his mouth and licked, and when he lifted his mighty neck, that immaculate muzzle was coated in her blood. It dripped from his whiskers.

"She is Medusa." I struggled to articulate her name. "She longed to fly." I am not sure why I said such. It just came out of my mouth, almost of its own volition.

Then Euryale gasped. "Stheno! Another."

A pair of hands emerged from Medusa's throat, and her body squirmed and then split as those hands became arms clutching at whatever it could reach—rock, sand, bone—to pull itself free. A boy child—hardly a babe—emerged. And I watched, in some horror, as it continued to grow, to enlarge, with rapid speed.

A giant.

In just a few breaths, he towered above us. He looked down at me expectantly with familiar green eyes that broke my heart.

These were Medusa's children, conceived under duress, harbored with reluctancy, and birthed in tragedy.

"Your mother is dead," I had to say, and the giant let loose a roar that shook our entire island. Euryale covered her ears. "A man—some unworthy human boy—killed her."

The giant pounded his fists in the surf, and his mourning raised the waves, blasting them out toward less fortuitous islands.

Good, I thought. *Drown them all.*

"You must leave this island. We are your mother's sisters, but we cannot care for you."

"Stheno, no."

"Euryale, they have to go. Their father's name will protect them."

That gorgeous horse lowered his head to my sister, and she stroked the path down his forehead. It looked so smooth. I wanted to touch it, too, but if I did, I would not remain hard enough to do what I must.

The giant moaned, bereft, and I wondered if his sadness could compare to mine. But how could losing what you never had compete with losing your everything? I crossed my arms over my chest.

Medusa's other child also sought compassion from Euryale. He turned to her and released a pleading sort of sound. "I'm sorry," she managed, though unable to meet his gaze. "I am so terribly sorry."

I pointed. "Head toward the island that turns red with the evening light. You will be safe there." I relayed this in a voice that brooked no room for negotiation. The horse turned and trotted down the beach, but as he broke into a lope, he lifted, rising into the early evening with a preternatural grace I envied. The giant lumbered behind and, just like any of the sea god's offspring, walked across the water's surface miraculously, as if it were no more than blue-gray stone.

The brothers—my nephews—did not look back at us, but I tracked them until the wings disappeared into cloud and the giant's head vanished below the horizon.

The murderous boy was also long gone. I could not have followed him even if I had the will.

I was left alone with Euryale. And our mess.

"You were supposed to wake me," I began, low and lethal.

"I did."

"Too late!" I snapped back. "You were too late."

Euryale's lower lip quivered, and her nostrils flared.

"You will blame me for this, too."

"You told me to rest. You told me it would be fine."

She would not fight me, not on this, not today. But neither could she stand by while I assailed her. Euryale turned, and she left me.

I shouldn't have slept, but that had been my decision. I allowed it to happen and now my sister was dead. I struggled to breathe, and my knees gave out. I sat in the sand, convulsing, my lungs fighting for air even if my spirit didn't care to live. I wondered if I could suffocate on my own suffering. I hoped I would.

I do not want to exist without her.

Euryale returned with a blanket from our pallet. She covered the gory remains of Medusa's corpse.

What were her last words? What did I say to her before I shoved that drug down her throat and doomed her?

Euryale sat nearby with her knees pulled in tight. She made no sound.

Do I light a pyre? Dig a grave?

I could not stop shaking. My teeth clattered against one another, biting into my tongue and lips. I drank my own blood.

Why couldn't the boy take Euryale instead?

I burned with shame.

For that thought alone, I deserved to die, too.

The ground rumbled. Euryale tried to get my attention, but I waved her away.

Come, fresh horror! I dare you, try to break what is already broken! I beg you.

And I sensed her gigantic form long before she beached. Echidna, pulling herself from the shoreline with her forearms, dragging behind that massive tail. I had never seen her above sea level before. Neither Euryale nor I spoke or moved as we watched our eldest sibling lift the makeshift burial shroud from Medusa's battered body.

Deflowered and then transformed, impregnated and abandoned. Mutilated. Abused.

Decapitated.

"Where is her head?"

"He took it."

Echidna ran her eyes along the body.

"Her hands are unchanged," she murmured, gently folding one in her own. "She showed so much love with these hands."

And I remembered Medusa's hands on Echidna's weeping back, on Cadmus's cheek and Semele's shoulders. Holding back my hair. Her fingers arching toward Athena's feet. Interlocked with mine and Euryale's.

Echidna held Medusa with a bravery I could not muster. She cradled her, laid a kiss against her chest. In death, in Echidna's arms, my sister became petite again. Returned to her girlish self. Or maybe it was only a trick of my mind—memories from our old life superimposed on a reality too ugly to process.

"I will take her body and bury her below the sea."

I thanked Echidna. Or I think I did. I might have just cried or grunted; maybe I spoke to her only in my own head.

Did it matter then? Does it matter now?

"Would you like to say goodbye?"

Euryale stood first. She murmured many words to Medusa's body, a lengthy message I will never know. Did she apologize? Profess love? Deliver one final barb? Does one use such a moment to make amends, settle scores? If Echidna overheard, she offered no sign.

And then it was my turn, and I could not touch her, this body that I had lain beside almost every night of my life. Because this assembly of fluid and flesh and bone had gone cold, and my Medusa was warm. This thing in Echidna's arms smelled like copper, but my Medusa was the sweetness of early summer. My Medusa was endless questions and honey-voiced laughter, calamitous dancing, and easy affection. My Medusa was gone. Stolen. So, no, I did not touch the figure Echidna held on display, but I remember what I said.

"You were magnificent."

Echidna, her eyes glistening, took Medusa and slid back into the water.

We had entered the age of heroes, and we were beasts. Standing on the beach that day, not one of us could have guessed how many of our tribe would fall. That Medusa was the opening attack in a losing battle. All of Echidna's children would be sacrificed to humans and demigods on quests for notoriety: Oedipus, Heracles, Bellerophon. Mortal men who would write their names in the viscera of Echidna's slaughtered offspring. She would spend the rest of her years roiling in a pain no mother could ever deserve.

For what?

For a story, for a song.

I TRIED TO sleep. Nothing made sense anymore, but it was night and that was what I was supposed to do. I was disturbed by the squawking sounds of a bird in the throes of some prolonged death. After far too long, I understood those were my own cries. I gave up on rest. I used the dark hours to remember the boy. His pathetic beard and scrawny chest, his awareness of our curse. Athena's aegis.

The morning sun inflamed my fantasies of revenge.

"I must know his name."

Euryale did not stop me. I journeyed from island to island, killing human men with my interrogations, leaving tombstones in my wake. But nobody had yet heard of a would-be hero, outfitted in magic gifts, ordered to deliver the head of a Gorgon.

Frustrated and circumvented, I redirected my bloodlust: Who told the boy of Sarpedon? They must be punished. I flew first to Delos, but Leto wept for Medusa. She tried to embrace me, but I shoved her away. If she was hurt by my coldness, I refused to notice.

"Your hate cannot bring her back," Leto tried to tell me. I fled from her advice.

Next, I arrived at the island of Cisthene. The Graeae were attendant upon their shore, roasting skewered eels over a fire. Flesh crisped, and bits of rendered fat slipped into the flames, sputtering and hissing.

I landed, purposefully kicking sand over their meal and flame. Pemphredo, who held the eye, protested.

"That was unnecessary, Stheno. And rude."

I ignored her. "You betrayed us."

"Perseus was tricky," defended Enyo.

"Perseus held our eye," added Deino.

Perseus. They did not realize the bounty they provided me.

"He murdered her. Your kin."

"Hardly kin," spit Pemphredo. "You and your pretty sisters always thought yourselves superior. When you were pretty, at least."

Enyo cackled.

I tackled Pemphredo and we tumbled backward. She was brittle bones and weak flesh, while I was muscle and monster. It wasn't a fair fight. The eye slipped from her grasp and rolled across the beach, collecting sand. Bits of shell stuck to its gelatinous covering.

"Sisters!" she screeched. "The eye!"

The other two blind women scrambled forward on their knees, hands swiping the ground, frantic and urgent. And I, with my two coral eyes, stomped across Pemphredo's back, shoved aside the other two bodies, and scooped up my prize.

"Stheno, no!" pleaded Deino.

I was merciless; I hardly recognized myself. *Who is Stheno?* asked the ghost of Semele. She is a Gorgon. Metamorphosis complete.

"Are we kin now?" I laughed.

"Ceto will curse you!" Enyo warned. "She will never forgive."

"Do not speak to me of forgiveness."

I flew away, leaving them to keen. In destroying their vision, I felt only perverse glee. When I was far enough away, I tossed the eye into the blue of Lake Tritonis. I wonder if it bobbed a bit before sinking into the ocean. And I wonder what creature chanced upon it, took a tentative lick and then a bite, making a meal of my petty victory.

(Perseus would be credited with this cruelty, but it was me! I threw the eye in Tritonis. I existed. I acted. I was there!)

My anger was no different from Hera's—a wrath born from one too afraid to name their sadness.

I never saw the Graeae again.

◆ ◆ ◆

TO COLLECT PERSEUS'S story, piece by piece, I became a handmaiden of Nyx, a creature of darkness. Dark soul, dark purpose. I taught myself to hide in corners and outside windows, to become shadow and ghoul, whatever necessary, to overhear the gossip of men. I followed the trail of information through cities and nights, and I heard of Perseus's journey home, about Andromeda and the sea beast. I discovered how Medusa's head was presented at King Polydectes's court, turning him and his minions to stone. My little sister became vengeance on another man—for another man—with no retribution for herself.

I learned Perseus and Andromeda named a daughter Gorgophone. *Gorgon Slayer.* That his mother married the new king of Seriphos, Dictys.

I found out he buried Medusa's head in the agora at Argos, under a new moon, so that it would harm no more.

I obsessed over Perseus, but the more I gathered of him and his family, the more I hated Athena. Goddesses made endings out of the mortal women who dared to break their hearts. Hera killed Semele as surely as Athena killed Medusa; yet they were cunning enough to sharpen the knives, then leave them within the grasp of a lesser male.

Could Medusa have done anything differently? Danaë? Leto? How do you free yourself from a god's lust? For it is a sentencing, usually fatal, and once you've been locked down, you can rattle the chains, slam on the bars, and scream at the wrongfulness, but you will never be innocent again.

These were the philosophical questions of my mourning. Then there were the more subjective: How does a person disappear so completely? Medusa had been beside me for ages—laughing and enduring and questioning and trying—and then she wasn't. What remained? A dress of hers. The cup and plate she favored. A collection of bird feathers. The blankets that smelled of her—but for how much longer? I didn't dare move them, lest her scent escape with the wind.

The scrapings of a life. She was everything to me, but she left behind so little.

I also heard of Medusa's children. The giant, Chrysaor, settled in Iberia amid the fields of golden wheat. Pegasus, the winged horse, reached Mount Helicon, and when his hooves struck ground, he released a sacred spring. The Muses called it Hippocrene and collected its water in chalices, imbibing for inspiration.

No doubt a white horse like Pegasus would stir the poets' imagination, would incite the violence of heroes. I knew it as surely as I was doomed.

Because I stopped hunting and fishing, I became quite gaunt. I suppose Euryale did as well, but I didn't much consider her. Or anything, really. I was senseless with pain. I did not bathe, drank only from puddles and ponds that made me sick. Our homestead began to collapse as my disarray deepened, and entropy consumed me. I was so tired of being resilient. I was no protector; I fixed nothing. I had been a negligent sister, not loving her enough to keep her safe, making too many reckless decisions. I was a horrible friend; I was a killer.

How many men had I murdered in my quest for information? Dozens, at least. And how many of my own kin had I banished? Two, as yet.

If only I could kill memory, as well.

I cannot recall how many days passed between Euryale and me in arrant quiet. Weeks? Years? We became fluent in silence, our preferred language with each other. I despised my own voice; I considered never speaking again.

But then one day, Euryale talked to me.

"Would you want this?"

Almost bashfully, she presented me with a mature tortoise shell.

"I found it washed ashore, the creature inside long dead. It might make a suitable lyre?"

I inspected the carapace, carefully turning it over. It was nearly without fault. With leather and wood, a bit of string, I could fashion something workable.

Did I want to? Music meant Ligeia; it meant Athens. Would I be able to strum chords without invoking memories—of Medusa in her priestess headband, of Thales, of dinners in the courtyard, the crowds and noise and complicated glory of the city that ruined us?

"I know you prefer the kithara," mumbled Euryale, "but I don't know the materials." She repeated herself. "You could make a lyre?"

"It is possible."

And with those three words, I gave slight acknowledgment to a future.

Despite my best wishes, I lived. I had survived, again, but why? Pain gnawed me to the bone, and what remained? A stone heart. A skin to shed. I had failed at who I was before, but I was a snake woman now, and just learning what that meant. Did I hold endless skins, endless selves, within me?

Must I prepare to live again? This time, without Medusa, without my polestar?

Disoriented, in disequilibrium, and destroyed, with my remaining sister and an empty shell, I began.

THIRTY-FIRST EPISODE

EURYALE

After they burned her,
she did not long for heat.
But neither did she mind the flames.

—Erastus of Athens, "Her Dark Love"

WHEN MEDUSA DIED, Euryale lost both her sisters.

While Stheno mourned and avenged, Euryale made herself scarce. She doubted Stheno wanted to see her, and Euryale was afraid. She had eaten the berry, after all. The travesty occurred on her watch. Would Stheno come for her head, too?

And Euryale could never say it aloud, was sometimes even scared to think it, but Medusa had wanted to die. Euryale remembered the threats. Medusa hadn't wanted those babies, the snakes or the wings. Had Medusa wished for this ending?

It was a dark thought.

And even darker was this one, which came in her most piteous moments: how unfair it was to be left behind. Euryale must make a life with Medusa's curse, in Medusa's exile. Another slight upon an eternity of amassed slights.

So Euryale walked. Endlessly. Memorizing and cataloging the trails of Sarpedon. In her explorations, Euryale uncovered a hidden cove. She first saw it through the brush above: a small inlet, a half circle of sand and shallow waters, protected from prevailing winds by tall cliffs. There was no path down and she could not fly, but she needed to see it, to claim it as hers. She descended by hand and foot, using her claws to gain purchase on the impacted dirt and stone. It was precipitous work, but worth it, for here was a beach not haunted by death, a space unassociated with either of her sisters.

And it felt, unmistakably, magical.

During Stheno's dark days, Euryale visited her cove often—especially after she confiscated rope from their shared stores and installed it at the cliff's edge. She climbed down to think; she climbed down to swim. As always, in the water, Euryale felt understood. She was a part of something immortal, yet also singular—a creature that belonged in the sea but happily traveled alone. An octopus, a sea turtle, a shark.

And time moved differently here in her cove. Often, she fell asleep in the sand, awakening only when the morning tide brushed against her toes. One day, the sea brought her the turtle shell and with it, an opportunity.

After Stheno accepted her offering, Euryale returned to the hut but kept a safe distance. The sisters did not acknowledge Medusa, though her ever-present spirit lingered, nor did they reminisce on the past. For if they spoke of blame and guilt, their tenuous trust in each other would surely rupture. Euryale was careful not to touch any of Medusa's things. When she accidentally stepped on Medusa's blanket, Stheno ululated with such sorrow: Euryale did not make such a mistake again.

They bided their time with the prosaic. Stheno tinkered with her lyre, cooked meals and cleaned, rebuilt their home, and cultivated a garden. Euryale dried kelp and treated her skin, the sole part of her that remained beautiful. Alone in her cove, Euryale touched herself and marveled at her own softness, her smoothness.

When he appeared one night in her sheltered bay, he was a surprise she should have expected. It was the paradox he operated within her life, shock and expectation, awe and disappointment.

Desire and disgust.

Poseidon stood before her, blocking the view to the sea with his billowing cloak.

"You do not greet me?"

"Great Lord of the Sea," Euryale gibed, holding up her arms, "our humble island is not worthy of such an illustrious presence. Bow, discarded clams and fish bones. Swoon, seaweed. Greet your king!"

He chuckled, amused. "Your tongue has become even more venomous."

"I can drip honey, but not for you."

"For whom, then?"

"Men who do not desire my sisters. Men who do not ruin my life."

"That was Athena, Golden Eyes, not me."

He sat beside her, but she kept rigid, not bending into him the way she once did. Too much separated them now—his timeless form and her new body, the ghost of Medusa, taken and torn on the altar.

"I watched you . . ." she began, and it was torture to speak of it aloud. "With my sister."

Poseidon shrugged. "Your sister is not you. Could never be."

"And now she is dead."

He whispered into her ear, his mouth grazing her neck: "I made her a legend."

Euryale recoiled. "You made her a villain."

"Only because I listened to you! When you told me of her sins with Athena, you wanted me to punish them both."

No, that wasn't right. Euryale had never wanted to hurt Medusa. She had only wanted advice, a confidant. A friend.

"You're manipulating my words," she protested, shifting farther away. "You are twisting what happened."

"I am a god, Golden Eyes. Do not expect an apology."

"And I am beast born, but I was beautiful. Do not expect any clemency." Euryale crossed her arms over her chest, closing herself off to him.

"*Was* beautiful?" Poseidon's eyes outlined her body, still curved by womanhood, lingering in spots that once warmed at his attention. "Then you cannot see how attractive you are to me, like this."

Damn him, damn him forever, for Euryale's mind flashed back to Mount Olympus, to the cliffs of Sounion, to the carnal memories of aching heat, lust and desire, the forbidden and unattainable.

And yet it was all wrong.

She was cursed, her sister was dead, and he bore responsibility for both.

"The time for us has passed."

Poseidon's eyes flashed like stormy skies. "Then explain to me, why do we still find each other?"

"That's hardly the truth, Lord. You found me."

"You wanted me to."

"I did, once," she relented. "But I do not love you anymore."

Euryale saw his jaw pulse once, then twice, as he fought for control of his emotions. And she finally understood him.

It was an amazing revelation, made almost hilarious by the stream of nights she spent cramped in a false wall, the endless hours perfecting Hasina and Annipe's beauty techniques. All she had ever needed to win Poseidon's heart was to hate him.

Euryale could not stop the laughter rolling up from deep within her, and she tossed her head back, lips parted in a dissolute smile.

Poseidon gaped. "You mock me."

Euryale covered her mouth with her hand. She shook her head. "I mock myself."

But he did not understand. Could never.

"I did not journey here to play the fool."

"Then leave, Lord of the Sea. Or kiss me. It hardly matters, either way."

He was speechless and shot angrily to his feet. She stood, too, and placed her palm against his bare chest. She stroked her thumb back and forth against his collarbone and watched the tension in his face begin to ease.

"I carry no sword, Golden Eyes. I wear no shield. I did not come to battle with you."

Shield.

Euryale drew in a sharp breath. She whirled from Poseidon and began pacing, for an idea had entered her mind, full-fledged and wholly wicked. She walked through the plan, quickly and frantically, seeing all the ways it could go wrong—the danger, the disgrace.

But if it went right? If she saw it through to the end?

Euryale felt reckless. Euryale felt it was worth the chance.

Poseidon watched her like she had gone insane, and considering what she was about to do, perhaps she was.

She strode back toward Poseidon, wrapped a hand around his neck, and pulled his mouth down to hers. She let him taste her, let him believe in her desperation, then broke away. His lips, slightly swollen, grinned.

"Change my mind about you," Euryale demanded.

"I will. Right now." And he grabbed her around the waist.

"No." She thrust his hands from her hips. "Not like that. Not yet. Get a message to Semele. Tell her I must speak with her."

"Who is Semele?"

Of course he had already forgotten. Another insignificant trophy on his brother's wall.

"The goddess Thyone. On Olympus."

Poseidon's hands flexed and Euryale held her breath. This was the first gamble. He could force her into the sand right now, and she would be powerless to stop him.

But she did not think he would.

"I am a god, Golden Eyes. Do not expect me to obey."

Semele arrived the next day.

THIRTY-SECOND EPISODE

STHENO

Pour out your cup of amber gold
and take up your sword.
We shall toast when this is done.

—Erastus of Athens, "Ode to Monsters"

EURYALE FAILED TO warn me that she had summoned a goddess, so when an immortal walked into our homestead unannounced, I leapt for my sharpest rock.

"No!" shouted my sister, grabbing my wrist. "Don't you recognize her?"

I looked again at the woman—her alabaster skin and dark lashes, the ebony curls of her hair—and stepped backward, hand on my chest.

Our visitor smirked. "I am shocked to see you as well, Stheno."

"Semele!" I embraced her as Medusa would have, kissed her cheek. Tears pricked the backs of my eyes, and I was confused by myself. It felt so good to see her, yet it hurt me, too.

"I am called Thyone now. Hera renamed me." Semele rolled her eyes, then grinned. "I brought wine."

I brought forth cups, and we settled outside at the table I built from fallen trees. Semele realized my miscalculation at the same time as me.

I had grabbed four cups.

"You know she is dead?" Euryale asked. With a somber nod,

Semele took the last cup from my hand, filled it with wine, and set it reverently before the empty space.

"Precious girl, you are missed."

I did not yet know why Semele was here, but if she came to talk about Medusa, she could leave. This was my island, after all. Not an open symposium. I changed the subject.

"We have heard of your son and your miraculous rescue. Tell us, how is life on Olympus?"

Semele somehow managed to both curl her lip and take a long sip of her drink. "It is nothing like Thebes."

"Naturally," responded Euryale. "Olympus is incomparable!"

Semele snorted. "At home, I was famous. I was celebrated. I had Desma, my parents." She laughed. "Even quail! I had everything. And then I died."

I remembered the thunderclap and the lightning, the wreck of her human body. She had experienced violent death—by her own lover—and descended to the grim and gloomy land of the dead, to the gray fields of asphodel and the bodiless departed. Then a full-grown stranger claiming to be her son dragged her to the Olympians' palace, where her murderers abided, blameless and royal.

Semele glowed with her gifted divinity, but trauma that glitters is still trauma.

"Nobody knows who I am. Hera made sure of that. I have Dionysus and I have wine." She raised her cup and winked, a failed attempt at flippancy. "Yet somehow you two found me."

I shot Euryale a quizzical look, but she was too focused on Semele to notice—alight with a strange energy and leaning forward on her elbows. I wondered at the enigma she continued to be. Would I ever know Euryale completely?

"I called for you," began Euryale. "Though I do not know Thyone, I knew Semele. She sponsored the best parties and made the most mischief. Is Thyone the same?"

Semele matched Euryale's posture, angling toward her at the perfect conspiratorial angle.

"Then, now, and forever."

Euryale beamed, and when she delivered her deliciously profane proposal, I decided that if these were the kinds of secrets my sister kept, I was more than willing to live in mystery.

WAITING FOR SEMELE'S return was excruciating. Euryale kept the final part of her plan to herself, and I allowed it, because the suspense gave me something to await. I felt hope spread through myself like an awakening.

I watched her labor on a tool with much fascination, for I'd never seen her work at anything before. She had a stick, whittled finely to the circumference of a finger, and she tied feathers plucked from her own wings to its tip. A brush of some sort? Even odder, she took tiny leftover bones from our meals and burned them, collecting the ash in a clay jar.

"What are you doing, Euryale?" I could not help but ask.

She gave me a sideways grin. "I'm practicing."

And some evenings we would sit together on the beach, watching for Semele. I practiced my lyre while Euryale lay beside me, lost in thought. Sometimes she asked me little harmless inquiries about music, which I answered to the best of my ability.

"But what about music with no words?"

"I argued with Ligeia over this," I admitted to her. "I thought I couldn't enjoy music if I didn't know what it meant."

Euryale lay on her side while we talked, and she propped herself up on an elbow. "And now what do you think?"

I tried not to look too flattered that she sought my opinion. "Maybe art is more memorable when its meaning is obscured," I said carefully. "If the artist reveals all their mysteries, who will care tomorrow?"

She nodded, then turned her head back toward the sea. "Perhaps life is like that, too."

When Semele arrived on the shore carrying a bulky item wrapped in a blanket, Euryale and I openly ran to meet her. Semele, too, seemed jumpy and excited.

"The bacchanal continues," she told us. "My son presides, keeping all the cups full, but I must return soon. She will notice it is missing."

Semele threw off the blanket, and there, on the beach of Sarpedon once more, was Athena's aegis. I tried not to think of it crashing to the temple floor or how Perseus's face reflected in its polished shine. I refused to touch it, wouldn't even stand too close to its ruinous presence, but Euryale shared none of my misgivings. She propped the shield against a rock and opened a pouch at her side, removing her handcrafted tool and a blade.

"What will you do to it?" posed Semele, in a mixture of thrill and fear.

My sister did not respond, and when she used the blade to slash a deep cut into her left palm, I winced, and Semele inhaled sharply. Euryale dipped the feathered end of her tool into the wound, coating it in her blood, then applied it to the ageless silver.

It *was* a brush, and she was painting.

Semele gaped. "You are vandalizing Athena and Zeus's aegis?!" She clapped her hands together. "Oh, Euryale, Desma was right. You are nasty!"

"With an immortal maiden's blood," Euryale explained as she added strokes to her design. "It is a sacred sacrifice; it will never fade."

"But you do not know how to write!" I protested.

Euryale smiled to herself while she worked. "I can still leave a message."

I stood back and let her work. Semele wandered the beach, impatiently extemporizing into her hand, signaling to Euryale that her time with the stolen aegis was limited. I, however, stood still, mesmerized by my sister's creation, for it did not take me long to comprehend whose image she painted.

The arching brows over eyes that lifted at the outer corners. The angular chin and full cheeks, rosebud lips, snakes in every direction.

"Do you remember, Stheno?" Euryale murmured. "Athena said, 'And now I can hardly bear to look at you'?"

Little beauty, you were my favorite of all.

"I remember every word."

Athena would learn to bear it, or she would suffer. Oh, Euryale, how I underestimated you! And I let a fierce love for my middle sister fill my heart.

I knelt beside Euryale and used her wet blade to slash my own hand. I held it up to her. "Take mine, too."

My sister nodded. She dipped her paintbrush gently into my palm and added my blood to Medusa's mouth.

"It is her very likeness," breathed Semele, coming up behind me. "Except the anger. I never knew her like that."

"The rage is for us."

Euryale finished and sat back on her heels, staring at her work. She crossed her arms, satisfied by what she had created. Medusa's perfect face rendered in her sisters' blood. I could think of no more powerful symbol. I tore a strip from my own dress to bind Euryale's hand.

"I wish I could see Athena's reaction."

"She cannot toss it away," added Semele in some amazement. "It belongs to her father, and it is too valuable."

"Will you be blamed?" I worried.

Semele snorted. "Nobody considers me, remember? My name won't even be mentioned." She draped the shield in her blanket and lifted the boon to her chest. "Perhaps I will return," Semele said, but I knew it for a good-intentioned lie. We all did. We were not the same girls who partied together in Thebes, and I could not comprehend how the new versions of ourselves could coexist with the old. Medusa had brought us together once before, and she had again, with unfinished business.

Now, it was finished.

Semele began to walk away, but a thought stopped her, and she turned back. Her face was drawn. "I should have never let her wear it."

"Wear what?" I frowned.

"The Necklace of Harmonia. It was cursed."

"How do you know?" pressed Euryale.

Semele's face changed—just for a moment—losing its ethereal glow. "They are all gone, my family, and our city has never been the same. That necklace doomed the House of Cadmus."

"Polydorus, too?"

"He died young, nobody can tell me how. Or why." Semele's eyes were tired. I didn't know that could happen to a goddess. "I never should have let her wear it. I'm sorry."

Her admission—and apology—confused me. Did Semele blame herself for Medusa's death? And then I realized how many of our souls hold regrets, how many of us feel responsible for another's evil and seek absolution wherever we can find it.

But this guilt belonged to Medusa's sisters, not the Theban princess.

"Medusa loved you," I said. "Let that be your memory of her. It is what she would want."

Semele dipped her head, and maybe I saw a tear on her cheek, or maybe it was just the shimmering magic of her divine nature as it returned, and she transported away.

I released a deep sigh. "Let us go home, Euryale. I will cook you something sweet."

But Euryale did not follow. "Forgive me, Stheno," she begged, avoiding my gaze and staring at the sea. "There is something else I must do tonight."

Her words chilled me to my core, but I chided myself for even momentarily doubting her. After her brilliant act of revenge on Athena, I could trust my sister. And her loyalty, to me, to Medusa.

Besides, even my worst suspicions paled in comparison with what she was about to do.

THIRTY-THIRD EPISODE

EURYALE

Lie to me, lay with me.
Undo me, renew me.

—*Erastus of Athens, "Her Dark Love"*

HE CAME TO claim her the night of the aegis, as Euryale suspected he would. Arriving in the moonlit fog like a romantic champion and not the devil he was.

"Have I changed your mind?" he demanded.

No.

"How is Athena?"

Poseidon grinned. "When I left the party, she was beside herself. Tossing wine and throwing spears, threatening everyone. She tried to scrub her shield, but for all her efforts, the paint clung harder, etching itself into the metal. It was great magic."

Euryale could not stop the smug smile that broke her lips.

"She blamed me, of course. 'You bait me, Uncle!'" And Poseidon did a surprisingly good imitation of her cool voice. "'I have no hand for art,' I insisted. 'And why would such a face bother you, Niece? Is there something you wish to reveal?'" He chuckled. "Now she is frantic, spinning a narrative that better suits her purposes."

Euryale's heart glowed with fiery vengeance. "Let her try."

"You are quite vicious, Golden Eyes."

"You say it like a compliment."

"Isn't it?"

"Tonight it is, perhaps."

And when she stood, Poseidon's eyes widened, for she was naked.

"Where is your dress?"

"I did not think I would need it."

Fully nude yet fully concealed. This was her mask, and he craved it.

And then he was upon her. Poseidon pulled Euryale into him, holding her tightly, as he kissed her mouth, her face, her neck. There was no tease to his actions, no hesitation. He wanted her—badly—and she had wanted this moment. He brought them down to the sand, and Euryale fell backward, welcoming his force but flinching as her wings bore into her back. She rolled Poseidon over, climbed atop him, and took the sea god in her way. He moaned.

It hurt less than she expected, but perhaps her tolerance for pain had shifted. Yes, there was blood on him, in the sand, but it was no sign of sacrifice. It was evidence of battle, the war she had won. Because afterward, Poseidon lay against her chest with his eyes closed.

"If only I had met you before Amphitrite."

She laughed. "You and I? Husband and wife?"

Oh, it had been a dream of hers once, too, of course, but she saw it now for the silly fantasy it was. They were wrong together, wrong for each other. If, in another life, she had married him, Euryale would've just been another Hera.

"We are drawn to each other, Golden Eyes. Admit it."

She brushed her fingers through his blue-black hair yet did not respond. He was selfish and cruel, full of tiny evils, but she could be, too. And there was no denying the pulsating heat of their bodies together, the throbbing she felt in her own marrow and knew he felt, too. Like calling to like, bodies responding in alchemical attraction.

"No other man can look upon you, can see you like I can."

"No *mortal* man."

"I know you," he insisted.

She stroked her thumb along his eyebrow, then turned her hand over, running the back of her loosely curled fingers down his cheek. "Once," she conceded. "Maybe."

"I have known you since I first saw you at Epimetheus's wedding, wild and defiant."

But Poseidon had not really seen Euryale at Epimetheus's wedding, for that girl craved belonging—never more so than at Mount Olympus, surrounded by opulence, hoping an affected attitude would distract from her bare feet.

Poseidon awaited her response, resting his chin upon her breast.

She had evolved, but he never would, and in this understanding lay power. Awareness. She held it tight while letting other things go. Euryale remembered the orange and purple crabs in Ceto's caves who outgrew their shells.

But tonight, for one last time, she would nestle here. It was not love; there was no name for this. She shifted beneath him, opened her legs.

"If you know me so well, show me."

And as he dove into her again, the fog wrapped the cove, covering the lovers in the act of their sin.

After he left, Euryale wept—not for grief, but neither for happiness. She cried with blessed release. From exhaustion. Deliverance. For her lost sister and their final conversation. She knew instantly that her womb had filled with a new beginning, and she rubbed the palm of her hand against her belly, already believing she could feel her son's kicks.

Because of course it would be a boy. She had always known.

She had seen him in the stars. And he would be worth it all.

THERE WERE ANY number of ways Euryale could tell Stheno of her pregnancy, but she opted against flattery or gifts, half-truths or outright lies.

One day Euryale simply announced, "I am with child."

Stheno went pale. "How?" she stammered.

Euryale smirked. "The usual way, sister."

"But . . . *who*?"

When Euryale did not respond, Stheno understood.

"After he . . . ?"

"Yes."

"Did he force you?"

Euryale shook her head.

"He came here? To our island?"

"Yes."

Stheno clutched her chest. "I can't breathe. I don't . . ." And then she slapped Euryale so hard across the cheek that Euryale's head spun, and her face hummed. Stheno had never hit her before. Not once—not as children, never even by accident. Euryale felt the bright vivid sting where Stheno's brass claws scraped away skin, and her golden snake rolled and hissed, but Euryale remained impassive.

Stheno wanted a fight, but Euryale would stubbornly refuse. Defiance, after all, comes in many forms.

"Say something, Euryale," exploded Stheno. "Tell me you're sorry."

"No."

"You should be begging my forgiveness."

"I won't."

"Just when I thought you had changed, you remind me how wretched you truly are."

"This is what I wanted."

"Then you are no sister of mine," she growled.

"I am happy, Stheno."

Stheno lifted her hand to slap Euryale again, and Euryale turned her face.

"Even the pain, at least. Hit me on this side."

Stheno brought her arm back down, looking at Euryale with such loathing, Euryale wondered if there had ever been any genuine affection between the two of them.

"I will never speak to you again."

Euryale barely listened. She held her palms below her navel, and she spoke down through her neck and chest, directly into her womb: *Ignore her, little baby. You are wanted. You are mine.*

Stheno collected her belongings. Before leaving their homestead, she picked up the cradle she had been constructing for Medusa and hurled it into the firepit. Euryale watched the destruction dispassionately. She would ignore this storm. She could weather anything.

And the sisters entered yet another era of silence. Euryale savored this time with her body; she welcomed the weight on her hips, the heavy breasts and bulge to her shadow. And she enjoyed communicating with the child inside her. *Live and breathe,* she cooed. *Grow strong and live. Please, my dear one, live.*

Moons passed, waxing and waning, and Euryale managed their home in Stheno's stead. She added to their stores and weeded the garden, and sometimes she made pictures. Drawing not with her blood, but the paints she created by harvesting ingredients and experimenting. She ground and mixed shellfish and tree resin, stem and petal, and with those colors she drew on the wood-paneled walls. Harmless, unassociated images for her baby: a goat, a bear, a lemon tree, a cloud.

A midnight tempest delivered another stocked boat to their beach, this one filled to the brim with swaddling clothes and a luxurious cradle trimmed in gold. Spoils befitting a woman of the highest class: perfumes, sandals, bracelets of jade, and exotic spices. A giant pearl on a golden necklace.

Euryale had always suspected, but now their benefactor's identity was without question. She was not alone in this discovery.

Stheno watched her unload the provisions, scowling from the top of a bluff.

"You called Medusa a slut once," called down Stheno, "but she did not barter her body for wealth."

"I learned from the best whores in Athens, Sister!" shot back Euryale, almost gaily.

For though Mistress Charmion would never approve of Poseidon, she and her girls would gladly accept such a bounty. During their night together, Euryale had not recalled a single move she learned at the little house, but she did retain the greatest lesson of all: give only your body, never your heart.

"All those presents are tarnished with blood."

Euryale set down the crib, which she struggled to carry over her enlarged belly. "Oh, Stheno. I am tainted, too. Are your hands so clean?"

Stheno dropped her gaze then and flew away.

Live and breathe, Euryale repeated, from her mind to her womb. *You are wanted. You are mine.*

Her baby kicked.

"EURYALE. EURYALE! WAKE up!"

But Euryale covered her ears with her hands, groaning as Stheno pried them loose. Her sister did not understand how it felt to foster a life, how she craved sleep with all of her being.

"Euryale, listen."

"Go away."

"Euryale!"

"What?"

"This is important." Stheno's snakes spiraled above her head in the moonlight. They, too, hummed with intensity. "If the baby is male and born without a caul, we will kill him. How do we live together if it is a mortal boy?"

Oh.

Euryale rose to her elbows on their shared pallet. "I don't know."

Was this the way of all sisters? That in the midst of a feud, after a hundred-day impasse, they could pick up again so normally? Had the urgency of the threat superseded Stheno's anger? Or had she momentarily forgotten Euryale's latest betrayal?

Euryale held her sister's gaze. "I didn't think you wanted my child to live."

Stheno's lips tightened into a straight line. "It is innocent of the crime of its conception."

Echoes of the past.

"He might be a horse," admitted Euryale, "or a giant, like Medusa's children. He could have a fish tail. But he is a man, I feel it, I know."

"Then I will find a way."

Stheno may hate her, but she would always offer protection—she knew no other way to exist. And so her sister departed Sarpedon the next morning. Euryale followed the flapping wings as they carried Stheno away, through the sky, to islands Euryale had never seen. There were plenty of questions she could have asked herself: How will Stheno "find a way"? What does that mean? And what if she fails?

How had they been so remiss when Medusa was pregnant? This potential problem hadn't occurred to any of them. Perhaps the terms of their curse were still too fresh. Or perhaps they suspected that Medusa would bear something otherworldly. Euryale barely recalled the creatures' birth. They must have had cauls, which they tore open themselves as they pushed through Medusa's neck.

She shuddered and chided herself. These anxieties might jeopardize her baby. Her delivery, her child, would be different.

Grow strong, she reminded him.

Many days passed, but Euryale did not worry for her capable sister and sure enough, when Stheno finally returned, she wore an accomplished look and carried armloads of cloth.

"It is the snakes that create the stone. If we cover our heads, your baby will live."

Euryale did not ask how many men died for Stheno to uncover this truth. And she could not be bothered. She would willingly forfeit islands of humans to keep her future child from harm, just like any good monster mother.

The sisters fashioned headscarves and practiced wearing them, mostly because the snakes objected and needed to become accustomed.

Which they eventually did, as all living beings must to survive.

When Euryale's labor pains commenced, Stheno's brown face

blanched. Euryale understood: Medusa's agony had been traumatic, for all of them. However, Euryale was committed to a different experience. She refused to birth her son into chaos—no errant swords or misplaced cords, no antagonists, no conflict. He could make his story later, but not today. He would know peace first.

"I am not scared," she assured her sister as she braved the clenching pains, the building tension, the insistent demands of a body in turmoil. She ground her teeth, steadied her mind.

But, oh! How it hurt!

Much more than she anticipated, with an intensity that stole her ability to think or remember who she was. Like being stabbed repeatedly through the gut. A murder recommitted with unending, increasing frequency. The snake writhed above her, uncomfortable and alarmed.

Her body was sturdy after years spent traversing rough terrain. Euryale walked through her contractions, slapping away Stheno's hand. She listened to her body—not her sister—and it told her to squat. When it was time to push, she screamed, straining against the pressure, certain some part of her was forever broken, torn asunder, but focusing her breath on five words:

It.

Should.

Have.

Been.

You.

It should have been you it should have been you itshouldhavebeenyou.

Bones cracked, Euryale opened, and life slid out on a burst of water. Another being in this mad, wondrous world. Stheno wept. Her bloody hands cut Euryale's wailing child free with the rock blade she no longer kept buried.

"A boy, Euryale."

An unnecessary announcement, but hearing it spoken aloud made it real.

Stheno wiped the baby down and wrapped him in a blanket.

Looking at him made her sister's face go fluid and soft, like a lagoon after a squall, and Stheno passed him to his mother like a sacred benefaction. A ritual act in this ceremony of reconciliation between sisters.

"No wings or tails, gills or scales. Just like us, Euryale. Beautiful. But with hair so black it is nearly blue."

Hair. Real hair. Euryale sighed and ran one fingertip over its matted strands. Would she ever tire of its feel? Two perfect lips. Dozens of tiny eyelashes. The smell of him and her and *them* that rose from the back of his head. A most blessed blessing.

"En caul?" she asked in a misty murmur.

Stheno hesitated, and then: "No."

Another mortal, another imperfect triangle. Euryale had lived long enough to understand how life was no more than a series of repeating patterns, some pleasant and some not. But she would not be disheartened, not when her child was more than she ever thought she would get, not when she was so close to fulfilling her promise to him: a peaceful beginning.

Euryale maneuvered the baby against her chest, and when his little mouth found her nipple so effortlessly, Euryale made an internal vow: *I will be content with every moment.*

"My son, my baby, my boy."

Mine.

Stheno smiled through her tears. "What will you call him?"

"Orion."

Heaven's light. A word from her dreams, in a language spoken long before this one.

"Welcome home, Orion."

THIRTY-FOURTH EPISODE

STHENO

Not renown or riches,
nor retribution either.
Beg only happiness of heaven.

—Erastus of Athens, "The Symposium"

AFTER ORION'S BIRTH, another boat appeared, this one full of boys' clothing and wooden toys. Bows and arrows. A handsome sword. A bevy of slaughtered goats—a tribute to the new son.

I accepted the offerings, though I banished any thought of their provider.

Before Orion, neither Euryale nor I had held an infant, and in our isolation, we had no reference or guidance. What experience did I have with babies? Little children? Even less. Nothing about handling this nascent life felt natural to me. *How do I carry him? What is that sound? Are his fingernails too long? Can he breathe? Is that a rash or a plague?* I worried for my nephew with a vigor I hadn't known in years. He awoke parts of me I missed—I laughed again, smiled until my face hurt—but he also rattled that dormant yet cataclysmic fear for my family.

The foreboding joy of loving someone you know you will lose. Another mortal for me to fail.

I checked on him while he slept, holding a finger before his tiny face until I felt his warm exhalation. I kept him tightly wrapped in blankets, afraid each time the weather changed. I stressed when he drank too much water—or too little—if he napped on his stomach, wandered too close to the fire . . .

In truth, I was exhausted by him—not because he was badly behaved, but because of his boundless energy. Always grunting and laughing, cooing or squirming, throwing himself from our arms, putting rocks and shells into his mouth. Falling forward on his face, backward on his head. Covering that sweet skin in contusions and cuts.

How was I to keep him alive if he wouldn't remain still?

Euryale rolled her eyes at my neuroses. For it seemed that as I grew increasingly anxious, she only became more composed. She whispered to him, rocked him in her arms when he fought sleep, kissed away his teardrops when he cried for no reason. Where did she find this endless reserve of patience? Euryale, as a mother, was unflappable.

She brought Orion into the ocean when he was only a few weeks old, despite my objection. He could swim like a seal within weeks, kicking his fat little legs and blowing out bubbles.

"He is too young," I admonished her. "He will swallow the seawater. Fall under the waves and be pulled by tides. Get eaten!"

"He will not," she returned, combing out his dark, wet curls with her fingers. "Consider his parents."

But that I could never do. To love my nephew—and I did, wholeheartedly—I had to pretend he was immaculately conceived, or some changeling we found in the forest. Even when Orion began to walk on water, our boy must remain a fatherless miracle.

Orion asked endless questions and begged for stories. At first, I stumbled along with little command of pacing or diction, but then I pictured Medusa in my place. How would she entertain our nephew? I added pauses, raised my eyebrows, and played with my voice. My storytelling would never be celebrated, but it certainly improved. I told Orion of three sisters who saw humans grow from clay, about a

Sphinx who enjoyed riddles, and of a dragon who liked honey cakes. Happy stories.

I might have told him about Pandora's vase or Hera, how Zeus betrayed Metis and Poseidon tricked Amphitrite, but I loved him too much and couldn't bear it. Innocence is sweet but insubstantial; why dilute his so soon?

One time, as I tickled his belly, our playful toddler tugged at my shroud. Immediately, I flipped his little body over and hit his backside three times as sharply as I slapped his mother years before. Orion wailed, from shock and pain, but also at the breach in trust. His wet eyes beheld me, his beloved aunt, with disbelief. I longed to wipe away those salty tears, to kiss his clammy skin and remind him how precious he would always be to me. Instead, I held firm.

"No, Orion," I scolded, trembling. "No. You never touch the shrouds. Not mine, not Mama's. If you do it again, I will hit you even harder. Do you understand?"

He mumbled, sniffled, wiped his nose. I repeated myself.

"Yes," he said, finally accepting my stern command.

"Good."

Nearby, Euryale watched in her own permanent headscarf, hands on her hips. I prepared myself for her disapproval and outrage: *How dare you strike my child? Wait until I tell his father!* But she met my gaze with a curt nod.

She understood. I would do the hard things to keep him safe. For we were a trio again—of sorts—and my responsibilities remained.

Far too soon Orion's toddles transformed into sprints, and he raced into little boyhood. No longer could we appease him with nonsense songs, with drawing stick pictures in the surf. He wanted stimulation, variety. Orion befriended trees, named rocks and carried them about for company. He tried training birds to rest upon his shoulder, then cried when they inevitably flew away.

"He needs a brother," Euryale decided, monitoring her son's restless energy with a frown.

I returned with a hard look. "Do not call for him."

Euryale shrugged a shoulder. "Then I leave it to you. Otherwise, I will do what I must."

My sister knew precisely which threats would spur me to action. I took flight that very afternoon, not entirely sure what I sought, but confident I would not find it on Sarpedon. I homed in upon a small island, a spit of earth birthed by volcano, attracted by its triangular shape. I landed past the shores and well into the verdant mountains, thick with pine, chestnut, and even some oak. There, I stalked the sounds and scents of humanity. Deep in this sylvan setting, I observed a pack of carousing boys, wrestling and whooping, hitting each other with sticks and fists, racing and falling, constantly—unnecessarily.

I wrinkled my nose at their antics. *Our Orion is another breed,* I thought proudly. Defter of hand and foot, composed, and far more comely.

Still, they exuded the joy and camaraderie Orion lacked. I considered abducting one of the smaller ones, then recoiled at my own savagery. Would I truly pluck some child from the woods like a hawk to a hare?

Besides, the boy would tell Orion of my wrongdoing, and Orion would hurt.

So I traveled farther inland, to the solitary streams and ranges, where the hot springs abounded and outsiders thrived. For Orion, with a family as ill-fated as ours, could never belong to a cadre. How did the human recluses maintain sanity, find happiness? I tracked these mortals past rich fruit orchards and petrified trees, following footprints and traces of fire, even feces.

At last, I spotted a boar-hunting man, whose auburn hair reminded me of Thales—though of an age Thales never achieved. The man whistled toward a companion beyond my line of sight. I folded my wings into my back and hid behind a tree trunk as a large breed of dog bounded from the brush.

It was a beast of a size and strength for battle: deep chested, with a thick, muscular neck covered in loose folds of skin, and a colossal head. I watched its dark brown eyes flash with ecstatic acknowledgment when it spotted its master, the gentle way it nuzzled into the man's thigh as the man ran a hand through its dense fur.

What an obvious answer! I wondered that I had not considered it earlier. A dog would worship my sister's son, would never betray him, lie to him, or leave him. A dog like this one could stomach difficult terrain and handle an adolescent's energy.

And an animal would be immune to our curse.

The hunter set off, but I purposefully cracked a twig below my foot. The dog whirled on me, instantly hostile, growling and lowering its head into its sloping shoulders. Bracing itself to protect its territory and guard what belonged to him.

I smiled. Orion deserved a companion who would brave the wolves for him.

I wished I could make off with this dog, but even Stheno the murderous hag wouldn't dare separate a bonded pair. And practically speaking, the creature was just too enormous. It took many more days and nights of searching and scouting, but at a secluded homestead, I found a litter of puppies. I waited among the trees, biding my time until nightfall, then approached the bitch while her humans slept. I bound my snakes under my shroud, and they seemed to understand my order: *Be still. This is important.*

I brought the mother dog a slab of stolen lamb meat—a shoddy payment, I know, for a beloved young one, but I hoped its message offered some solace. *I will take your offspring, but I do not take this transgression lightly. I will care for them.*

She growled at my approach, so I hummed one of Ligeia's tunes. Slowly, surely, her guttural alarm began to decrescendo. When it reached a light vibrato, I took a seat, assembling myself cross-legged a few steps away, never wavering in my song. Eventually, she accepted my submission and ignored me. The puppies harbored none of their mother's reservations and bounced upon me with their wet, effusive ministrations, all tail whips and teeth, elastic muscles and ungainly moves.

I settled upon a docile male who had taken right to my lap. He was hefty but sweet-tempered and closed his eyes when I petted his silky head. But then a runty red female bounded forward, nipping at her brother until he roused and moved aside.

She assumed his position and looked up at me expectantly.

"Tenacious one," I murmured, placing a clawed fingertip on her moist pebble of a nose. "You will do."

Even a dog must be tough to survive Sarpedon.

I flew the pup home in a sling of fabric across my chest, and the sound of my beating wings with the whir of wind lulled her into the deep sleep of youth. We arrived home in the morning. Euryale and her son collected shells on the beach. I joined them on the shore, the dog still hidden.

"Where did you go, Aunt?" asked Orion, hands on his hips, studying the pulsating sack with cautious suspicion. I unwrapped the dog and lowered her into the sand, where she tumbled away from my warmth with a yawn that seemed to stretch through her whole body. She blinked, righted herself, and shook back to life so thoroughly that her back legs left the ground.

"I brought a friend."

Orion's eyes widened. "For me?"

I nodded, but then Orion edged backward, returning to his mother and clutching at her leg, overcome with shyness.

"Watch me," I said, and I showed him how to pet the dog. "She may nip at you, but she is young. You must be patient as you teach her."

He listened but would not move.

"Come, Orion," I urged. "She is yours."

He mumbled something into Euryale's dress, words he did not want me to catch.

"Speak louder," she chided, pulling him from her protection.

Orion stared at his bare feet, brushing them back and forth in the sand. "What if she doesn't want me?"

His question threw me. I made to answer with some sort of tease, to reassure him that a dog would love whoever brings food, but Euryale spoke first.

"I worried the same for you," she began, brushing the hair from his forehead. "When you were still in my belly. But I decided that even if you rejected me, I would never give up on you. I would love you until you tolerated me, until you trusted me. I would love you until you liked me. I would love you so unconditionally, every day, until my love became a part of who you were and we could never be truly separated."

She placed a hand under Orion's chin and tipped his head upward so that her golden eyes met his own.

"When you want something, Orion, you must be prepared to wait."

He took a deep breath, nodded, and then knelt in the sand. He put his hands on his knees, then flipped them over, palms upward, as if to say, *I hold no weapon. I am no enemy.* The puppy sniffed in his direction, made a few circles, and then raced into the surf. She repeated this neurotic process, over and over, but Orion did not call out or get up, he did not move his hands.

He waited.

At nightfall, she let him touch her without darting away, and by midnight, they had fallen asleep, curled together.

Come dawn, they were inseparable.

And Orion, who was our light from heaven, named the dog Sirius, for she was as red as the scorching sun.

She would remain by his side until the last day.

SOON ORION STOOD taller than me, an achievement he greeted with great mirth. He loved to rest his elbow upon my shoulder and laugh, to call me his "little aunt."

And he was handsome, more so than any earthborn boy had right to be. He hunted expertly, for it came to him as effortlessly as swimming, and I no longer had to set traps. But he tired of our simple prey. Sarpedon had some wild pigs, but no stags or lions, and Orion found the effortless killings of rabbit and fish almost unfair. As much as he cherished Sirius, a dog could never replace human intrigue, nor mitigate adolescent lust. Our boy hungered for more—more challenge, more stimulation, more danger.

Orion considered himself invincible, not because of his Olympian father, but because of two mothers who adored him too much.

After foraging one evening, I came to the homestead and found Euryale relaxing by the indoor hearth. Sirius snored happily at her side. Our home had also grown. With materials I stripped from the tribute boats, I built an additional room—even a serviceable door.

"Where is Orion?" I asked, setting down my gatherings and joining them.

"With his father."

I shuddered and felt my face twist in revulsion. Poseidon had visited Orion a handful of times, and in each instance, I exiled myself from Sarpedon until the winds and waters whispered of my immortal enemy's exit.

If he and Euryale interacted while I disappeared, I cannot say. I refused to ask. He was a quagmire where we lost our footing, so I avoided his presence and his name, and walked around his memory as best I could. Otherwise, I could not exist as Euryale's sister.

"And he did not take Sirius?"

"Apparently not," she responded dryly.

Her insouciance irritated me, for I worried each time Orion vanished. What stories did Poseidon spin, what spells did he weave? With what vile obscenities did he poison our good boy?

I selected a mushroom from my basket. "Do you ask him what they discuss when they are together?" I inspected its convex white cap, then took a nibble.

"No."

Her apathy wasn't bothersome, it was enraging.

"What if he tells him about Medusa?"

Euryale shrugged. "Orion already knows."

I spit the mushroom from my mouth, and it tumbled back into the dirt from which it came. Euryale did not flinch but maintained her steady scrutiny of the flames. Neither did Sirius stir.

"How?" I sputtered. "Why?"

"I caught Orion pleasuring himself years ago."

I am sure I blushed, for I burned with secondhand embarrassment.

"And I spoke to him of men and women." Euryale paused. "And men and men. And women and women, too."

"Euryale!"

She met my glower with one of her own. "What?"

"That is not what mothers do."

"It is not what our mother did. But she did nothing." Euryale bristled. "We were forced to learn by ourselves, and it was a hard lesson. I told my son everything, and I taught him how to handle his urges without hurting another."

"And he is aware that his father *hurt* our sister?" I borrowed her word, returning it with scorn.

"He is."

"And he accepts that knowledge? Of his father? Of us?"

"He accepts the truth no better or worse than the rest of us do."

All the years I spent protecting Orion, like a fool, for Euryale to fill his head with our horror. What else had she revealed? Did he know of all the men I turned to stone, of Medusa's children, whom I abandoned to the wild—tossed from our island like detritus? Of all my catastrophic, ugly failure?

"I will never understand you," I said. I was so angry with her.

"Because you never trust anyone besides yourself. Not me or Orion. Not Medusa."

I scoffed, dumbfounded, then stomped outside, marching inland and away from my sister, and finally settling upon a rock where I could think and breathe. I studied the colors of displaced dust as they hit the sun's final rays, floating—glorious—evanescent, and I sat with my feelings.

The truth.

I hated that Orion would associate Medusa with Poseidon or Athena and not with my curated memories: a hand upon a grieving king's cheek, feet moving in a fumbling but euphoric dance, a crown of fresh violets in sun-streaked hair.

I wanted control—of one sister's legacy and the other sister's son.

Impossible dreams, like a garden that has never known a weed or a fruit that won't go soft. Like a mortal that will not die.

Euryale was correct: I had trouble trusting. But she was wrong when she assumed I trusted myself.

I hadn't in a very long time.

I was old, set in my ways. Was it too late to start?

WHEN ORION RETURNED, he looked guilty, and I knew.

In a voice mild but convicted, he informed us of his decision to leave Sarpedon. "It is time, and my father agrees with me." He took each of our hands. "I cannot go without your blessing."

Euryale brought his hand to her lips, laying a kiss against his knuckles. "You've always had it."

"And you, Aunt?"

I glanced at Euryale and the lips she valiantly kept from quivering, and I wondered, Was she beside me again in that awful cavern, shouldering Ceto's laughter as we announced our plans for Thebes?

We weren't asking permission.

You three are due for a reckoning.

My mouth went dry. Orion awaited my response.

It was inevitable he would outgrow our island, but now? So soon? Hadn't he just been a boy, crying over scraped knees and playing pretend with his sticks and his dog?

"Orion," I answered him. "Go and be great."

He beamed and pulled us both into his arms.

I thought my act of goodwill could undo what my mother had done to me, but nothing in life is so tidy. Moments of heart cannot be measured, nor can the scales perfectly rebalance by counteraction. For instance, raising Orion could never compensate for denying Medusa's children. And yet I wanted to believe in reciprocity, in the possibility of restoring the damage I had caused.

I convinced myself that letting Orion go was brave—magnanimous, redemptive—but it was just another mistake.

THIRTY-FIFTH EPISODE

EURYALE

So many have tried to kill me.
I will not die tonight.

—Erastus of Athens, "Exile"

NO MOTHER, MORTAL or otherwise, can ever prepare for the day her child says goodbye.

On that day, when Orion left, Euryale sought sanctuary in her secret cove. She had never revealed its location to Stheno, and she stopped bringing Orion once he learned to walk and talk, once he was of an age that remembers. As much as she cherished her son, this pocket of Sarpedon belonged solely to her.

Settled upon the same shore where she conceived her boy, Euryale removed her shroud. For the first time in nearly two decades, she could do so without any apprehension. Orion was safe from her, at least. Her lemon-colored snake arched and stretched, reveling in its return to freedom, tongue flickering in the moist sea air. Euryale dropped the linen in the wet sand and let the tide tease it back and forth, until a wave curled and dragged it away for good.

Another farewell.

"Three sons," Euryale mused aloud, "born here, then gone."

The horse, the giant, and now her Orion.

They all could leave, but she could not.

Euryale did not torture herself with regrets. She could not keep

Orion small, nor could she hold him here forever. And there was nothing more she or Stheno could have done to prepare him for what awaited. Stheno spent days preparing food for the journey: dried meats and berries, nuts and herbs. Euryale's older sister reinforced the hems on his tunics, polished the wood of his bow, tested the integrity of his leather sandals.

Funny how Euryale still thought of Stheno as her older sister when she was her only sister.

And Euryale? She did as she always had. She disappeared and she walked. Returning to the trails she'd forged in their early days on the island. She would not watch him pack.

When he was ready to depart, Euryale fussed over the dog.

"My Sirius," she murmured, on her knees, stroking the mutt's muzzle and running her hands along Sirius's neck to the spots she liked most. "What will you do without me, sweet girl?" Euryale pressed a cheek into the dog's fur, imprinting herself, but then Orion pulled his mother to standing.

"Sirius will miss you," he insisted. "Very much."

Euryale held her head straight and proud. "Remind her of me, Orion. Do not let her forget this life we had here, all together."

"How could she? You loved her so unconditionally, Mama, every day. Your love is so much a part of her that you cannot truly be separated."

"She is a good dog."

"Yes."

And he kissed her cheek. Euryale closed her eyes and held her breath, held on to her boy. He still smelled like a baby, like sweaty curls and warm oil, the hint of milk.

Orion sailed away in the best of the boats his father had banked, the only one Stheno never repurposed. Stheno stood sentinel on the beach, waving to him until he passed beyond range, shouting unnecessary advice. But Euryale did not stay, could not. She left and did not look back, skirting their home and entering the wilds. Pacing until she ended here, in her cove.

She admired the smooth surfaces of the beach's boulders. Perhaps she would return here with her brushes, requisition some fresh paints. There would be time for that now.

It was evening, and she wondered if Poseidon would come. She hoped not. Euryale was too tired to play their game. All these years she avoided him, leaving him alone with Orion when he appeared on Sarpedon. They were not a family, and she would not pretend to be, especially not for Orion's sake. For seventeen years she had done nothing but mother, been nothing but a mother, and while it had been the apogee of her life, she was on her way back down, and she was exhausted.

On that night, the night Orion left, Euryale wanted to feel enveloped by water, to submerge and be crushed. She needed its weight against her empty chest, for only in the sea can nobody tell tears from salt.

So she glided into the kelp forest seeking serenity, past the stems and through the fronds that brushed against her skin, touching and tangling. Bypassing shades of brown until she happened upon green and startled.

Green seaweed. Green snakes. A pair of kind green eyes.

Orion had been a distraction. Now that he was gone, Euryale's mind returned to Medusa. Euryale rose to the surface, gasping.

No.

It was too much for one night.

She swam back to the shallows, trudging up and onto the beach. She needed to rest, to reset her mind. Curled in the sand, arguing against images of the past, Euryale fell asleep.

In her dream it was also night, and she swam, deep beneath the water. Only in her dreams could she swim like she used to, unencumbered by wings and a snake on her head. The strokes of her arms, the kick of her legs drew her forward, compelled by some unknown force. For what did she search?

Or maybe the better question was for whom? When Euryale opened her eyes, floating before her in green waves, billowing and beckoning, was Medusa.

Euryale jolted forward, frantic, arms outstretched, but her sister faded before the touch of her clawed fingertips. The sea swallowed Euryale's screams—*Wait! Wait!*—as she searched amid a tangle of weeds and seagrass. Where had she gone? It had been no trick, no ruse of mind and light and color. Medusa was here, somewhere. There was only one beauty with such undulating serpent hair in this world.

Euryale turned in circles, and—*there!*—once again, and just out of reach, was the lithe shape she remembered. The exact length, the same slender waist. Though Medusa did not show her face, Euryale knew it was her sister, exactly as she looked before she died.

There are some things you can never forget.

Euryale was careful not to scare Medusa away. She held herself back, biding her time, exhaling bubbles, until the sea ghost neared.

It is you, Euryale?

It is me. Come closer.

I cannot.

Where have you been, Medusa?

I have been below, but now I am here, waiting.

For what? For whom?

For your son to die, for you to tire of this island and join me.

My son lives.

Yes. But he is mortal, like I was.

And he is strong, like me.

Euryale, death is not a weakness. It is a transformation.

Are you still an idiot? I am an immortal. Do not speak to me of dying.

The phantom Medusa smiled. Euryale saw her teeth, even in the dark, even from afar.

You are also ocean. You can be whatever you want to be.

And what are you, Medusa? Now?

Right now? Just a dream.

And when you're not bothering me, then what?

I am free.

Medusa's snakes disappeared, her wings faded, her claws retracted, and she was a golden girl again. She held out a slim hand and offered Euryale a violet.

When you are ready, I will guide you.

Oh, go away, Medusa.

I'm trying to tell you: we are not so different, you and I.

Ha! We are night and day.

Yet every day becomes night, and each night becomes day.

The violet floated across the watery expanse between them.

I do miss you, Euryale.

And then Medusa dissolved into the kelp.

Euryale awoke gasping. She placed one hand against the disordered breath of her chest, holding it there steadily until she calmed. She scowled. *You can be whatever you want to be?* Even dead dream Medusa was a maudlin fool. Orion was fine, Euryale was fine, everything was fine.

And she was free enough.

But her heart lurched in her chest when she noticed a violet clutched in her other hand. Euryale dropped the flower as if it were scalding hot, and scrambled to her feet, grinding its lavender petals into the sand with her heel.

She could not sleep here, could not dream here, anymore.

Euryale would not return to her cove at night until the end.

ORION WOULD KEEP to the islands. Keep to his promise.

Avoid palaces and temples, Stheno had warned him. *Royalty and religion will bring you nothing but problems. And above all else, do not enter Athens.*

Euryale's son swore on Sirius, which was better than blood.

But Euryale understood the lure of the mainland, the pull of the cities. Would a boy like Orion—with such capabilities, with such a face—be satiated by quiet islands and fishing villages?

Not for long.

And she imagined him stabbed in a tavern brawl, lost in a forest fire, poisoned, pummeled, infected, and sick. Euryale could release him from this island, but she would never stop worrying.

But Stheno could fly, and she had mastered anonymity—the clandestine way of hiding in trees and upon rooftops, collecting whispers. She alone could monitor Orion's whereabouts.

"I will cook," Euryale announced. "And I will clean. Just go. Follow his story."

Stheno raised an eyebrow.

For Orion, Euryale would beg, but Stheno did not require additional convincing. She could not bear his absence either.

By their arrangement, Stheno flew away for lengthy periods, returning home with accounts of varying integrity, a mix of gossip true and egregious.

"He is in Rhodes."

"That far?"

"No, Samos."

"Samos. All right. I can accept Samos."

"Maybe Laconia."

"No, not Sparta!"

"I will keep looking."

Finally, Stheno arrived home, confident in her report. She sank into her pallet, wearied by constant travel and fact-checking.

"Orion arrived at Chios," she informed Euryale, stretching her feet—flexing her toes and rolling her ankles this way and that. "And he has settled there. I am sure of it."

"Chios . . ." mused Euryale, racking her brain for references. "It is famous for its wine."

And Euryale considered Semele's fate, whether it was brought to fruition by her drunkenness or despite it. She scolded herself: Why hadn't she practiced drinking with Orion? Alcohol was a threat she had not prepared him for.

"The king is Oenopion," continued Stheno, "and Orion has made himself a favorite. Chios teems with wild beasts, and he has promised to tame the island."

Nobody could track prey or understand terrain like Orion, nor could anyone shoot a bow with such accuracy or swing a blade with comparable veracity. As a hunter, he would remain far from court. Euryale released a breath she'd been holding for months. A breath she had contained in her clenched shoulders and tight neck. Orion was safe. No natural-born creature could kill her boy.

Stheno looked about their barren home, at the dust and cobwebs, the moldy barley and cracked roof, and she sighed. "I thought you were going to cook and clean."

Euryale tossed her a bunch of red grapes, only slightly brown and scented of ferment.

Stheno rolled her eyes. "You are a domestic goddess."

Stheno stayed home for one full cycle of the moon, repairing all that Euryale had neglected, before Euryale sent her away again.

"I must know more. Go to Chios." Euryale pointed a finger outward, toward the sea and sky.

"That's not even the right direction."

"Add it to the list of things I don't bother to know."

Stheno groaned, but one of her snakes rose and stretched. Euryale smiled, smug, and Stheno set forth after breakfast.

The following period was a dizzying relay of information. Stheno flew back and forth between Sarpedon and Chios with fragments of Orion's adventure. Sometimes, she stopped for only a few hours' rest before taking again to the skies, such was the intensity of her intel.

> *"The king has a daughter, Merope. She and Orion have formed an attachment. He brings her trophies of his most dangerous kills."*

"No, Stheno! Not a princess."

"The king has promised Princess Merope to Orion in gratitude for his service to the island."

"He is too young! Why must he fall for the first girl he meets?"

"The betrothal's announcement is postponed."

"Why? But also, good."

"It is postponed again."

"Does this human worm not approve of my Orion? Impossible."

And then Stheno came with the news Euryale had dreaded, like the arrival of a distant storm eyed warily, ever long. She had sensed its approach, and now that it was here, an abrupt calm fell upon Euryale, like the gray sky before the winds change and the temperature drops, before a strange pressure hits the bones and the clouds darken.

Stheno took Euryale's arm, guided her to a seat.

"There was a feast," she said. "Oenopion claims that after the party, Orion took Merope's virginity." Stheno closed her eyes. Pain shaded the contours of her face. "He claims Orion lay with her under force."

Euryale shot up. "I will hear no lies. He would not do it. Never."

"Oenopion walked in on them together and went mad. He has punished Orion."

Punished. Euryale chilled at the word. Hadn't their family been punished enough?

"How?" she managed to ask.

Stheno clammed up, and hysteria stampeded across Euryale's soul. There is no panic like that of a mother mortally afraid for her child. She clutched her sister's face, shook her, squeezed her, slammed closed fists into Stheno's chest.

"Tell me!" she cried. "What has that degenerate done to my son?"

"It is my fault, Euryale. A repayment for my sins." Stheno moaned, and she fell to her knees, burying her face in her hands. "Forgive me."

"Do not dare speak any way but plainly to me, Stheno."

And her sister's back jerked with sobs.

"The king took Orion's eyes."

THIRTY-SIXTH EPISODE

STHENO

But I would challenge the sun itself
for you.

—Erastus of Athens, "Ode to Monsters"

I WOULD NOT TARRY on Sarpedon, for I could not close my eyes without seeing a vision of Orion, blind and bound. While I ate some dried fish, Euryale packed for me. She handed me my sack.

"What is in here?"

"Only what you need. Make haste."

Curious, I peered inside the bag. Would Euryale pack essentials like food or water? Of course not. Instead, I found my favorite rock, honed to deadly precision over decades of sharpening. A tiny tooth. A feather, fine and flaxen.

I held up the molar, no more than a pebble in my hand.

"Orion's?"

"I saved all of them."

I allowed myself a small smile. "Perhaps if we plant them in the island soil, we can raise our own army like Cadmus."

"We have no need of sown men," corrected Euryale. "We have you."

It was the greatest compliment she ever gave me.

I turned over the ivory relic, pressed its tiny grooves into the pad of my thumb, soft and rounded for munching nuts and leaves. Our boy had shed childhood, but this sweet evidence remained. *He was real!* my heart sang. He used this tooth to chew the meals I cooked! And as he grew, it began to wiggle, to loosen, to make room for a young man's mouth and hunger and bite. He brought it to me when it fell out, proudly pointing out the bloody root still attached as he grinned and poked his tongue in the empty spot.

Oh, that a little bone could mean so much.

I held the feather next and ran its silky fringe against my cheek. It was Gorgon gold, long and thin. But it did not smell of Euryale. My hands shook.

"I found it on the beach after Echidna took her." Euryale faltered a bit, and her eyes trailed away from me, losing focus. "I should have given it to you then. I'm sure she left it for you."

"No," I demurred. "I am glad you had it all these years. And I am glad I have it now."

She did not bid me farewell, but Euryale never did. I launched into the sky but reined in my pace. For I was worn down by the constant trips to Chios, and this would be my most consequential journey of all; I could not aim too high, burn out, and drop into the sea.

I went to save Orion. I would save Orion.

I flew in and out of winds while questions whisked through my mind.

Did Orion hurt that girl?

If Oenopion already has his eyes, what will he take next?

Will I make it in time, this time?

For here it was again, that dreaded number three. The third time I raced against the acts of men to circumvent death or disaster.

Usually, I did not tread past Chios's seaside villages, but today I had business with the king. I flew directly into the center of the city, over the palace walls, and into its central courtyard. I reassembled my headscarf and apologized to my hissing snakes.

But stay alert. I may need you.

Servants and courtiers spotted my descent and sought cover. They screamed, *Beast! Fiend! Creature of death!* I bared my fangs and extended my claws, spreading horror through the sentient masses like plague. Let them fear me. Humans ducked and fled as I landed and entered the vestibule.

"Where is the king?" I demanded of a servant girl hiding behind an urn. She pointed down a long hallway. At its end was a pair of doors, which I gleefully kicked open. Beasts, fiends, and creatures of death require no invitations.

Inside the royal chamber, an intimate collection of unimpressive men drank wine around a wood table. But they stopped midsentence, mid-drink, when I stretched my wings and gnashed my teeth.

"Which of you is Oenopion?" I snarled.

Four ashen faces, four cowardly moons. But one pair of weaselly eyes exposed the king. I followed the traitor's darting glance to the man holding an ornate drinking vessel. He had a face marked by large pores and the ruddy nose of the oft inebriated; he had soft hands befitting one who is lazy and useless.

I might have guessed.

"Where is the hunter Orion?" I demanded, stepping forward and homing in on my enemy, the king.

The man sneered. "Hardly a hunter. Do you mean the predator who preyed upon my innocent daughter?"

"They were promised."

Oenopion chuckled. "Yet never formalized. And he dared to look upon Merope unclothed. I will not suffer such disrespect in my own home, not after I offered him hospitality."

"They were attached to each other. It is widely known."

"Merope is young and stupid. I would never sacrifice my daughter to the offspring of a Gorgon. We are descendants of Ariadne!" He slammed his full cup down against the table, sending crimson waves crashing over its rim. I understood he was quite drunk, foolishly so. His acquaintances squirmed.

"Orion tamed this land for you, and your people rejoice. He honored your arrangement," I repeated calmly. "Chios is free of beasts."

Oenopion ran an eye over my form, relishing in his disgust. "Not all of them."

I sighed at his arrogance, at his belief that I cared for his opinion. Because we spoke face-to-face, he assumed himself immune to my curse, but would he say as much to my snakes?

"I will ask only one more time. Where is Orion?"

Oenopion's men stared down at their laps, scanned the walls and ceilings, looked up and away, while the king drank long and hard from his cup—clearly avoiding my question.

"You have no weapon," he said instead.

Oblivious, insipid man.

I could not hold back my smile. "I am a monster. I need no weapon."

"He was in a cell below the palace," the man with the shifty eyes offered hurriedly, though the king spewed invectives his way.

He *was*?

My heart flapped against my ribs like a caged bird in the throes of death. I was too late. Again.

"And now?" I growled.

The king flushed and sputtered, his ugly face turning purple and mottled. "I do not know." And he shot his garrulous companion a scathing look. "He escaped. Him and that disagreeable dog. A few days ago."

"I freed him."

A girl emerged from the walls, surprising me, surprising us all. How long had she been here, watching and listening? How had I overlooked her? She was petite, with light hair and a plain, honest face. She spoke directly to me. "I led him back to his boat and sent him toward Hephaestus's island."

Oenopion grumbled—apparently, this was common knowledge.

She took several light steps toward me. If she was afraid, she hid it well. "You are his mother's sister."

Amused by this nomenclature and touched by her courage, I nodded.

"Then you must hurry," she pleaded. "He cannot see at all. I am so worried."

"Shut your whore mouth, Merope!" shouted the king.

Merope brushed aside the slight. "My father burned Orion's eyes with a scalding iron. I pray the god of the forge can heal him."

I imagined Orion's handsome face with charred eye sockets and recalled—so vividly—the odor of Semele's immolation. I would have gagged but for my ire. Hatred kept me focused.

"Thank you, Merope. Your spirit becomes you." And then, under my breath, I told her, "You are your own daughter now. Close your eyes."

Her eyes widened before she covered them with both her hands. Turning to face Oenopion and his enablers, I tugged at the end of my shroud.

It fell to the floor . . .

Onward to Hephaestus's island.

Lemnos.

I FLEW NORTH. It was not long before I spotted Orion's boat from the sky—crashed into the rocky coast, mast shattered, and sail torn. Our boy nestled in its remains, curved like the fetus I pulled from his mother, with Sirius standing guard above him, a red sentinel. When I landed, she ran to me, over boulders and through the surf, joy and relief evident. The poor thing's dry tongue hung from her mouth. I threw my arms around her trembling body. "Good girl, Sirius. Good girl."

I waded out toward the boat, calling Orion's name.

"Aunt?" He sat up, and the hull lurched sideways with the sudden movement. I caught the bow and righted it. Orion swayed.

"Wait, Orion. Let me help you."

Hand in hand, I freed him from its wreckage and slowly led him into a cave along the shoreline.

"How did you find me?"

"Merope."

He moaned. His lips were cracked, his skin burnt, and sores wept from the place where his eyes had been. Purple contusions circled his eye sockets, and his sunken lids were swollen shut—with blood and ash and a pus that reeked of infection. I swallowed my nausea guiltily. What was my discomfort to his excruciating pain?

If only I could kill Oenopion again.

"I will find water."

But then I was overcome by a haunting memory: making this precise declaration to Medusa in another time and place. Oh, I had lived long enough to know there is nothing new. My immortal existence circled, repeated a pattern of actions I thought were choices but were only a set course, while ghosts of the past gyred around me.

Orion collapsed to the ground.

Oh, I had also lived long enough that I sometimes lost track of time, of reality, just as the elderly do. Do not be fooled by my youthful face!

Water, Stheno. Focus.

On Lemnos, I found no freshwater stream but a strange, swollen plant growing on the ground like a pumpkin. When I cracked its green rind, I discovered a juicy red fruit. I took a tentative bite; it was delicious. I brought half to Orion and gave the other to Sirius. They ravished the meat and sucked down the juice.

"More."

I retrieved gourd after gourd, placing the refreshing food in Orion's uncertain hands, feeding my family as I had always done, as I would never tire of doing.

"Careful," I teased, "you will devour the island."

But he was too badly broken to smile.

Sirius, fed and finally able to drop her guard, dozed while I disposed of the rinds before they attracted flies. Orion was awake but quiet. His head followed my movements by their sound, so I made a special effort to be noisy. He needed to know I was still here.

"Aunt?" he asked me. "Do you wear your shroud?"

I was taken aback, by his question, his intuition, but also the reality.

"No."

"I am glad."

I held my breath and knelt before him, taking Orion's trusting hand and guiding it to the trio atop my head. He touched the first snake, and it slid beneath his fingers. Orion jerked back, but only for a moment. He reached out to me again.

"More."

And so I introduced him to my snakes, one by one. "There are three," I explained softly. "This one is feisty and this one is shy. This one never rests."

And my snakes met Orion, as well, at last, tasting the air and welcoming him into their space.

"And what of Medusa's?"

I startled, for he and I did not speak of my missing sister. Even hearing her name on his lips felt specious somehow—like a word I was supposed to know but whose meaning I couldn't recall. Still, here, on this foreign isle, Orion was blind and forsaken, and I stood before him, unveiled. Here, today, I could let him see.

"They were green. And plentiful. One for each of her passions."

"She loved many things."

"She loved everything," I emended. "With no reservation. It was her hamartia."

Orion nodded his head, accepting what I told him—agreeing with my judgment—and perhaps for the first time in seventeen years, I beheld the burgeoning adult in him. Orion, a man.

No, I would not cry. Not now, at least.

"Tell me about my mother's snakes."

"She has only one. An exquisite amber and so strong, so perfectly coiled around her head." I grinned. "It conserves its energy, but when it strikes, her snake has the longest, sharpest teeth of all."

"I am glad," he said again, with a hazy hint of a smile, and then he lay down, groping in the dirt until he found his place beside Sirius.

Glad for his mother and her snake? Glad that I removed my shroud? Glad to rest in a cave?

I could not clarify; he was already asleep.

◆ ◆ ◆

MEROPE'S PLAN WAS sound; if there was any hope for restoring Orion's sight, I needed to summon Hephaestus. A grand temple stood in the city, but I dared not bring us before humans in the daylight. Of course, I could guide him there in the dead of night, but some enigmatic force held me back.

Why this reticence? I questioned myself.

Because you hate temples.

And I did. I despised their convictions and their rules, their hypocrisies. How could a temple ever be our sanctuary, after everything we had suffered on the altar?

I thought of Ligeia's songs, the ones commemorating the paeans of old. When there was no need of marble or wall, just element and intent, humans worshipped with what they had: earth and fire, hands and voice. Were these elements sufficient for a creature like me?

I built a bonfire on the beach below the cave, feeding it a steady diet of driftwood until it blazed with sublime flames, taller than me. Then I lowered myself, clasping my hands and praying for the first honest time in my existence.

"Hephaestus, Lord, god of fire and bronze. I beseech you—though you do not know me and owe me nothing—to help this boy. Unjustly maimed by a wretched king before he had the chance to live."

I repeated my plea in different ways, hoping that Hephaestus, the ugly god, made lame by his own mother's disgust, would find sympathy and respond. For Orion I would do anything. I would be made pitiful; I would sob and tear my cloak. I would lie naked with my legs spread. I felt no shame at the depths to which my soul would descend.

And just as my voice began to run hoarse and my own words scraped against my throat, a hum entered the air, the light of my conflagration dimmed to blue, and a god rose up from the flames.

I bowed my head.

"Lift your chin, daughter of Phorcys," said Hephaestus, in a voice orotund but kind. I did as he commanded. His beard covered enough of his face that I could not gauge his infamous ugliness. I nearly laughed; who was I to judge? He wore a hammer at his belt, and his right hand held a cane. Though his arms and chest were heavily muscled, his legs were atrophied—thin and awkwardly shaped.

"Why do you call on me? I doubt you desire armor. Or a necklace."

I told him of King Oenopion's betrayal. "My sister's son was true to his word," I insisted. "But punished for his parentage."

"And who is his father?"

I swallowed. "Poseidon."

Hephaestus frowned. "Why, then, do you not beg his aid?"

I carefully assembled my response: "Lord, I seek not water today, but light. Vision. And there is no element more lucid than fire."

He smiled. "A fine answer."

"Then you will restore his sight?"

"Alas, I cannot forge eyes."

My heart dropped.

"But I may know a way." He paused. "What are you willing to do for him?"

I answered truthfully: "Anything."

"Then bring him to the Titan Helios in the farthest east. Let the first rays of the rising sun fall upon his eyes, and the boy will see again."

My troubled, exhausted heart rose with elation, with eagerness. I bowed again and again. "I am so grateful, Lord. We all are."

"You are Medusa's sister, but what is your name?"

I told him. He repeated it once, then sank below the fire.

He was so gracious, unlike any Olympian I had met before. And maybe if I had been bolder and had imagined a future beyond the sunrise, I might have asked him for armor.

Not for me, of course, but for Orion.

◆ ◆ ◆

I FLEW EAST with Orion tied to my chest. He clung tightly to my middle while I used every muscle in my body to maintain flight. He was massive; I still cannot fathom how I found the strength.

Perhaps I invoked it from the golden feather tied across my forehead.

We were forced to leave Sirius at Lemnos, in a cave with a stock of melons.

"I will return for you," Orion promised. She laid her head down between her paws, and I knew she would wait for him, even until her own death.

We pushed east, passing underneath the sun in a race of opposing directions. When we met again, it must be at dawn. I flew with a falcon's speed. I was no crane; I was a raptor. I did not worry about time, because I did not think. I forfeited my mind to the animal inside me.

The sky graduated in color, from pale to cyan, cobalt to midnight. Orion and I landed on a rock at Oceanus's eastern edge in the inky black night, the outline of Helios's palace barely visible. I lay flat, thoroughly depleted, and wondered, somewhat dispassionately, if I would die. There must be limits, even to the immortal body. As long as Orion healed first, Hades could have me.

While I contemplated my death, Orion paced like Euryale.

"How much longer?" he asked me, repeatedly.

I reminded myself to be patient. *He cannot see.* "It is still quite dark, Orion."

He lessened his pace, slowing to a stop. "We have made it to the very opposite of Sarpedon, Aunt."

True. For Orion had been born in the farthest west.

"We have been to both ends of the earth together."

Had I ever loved him more? Could I? But then I sensed a flicker of activity and shot up. We could not miss this moment.

"It's happening!" I exclaimed, expertly reassembling my shroud. Orion tensed, and I turned his body toward the horizon. "Do not move," I ordered. "Keep your head still."

He panicked, and in the crease of his forehead, the tremble in his chin, I saw him again as a little boy, frightened of storms and spiders. "What if it doesn't work?"

"Shh," I soothed, smoothing over my own trepidation. "Soon."

In Sarpedon, I ceased to care about sunrises. I'd become spoiled, immune to their charms. As such, I hadn't properly considered what we were primed to witness.

Helios in his chariot, crowned in aureole, emerged with the dawn. Four white horses galloped upward, breaking through cloud and banishing the dark. Riding toward us in the vanguard of day—of light—of life itself.

Rays so bright they should have seared.

A yellow that begot all other yellows. The core of a cracked egg. A bumblebee's stripe. A lemon, a tulip, a butterfly's wings.

We were awash in color and warmth, cleansed, glowing. Reborn.

I am so thankful that I have seen this. And that I did so with him.

For Orion turned to me and his beautiful, recovered eyes cried beautiful, healthy tears. He leaned his face against my shoulder, and I held him close, humming in his ear, "You are saved, you are whole, you are loved."

At the edge of the world, another hero received another chance. He sobbed.

THIRTY-SEVENTH EPISODE

EURYALE

Mother, Mother, why do you cry?
Your boy is stars, but mine is stone.

—Erastus of Athens, "Thales"

EURYALE NEVER TIRED of the story, and she made Stheno repeat it over and over again. How Merope defied her father and Stheno turned the king to stone. How they summoned Hephaestus and basked in the colors of the morning sun. She craved every detail of Orion and Sirius's reunion in the cave on Lemnos.

"Tell me again his last words."

Stheno sighed but humored her. "'Tell my mother that Sirius does not forget her life on Sarpedon, when we were all together. Tell my mother that Sirius remembers, every day.'"

For Orion had chosen not to return home. Instead, he headed far south, to Crete, where Artemis needed huntsmen.

Another Olympian. Another virgin.

Stheno did not resume her surveillance of Orion, and Euryale never insisted. Was this what it meant to let go, to let be? Perhaps, for Euryale had conceded to herself that they could not prevent fate again.

She brought paints and a brush to her cove, and she got to work. She drew her son and his dog and other things she did not necessarily want to analyze. Euryale gave the brush control. But only in daylight did she decorate each rocky surface, for once night fell, Euryale returned to the homestead and the safety of Stheno. She would not risk another slumber in the cove, another dream's chance encounter with Medusa.

Stheno roused her one morning, and Euryale responded as she always did, by swatting her away.

"I am sleeping," she grunted.

"I don't care."

Euryale peered through bleary eyes. Stheno's face, her every fiber of being, seemed grave. "Leto has come."

"Leto? Why?" Euryale sat up. Her arms were covered in gooseflesh though the day was warm. "What does she say?"

"Nothing yet. She waits for you."

The sisters walked side by side. Euryale, with her chest hollowed out, felt oddly light, and she marveled that her feet stayed on the ground. It is a rootless life when you give away your heart.

Leto sat before the outside firepit, atop the same hewn log as before. The shimmer of her veil caught the rising light.

"I have brought my sister. Will you tell us now? What has happened?"

"Sit down, please."

Leto removed her veil, folding it carefully and laying it across her lap.

Euryale sat. This time, she would not censor her tone nor school her facial features. She would not cover her snake, no matter how gruesome it appeared. Euryale did not convene with Leto as a lesser being anymore, but as one mother to another.

Leto seemed to understand, and she began her tale.

CRETE'S FORESTS, BEING so vast, provided Orion with ample challenges, and in Artemis he enjoyed a kindred spirit, another soul with the same talents and obsessions. To observe them hunt in tandem was akin to watching a choreographed dance; they moved alike, tackled obstacles with a perfectly coordinated mind-set, and reacted as one. They slew bears and wolves, feral goats with fatal horns, mountain lions, boars, and legendary stags.

And as their hunting parties feasted and toasted, Orion proclaimed their preeminence: "There is no beast we cannot kill!"

Artemis had a deerskin cape fashioned for Orion, identical to her own, and even when the season ended, the two remained together, celebrating their companionship by camping and hiking, swimming in springs and leaping from waterfalls.

People began to talk, as people are wont to do.

Has Artemis found love, at last? the women wondered. For Orion was considered the most handsome man on earth.

Is she still a virgin? snickered the men.

Artemis met their accusations with laughter. *Orion is my other half,* she maintained. *We are formed of the same spirit.*

But this was an unfortunate choice of words, for the mischief-makers of Crete immediately relayed the message at the altar of Apollo.

Apollo, Artemis's twin and other half, was also a god unaccustomed to sharing.

Soon after, a gigantic scorpion was spotted on the southern isle, sowing chaos. The locals named him Scorpios, and he was a monstrosity—a blight—of unknown origin.

It came from Gaea herself, some believed. *For humanity has slain all her favorite creatures.*

No, this is Apollo's design, others argued. *He punishes Orion for stealing his sister.*

These troubling rumors reached Leto, and she departed Delos almost immediately. She alone could heal the rift between her twins and banish this eight-legged monster.

But Leto did not find Artemis when she reached Crete.

"The goddess hunts Scorpios," the priest told her. "Alongside the mortal hero Orion and his dog."

Fear stricken, Leto followed the beast's trail: the tracks of its legs and claw-marked tree trunks, the endless carcasses of owls and lizards, bats, shrews, and mice. She worried about her son's involvement as much as she agonized for her daughter's safety.

She had been a good mother. How did she end up here?

And as fate would have it, she found Artemis and Scorpios at the same moment.

In a sleepy glen, her daughter and the mortal boy battled the scorpion. Artemis dodged its dual pinchers as she inched closer, swords aimed at the beast's eyes. Meanwhile, Orion swerved around the scorpion's massive articulated tail. In his attempt to slice off the venomous stinger, Orion leapt upon the armored back, riding the monster as it bucked and bellowed.

Then Scorpios spotted Leto, unarmed and soft, the easiest of prey. It scurried in her direction, clicking and hissing.

Artemis screamed. "Mother!"

And Orion leapt.

He landed atop Leto with a roar, smashing her into the ground. And the stinger meant for the Great Mother, the gentle goddess, the most holy and demure, stabbed Orion in his back, injecting a venom designed not only to kill but to torment.

"No!" keened Artemis, dropping her sword and dashing to her fallen hunter. "Not him, not like this!"

Orion agonized in delirious death. He could not breathe; his body thrashed; his muscles twitched. His head circled around his neck, and his eyes rolled backward. Leto opened Orion's tunic and laid a hand upon his chest, flushed and wet with feverish sweat. Beside her mother, Artemis wept. She held her hunter's hands and laid kisses upon his forehead. She told Orion how much she loved him.

Gods, Olympians especially, never stay with any mortal until their final breath. Doing so risks pollution. But for this hero, Leto and Artemis would humbly extend such an honor.

After Orion died, Artemis could not persuade Sirius to leave her master's body. No poking or prodding, no yelling or cuts of meat could sever their union. So Artemis did what any merciful hunter would do. She drew her blade and slit the animal's throat.

Now, Crete belongs to Zeus's mythology. It is where he was fostered during the reign of Cronus; it is the land that kept him alive for vengeance. And so, in the heart of its forest, Artemis called upon her almighty father.

"Return Orion to me!" she demanded.

Zeus's voice filled the sky. "I cannot. He was mortal, fairly slain."

"Then you must reward the boy for his service to me," appealed Leto. "The mother of your esteemed twins."

"He must be remembered, Father, please."

And so Orion's body lifted into the air, his dead dog beside him, and by the divine magic Zeus alone commanded, he transformed the pair into stars and placed them in the sky to the far east.

Where Orion's mother lived.

But Zeus always hated to choose sides, so he also raised the stumbling Scorpios, wounded and confused, and reconstructed its essence into pinpricks of light, which he set in the farthest west.

Hunter and hunted. Killed and killer. At odds for eternity.

"Make peace with your brother," Leto ordered her bereft daughter. "I will speak to the Gorgons."

"I AM SO sorry, both to tell you this and that it happened. Your son rescued me from great pain."

Leto stood. She would not linger, would not press the wound.

Euryale said nothing, so Stheno performed the customary farewell. Her sister's body and mouth could work independently of her heart. Euryale's could not. She could not say, "Farewell," now that her child was dead. Could not say, "Thank you," ever again. The baby she rocked to sleep and taught to walk, the toddler she carried on her hip and fed berries from her fingers, straight into his little gaping mouth—*More, Mama! More!*—was no longer here, and nothing else mattered.

How could she wish safe travels to anyone now that her gorgeous son had gone? The boy whose curls she brushed each night. The young man she swam beside and shared the secrets of the ocean with—*More, Mother! Tell me more!*

No, Euryale's life had fractured. Her pain was irreparable. There would be no more formalities.

Orion. Heaven's light. The promise of every dream. He had been killed, so why would she ever bother with *please* or *thank you*? Why change her dirty clothes or wash her hands or sip wine or laugh or eat or drink?

Or breathe?

Leto must have left, but how long did Euryale sit before a weak fire? She was dimly aware of Stheno's presence. Crying and touching. Hugging her? Pleading?

"Say something, Euryale, please."

When she was ready, Euryale stood.

"Do not follow me," she ordered.

And Euryale walked to the cove.

POSEIDON LEANED AGAINST one of the larger boulders, facing the sea. Euryale's feet met sand, and she released the sturdy cliff-side rope. Hearing her arrival, the Lord of the Sea pushed himself from the rock and turned to her, arms open.

"Our son is dead."

"*My* son."

She would not meet him, so he approached her instead, palms up and open, proffering peace.

"Golden Eyes, must you always battle me?"

Euryale ceded; she accepted his embrace. Maybe his touch would feel like something, would rouse her from this stupor. But then Poseidon's mouth was on her neck, tasting her, needing her, whispering, "Let's make another."

She shoved him away, revolted, appalled. "There could never be another Orion."

"That's not what I meant."

"A new baby would not replace what I have lost." Euryale felt tears sting the backs of her eyes, but she would not cry. No, it was her nature to fight. She clenched her fists. "You have countless lovers, so many children. I have you. I had him."

"You think that brings me happiness?"

She didn't.

Her life had been marred, yes, by a vengeful goddess, but also by obscurity—*the lesser offspring of lesser offspring.* But amid the dull and dark difficulties, the disfigurements, sparkled diamond-bright moments: picking apples with her sisters in the Hesperides, giggling with drunken Medusa as she careened into walls, sharing bread with Stheno in the Athenian agora, stealing Athena's aegis.

Brushing Orion's black hair from his forehead while he slept. Kissing his eyelashes, his plump cheeks, the most perfect tips of his ears.

Euryale had known real love, a legacy in itself, and she pitied Poseidon his godliness.

"You have never sought happiness," she challenged. "Only power."

Poseidon stood taller. "My power is a duty," he proclaimed. "I protect sailors and fishermen. I control the waves and the storms."

Euryale let loose a laugh, as quick and sharp as any arrow. "Your power is a poison."

"You wanted me, Golden Eyes, because I am a god."

"I did." She nodded, apparently acquiescing, and Poseidon relaxed, reassured, only for Euryale to deliver one more dart: "And yet I might have kept you if you were more of a man."

Rain came, suddenly and completely, and there was no mistaking its provenance. Euryale's snake lifted its head, refusing to be cowed, as the Lord of the Sea demonstrated his might.

"I have treated you better than any other," he commanded, and when she gave him a hard look, Poseidon's nostrils flared. "I made one mistake. Once."

"'One? Once?'" Euryale threw her arms in the air incredulously. "Which mistake are you referring to? Please tell me you do not mean Medusa."

He frowned. "You forget, I will not apologize."

"And that is precisely why there is nothing here for you anymore!" She closed the distance between them only to shove him backward with such force that he struggled to maintain his footing. "You still think what you did to Medusa was a simple mistake. You continue to believe that I have forgiven you. You cannot change; you never learn or grow. You are stagnant water."

He was shocked; he fumbled for words. "I am not your enemy."

Euryale dismissed him, waving her hand. "Leave me to mourn."

"He was my son, too!"

A thunderhead clapped above the beach. Rain pelted their faces, and Euryale squinted, seeking Poseidon's face in the downpour. A stillness had fallen upon him, and with his soaking ebony hair and distraught eyes, he became, for a brief moment, both younger and older than she knew him to be. His voice was low, softer than she had ever heard before, as he lifted a finger. "You're wearing it."

"What?" But her fingers instinctively clasped the pearl necklace at her throat, the one from the boat after Orion was born.

"You never do. Why tonight?"

"Because . . ."

Because a pearl is a symbol of wisdom gained through experience.

Because a pearl is a treasure that needs no cutting or polishing by man.

"Because this is the last night. For us."

Was it her imagination, or did the earth shake?

"You think you can be done with me? I am as immortal as the ocean."

And she nearly laughed, but she would not explain how amusing she found such a statement, considering everything she planned to do. Instead, she took his face between her palms.

"Go."

And she saw the pair of them reflected in his eyes, witnessed their relationship as he did. He thought they could continue like this forever, that Euryale would always await him on island or cliff, some forgotten beach. That they would argue and reconcile for another century.

His vision was so limited.

"I want you to go, I need you to go."

He tilted his head, leaned his cheek into her hand. He still didn't believe her. "May I kiss you goodbye?"

She recalled a night nearly twenty years ago, when she first began to understand him. "It hardly matters either way."

So Poseidon kissed a Gorgon, one last time, slowly savoring her. It was so easy—too easy—to fall into their routine, and she pulled away.

"Euryale . . ."

When had he ever called her by her name? Never.

"This is enough."

He moaned, made to protest, and then—

"You heard her. That is enough."

Stheno was in the cove.

She had flown over the precipice and descended on spread wings. Stheno hovered in the air, just before them, and Euryale bit back a smile. Her sister, with her red eyes and snakes, made for a redoubtable appearance.

Did Poseidon seem a bit nervous?

"This is my island," Stheno asserted, as flippant and cold as any human queen. "And you have been asked to leave."

He affected a shrug, assembling his body into its godliness as if donning a cloak and crown. "I am Lord of the Sea. They are all my islands."

Stheno chuckled. "Not this one." And she landed.

"Golden Eyes?" he asked Euryale, keeping one eye on Stheno.

"I am only a middle sister. Nobody cares what I think."

Stheno looked him in the face, for she was nearly of his height. There was only a slight twitch in one eye that hinted at how desperately she fought to maintain her composure. "I have playacted all the ways I would hurt you. But it is out of my hands. Time will take care of you, Poseidon."

He scoffed, but his cynicism fell flat.

"One day, sooner than you realize, the humans will know you for what you are. And all the many, many things you are not. The altars will run dry with dust; the fires will die. Your temples will empty and fall to ruin."

Poseidon's brows narrowed as he glared at Stheno. "You are no sibyl. You are just the shunned sister nobody wanted. I do not care what you have to say."

Stheno smiled, delighting in his abuse, for she was far from finished. "Without their worship, without the women, you will wither away. And as your power wanes, I want you to know, I will be there, watching with rapture. Because I'm just the cast-aside sister, I don't demand veneration to survive. I will witness it all."

"I am an Olympian," he fumed.

She shrugged. "For now."

Poseidon sputtered. He looked, one last time, to Euryale. Did he expect her to defend him? To renounce Stheno?

"Go," Euryale repeated firmly.

"I am not lifeless. I have . . . felt things," he said to Euryale privately, pleading with her to understand. "You must know."

She nodded once noncommittally, and then exasperated, confused, and defeated, Poseidon vanished, gone to wherever the gods go in between their devastations.

Euryale stared at the space where he had been, the space he had taken, and waited to feel something.

Nothing. Only hilarious emptiness. She giggled.

"I think he might be afraid of you."

She clasped her sister's hand.

THIRTY-EIGHTH EPISODE

STHENO

When I choose myself,
do not be afraid
if my choice looks different from yours.

—Erastus of Athens, "The Theater of Sisterhood"

FREE OF HIM and determined to forget, I took in my location. After Leto's visit, I worried for Euryale and tracked her across Sarpedon. How had I, in all the years of flying over the island, never chanced upon this enclave?

"What is this place?" I mused, enchanted.

"I do not know. I needed it one day and it appeared."

The aura of magic was made more real by the art. Every single surface was covered in Euryale's paintings, some crude and others detailed.

"May I look?"

She nodded, somewhat shy, somewhat proud, and I passed before her work, hand to my mouth. Some images I immediately recognized: Polydorus's smolder and Poseidon's trident, Ceto's octopus and Semele's kantharos. Others, I did not understand. A girl with a dimple in her left cheek. A scallop shell, a pair of bejeweled and gnarled hands. We would never know everything about each other, and that was all right.

Maybe Euryale and I were a song with no words.

Across the largest of the rock faces was a composition of colorful images somehow separate yet united by Euryale's touch: Medusa's wreath of violets. Sirius's paw prints. Orion's bow. Me, holding a kithara.

Our family.

"But where are you, Euryale?" I asked, looking back at her over my shoulder.

"I am the golden paint mixed into all of them."

Small surprises become rare as you age. For me, Euryale's mural was a laconic taste of unexpected sweetness.

"Look up," she trumpeted, pointing into the cluster of stars.

And so we beheld the new set of stars across the firmament together. So bright and distinct, so recognizable. A wonder upon wonders.

"There is his belt and his sword," Euryale murmured, both awed and exultant, tracing the sky. "And look, Stheno! There, following him!"

The unmistakable shape of a dog.

"My son will be remembered. A legend written in light."

But I already worried that he wouldn't be remembered correctly. How would he be cast in lore? As a brute and a killer? A seducer? Would the poets mention his loyalty? The benign, common ways he showed his supernatural strength?

Oh, yes, I worried.

But Euryale did not share my misgivings. She was lost in a reverie.

"What we shared with Orion, that was truly something, wasn't it?"

"It was our best thing."

My sister stood before me, just within reach of the waves, arms wrapped around herself. I could see how she might have aged if she were human—the silver hair that would've framed her proud face, the lines drawn at the corners of her mouth. She would've gained weight about her hips; the breasts that fed her child would've hung low and flat.

Her indomitable hair would still curl and tangle.

I began to cry. After all that had transpired over the day, this was what got me. I missed that hair—the way it fell in Euryale's face when she slept, how I'd find it everywhere. What I wouldn't give to pick up one loose hair again! To hear Medusa's complaints and Euryale's dry retort!

There, beside the cold dark sea, I recalled the warmth of my sisters sleeping beside me, our limbs braiding us together. I could nearly feel their ghostly touch, could almost hear the faint echoes of breath and sigh.

"I was a terrible sister," continued Euryale, "but a good mother."

"You weren't a terrible sister," I admonished.

"I was." Her eyes locked upon the black waters. "I wasted too many lifetimes consumed by jealousy."

I did not respond. I think she needed to speak; she needed somebody to listen. I could do that for her. I would do anything for her.

"I am sorry you were left with me. I know you would've preferred her."

I stepped closer, but she barely noticed my presence. "Don't say such a thing," I remonstrated.

"I don't blame you. You two always had such a bond, I could never compete." Euryale cocked her head, rested it at a contemplative angle, as she studied the waves. "But Medusa was my sister, too, and I miss her. It's important to me that you know that."

"Of course I know that."

"You should know, too, why I did it."

"Why you did what, Euryale? Must you speak so cryptically?"

"Why I needed Poseidon."

Oh. That.

"After we were changed, I needed to feel like a woman." She dropped her hypnotic gaze and looked at me, finally focused on me. Oh, that face! Euryale never trusted in her own beauty, was never satisfied, so she could not comprehend its perfection, her own crushing charm. "But it wasn't taking a lover that made me myself, it was the baby. Orion made me a mother, he made me a woman again. Poseidon gave me that.

"I know you struggle with me. That you have hated me." Euryale laughed a little, under her breath. "Rightfully so. I'm well aware how difficult I can be."

She glanced upward, lifted a hand to the stars. "But I will not be a collection of my regrets, Stheno. No. I am all the things I loved."

Her paintings. That was what she had been creating here, curating a collection of her heart.

"I thought I had to be perfect to be loved, but my son did not care."

"Neither did I," I whispered.

"I only wanted to be adored, my whole life, but I learned—too late, definitely too late—that giving love made me whole."

"Euryale, I—"

She held up a hand, cutting me off. "Stheno, I am tired of this island."

"Then we will leave," I countered, sickened by a seeping panic. "I will teach you to fly. We can go anywhere!"

But my sister hushed me a second time and strode into the sea, past her ankles and up to her knees.

"I spoke to Medusa, here, in the kelp."

My mouth fell open. Had Euryale gone mad, and how had I overlooked the signs?

"I'm not crazy," she insisted. "Sometimes I dream . . . I have always known, somehow, about the white horse and the snakes, the sword, my son in the stars. Stheno, don't look at me like that. It is all right. I didn't understand at first, either, but then I saw Medusa."

Grief over Orion's death had clearly pushed her beyond the bounds of reality, but was she redeemable? Could I save her?

"I used to care so much about hierarchy, but none of that is real. There is only the ephemeral nature of things."

"I want to understand you, Euryale, but—"

"We all share the same essence, Stheno. Gods and humans, monsters and earth, everything originates within the same life force. And there are an infinite number of unlikely outcomes when these forces are brought together. Which is why lovely women descend from beasts and beasts sire gods that raise men out of earth."

Euryale stepped farther into the water until the bottoms of her wings broke the surface. I trailed behind.

"I think I agree with you, but where is all this coming from? I did not know you thought this way."

She acknowledged me, frankly, eye to eye. "We didn't share our thoughts enough, did we?"

"No, I suppose we did not."

Euryale dipped her fingertips into the sea. "Poseidon only understood the physicality of water, never its spirituality. But I understand that the sea is a conduit." She paused, considering. "Maybe it's because women and water are both life bearers."

A conduit? My mind reeled. *To where?*

"What are you doing, Euryale?" I could barely mask my apprehension.

"I'm ready, Stheno. To go home, to *be* home. This is my freedom." Euryale's voice was so gentle, in a tone I hadn't heard since Orion was an infant. "You don't have to fight anymore. You needn't worry." My sister reached for me. She took my hand and squeezed once. "If I can abandon jealousy, you must let go of fear."

Tears fell from my eyes with abandon, and I gripped her tightly.

"Do not let me go, Euryale," I begged. "Do not leave me. Please."

"Don't tell me what to do." And she winked. Her eyes had never shone so gold.

I dropped her hand and Euryale moved forward; the sea lapped about her waist in concentric circles.

"She would have forgiven me his father. Once she met my boy."

A sob caught in my throat, and I clutched at my neck with an empty hand. For I knew I heard her final words; I would never see my sister again.

Euryale waded into the water she cherished beneath the son she loved, and then my last sister disappeared.

EXODOS

ENTER STHENO, ALONE

With or without a name
for what I became,
for whom I had to be,
I sing beautifully.

—*Anonymous, "Anonymous"*

I HEARD A MAN say once that Athena never punished Arachne, because turning her into a spider allowed her to weave forever. It was a gift! So I am forced to wonder: Do some people consider Medusa's curse a blessing—a revenge upon the men who rape?

I cannot accept that explanation, for if so, why, then, was I punished? Or Euryale? To agree would be to admit that I do not matter.

I may be anonymous, but I existed.

I was there.

And I am ageless. No blade may kill me, no matter how divine. But I can transfer. I can fade. I see that clearly now. Medusa went below the ground, and Euryale into the sea.

Me though? I belong to the air.

I thought I'd experienced alienation in Thebes or Athens, on those days when my sisters left me behind, or on Sarpedon when Euryale and I did not speak. But I have learned that loneliness is a human construct, created by mortals who need to fill time and space so that they can die well.

Their heartache does not belong to me.

I will be all right on my own.

Before I left, I walked the famed Gorgons' isle one last time, its beach strewn with intersecting specters in the great spiral of my life: Medusa and I on our stomachs watching the birds, Euryale swimming, Orion and Sirius racing the waves. Apparitions coexisting and circling, ghosts that will follow me, appearing again and again, in different forms and feelings, forever on. I welcome their memory. Some believe forgetting is the key to an immortal existence—because love can be painful, memories can be painful—but to forget them, Semele and Desma, Erastus and Ligeia and Thales, my sisters, our boy—would be to deny myself, to forget myself.

I broke away from all of it with only a tooth, a golden feather, a kelp frond and brush, a sharp rock, and my headscarf.

A veritable treasure chest.

I left behind my handmade lyre but stole a well-made kithara from the first human village I spotted. I've remembered the coordination and regrown my calluses. The notes, the melodies, never left. I play as I travel—vacillating between time and tense and place. I am old enough to know that sometimes moving forward means looking back.

Who is Stheno? That damned question, so many times over. I can answer it now: Stheno bears the story—and it is a heavy weight, for there are many.

I could never articulate love before, or freedom. But now, at last, I sing of us, to my own melody with my own words.

This is my truth and my autonomy.

My release *from*. My freedom *to*. My absence *of*.

Because I loved her
I met punishment.
Because I loved her
I received a child.

I was vengeance
yet restored.

I was deconstructed
but unbroken.

Strings and snakes,
shields and scales,
sisters and stone.

Son. Sun. Sight.

I was three but I am me
me
me
me.

I guarded my shame and did not share,
but I ate my sadness and am sated.
I am a story, too,
after all,

and I am so grateful.

The wind whispers, susurrations of war on the beaches of Ilium, where my cousin Thetis's son longs to put glory on his name. And where a man from my father's favorite isle, Ithaca, will be the latest human plaything in the war between Athena and Poseidon.

Perhaps I will fight; perhaps I will rescue.

Perhaps I will find the giant and the winged horse and make things right with Medusa's children.

And perhaps I will learn Medusa's way of writing—those one hundred eighty-seven pieces of useless information—and commit all my verse to perpetuity. So the Gorgons can be remade without bitterness and rage.

Perhaps, perhaps, perhaps. A thrill to each syllable.

And so I fly.

Ever onward.

Until myth becomes mist, and I blend between fog and fable.

AUTHOR'S NOTE

Medusa's Sisters is a work of fiction. However, it is pieced together from stories in the mythological canon. In the *Iliad,* Homer first mentions a singular Gorgon, whose snake-haired head decorates the aegis. Later, Hesiod makes the Gorgons a trinity and gives them names. In *Prometheus Unbound,* Aeschylus describes them with wings. I leaned most heavily on Hesiod's *Theogony* as I researched the Perseus myth, the details of which are echoed in Apollodorus's *Bibliotheca* and Ovid's *Metamorphoses.* While Semele and Leto do not appear in the traditional Gorgon story, the "facts" of their lives are supported by these same sources. The tale of the hunter Orion, one of the earliest Greek heroes, also appears in the *Iliad.* In Ovid's *Fasti,* Orion sacrifices himself to Scorpios to save Leda. Hyginus, in *De Astronomica,* blames Apollo for Orion's death, as he became jealous of Artemis's love for the mortal hunter. Euryale is named as Orion's mother in fragment 4 of Hesiod's *Astronomia* and by Apollodorus. She could be a princess of Minos, but it makes one hell of a story if she's Medusa's sister.

And with all due respect to Jane Ellen Harrison, no woman is ever an appendage. Every woman has a voice that matters, a story worth telling.

LIST OF PRIMARY SOURCES

FROM THE ARCHAIC PERIOD, 800–500 BCE

Iliad by the Greek poet Homer

Theogony and the *Astronomia* fragments by the Greek poet Hesiod

FROM THE CLASSICAL PERIOD, 500–300 BCE

Prometheus Unbound by the Greek tragedian Aeschylus

FROM THE HELLENISTIC PERIOD, 300–100 BCE

Bibliotheca by the Greek scholar Apollodorus

FROM THE IMPERIAL ROMAN PERIOD, 100 BCE–200 CE

De Astronomica by the Latin scholar Hyginus (translated by Mary Grant)

Metamorphoses and *Fasti* by the Latin poet Ovid

ACKNOWLEDGMENTS

Every hero's quest worth its salt must include divine intervention and a meeting with the mentor. This book, the culmination of a long journey, wouldn't exist without either. Thank you to the goddess Jane Dystel for descending upon my life with all your agent magic when I needed you most. Thank you to Anne Sowards for your editorial guidance, showing me the way to better writing—and reading. What can't I achieve with you two by my side?!

To Miriam and the rest of the DG&B staff, I am so grateful for your warm welcome and expertise.

Thank you to Angelina Krahn for your thoughtful copyedits. And to the Ace / Berkley / Penguin Random House team, I couldn't be happier that Medusa, Stheno, and Euryale found a home with you.

To all the educators: The teachers back in Long Beach public schools who told me I should be a writer. The brilliant minds I've met at Seattle's Hugo House and Holocaust Center for Humanity. The staff I worked alongside at Viz and HFK. You are everything.

To the students I've taught over the years. You made me more compassionate. Because of you I ask better questions and think more critically. I'm so relieved that the future is yours!

ACKNOWLEDGMENTS

This book would not exist without childcare. Thank you to everyone who watched my babies so I could work.

I owe so much to Rachael, my chosen soul sister, and the best girlfriends in the world. To the inimitable Katie O., Liz, and the ladies of my book club for the many, many bottles of wine. To Nancy and Nicole for fueling me with laughter and love. To Heather, my constant cheerleader (should I pop that Dom now?), and Jessica, my nefarious, original writing partner in crime. To my first friend, Kristin/KPH—cheers to our hobbies! And to everyone else who has listened to me, supported me, fed me, and celebrated with me throughout this crazy experience.

Thank you to my Andrews-Chapman-Hurley-McGurk-Alessandro-Lydeard-Portner-Bear-Howard-Helman-Rively family. And Sharon Honig-Bear, who has always believed in me.

R., D., and S., my Muses, my very own trio of malevolents! Thank you for all the snake pictures and snuggles. Everything is for you.

And Dan, my lodestar, my love song. None of this would mean anything if you weren't by my side.

I'm a lucky monster.